THE SILENT TOWN

ANNI TAYLOR

bookish
COAST

THE SILENT TOWN

Tallman's Valley Detectives: Book 3

ISBN: 978-0-6484380-3-8

Dedicated to the people of the Blue Mountains, NSW, Australia—who lived through devastating fires in the time and place in which this book is set.

Although this is a story, the fires and the anguish they caused were very real.

The fires raged from October 2019 to January 2020, becoming the worst fire season Australia has yet known.

PART I

CHAPTER ONE

TALLMAN'S VALLEY FUNFAIR, 1989

The smell of burnt popcorn lingers behind the line of carnival stalls, curling into the dark forest, where it's overpowered by a deeper stench.

It's as if the forest is rusting, sweating… decomposing.

A distant spotlight from the carnival casts its glow just far enough to reach a clearing. Here, the sickening, yellowish light reaches two figures hanging from a low branch. A man and a woman.

The faces of the figures are disfigured and bruised from ropes knotted tight around their necks, dirt caked through their hair. A mess of blood clumps on the white shirt of one of the figures, just below his rib cage.

A rusty odour emanates from their blood, mixing now with the smell of a coming downpour.

Raindrops begin to fall on the mottled skin of the pair, but they are beyond feeling its patter.

CHAPTER TWO

DETECTIVE KATE WAKELAND

THIRTY YEARS LATER,
DECEMBER 2019

A fading, peach-coloured sunrise lit the empty streets that I drove along.

Bushfire haze veiled the sky, the smoke making my throat scratchy.

The fires had been burning for two months now. It'd been our worst and most dangerous fire season. The fires hadn't reached our valley, but there was the constant threat that they might—and soon.

There weren't many houses down the end of the valley where I was headed. Nor were there many reasons for anyone to come here. It was mostly scrubby, boggy forest.

This morning, I'd driven out this way to watch something that was about to happen.

The old Tallman's Valley Funfair was being torn down. And I intended to watch every moment of it. I wanted to see it gone.

For the past three decades, the abandoned carnival had squatted in the back fields of town. Until it was completely hidden behind trees and dense foliage.

There were some who'd call my feelings about the carnival a personal vendetta. After all, this year was the year I'd discovered that people connected with the carnival had harmed my family. I'd been twisted inside out and left raw.

Yes, it was personal.

But it was much, much more than that. This affected everyone in our town. And I suspected that what I'd experienced had barely scratched the surface.

The carnival had been part of the history of this town, knitted deep into its bones. My parents used to take me there when I was a child.

It'd all ended in December 1989, when the police raided the carnival. But the criminal activities had just burrowed in, continued on, undetected.

I'd grown up in this town. There were pieces of my family and me all over—in the lakes and the forests and the mountains that edged the valley.

That was the side of life in Tallman's Valley that was always intensely sweet to me.

But lately, I'd sensed a deep cold in my bones—an ache that refused to go away.

There was a silent town sitting beneath this one. I was certain of that. This silent town was a place where the streets and landscapes were the same, but where daylight never reached.

I scarcely knew who walked the streets of the silent town. I didn't know what had happened there decades ago, and I didn't know what was happening there right now.

But I was going to find out.

I parked outside the field where the decaying buildings of the Tallman's Valley Funfair stood.

Contractors with bulldozers and heavy excavators were at the ready. A wide swathe of trees had been knocked down to let the machinery through, leaving an open viewing area.

I waited, watching.

The excavator's long arm shattered the sagging roof of the former funhouse. Timber shards scattered high and wide.

There was something cathartic about seeing the excavator smash the building again and again.

With a loud boom, the entire framework of the funhouse collapsed.

Within minutes, the remaining office buildings and stalls were squashed, too. An excavator dug up the Ferris wheel. The giant wheel had lain on its side for decades, gathering vines and sinking into the soil.

Everything was gone now. Gone from view anyway.

I was close to leaving the police force. At age 64—almost 65—I'd stayed longer than most, and I was just a whisker away from retiring. I'd assured my family that I'd soon be leaving the job that had claimed so much of my time and energy over the past decades.

My husband Pete was already retired and wanted us to go travelling the world—to visit all the places we'd been dreaming of for so long. My daughter Abby and my two beautiful grandchildren, Ivy and Jasper, wanted more of my time, too.

But I couldn't leave my job just yet.

Whatever it took to expose the silent town of Tallman's Valley, I was ready for it.

CHAPTER THREE

A name flashed up on the police radio unit in my car.

Detective Jace Franco.

"Wakeland, where are you?" came his gravelly voice.

"On my way," I told him.

"Hey, did you stop off somewhere? I can't hear your car engine. You got coffee without me, didn't you?"

I grinned, glancing out at the field before me. "No, I didn't get coffee without you. Be there in fifteen."

"Okay, great. We'll grab coffee on the way."

He ended the call there. He'd sounded sleepy. Franco wasn't a fan of early mornings, especially not on a Saturday. And today was Saturday.

Superintendent Andrew Bigley had requested that Franco and I attend a fair today.

Franco and I were both due to receive police medals, and Superintendent Bigley wanted the whole community to witness it. Typical Bigley. He was fond of anything that made his local police command look good.

The fair was a community event—to celebrate the end stage of a ten-year project in our town. A decade ago, developers had begun a project that was meant to be like a mini *Silicon Valley*. They named it *Close Quarters*. Or, CQ for short. Its four quarters consisted of hospital, university, retail, and technology sectors. CQ had brought in workers from many countries—the UK, the

Americas, India, Asia and others. An enormous village had been built to house them all.

The fair was kicking off an hour earlier than originally scheduled, due to the awful heat spell we'd been having. And it wasn't just the heat that was bothering people in our town—there were fires ringing the Blue Mountains. Smoke had squatted in the air for weeks now. People's eyes and throats were burning because of it.

I drove away from the field and along twisting roads. The carnival was all gone now—I'd seen that for myself. But an image of the Ferris wheel still turned in my mind.

Far ahead loomed the mountain that bookended Tallman's Valley. Witness Mountain.

A sound had me jerking my head up high.

A gunshot.

Then two more of the same.

The echoes of the shots pin-balled, making it impossible to tell the direction from which they'd come. Gunshots weren't uncommon in the mountains, but still, it was a sound that always got your attention.

The shots seemed to me as if they had been fired from a .303. They were *noisy*.

When I reached Witness Mountain, the whole side of it was dark. The morning sun hadn't touched it yet.

I continued to Franco's house. It was right at the base of the mountain, shrouded in a deep sepia light. The brownish tint had his house looking even more rustic than usual. Clad in wood with a stone porch, it resembled the old farmers' cottages I remembered from my childhood.

Franco ambled out as I walked up the path, munching on a piece of toast and tucking his shirt in. His shaggy mane hung over one eye. "Better late than never, Wakeland."

"I'm not late. Check your clock."

"I was in the bathroom."

"While you were eating toast? Actually, never mind… Did you hear the gunshots?"

"Nope?"

"You must be deaf."

"I had earphones in."

"Someone was shooting up on Witness Mountain. Sounded like a .303 to me."

"The good old Lee-Enfield .303, huh? Could be teenagers shooting targets. Or maybe loose dogs got to someone's sheep, and they had to put them down."

"Yes, maybe."

A kitten slipped through the open door. It was the scrappiest looking creature I'd ever seen—its calico fur spiking every which way. The kitten wound its way around Franco's ankles and then came to sit at my feet.

I stooped to pick him up and stroke his tiny forehead. "So, this is your new kitty? He's a little charmer. What's his name?"

"I'm working on it."

"You got him about two weeks ago, right?"

Franco flicked toast crumbs from his shirt. "Right. Just can't think of a name that suits him."

"It's because of Mugs, isn't it?"

"No." He sighed. "Yeah. I guess I wanted another cat just like her. But then I saw this one at the shelter. Just a month old and already looking like an old-timer who's given up on life, y'know?"

"Awww, he's beautiful." The kitten wrapped itself around my fingers, play-biting my thumb. "You deserve a name, don't you, little one?"

"Yeah, yeah, I'll get to it. The way he's scratching the furniture, I should call him *Claws*. Anyway, gimme the little monster."

Franco took the kitten from me in a way that was far more tender than his words, and he carried him into the house.

He returned a minute later. "C'mon, Wakeland. Let's get this shindig over and done with."

"Yep. Let's do this."

We walked down the pathway and into my car. The dry dirt road kicked up dust as I drove away from the mountain.

"How 'bout we get coffee at Esposito's?" Franco said. "They make a damned good Italian brew, and it's on our way."

"It's a plan."

The horizon remained smudged with smoke as we drove past lonely stands of gum trees and fields with grass as dry as toast. The long dry spell had snatched our normally green valley away and replaced it with a landscape I barely recognised.

Franco shifted about in his seat, whistling and repeatedly pressing his shoulders into the back rest.

"What's up?" I asked, shooting him a curious glance.

"The speeches. Why the Dickens is Bigley making us give speeches? I hate talking about myself."

"I beg to differ."

"Real funny. I don't like talking in front of a crowd. I mean, what am I supposed to say?"

"I don't know. Why don't you talk about you being a volunteer kids' soccer coach? That'll be a crowd pleaser."

"Maybe. They won't know I do it just because I'm bored outta my brain on Sundays."

"That's not why you do it. I know you, Franco—your heart's pinned in the right place."

"Yeah, right on the donkey's butt."

I laughed. "Say *what*?"

"You know, like in that old *pin-the-tail-on-the-donkey* game? Ah, never mind. I'm ranting. Losing the plot."

"Just… chill. Okay? You'll be fine."

After getting our coffee in town, I drove across to Valley Square. People were already streaming through the front gates.

As I parked the car, a teenage boy in a shapeless, oversized tee-shirt rode past on a rusted bicycle. As soon as he spotted our police vehicle, he was quick to whip his head away. There was something in the head turn and hunch of his shoulders that prickled me. Perhaps he'd carried out a petty crime or two recently.

The boy steered his bike around the perimeter of the crowd, and I soon lost sight of him.

CHAPTER FOUR

Franco and I exited the car and headed for Valley Square—the building of which had been the last stage in the CQ development. It was meant to be an open, green space for community use.

Stone pillars and high iron gates guarded the entry of Valley Square.

"Looks a bit fancy for Tallman's Valley," Franco commented.

"Sure does," I agreed.

We pressed our identification passes onto the electronic reader that stood just outside the gates.

An automated female voice greeted us: *Welcome, Detective Sergeant Kate Wakeland and Detective Sergeant Jace Franco. You are currently three minutes past scheduled time. Please make your way to the stage at your earliest convenience.*

Franco shot me a side glance, scratching his chin. "Ehhh, I feel like I just got told off by a bloody robot."

"All a bit pretentious, isn't it?" I tucked my pass back into my pocket.

We stepped through the gates. Ahead lay a vista of greenery, the sprawling square of grass so luridly green it almost hurt my eyes to view it. White mulberry trees edged the square. Fountains bubbled with water. Food and technology stalls had been set up around the perimeter of the square.

The smoky smell from distant fires mingled with the scents of cinnamon doughnuts and fresh fruit juices—making me slightly queasy.

Family groups sat on picnic rugs. Students from the Valley Grammar school gave a violin recital on the wide stage. Enormous screens positioned above the stage showed close-up views of the students and their violins.

A girl with braces and a nervous smile hurried up to Franco and me. She eyed the suits we were wearing and then nodded enthusiastically. "Are you two CQ workers? Are you planning on looking at our newest display homes in the village today? We have lots of options for… older couples."

"We're not a couple," I informed her. "We're *detectives*. Here to speak at the opening ceremony."

A look of dismay had the girl's eyes opening wide. "Oh. *Oh no*. I didn't realise."

"Don't sweat it," Franco told her, shrugging nonchalantly.

But as we walked away, Franco hissed out of the side of his mouth. "She thought we were a *couple*? It's the grey hairs, isn't it? I'm sprouting a lot of them this year."

I smirked at his discomfort. At age sixty-four, I was almost seventeen years older than Franco. "She's just a kid trying to do a good job."

Still, he seemed to grit his teeth. "I know what it is. It's *you*. You look… fit. Bigley said as much."

"Bigley said *what*, exactly?"

"Uh… he said you've got a good rig."

I stared back at him, aghast. "A good rig? Really?"

"Yeah. It was at the Christmas party bash. Bigley threw back a few too many beers and got a bit loose with his tongue. He cut a bit loose with his feet, too. At one point, he was showing us all his best dance moves."

I pictured Superintendent Bigley drunk and dancing. It wasn't a pretty image. "Hmmm, I'm glad I didn't go."

"You didn't miss anything good."

I'd skipped attending that police party and a few other events lately. After the cases this year that had involved my own family, I'd just wanted to spend as much time as possible at home, with the people I loved.

As we reached the stage, the Valley Grammar school finished its violin recital.

A woman stepped out on the stage. Her bright red lipstick matched her red jacket. She was either in her late sixties or early seventies, with immaculate silver hair.

She offered the crowd a beaming smile, speaking in a clipped, cultured voice. "Hello and welcome to a very special town fair. This is the opening of Valley Square—a place for everyone in town to gather. I am Nancy Upchurch, the manager of NineOak—the company behind the CQ developments. I'm normally working hard behind the scenes, in our city offices. It's wonderful to be here today in your lovely, lush Tallman's Valley."

"Lush?" Franco grumbled, pulling at his collar while sweat gathered at his temples. "Does that lady realise we're in the middle of a *drought*?"

I shrugged. "I bet she flew in by helicopter and hasn't strayed far from CQ."

As if on cue, images of intensely green hills began displaying on the large screens just above Nancy Upchurch and the stage.

Franco crossed his arms. "Someone's been busy with the Photoshop work."

Nancy waited for the audience to finish clapping. "Over a decade ago, our plan was to search for a green, unspoiled area within reach of Sydney city. Our project was to build a centre for cutting edge technology. And we found the perfect place for that right here in Tallman's Valley, nestled as it is at the foothills of the majestic Blue Mountains."

Photos of the enormous CQ building displayed on the screens, with its expanses of plate glass and the green plants on its rooftop.

Pointing upwards at the screens, Nancy nodded. "And there it is. CQ. We couldn't be prouder of what we've achieved. The facilities are world class. Tallman's Valley has gained a thousand new people a year on average—from around the world. Amazing, isn't it? The houses we've built for them are ecologically friendly living spaces, with lighting technology adjusted to match natural circadian rhythms…."

Nancy rabbited on and on about the merits of CQ Village, prompting a yawn from Franco.

"The next item on our agenda," Nancy said, "is our wonderful Royal Fire Service. We are all aware of the terrible fires Australia is experiencing at the moment. The RFS is an organisation of firefighting volunteers—and is the largest in the world. Please welcome long-serving member and team leader of the local branch, Pete Wakeland."

I watched, surprised, as my husband walked out on stage. It was so typical of Pete not to say anything about his part in today's event. He'd always been such a laid-back kind of guy. Pete gave a short talk about what we all needed to do to stay safe during the fires, and who to call if we spotted any injured koalas or other wildlife.

Nancy Upchurch clapped as Pete finished his speech and left the stage. "I now introduce you to four computer programmers from CQ Technology—Elliot Calladine, Anaya Malik, Leo Dubois, and Benjamin Tremayne. At CQ, we have an entire room of supercomputers that run billions of processes per second. Our programmers work on many exciting projects, using artificial intelligence and digital imaging."

The faces of the computer programmers appeared on the big screens as they walked out.

Elliot, from England, looked older than the other three—perhaps in his mid-forties—with a shock of dark hair above intense pale-green eyes. Anaya was a pretty woman of Indian background, with her short hair dyed pink. Leo was a blond Frenchman with a gap-toothed smile, round frame glasses perched on his nose. Ben was American, with a serious expression and mousy-brown hair down to his shoulders.

Franco made a dismissive sound from between his teeth.

"What's up?" I asked him.

"That guy—Elliot—Martina started dating him a few months ago."

"Really? He doesn't look like her type."

"He doesn't look like *anyone's* type," Franco muttered.

"Still holding a candle for Martina, huh?"

"I think she could do better than him, that's all."

Four years ago, Franco and Martina had planned on getting married. I didn't know all the details, but Franco had ended up with cold feet and he'd wanted more time. Martina hadn't been prepared to give him that time, and she'd ended the relationship.

After Elliot, Anaya and Leo finished their presentations, the American—Ben—gave his. He laughed nervously before speaking. "Hello, uh, people of Tallman's Valley. What I'm here to show you today is called *digital mapping*."

Ben fitted himself with a strange silver vest and gloves and then switched on a computer. "What you see on the screens above is actually a virtual-reality world."

The screens displayed a video of a street within CQ Village. The houses were all neat and modern, on small blocks of land.

"The suit I'm now wearing has a series of sensor pads." Ben explained.

"With this special suit, I can open doors and pick up objects… and get the full experience."

He pulled on what looked to me like a set of chunky black goggles over his eyes. "This is the headset that allows me to view the virtual world."

To demonstrate, Ben opened the door of a house and walked inside. He entered a theatre room and switched on a movie, then he continued to the kitchen and tried out the inbuilt coffee machine.

"This is a new way of viewing real estate," Ben said. "Someone in Canada, for example, could view this house while wearing this sensor suit, and make a well-informed decision on whether he or she wanted to buy it."

I listened to it all, fascinated. I barely knew what the technology sector of CQ did. I couldn't help but like Ben, who was very obviously uncomfortable with the sudden attention on him.

After Ben's talk, our police superintendent—Andrew Bigley—took over the stage. Bigley had no problem whatsoever with the attention of the crowd. In fact, he seemed to bask in it, puffing up his wide chest and sucking in his stomach.

Nancy Upchurch waved frantically at Franco and me from the side stairs of the stage.

"Goodness," Nancy said as we approached her, "I thought you two were already up here and waiting to go on. It's been a bit of a mess today, all told. I scarcely know what's what, I can tell you." She exhaled with a hooting breath.

"Sorry," I said. "We weren't certain where we were meant to be. The talks have been great so far—I found the young tech guy so interesting."

She nodded enthusiastically, guiding us forward. "Oh, yes. Ben's a wonder. We've got lots planned, with Ben at the helm. Okay, now just stand here, and Superintendent Bigley will call you."

She clattered away again on her red high heels.

Franco clamped his eyes shut, drawing in a series of deep breaths.

"Don't spin out," I told him. "You've got this."

I could see a side view of Bigley on the stage. He was giving the audience a rundown of his time as the superintendent of the Blue Mountains Area Command. It was… *lengthy*.

"And now," Bigley went on, "we celebrate the recent bravery of two members of our force—Detective Sergeant Kate Wakeland and Detective Sergeant Jace Franco. Both have just been awarded the highest medal that police can receive—the prestigious National Police Bravery Award from the

Police Federation of Australia. Among their acts of service over the past months, they have brought five missing children back to us, solved the murders of two of our beloved citizens, and raced headlong into dangerous situations in the pursuit of criminals."

I whispered in Franco's ear as we walked out. "Relax, okay? They'll love you."

I stepped up to the microphone stand. "Good morning, everyone. We're very happy to be here with you today, and we're honoured to be Tallman's Valley police. Detective Franco and I were born and bred here. We've seen many changes in our small town over the years, but the people of our beautiful valley remain the same. We come together in crisis, and we enjoy every minute of the good times. I'll soon be leaving the force and retiring, but with Detective Franco, you'll be in very good hands."

As I continued my speech, my gaze fell upon the faces of my family in the audience. My husband Pete, our daughter Abby, Abby's partner Logan, and their children, Ivy and Jasper—all wearing proud expressions. It was a moment I wouldn't forget. They were my everything.

Franco took the microphone after me, and he did end up relaxing into an inspiring speech, sprinkled with his usual style of dad jokes and humour.

Bigley presented us with the medals. The police ceremony in which we would officially be awarded the medals wouldn't happen until next year, but Bigley had wanted this mock-up ceremony for the fair today. He looked pleased. His star detectives had engaged the crowd, just like he'd wanted. I couldn't help but feel a little like his puppet. He'd too often treated me that way over the years.

As Bigley, Franco, and I returned to the side of the stage, Nancy Upchurch returned to the microphone. "And now we welcome one of the founding members of CQ—Doug Overmire."

Doug Overmire walked out from the opposite end of the stage.

I whirled around to Bigley. "What on earth is *he* doing here?"

Bigley looked at me impassively. "Cool your jets, Kate. I'm not responsible for the itinerary."

"But you knew he'd be here. He's a criminal. And he stood by for years while knowing the terrible things his brother was doing. That family hurt mine… in every possible way."

"You can't call him a criminal without evidence," Bigley said in a hushing tone. "He's the main financier of the CQ development. He's brought thousands of jobs to our region. Doug's done a lot for this town."

A burning sensation spread through my neck. In his late fifties, Doug was the oldest child of Mickey and Henrietta Mulden—the owners of the old carnival. He'd changed his name from Mulden to Overmire soon after the carnival closed down. He was number one on my list of people to investigate, but so far, he'd had a lot of layers of protection around him.

I blocked out everything Overmire was saying to the audience. I was seething that he was even here.

Nancy Upchurch concluded the morning's speeches and then asked everyone back on the stage.

As my husband walked out, I tried to position myself between him and Franco. But Bigley moved in, putting himself beside me and shuffling Pete further along. The students who'd played the violins earlier joined us on the stage, and now I was hedged in.

Nancy Upchurch smiled expansively at the crowd. "I think you will all agree that this stage represents the very best of Tallman's Valley. And now, Superintendent Andrew Bigley has an announcement."

I frowned in annoyance. What else did blowhard Bigley have to say? Hadn't he said enough already? *Apparently not.*

Nancy handed a microphone to Bigley.

Clearing his throat, he began. "As you all know, the Blue Mountains Police Command has some very big shoes to fill with our beloved lead homicide detective, Kate Wakeland, soon leaving us. But I'm pleased to announce that we have a very experienced detective joining us from Sydney."

I couldn't believe what I'd just heard. They were bringing in someone *new*?

Franco muttered something under his breath that I couldn't catch. But I could guess it included a few swear words.

A man walked out onto the platform. His was a face I knew only too well. He'd lost his hair, and the vertical lines at each side of his mouth had deepened, but his boyish blue eyes were the exact same as I remembered.

He'd been my police partner during the decades I'd worked for the state homicide squad.

"Please welcome Detective Sergeant Trevor Melainey," Bigley said.

Bigley's face cracked into a wide grin. In some type of horse play move,

Bigley tossed the microphone to Melainey, and he caught it as if it were a football.

"Wow, well, so happy to be here in your wonderful Tallman's Valley," said Melainey into the microphone. His accent was still that same mix of rugged Irish and broad Australian that he'd had all those years ago. "I've just spent the morning with Superintendent Bigley and Nancy Upchurch, catching up over a long breakfast of pancakes and berries, and finding out all about the valley. I want you to know, in everything I do, I give it a hundred percent. I'm ready to serve and protect the community."

Melainey was a good detective. We'd solved many high-profile cases together. But I was devastated for Franco. Franco was more than ready for the role as lead detective.

That role had just been taken by Trevor Melainey.

It was an unexpected blow.

CHAPTER FIVE

Franco took the wheel on the drive back from the fair. His driving was jerky and his expression numb.

I still felt burned from seeing Doug Overmire on the stage, but it was Franco who'd received the worst shock. Bigley had certainly sprung it on us that Trevor Melainey would be joining our team.

"Bigley's not making any sense," I told Franco. "You're perfect for the role. Why bring in Melainey?"

"Shintani didn't say anything, either."

"Do you think he even knows? I'm not so sure."

Shintani was the police inspector of our homicide team. I held a lot of respect for him.

Franco didn't answer.

I released a tight breath. "I've got a feeling this has been rushed through. And what a time to make the announcement—while we're both in the public face and can't react."

Franco, shaking his head and biting down on his tongue, shot me a bitter glance. "You're dead right, Wakeland. They couldn't have planned it better."

Franco fell into a dark silence as he drove along Kirk Road—the long, straight stretch that led to Witness Mountain.

Nancy Upchurch's images of neon-green hills were nothing like the dry, drought-affected fields on either side of us.

Ahead, a scene suddenly came into view that looked like trouble.

An SUV had stopped at the kerb, the driver standing in the middle of the road.

As we drew closer, I spotted a bicycle with a twisted wheel. A teenage boy sat on the grass at the roadside, his head resting on his knees.

Franco parked just behind the SUV, and we jumped out of the car.

The driver came jogging up. He was sweating in the morning heat, a sports shirt stretched tight over his protruding belly.

"The kid came out of nowhere," the man told us. "Straight in front of me. Just a minute ago."

Franco cast a dubious look at him. "Mate, this is a straight road. Nothing on either side but fields. How'd you fail to see the boy?"

"I swear he just shot out of nowhere," he said. "I swerved, and the kid fell off his bike. My wheel caught one end of the bike and mangled it a bit."

"Did you call an ambulance?" I asked.

He shook his head. "The kid got angry when I said I'd get him one. He seems fine, just a bit shaken up."

Franco crossed his arms. "What's your name, mate?"

"Kenny Mosely."

Franco gestured towards our police vehicle. "Okay, Mr Mosely. I'm just going to conduct a breath test. And then I'll take down some of your details."

"Is that necessary?" Mr Mosely protested. "I haven't been drinking. I didn't even—"

"Just procedure," Franco assured him.

While Franco conducted the alcohol and drug test with Mr Mosely, I walked across to the boy. His face was half-hidden beneath a cap. He wore a faded, oversized tee-shirt and chain store running shoes. Apart from a few scrapes on his hands and left knee, I didn't spot any obvious injuries.

"Hi." I crouched down to him. "How're you feeling?"

"Okay."

"Can you tell me your name?"

"Jordan."

"Last name?"

"Green."

"And your age?"

"Sixteen."

"So, tell me what happened, Jordan?"

He shrugged a shoulder. "Didn't see the car. Sun got in my face."

"Can I see your eyes, please?"

He lifted his cap, looking up for the first time. I caught sight of intense aqua-coloured eyes beneath a set of dark eyebrows. I wasn't sure what I saw in his expression. *Alarm*? *Dread*?

I realised something. This was the kid I'd seen just as Franco and I arrived at the fair earlier, the one who'd turned his head away from me.

I checked Jordan's eyes for signs of dilated pupils. They looked fine.

"Did you get knocked out cold at all?" I asked.

Shaking his head, he raked his teeth across his bottom lip. "Nah."

"Did the car hit you?"

"Nope. I got out of the way fast."

"Does anything feel sore?"

"No."

"That's good. But we'll still get you to a doctor to get checked out."

"Don't need one."

"You must be sitting down for a reason. You're not feeling good, right?"

"I'm just waiting for a lift."

"Okay, great. You've got someone coming to pick you up?"

"Yeah."

"We'll wait with you until they get here."

"No, I…."

I frowned. "Were you going to try to hitch a ride?"

He hesitated, then nodded. "I asked the guy over there for a lift. But he said his car insurer might take that as an admission of guilt if I decide to sue him."

"Right. Okay. Where were you headed?"

"Home."

"Where is home, Jordan?"

"Just up there. On Witness."

"Witness Mountain?"

"Yeah."

"Is someone there now?"

"Yep. Mum and my little brothers."

"Well, don't worry, we'll get you home. I'd like to have a word with your mum, too. She can decide if she wants to take you to a doctor or not."

He glanced away from me. "Okay, thanks for the ride. But mum's sick. She can't talk to you."

"Oh?"

"Yeah. Like, she was throwing up and stuff this morning."

"Hmmm, that's no good. Well, come and get in the car. I'm afraid the bike won't fit, though."

Jordan pulled himself to his feet. "S'ok. The bike's *cactus* anyway."

I eyed the bike. Jordan was right. Besides the twisted wheel, the frame had a fair amount of rust. We didn't have to worry about leaving it behind. No one was going to steal it.

I walked Jordan to the car.

Mr Mosely had returned a negative alcohol reading. He was free to go.

Jordan slid into the back seat, keeping his cap low on his forehead.

I had an uneasy feeling about him. He was hiding something. Whatever it was, I hoped it was something minor.

CHAPTER SIX

Mr Kenny Mosely drove away.

Franco eased our police vehicle back onto the road. Jordan remained quiet in the back seat.

Franco half-turned his head to the boy. "So, your bike is pretty banged up, huh?"

"I guess." Jordan pulled his cap off and ruffled his hair in an agitated way.

"Tell you what," Franco said. "I've got a mountain bike sitting in my back shed doing nuthin'. You can have it."

"Really?" Jordan said incredulously. "Why would you do that?"

Franco shrugged. "You look like a boy who needs a bike is all."

"Thanks," Jordan mumbled, still sounding puzzled.

"So, which street on Witness Mountain, Jordan?" I asked.

"Lone Oak."

"Okay," I replied. "I don't know it, but you can direct us."

We reached the base of the mountain. Ahead, the road sloped upward at an extreme angle.

It'd been years since I'd been up here. Pete and I never came on runs on Witness Mountain. The pebbled roads were too slippery and steep.

Franco drove on. The road climbed around and around the mountain.

The tarred section soon ended, and then we were bouncing along a dirt road that was strewn with small rocks and gravel. Potholes and ridges were a constant feature. The road twisted and meandered around fields that were dotted with cows and goats. It was pretty—apart from the browned grasses.

Franco steered onto Lone Oak Close.

"This is it," the boy stated. "You can drop me where the gate is."

I spotted a house quite a distance away. "Jordan, open up the gate. We'll take you up to your doorstep."

"Uh, no, it's better I get out here," the boy replied, grabbing the handle of the car door. "Mum might be sleeping. Don't wanna wake her."

Maybe his mother really *was* sick and sleeping. Teenagers were sometimes hard to read. But at the same time, there was a slight tremor in his voice. He seemed... *cagey*.

Franco had a frown on his face, as if he'd noticed Jordan's odd behaviour, too.

Something beyond the gate and to the right caught my attention. A mass of flies was swarming, just above grass level.

"Have you got any pets or animals here, Jordan?" I asked gently.

"Nope, no animals."

"Okay, good." I pointed towards the cloud of flies. "Because I think some animal must have wandered onto your land... and died there."

He shrugged. "Probably a bird or something."

"That's a lot of flies for a bird." My mind went somewhere I didn't want it to go. Last year, Franco and I had come across a group of teenagers who'd been torturing animals and uploading the videos online.

Franco shot me a concerned look.

"Hey, Jordan," Franco said. "Whatever it is, I'll help you bury it. Just go grab me a spade."

"No," the boy replied in a tense voice. "I mean, you know, I can do it myself. I don't want to put you out."

It was the kind of conversation that could go nowhere fast. We couldn't force Jordan to get the spade.

"How about I just go take a look and see what it is?" I said. "Then we'll know what we're dealing with."

Jordan protested as I exited the car and walked away, but I pretended not to hear.

Unlatching the gate, I stepped through. To my right sat a thick band of shrubs—all of it *holly grevillea*. I navigated the best path I could find through it. It wasn't easy. The grevillea's red flowers were pretty, but their holly-shaped leaves had been made even more brittle and sharp by these hot summer days. My hands were quickly getting scratched up.

I could hear the flies now. There were blow flies as well as bush flies swarming.

If it was a bird attracting all that attention from the flies, then it was a large one—an eagle, perhaps. I'd never known an eagle to die like that, though. Birds didn't tend to die on the wing.

As I drew closer, I put aside all thoughts of birds and eagles.

Whatever was lying dead on the other side of the bushes was longer and larger than any bird we had here in the Blue Mountains.

Swatting away a fly that came close to landing on my tongue, I quickened my pace.

CHAPTER SEVEN

The next step I took had my heart sinking.

I'd been prepared to find an animal.

But I hadn't been prepared for *this*.

A woman was lying on her side, blood blooming through the light check shirt she wore on her back. There was a small wound to the side of her head, a rust-coloured trickle of blood across her closed eyes. Her skin had a greyish hue.

Both wounds looked as if they'd been sustained from bullets.

A trail of smashed hens' eggs littered the ground near the woman, their gooey contents congealing in the hot sun. I guessed she'd been carrying them in the open bag she had strapped around her waist. The flies were feasting on the broken eggs.

Instinctively, I knelt to brush the flies from the woman's face. When I checked her vital signs, I was surprised and relieved to find she had a pulse.

But there was no breath.

No breath.

Cradling her back with a hand tight over the wound, I began administering rescue breaths.

The woman was in a short window of time between losing her breath and still having a faint pulse. I knew that soon, her pulse would be gone, too.

It's not working... she's not breathing....

Grabbing my radio, I alerted Franco to call for police backup and ambulances. And told him to race the first aid kit over here.

The last thing I said to Franco before ending the call was to tell Jordan to wait in the car. This woman was most probably his mother.

God, the shots I'd heard earlier—were they from this shooting?

Raising my head, I looked around in a tight circle. There were no signs of the children, and no other clusters of flies.

I turned to the house. Were the children in there? And were they alive… or dead?

Franco rushed towards me with the medical kit—Jordan running ahead of him.

Franco muttered as he reached me. "Sorry, couldn't keep him back."

Jordan stared down at the woman, arms over his head in a gesture of shock. "No. *No, no, no….*"

"Jordan," I cried, "get down to the ground. The person who did this might still be here."

Obeying, he crouched down.

"This is your mum, isn't it?" I asked. "What's her name?"

"Angie. Yes, she's my mum. What can I do for her? Tell me what to do?"

"Pray," I replied.

I helped Franco administer surgical bandages and emergency oxygen to Angie. Her breaths slowly restarted. She was still weak and unresponsive, but for now, she was alive and breathing.

Jordan's bottom lip trembled. "I need to find my brothers. Toby and Oliver."

"No, mate," Franco told him. "I'm gonna go. You stay put."

I eyed Franco in alarm. "We need to wait for backup."

Franco's face held a determined expression. "But there are kids here…."

I knew exactly what he meant. If one or both of the kids had been shot, there was a chance they could still be hanging onto life by a thread—like their mother. Every second counted. Even so, this was a shooter situation, and it was damned risky.

"I'll go," I said.

Franco shook his head. "I'm faster than you, Wakeland."

Not giving me a chance to debate him further, Franco charged back to the car and began driving it along the driveway to the house.

I checked Angie again, brushing the ever-swarming clouds of flies away from her. At the same time, I kept an eye on Jordan, one hand close to my gun holster. I didn't know him, or what he might have done, or what he might do next.

Jordan's breaths were hard and strained. "Is she—?"

"She's doing okay."

Angie wasn't doing okay. But I couldn't tell Jordan that.

"Will she live?"

"She's trying hard—giving it all she's got. Jordan, I need you to answer my next question honestly. Do you know of anyone who might have shot your mother? Anyone else who lives on the property?"

"No. We don't even live here, anymore. Mum only brought us back for the school holidays. We've been here, I don't know, maybe two weeks."

I turned this new piece of information over in my mind.

They'd only just been here for two weeks?

It raised new possibilities. Was this a random shooting? The whole situation was about as unclear as it could get.

"What about your dad?" I asked. "Is he in the picture at all?"

Jordan shook his head. "My mum and dad split up over a year ago. Dad went to Sydney for work."

"In the city?"

"Yeah."

I calculated the distance. Sydney city was about two hours away from here. If the father was in the city right now, he wasn't the person who'd shot Angie.

"How old are your brothers?"

"Six and four."

"Okay, they're just little. Don't worry, we'll find them."

I radioed Franco, relaying the age of the kids. Kids that young could be hiding in some tiny spaces in the house.

Jordan half pulled himself to his feet. "I gotta go help find them."

"Don't," I warned. "Stay here and stay down."

Franco pulled the car up sharp next to the house, the wheels crunching on the gravel.

"Police!" he called. "If anyone's in there, come out now. Hands in the air."

All was quiet. My heart in my mouth, I waited for a response.

Two magpies chased each other across the sky, completely unconcerned about the scene unfolding beneath them. Their raucous calls broke the silence.

Franco entered the house, his gun raised.

I monitored Angie, willing the ambulance to get here quick. She was fading.

Twelve minutes passed. In the distance came a wail of sirens. The ambulances.

Franco emerged from the house.

Alone.

He headed towards a shed that looked large enough to house tractors.

My radio crackled.

"The kids aren't here," came Franco's voice over the radio. "I searched everywhere."

That was both good news and bad news. He hadn't found them dead. But he hadn't found them alive, either. Where were they?

I tried to think of the places my granddaughter Ivy liked hiding.

"Are there any playhouses outside?" I replied.

"Negative," said Franco. "No playhouses. And no toys. The house is practically empty."

No toys? A terrible thought struck me. What if Jordan was just making it up about having younger brothers? Just to force us to search for them so he could get rid of us?

Taking my eyes off the house and shed, I whipped my head around to Jordan.

He was gone.

CHAPTER EIGHT

The ambulances arrived first, clouds of reddish-brown dust blooming from their wheels.

I gave the care of Angie over to the paramedics, protecting them while they worked on her—my gun in hand.

The situation was still highly dangerous. Whoever shot Angie might still be on the grounds. If it was Jordan, then the shooter was definitely still here. Jordan must have crawled away through the masses of grevillea bushes that surrounded us. I couldn't guess in which direction he'd gone.

I watched Angie being carried into a waiting ambulance. I took a short walk around the area where Angie had been lying. There were more eggs, all smashed, as if she'd been running and dropping them from her bag at the time she was shot.

Franco ran up to me. "Strange house. Almost no furniture. Just the bare essentials. Hey, where's Jordan?"

"He took off while I was talking to you on the radio."

"Damn."

"I'm kicking myself hard for taking my eyes off him. Hey, if I can believe what he said, the family don't live here. They just returned for the summer holidays."

"That'd explain the empty house."

"Did you spot anything that looked like it belonged to two little boys? I'm starting to doubt they even exist."

He caught his breath, staring back at me. "No kids, huh? I wouldn't put it past Jordan. He was kind of shifty."

Taking out my phone, I called the station. "Thea, could you look up a name for me? Angie Green. We're currently at number eight, Lone Oak, Witness Mountain—but apparently this is an old address of hers. I need to know her current home address and names of her children. Thanks."

I inhaled a quick, deep snatch of air as I ended the call, looking back at Franco. "Okay, well, until we know differently, we have to assume the kids exist."

"Yeah," he said. "Problem is that this is a big property, surrounded by a lot of other big properties. They could be anywhere."

I brought up a map of the area on my phone. "The nearest neighbours are just on the other side of that fence. Maybe the kids ran there." I pointed to the fence line north of where Angie had been lying.

"Yep," he said. "And Angie was carrying a dozen or so eggs. I'm betting on the neighbours being the ones to supply them. I mean, she wouldn't have chickens here if she'd only come for the school holidays."

"You're right. We need to go check this out."

Franco ran a hand through his thick hair, sweat gathering at his hairline. "Wakeland… if the neighbours had just given Angie the eggs, at least one of 'em would have been right there as it happened. I mean, even if they didn't see the shooting, you'd think they'd have noticed the sound of someone firing off rounds of ammo. But we didn't get any police reports come through."

"The shooter could be the neighbour…." I breathed.

"Yeah."

I pulled my gun out again, tension running in waves along my arms. "Let's go."

CHAPTER NINE

The neighbouring house was dead still on our approach.

Nothing but the faint drone of a TV set.

The house was located close to the fence line, just on the other side of a low stone wall. There was a gate between the two properties.

As Franco had guessed, there was a chicken coop here. Ten or so brown hens placidly pecked away at the soil.

We moved through the gate and towards the house.

"Hello?" Franco called. "This is the police. If anyone's here, show yourself. Come out slowly. Hands in the air."

I made my way along the stone wall. "Toby! Oliver! If you're here anywhere, please come out. We're the police. We can help you."

No one answered our calls. No one came out from the house.

One more step had my foot kicking something hard in the tall grass. A boot. I walked around the edge of the wall to find a man of about eighty lying there.

Angled across his arm and chest was a rifle. An old .303 bolt action sniper rifle.

The flies were thick on the man's body. He'd been shot just below the chin. The blood had drained from his cheek, pooling darkly on the side of his face that lolled against the ground.

Before I crouched to check his pulse, I already knew I wouldn't find one.

He'd been dead for some time.

Franco walked up beside me, his expression grim. "I think we've just found our shooter."

"My God, what went on here?" I breathed.

Taking out his phone, Franco snapped some photographs.

Still crouching on the ground, I made a quick study of the man's body. I noticed that the glass face of his watch was cracked. The watch was no longer working, with the time set close to 7:15.

Guns raised, Franco and I continued to the back door of the house and entered the kitchen.

A second body was sprawled across a broken kitchen chair, clad in a floral dress. The woman looked a little younger than the man outside. She'd been shot in the chest, and she was very obviously dead.

I guessed she'd fallen on the chair when she'd been shot.

A mobile phone sat nearby on the kitchen bench. She might have been trying to race for the phone. But she hadn't made it.

I hated to leave her draped over the broken chair, so undignified in death, but I couldn't touch her or even close her eyes. The forensic team would need the scene to remain as it was.

Franco stepped around the kitchen, examining a small round hole in a cupboard door. "A bullet made that hole."

My phone rang. It was Constable Thea Georgiades, calling me back after my request to her earlier. I put the phone on speaker so that Franco could hear.

"Detective Wakeland," Thea began, "I can't pin down a recent address for Angie Green. Last address I can find is Lone Oak Close, Witness Mountain—the one you already mentioned. She has three children. All boys. Jordan, Toby and Oliver."

"Thanks, Thea. That's a great help."

"Oh, and her parents are Gus and Perdita Iverson. They live on the property next door."

"*Right next door*?" I cried.

"Uh, let me check again. Yep, their property borders Lone Oak and Orphan. Theirs is the only house close to Angie's."

I eyed the dead Mrs Iverson. "Thank you."

As I put my phone away, I raised my face to Franco, sighing heavily. "These people are Angie's *parents*."

Franco pressed his lips together so hard they went white. "Her parents? Hell. Okay, Her own dad's the culprit."

"What possessed him to do this?"

At the same time that the words left my tongue, something didn't seem right with this whole scene. The elderly, deceased man outside looked frail. How had he managed to shoot two women over such a large distance—with neither of the women being able to get to a phone… or a car?

But I didn't have time to think on that right now.

"Where on earth are the kids?" I breathed.

The children had possibly been shot, too. Or maybe not. There were other, silent ways of killing people. And in a multiple killing spree like this one, the odds were high that the children were dead.

Still, Franco and I took one look at each other, then turned and stormed through the house—searching every room, calling the two younger boys' names over and over.

The elderly couple's house was cluttered. If the children were here, hiding, they could be in any number of places.

Family photos of Angie and her three boys adorned the walls. A sad sight after what had just happened here.

I stopped to call Inspector Jiro Shintani. "Jiro, we have a multiple shooting situation. Besides the female victim we notified you of, we have two elderly victims on the neighbouring property. Both deceased. As far as I understand, they're Angie Green's parents."

"Noted," he replied. "And, as for Angie's children?"

"Still searching for them. No sign so far."

"I'll inform backup. Should be only a minute away now. I've got forensics on their way, too—they'll get started once you tell us the site is secure. Take care, Kate."

As the conversation ended, I heard the faint blare of police sirens.

Twenty minutes later, despite a team of a dozen officers searching with Franco and me, we still hadn't found Toby or Oliver. We hadn't located Jordan, either.

I made the call to bring in additional search teams and search-and-rescue dogs. Then I called Shintani back to tell him that the area was safe for the forensic group to come in.

Out in the forest, someone was bellowing commands in a vaguely Irish accent. At first, I was confused as to who it was.

But then… of course, it was Trevor Melainey.

I'd been so intent on finding the children that I'd put all thought of him on the back burner.

He crossed his arms as I turned in his direction. "I wonder what caused the old man to pop his cork and try to kill his family?"

"I'm hoping Angie Green can shed some light—if she pulls through."

"For sure. Sometimes, I miss the old days of the good old shootouts. At the end of the siege, we'd either shoot them dead or take them into custody, leaving the rest of the family alive. Nowadays, family shooters just kill everyone."

"I really wish they'd just… turn themselves and their guns in, before they do something like this."

"Yeah, true enough. Anyway, congratulations on your medal, Wakeland. Impressive. I didn't get a chance to say it before. You left pretty quickly."

I wondered if he guessed that Franco had been angered by the decision to bring him into our team.

"Just as well I left when I did," I answered, "given the circumstances."

"Can't debate you on that one. I certainly didn't expect to walk into anything like this on my first day on the job."

"It's been a long while since we had a multiple shooting in the valley. Strange set of circumstances. The young woman—Angie—she'd only been here for a couple of weeks. Sounds as if she'd brought her kids back to her hometown to see their grandparents. Then *this* happens."

He winced. "Must have been something dire brewing in that family. And it all came to a head."

"Seems that way." I shook my head. "Melainey, can I ask something? Why the move out here to the valley? As I recall, you once said you hated the thought of country life."

"I've mellowed."

I searched his face for the truth in that statement. But I couldn't tell if he was being sincere or not. A humorous look always used to lurk in his eyes, and that hadn't changed. He'd be fifty-seven years old now. He'd been a handsome guy once, and he still retained a commanding look. There'd been a time when Pete had grown a little jealous, when I used to work alongside Melainey. But Pete never had anything to worry about.

Choosing to hide my thoughts, I said, "Well, welcome to the mountain command homicide crew. Enjoy your slower pace of life. It's *usually* slower here. This year has proved the exception."

"Won't take me long to get into the rhythm of things. Can't believe I've never been out to the mountains before. No, actually, I can. I'm just a hopeless city boy. To be honest, it was Siobhan who was pining for some country life."

I gave a small laugh. "Now, *that* I can believe."

Melainey's wife, Siobhan, had grown up on a farm in Ireland.

"To tell you the truth," he said, "I was a bit shocked when Bigley ran this past me. But Siobhan talked me into accepting the role. And here we are."

"Will you be renting or buying here?"

"Already bought. We'll be moving in during the week. Siobhan picked the house. She's all excited about renovating it. Eh, I couldn't give a toss about that sort of stuff. A house is a house." He shrugged. "Okay, back to the task at hand. We need to get those kids found. What are your thoughts so far?"

"I'm forging ahead with the idea that the kids are alive—until something tells me different. Any ideas?"

"No, I'm stumped, to be honest. Grandpa goes nuts and tries to kill his daughter, then goes after grandma… but the grandkids are missing. We should have found the little ones by now, cowering under a bed or something."

It was worrying that we hadn't found them.

I hated the images rearing up in my mind now. Raw, ugly images. Homicide crime scenes were always awful, but especially so when they involved children.

"And the teenage boy took off?" Melainey said. "Destination unknown?"

"Yes," I said from between my teeth. It was my fault the boy was missing, and I guessed that Melainey knew that.

"Well, let's keep going hard in the search for the kiddies. Perhaps they ran off further than we think they could have. I'll spread the teams out."

"Go for it," I said.

Melainey gave me a nod and then turned and jogged away.

I walked across to Franco. He was over by the chicken pen, studying something on his phone. He looked up on my approach. "Did Melainey find anything?"

"No, not so far. He's taking the search field wider."

I wasn't going to admit it in front of Franco, but it was good to have Melainey here with us today. I'd been on investigations with him in the past in which we'd found missing children after one or both of their parents had been murdered. He had a ton of experience.

I gestured towards Franco's phone. "What have you got there?"

"Just doing some digging, trying to see what family Angie or Carlson might have here in town."

"Find anything interesting?"

"Nope. Can't find anyone for Angie. Carlson's parents live in the UK."

"Okay. Worth looking into."

He turned his screen to me, displaying a photo of a blond man in a suit and tie. "This is Angie's ex-husband, Carlson Green—the father of the three boys. I used to see him about town."

"Oh, yeah, me too. Isn't he a real estate agent?"

"Yep. Lives in the city now. Shintani tried to call him, but he couldn't get him on the phone. He left him a message."

"He'll be going out of his mind once he gets that message. A multiple shooting and all three of his kids missing."

I exhaled, sweat pricking my scalp and the back of my neck. I was desperate to know what happened to Toby and Oliver. But so far, all the frantic searching had revealed nothing.

CHAPTER TEN

"Hey," I said to Franco, "I'm going to take a wander and have a think. Carve out a bit of headspace."

I made my way through the gate of the Iversons' land and back onto Angie's property. I walked to the spot in which I'd found Angie.

Letting my eyes close, I pictured the scene as it was when I'd first seen it. Before police search teams had stomped all over the surrounding grass.

Angie had been shot in the back and the side of her head. The head wound appeared to be the less serious wound, and I guessed it'd come first. She might have stayed on her feet after that shot—the blood I'd seen on her face had dripped down in a vertical path at first. Gus Iverson had fired again, the bullet entering Angie's back and this time making her drop to the ground. He would have been fairly certain he'd killed her.

I recalled the line of smashed eggs leading up to where she fell. It told a story of a woman who'd been making a desperate dash.

She must have been running to the house to get the children.

So, why weren't they there? If they'd run away, why hadn't we found them?

The only real possibility left was that Jordan had done something with them. We had to find him.

But… there was the tiniest detail about Angie Green that confused me. She'd been wearing a loose, lightweight, unbuttoned shirt over her tank top, and somehow, she'd managed to keep it on while she was running. If she'd run all the way from her parents' property to where I'd found her, the shirt should have fallen off her shoulders.

I went for runs every week. I knew well that if I wore a loose, unbuttoned shirt over my top, I couldn't keep the damned thing on for longer than a few seconds. It was guaranteed to fall off.

It seemed to me that shortly before Angie had been shot in the back, she'd suddenly stopped—at which point she'd pulled her shirt on.

If so, why had she stopped? Had she tried to talk with her father and convince him to throw his gun down? Or… had the children emerged from the house at that time? If the children had done that, she might have been terrified of drawing the shooter to them.

The first scenario didn't seem likely to me. I assumed he'd already shot Angie in the head by this point—she'd have had little reason to believe he'd spare her.

The second scenario made the most sense. If the kids had come out of the house, she might have stopped—pulling her shirt back on and gathering her nerve—trying to figure out how to prevent her father from shooting them.

Maybe she'd even called out a warning to the children, telling them to go hide somewhere specific. The hiding place could be that good that it was fooling us.

It was a flimsy theory. Super flimsy. And even if my theory was right, I had no way of knowing where she'd told the kids to go. Not even a whisker of an idea.

Franco's voice came from behind me, making me jump. "A coin for your thoughts, Wakeland."

I turned around. "I think I'm going to search in and around the house again."

"The team has done a pretty thorough job of that."

"I know. Look, this is just a wild thought—what if Angie told the kids exactly where to go and hide? So far, our thinking has been along the lines of places that small children might choose to go hide. But what if the kids are in a hiding place that an adult thought of?"

He flung a sceptical look at me. "It would have been hard for Angie to come up with something on the fly—'specially while being shot at."

"You're right. Maybe I'm just having trouble grappling with the alternative —of the kids being dead this whole time."

"Hey, I wasn't discounting your idea."

"I know. If I seem a bit sensitive, it's just been a hell of a day."

"No argument there. Okay, let's just go with your idea. It'd have to be something the kids would understand, and that Angie thought her father wouldn't. What would that place be?"

I shook my head. "Nothing's coming to me. Nothing that hasn't been searched already."

"Let's just go look around."

Franco and I walked up to Angie's house and through the rooms, stepping around the forensics group, who were now at work in the kitchen. The house seemed so, so empty. Not just because of the lack of furniture and normal household things, but because it was devoid of the noise of the children who were supposed to be here.

There was really nowhere in the house where two children could be hiding.

We headed outside into the bright, hot sun again.

Near a stand of trees sat some wooden crates with empty food cans on top—cans that had once held corn and beetroot.

Rusted cans with bullet holes in them were scattered on the grass nearby, along with old bullets.

"Someone's been using these as target practice," Franco remarked.

"Possibly Jordan."

"I'd lay bets it was him. That tells us he knew how to shoot. I'm guessing those bullets were shot from a .303, too."

A numbered identification marker had been placed by police at the scene. A search team would have found this corner of the grounds earlier.

Franco and I walked from that spot over to the shed. Everything inside the shed had been pulled out or apart in the search for the children.

We continued. At the back of the shed, a large awning threw some welcome shade. Four sizeable dog kennels stood beneath the awning.

"They must have had some large dogs at one point," I remarked.

They'd probably been herding dogs. I knew many herding dog breeds liked to remain outdoors, even during our freezing cold Blue Mountain winter nights, when the temperatures got down to zero or less. My two Maremma dogs were like that.

The kennels were long, and custom made, with tiny porches and canopies. Someone had carefully constructed these, ensuring that the dogs could keep out of the rain. They were overgrown with a climbing grass that had knotted.

Stinging nettles stood tall and spindly all around. There hadn't been any dogs here for quite some time.

An old dog kennel might be a place a desperate parent would tell a child to hide, but a police number marker showed the kennels had been searched.

Getting down on our hands and knees, Franco and I shone the light from our phones into the dark space of each kennel. There was nothing inside any of them.

Franco pulled himself to his feet, frowning. "The kennel on the middle left looks longer on the outside than it does on the inside."

I glanced at the kennel he gestured at. "It does?"

"I might be imagining it." He stood there for a moment, chewing his lip. "Nah, not imagining it."

He ducked down and crawled right inside.

Crouching, I stared in after him.

He pushed at the end wall of the kennel.

The wall swung slightly. It was actually a door.

Franco was right. There must be a small, additional chamber beyond that internal door. I guessed it had been made for an old-timer herding dog that thought it could brave the winters—but in reality, its fur was getting a bit threadbare.

Franco's voice was taut as he turned his head. "Something's stopping it from opening."

Panic swept through me.

The kids couldn't possibly be in *there*, could they? It would be the tiniest space—barely big enough for a dog. And with the heat today, it'd be airless.

Franco jammed himself into a corner, attempting to shine some light through the sliver of an opening.

"Hell," he cried, fast-crawling back out of the kennel. "I spotted a hand—a little kid's hand."

CHAPTER ELEVEN

I radioed the paramedics, who were still waiting in the ambulances outside the property gates. "Requesting urgent assistance. We've found at least one of the kids. Condition unknown. He's trapped in a dog kennel near the shed at Angie Green's house."

Next, I radioed our homicide team. The more hands, the better.

Franco returned with hammers, a saw and crowbar that he'd grabbed from the shed. Working faster than I'd ever seen him go before, he had some planks off the kennel roof within seconds. I worked from the opposite side of the roof, knocking out nails with a hammer.

A view inside the back chamber of the kennel opened up.

The boys were curled up together, their faces pale and perspiring.

"Toby... Oliver," I breathed. "Hold on. We're getting you out of there...."

The smaller of the boys moaned for his mother in a soft voice, but his eyes remained closed. The other boy didn't respond at all.

Trevor Melainey charged up to us. With his bare hands, he wrenched off a plank of wood that I'd loosened.

Two ambulances drove straight up to us, paramedics jumping out as they parked.

Franco, Melainey, and I moved back to allow the paramedics to assess and retrieve the children.

My pulse raced as I waited to hear the condition of the older boy, Toby.

Within the next minute, we were told he was weak but breathing.

The boys were treated at the scene and then swiftly escorted away.

Franco and I walked behind the ambulances and out to the road. I'd called a quick meeting of my team at the entry gates to Angie's property. Now that the children were found, we needed to plan our next steps.

While I waited for everyone to make their way here, I tried to stretch out my back muscles. They were knotted and sore and giving me trouble.

A figure stood at a distance up the road, watching the departing ambulances.

Jordan.

I jogged up to him, half expecting he'd run. And we'd have to chase him by car. But he didn't run.

There were smears of dirt on his hands and forehead, and his clothing was partly wet.

"Jordan, where did you go?" I demanded.

"The creek. I thought Toby and Ollie might go there."

"You've been gone for almost an hour. The police have been looking for you, calling your name—didn't you hear them?"

"Yeah, I heard. But I was looking for my brothers."

He stared back at me, a dull anger entering his eyes. The anger was a little chilling. Very different to the usual look I'd see in the eyes of a teenager who I was confronting.

"Tell me why I should believe you?" I said. "You know, we could have used your help when we were trying to find them. You'd know things we don't."

He looked at his bare, muddy feet. "How are they? They're okay... aren't they?"

"No, they're not okay. They were in the back of one of the dog kennels. Fast running out of air."

He jerked his head up. "What? Why did they—? Oh... crap, they used to like playing in there, pretending to be dogs."

He sounded genuine. But was he expressing astonishment because he'd been anxious to save his brothers... *or to kill them*?

Jordan glanced away from me again, the muscles in his jaw flexing.

"Come with me now, Jordan—we'll drive you to the station." I drew a breath, reminding myself that this was a kid who'd just lost his grandparents—

and he might lose his mother, too. His erratic behaviour might have a viable explanation.

I softened my tone. "Jordan, I'm afraid we have some bad news. It's about your grandparents."

"My grandparents? Where are they? They were going into town—to get groceries."

"I'm afraid they didn't leave their house."

"But they're okay… aren't they?"

I shook my head.

He trembled now, staring at me as if I must be lying.

"I'll explain as we walk." Putting an arm around his shoulders, I walked him along the road.

When we reached the police vehicle that Franco and I had driven him here in, he got in silently. His expression was numb.

"Wait here," I said.

I stepped up to my team, who'd assembled at the gate.

"A good result in the end, as far as the children are concerned," I said to the team. "We can leave the site in the hands of forensics now. Except for one thing. I want a few people to search the area around the creek again. That's where Jordan said he was, and his wet clothing seems to back that up. But, just to be certain, I want to know if he was doing something there other than to look for his brothers."

CHAPTER TWELVE

Inspector Shintani walked up to my desk at the station. "Kate, are you ready to begin the meeting? I've organised some lunch to be brought in. I know none of you who attended the case this morning have eaten."

"Yes, I'm ready. And thanks for the lunch." I hesitated, tapping my fingers on the desk. "I need to ask you something. It's about Melainey. Did you know he was joining the mountain command?"

His expression grew heavy. "Not until this morning."

"The way Bigley phrased it, Melainey will be stepping into the role of lead detective?"

"It does seem that way. I'm as surprised as you are."

"I understand. I'm cranky I wasn't given advance notice. I mean, I *am* still the lead at the moment."

"It was poor form. Unfortunately, the superintendent will be attending the meeting. He's on his way."

"Oh, what? I thought Bigley would have buzzed off straight after the fair."

Although Superintendent Bigley kept an office at the Tallman's Valley police station, his main office was in the Sydney suburbs—and he spent most of his time there.

Shintani shrugged. "Apparently, he's been at CQ with Nancy Upchurch. Hey, I'll sit in on the meeting and be your wingman if you like."

That drew a grin from me. Shintani had a serious, reserved character, but he wasn't lacking a sense of humour. He'd been a senior homicide detective himself before going onto become an inspector, and his presence in our meetings was always welcome.

I put my paperwork away in a file and walked with him to the meeting room.

The room was full of police. The multiple shooting had prompted a big investigation.

Shintani cleared his throat. "Good afternoon, everyone. I'm very proud of what was achieved at Witness Mountain today. The lives of a woman and two young children were saved. Detectives Wakeland and Franco did an outstanding job. And everyone put in a fantastic effort during the very trying conditions. It's unfortunate that before anyone arrived on the scene, an elderly couple died in what appears to be a murder suicide. This terrible incident will send shockwaves through our community, and beyond."

Franco and I went to stand next to Shintani. Together, we gave a timeline of everything that had happened, from the moment I'd heard the gunshots.

Shintani took the job of writing up the timeline on the whiteboard.

I glanced across at Constable Thea Georgiades. I'd tasked her with researching the backgrounds of the Iverson couple and their daughter, Angie.

"Constable," I said, "what have you been able to find out so far about the family?"

Thea took out a couple of pages of notes. "Okay, well, it seems that Angie Green and her parents lived at Witness Mountain a long time, in the two adjoining properties. Angie's parents—Gus and Perdita Iverson—seemed to have lived pretty quiet lives. Church on Sundays, volunteering with the local historical society—that kind of thing. Perdita did waltzing on Saturday nights. They owned a bakery, where Gus worked. Gus gave up the bakery about ten years ago, because of his bad legs. Gus has severe arthritis, apparently. Angie divorced her husband about 18 months ago, and then she moved away from town a year back. Her ex-husband, Carlson Green, moved into CQ Village after the divorce. And then, more recently, he moved to Double Bay, in the city. That's all I've got for now."

"Thanks, Constable," I said warmly. Thea had only been on the team for about four months, but she was shaping up well.

I turned to the whole team. "So, it seems we have nothing out of the ordinary in the backgrounds of the family. What we need to establish now is the order of events before we arrived at the scene."

"I'd suggest that Gus shot his daughter first," Melainey said. "Because she'd be the fastest out of the two. And then Gus went after his wife. Then he shot himself."

Franco crossed his arms. "Eh, I'm not so sure. Constable Georgiades just told us that Gus Iverson had bad legs. That's a lot of running about for an old guy on wobbly legs."

I nodded. "That's a big problem. It doesn't add up. Two women, running in different directions, were unable to get away from one elderly man with bad arthritis."

"Perhaps the granddad and grandson planned this together?" Melainey offered. "I've investigated a couple of family shootings where two members of the family were involved."

Constable Thea Georgiades lifted her hand. "Jordan does seem a bit suspicious. I mean, it sounds as if he knew something was up before you guys even found his mother? And then he vanished. Your timeline says Jordan was down at the creek the entire time police were looking for the kids? Well, what was he doing there, exactly?"

"Right," Melainey said. "That's what I want to know."

"I led the team that searched the creek," Franco put in. "We conducted a thorough search. We found evidence that Jordan was there—his footprints were along the banks of the creek. But nothing else."

I nodded at Franco. "I wonder if he was trying to hide something?"

Franco gave an uncertain shrug. "Seemed more like he was looking for something—like his brothers. The footprints went a long way along the creek."

That correlated with what Jordan had claimed, at least.

I turned to address the room. "Well, hopefully, things will become clearer once we're able to question Jordan. Of course, being that Jordan is a minor, we need the permission of his father. Carlson Green has only just answered the text message and so he's only just found out about the shootings. He's driving over here now. We've scheduled an interview for tomorrow morning."

Lunch arrived—a mix of chicken, meatball and salad subs. Shintani had ordered it from our usual sandwich shop.

We'd barely finished the lunch before Superintendent Bigley strolled in.

Bigley made a sweeping glance around the room, sighing deeply. "Well, of all days for something like this to occur. While we were all at the fair, reassuring the public that all is well again in our valley… there was a shooting event at play."

He almost sounded disappointed in us, as if we should have been able to prevent such a thing from happening.

"Sir, we're taking a lunch break," I pointed out.

"My apologies," he replied. "I'll be short."

I exchanged glances with Franco. Bigley was *never* short.

He asked a rundown of everything that had occurred on Witness Mountain, and he wanted to know what next steps had been planned in the investigation.

Bigley's intrusion was lengthy, and it was wasting time.

And we didn't have time to waste.

CHAPTER THIRTEEN

Fatigue weighed on me as I walked onto the front deck of my house.

It was late. Near midnight. The sky was a clear indigo, apart from a smoky haze sitting at the horizon.

Franco and I had stayed at the station long after everyone else had left, collating and analysing all the information that had come in so far.

Elsa and Snowdrop bounded up. Collapsing on the swing seat, I hugged the two Maremma dogs, burying my face in their white fur.

Pete stuck his head out the front door. "Thought I heard you."

"Hi. You're still up?"

"Yeah, waiting for you." He came to sit beside me on the swing seat. "How'rc you doing?"

"I'm okay."

"Haven't heard from you since midday. But I was expecting you'd be late home."

I exhaled, crinkling my eyes shut. "I'm sorry, Pete. I got caught up."

"Don't be sorry. I know it's all systems go when something like this happens."

I breathed in and out slowly, collecting myself. It wasn't okay not to stay in contact with Pete. It never had been. This was the kind of thing I used to do too often to him—get so intent on a case that I forgot everything else. Today,

I'd burned through every scrap of energy I had. But still, I needed to keep in touch with Pete and keep him in the loop. He deserved that.

I explained to Pete how the day had unfolded, filling in details to which the media hadn't been privy.

Pete listened carefully. "Awful stuff. This whole thing is going to leave a lot of people feeling pretty shaken. That feeling like anything could happen."

"True. I was there, and it's hard even for *me* to grasp. Three people shot. Two dead. In *our* town."

"Kate… are you sure you're okay? After all, you and Franco were the first ones on the scene."

"I don't know what I'm feeling, to tell you the truth. I'll be sure to book in for some counselling if I need it. But I think finding the little boys alive lifted my spirits. It's what I needed to keep going today."

"How are they?"

"Much better. They're going to be fine. But their mother's in a coma—due to the headshot wound, the doctors think."

He was silent for a moment. "I was proud of you this morning at the fair."

"Thanks, honey. I was proud of you, too. I felt like calling out to everyone in the crowd, *hey, that's my husband up there*!"

He gave a low chuckle. "Well, aren't we just a mutual admiration society?"

"Yep." I smiled.

"Couldn't believe it when I spotted Trevor Melainey, though. He's a blast from the past."

"Yeah. He sure is."

"Maybe it'll be a good thing—take the pressure off you."

"Yes, maybe. Stings for Franco though."

"True. How'd he take it?"

"Not well. But neither would I. If there's a silver lining in this, maybe it's that Melainey can help take on the problems of this town. I mean… the problems stemming from the past. He was around in the 80s. He knows exactly the kind of thing that went on. You know, with him, Franco and me pulling together, we might be able to get somewhere. Someone's got to start digging under the surface."

I was intent on finding out all I could. It was only this year I'd caught glimpses of terrible things that had ties to the past, and my eyes were open now.

I'd moved away from our valley in the mid-1970s, when I was 20. I'd recently joined the police force then. I lived in Sydney to the end of the 1980s.

The 70s and 80s had been the era of mobsters in Sydney. And it was the *police* who'd been the mobsters. The drug lords and crime kings of Sydney had been the detectives in the drug squad and the homicide squad. There'd been cold-blooded murderers in our police force.

No one believed the extent of the rot. Until it was all dragged kicking and screaming into the light.

It had been a rough time and place to be a cop.

The roughest.

But not all of the cops back then were bad. There'd still been detectives who'd wanted to make a difference, make things better, make things right.

I'd believed that Tallman's Valley had been immune to the rot—a place that was untouched. But I was wrong. There were deep shadows here.

Pete had gone quiet while I'd been caught up in memories. He bent to ruffle Elsa behind the ears.

"Pete?"

"Yeah?" He didn't look up.

"I know I need to leave all this behind me soon," I said softly.

"You sure you can do that?" His voice had a tired, frustrated quality to it.

"Yes, I can."

"Good." Turning his head slightly, he shot me a tight smile. "You can't keep going forever. You've gotta hand over the baton."

"I'm getting ready to do that."

"Are you?"

I nodded and then put my head on Pete's shoulder. I gazed out at the low hills of our property and the thick line of trees that I could only just make out in the darkness.

I wasn't being entirely truthful with Pete, and I hated that I couldn't be.

"Abby made tiramisu," Pete said. "Interested in a late-night snack? I wouldn't say no to another helping myself."

I wasn't much of a sweets eater, but tiramisu was my kryptonite. "Love some."

I hugged the dogs goodnight. They zoomed off for their nightly routine of checking that the perimeters of their property were safe and not breached by strange animals or humans.

Pete and I had our snack together and then headed upstairs.

I hung back to peek into my grandchildren's rooms, as I did every night when I came home late—just to see their little faces as they slept.

Ivy, with her dark hair fanned out on the pillow, looked so much like Abby at the same age. When I looked in Jasper's room, his cot was empty.

A light was on in the bathroom down the hall. I poked my head in through the open door. Abby was kneeling beside the bath, baby Jasper splashing in the water.

Abby looked up at me through damp locks of hair. "He's got bad wind pains again. This seems to be the only thing that settles him."

"Poor little mite." I crouched to brush Abby's hair back and then trickled a scoop of warm bath water on Jasper's belly. "Hello beautiful boy, is your tummy giving you trouble again?"

Abby sighed, stretching her arms and back. "He's a lot better than he was half an hour ago."

"I can rock him for a while, if you like? Is he nearly done with the bath?"

"Yeah, I think he's done. Are you sure, though? You look tired. You've come home really late tonight."

"Have you seen the news?"

"No? I haven't had the TV on all day. Why, what happened?"

"I'll tell you all about it tomorrow."

"Anything to do with the fires? Are we safe?"

"It's nothing about the fires."

She nodded. "Maybe I'll sleep better without knowing what it is." She gathered Jasper up from the bath with a towel, and she carried him into his room.

I changed him into fresh clothes while she collapsed into the rocking chair.

Picking Jasper up, I cuddled him. "You're going to have a lovely snooze now, aren't you, little one?"

Abby glanced out the window. "I'm wondering if all that smoke in the air is bothering him. Logan and I took the kids to a park after the fair, but the air was so bad that we just came home."

I tutted, frowning. "Yes, it could be the smoke. I've heard of a lot of people having issues. What if we put up some play equipment here for Ivy and Jasper?"

"No, Mum. You and Dad have done enough for us. You've been letting us stay here. And you're giving us your old house. I feel like we're taking too much."

"Never. Don't talk like that. We're a family, okay?"

She gave a weary smile. "Logan's almost finished painting the inside of the house. We'll be moving out soon."

"I'll miss you. I know you and Logan need your own space. But your father and I have loved having you and the kids here."

"Really? Even when we're noisy?"

"Even then."

Jasper eased into a deep sleep. I laid him down in his cot.

I really *was* going to miss things like this after Abby moved out. After the haywire years when Abby was a teenager, and then the years after that when Abby was feeling lost—when she thought she needed to stay away from Pete and me—it'd been an intense, wonderful experience to share a home with her again. It'd been healing.

Life seemed like a constant stream of phases. Some things ended. Other things began. And some things just drifted away on the current. You couldn't keep hold of everything that you wanted to, no matter how hard you tried.

PART II

CHAPTER FOURTEEN

A horde of reporters was waiting outside CQ Hospital when I arrived.

They rushed at me, clamouring for updates on the survivors of the Witness Mountain shootings.

I made a brief statement—telling them I understood that people in our community would be eager to know how Angie and her boys were doing. But I hadn't spoken to their doctors yet and I had no news.

The reporters began asking questions about the crime scenes then, at which point I begged off and continued to the hospital.

In a room up on the third floor, the machines that were hooked up to Angie Green beeped and hummed. The monitor screens beside her displayed steady results. But Angie herself was silent and motionless, lying in her hospital bed.

The morning light shone weakly through a window on the opposite side of the large intensive care room. Angie was alone in here. I'd requested a private room and security guard for her. I couldn't be certain whether Jordan had any involvement in the shootings, and I wasn't taking any chances.

Gently, I squeezed Angie's arm. "Angie, if you can hear me, this is Detective Kate Wakeland. I'm not sure if you know how you came to be in a hospital. But I want you to know that you're safe, and your three boys are safe. Lots of people out there are thinking about you."

No response came at all, but I hoped she'd heard me.

A nurse walked in. Touching Angie's hand, he bent down to her. "Hello,

Angie. This is Joseph. I'm just going to take a look at some things. You're doing well."

Peeling back a soft cap from Angie's forehead, he checked a set of wires there, then replaced the cap. He checked the screens after that, recording the results on a clipboard.

I waited until he'd finished and then stepped away, motioning him over. "How is she?"

"Angie's operation went well," he told me. "They were able to reduce the swelling on her brain. The second bullet, in her back, didn't hit any vital organs."

"That sounds positive."

"Yes, it is. But she's also pretty fragile after the surgeries. You're Detective Wakeland, right?"

"Right, yes. And you're Joseph? Thanks for talking with me. I'm very much hoping that Angie recovers—for the sake of herself and family, of course, and so she can tell us what happened."

"Well, it's certainly a good thing for Angie that you found her when you did. Due to her blood loss, she was right on the brink. I was on the emergency care team when she was brought in. It was very much touch and go. She was very lucky not to die at the point that the bullet grazed her skull. If it had hit a few centimetres to the left, then… not so lucky."

"I see. Has she responded in any way as yet?"

"Her eyelids have fluttered, and she's made some noises. Those are good signs… but she's still in a coma, and there is unfortunately no guarantee she'll come out of it. You'll need to speak to her doctor to get the full information. Doctor Castile should be coming in soon if you want to talk with her—in about half an hour."

"Thank you. I don't have time to wait at the moment, but I'll try and see Doctor Castile soon."

After leaving Angie's room, I walked to the other end of the hospital, to the children's ward. I was due to have a chat with Toby and Oliver—Angie's two youngest boys.

A child psychologist that I'd had dealings with before—Dr Li Zhang—met me outside the room where the boys were.

"They've both recovered well, physically," she told me. "But they're both highly traumatised, as you can imagine. I'd say they're not up to more than five minutes of questions."

"Poor kids. I'll be brief."

The two little boys were sitting together on a bed.

"How are you both?" I asked them.

"Where's Mummy?" Oliver said with a sniffle.

"I've just been to see her. She's sleeping," I said. "I'm Detective Kate. I'm just here to have a little chat with you."

The boys looked back at me quietly.

"We found you two in a dog kennel yesterday," I continued. "That's a funny place to be. Can you tell me why you were in there?"

"Mummy told us to," answered Toby in a serious voice. "She told us the dog's name, and we knew where to go."

"Why did Mummy tell you to do that?" I asked.

"To get away from the bad man," little Oliver piped up.

I held a breath, knowing I needed to phrase my next question very carefully. It was important not to put ideas or images in their heads.

"Okay," I said, "so, there was a man? Who was he?"

Toby shook his head. "We couldn't see. He was too far away. But he had a gun. And he shot Mummy."

Toby's bottom lip trembled, and his eyes grew distant.

Oliver began crying.

I couldn't continue from this point. I glanced across to Dr Zhang, and she nodded in acknowledgment. This was all I was going to get from these two little boys. They hadn't named their grandfather as the shooter. Perhaps Angie had tried to save them from knowing that, and she'd just called the shooter a bad man.

I left the hospital and drove to the police station.

The smoke was thick today, the smell of it acrid in the air. The shopping strips that were usually full of people were almost empty.

A line of fire engines passed by me. I knew where they were probably headed. Gospers Mountain. The fires there had merged into a monster, and the monster was bearing down on Sydney, the coastal regions to the north, and the inland regions where the Blue Mountains stood.

I walked into the station, ready for the interview with Carlson and his son.

Melainey handed me a coffee as I headed to my desk. "Still like it with milk and no sugar?"

I flashed a tired smile. "Yep. And thanks."

Franco swivelled around in his chair, pushing himself back from his desk.

"I spoke with Jordan's father on the phone a few minutes ago. Said he'd be here in half an hour."

"This isn't going to be an easy interview for Jordan," I replied.

"Nope," Melainey agreed. "And things are gonna implode if Green catches on that we're holding a few suspicions about Jordan."

Franco groaned under his breath. "I'm guessing he'll shut us down and get a lawyer if he realises."

"Let's lead Jordan in slowly," I said. "You two do the gentler questions and I'll go in for the prickly end of the questioning."

Franco and I usually conducted interviews like this—he'd take the suspect's side and try to relax them. And then I'd move in later with the grittier questions. It was a technique that often—but not always—gave us quick results.

I sipped my coffee, looking over the notes that Franco, Melainey and I had written up the day before. We really needed to nail down this interview.

Franco looked from me to Melainey. "What about Carlson himself? He's the ex-husband. Could be an angry ex for all we know. Should we direct a couple of questions his way? See if he has an alibi?"

Melainey frowned. "He was two hours away at the time of the shootings, right?"

"Maybe," I said. "We don't know that for sure. I think we need to gather some information before questioning him. We'll look into his mobile phone data and social media. That way, we might catch him out if he tells us a lie about his whereabouts. But that'll take a while. For today, I think we should focus on Jordan."

We had ten minutes up our sleeves before the Greens were due to arrive.

I played the footage of the town fair that I'd obtained from Nancy Upchurch earlier today. Jordan had been at the fair, and I wanted to know why.

But the footage was grainy and murky. I decided to send it away to be fixed—we had an expert who could work magic on footage, with forensic video enhancement.

I hoped Jordan could tell us himself why he'd been at the fair.

A few minutes after that, Carlson Green arrived at the station in casual business clothes, looking anxious. Jordan was beside him, head down, wearing an ironed shirt and long pants. He stood in an awkward pose, as if he didn't know what to do with himself.

"I took a quick detour to the hospital," Green told us as the two of them sat in the interview room. "I wanted to see my younger boys again—and Angie. She seems to be stable, but I'm worried, of course."

"We're all hoping for the very best for her, Mr Green," I said. "Can we get you and Jordan anything? Coffee, tea, juice?"

"Tea," answered Green. "And a juice for Jordan. Oh, and call me Carlson."

I made a call to Constable Georgiades to bring in the refreshments.

"How are your little boys doing, Carlson?" Melainey asked.

Carlson pressed his mouth into a hard line. "They're doing okay, considering. A bit confused about what's going on. They don't know their grandparents are dead, yet."

"That's going to be a tough conversation," Melainey commented.

"Yeah." Carlson sighed. "I want to thank you three for all that you did yesterday. It still doesn't seem real."

"That's completely normal," Franco said. "It can take quite a while to come to grips with something like this."

Jordan remained quiet. Stone cold quiet, actually.

"How are you today, Jordan?" I ventured.

"I'm okay," he mumbled.

"Are you sore, mate?" asked Franco. "You had quite a tumble from your bike."

"Nah," Jordan replied. "Just scratches. Anyway, it was a good thing I had the accident. You know, because then you took me home… and you found Mum."

He didn't look up at us the whole time he spoke. His speech sounded rehearsed to me.

"I'll get that mountain bike to you soon," Franco told Jordan.

Carlson raised the palm of his hand. "That's all right, I can replace Jordan's bike. I'm here now." He shot a warm smile at his son that went unseen.

Constable Georgiades brought in the tea and juice and then left the room again.

I waited for Carlson and Jordan to sip their drinks before speaking. "Are we ready to start with a few questions?"

Carlson glanced at his son and then gave me a nod. "I think so."

I sat back, letting Franco and Melainey take on the first stage of the questioning.

Franco gave Jordan a small smile of encouragement. "You'd been staying at the house at Witness Mountain for about two weeks—is that right, mate?"

"Yeah, 'bout that long."

"Okay," Franco said. "Can you tell us about yesterday, from the time that you woke up?"

Jordan's shoulders pinched inward. "I woke up 'cos Toby and Ollie were having a fight—they argue a lot. Mum was in the kitchen. She asked if I wanted an omelette. I said no 'cos I wanted to get out for a ride. Then I left."

"Did you hear gunshots at any point after you left?" Franco asked.

"No. No gunshots."

"You're sure about that?" Melainey added.

"I'm sure."

Franco slid a photocopied map of Tallman's Valley over to Jordan. "Can you show me the route you took from your house to Valley Square? Just draw it on here."

Jordan picked up the pencil Franco offered him and drew a path that went along Kirk Road and then through a field and over the bridge of a creek.

Franco took the photocopy back. "This is really helpful, thanks." He paused, flicking his gaze up at Jordan. "All right. Is it okay to ask some questions about your grandparents?"

Jordan nodded. "I knew you'd have to ask about them."

"Yeah, no getting around it, unfortunately," Franco said gently. "Did you hear your grandparents arguing at all that morning?"

"No."

"What about in the past days or the past couple of weeks?" Franco asked.

"Nope. Nothing."

Franco waited a beat. "What about your granddad—did you think he'd been acting a bit different?"

"No different than usual. Just cracking jokes and stuff. And getting me to help him fix the fences."

"Hmmm." Franco tapped his fingers on the desk. "Did you two happen to do any target practice together? I noticed all the tin cans with bullet holes in 'em."

Franco had asked the question casually, but the intent behind it wasn't casual at all. I hoped that neither Jordan nor his dad would realise that.

Jordan shuffled his feet like a small child would. "Not these holidays. Back when we used to live there, yeah."

Melainey crossed his arms. "Okay. Hard question coming, Jordan. Did you see your granddad with his gun at all the morning of the shootings?"

"No. I don't know why he did… what he did. He must have gone crazy. Granddad wasn't a bad guy." Jordan's eyes grew wet. He swiped the tears away with the back of his hand.

It annoyed me that Melainey had gone to a difficult question so soon. It wasn't what we'd agreed on. Melainey always did have a totally different way of conducting interviews.

Carlson curled a fist around the side of his son's chair, his expression growing dark. "I never thought Gus would do anything like this. You okay, Jordan?"

Melainey gave Jordan a minute to compose himself before continuing. "Did your mum seem upset about anything that morning?"

"Um… no. Not really."

"All right," Melainey said. "Thinking back to the past weeks or months, has your mum seemed anxious or upset at all?"

Jordan stared down at his fingers as he shook his head.

"Are you sure?" Melainey pressed in a gentle tone.

"Sure," Jordan answered. "Nothing more than usual."

Melainey let a second pass. "What do you mean by *usual*?"

"She'd stress out and yell at us sometimes. Just *mum* sort of stuff."

"Okay," Franco said. "Can you tell us where your family has been living?"

"Fraser Island," Jordan mumbled.

I was surprised by that answer. Fraser Island was on the east coast of Australia, way up in the northern parts. Although the island was large, I knew there were few permanent houses—apart from the resort cabins.

"Wow, island living," Franco said. "What's that like?"

"Nice, I guess. Kind of basic. There's no school, so Mum homeschools us. You have to pump your own water… and you need solar for electricity. So, we have hardly any internet or TV."

Jordan's expression tightened.

Had life on the island angered him? He was a teenager, perhaps kept away from all the usual things teenagers these days took for granted. And, as far as I understood, the family would have been heading straight back to the island after their holiday in Tallman's Valley.

Franco inclined his head, studying Jordan. "Did you do any boating there… or kayaking? I admit I don't really know Fraser."

"Yeah, a bit of kayaking," Jordan said. "Only on Lake McKenzie and a few creeks. Not on the eastern side of the island. You know, 'cos of the sharks and stingers… and crocs now and again."

Franco blew out a breath. "Oh, wow, right. And there are dingoes there, too, aren't there?"

"Yeah. You've got to be careful of the dogs. I had to keep a watch on my brothers."

There was that tone again. That vaguely angry, dark tone. I was building up a picture in my mind of a boy who'd been taken to live in a remote location, away from his friends and school, and tasked with minding his little brothers.

Carlson took a gulp of his tea and then set the cup down a little too hard. "The dingoes… they had me worried. Beautiful place, but Jordan's not joking about the dangers."

Franco turned to Carlson. "How long were Angie and the boys on Fraser?"

He sighed, crossing his arms. "About a year. I'd gone to the city for work by that stage, so I had to respect her decision. Still, the thought of the kids being out of the school system—that concerned me a lot. And… she sounded pretty down whenever I spoke to her."

"Did you know that Angie and the kids were back at Tallman's Valley?" Franco asked.

Carlson shook his head. "No. Angie didn't tell me. I thought they were still up north."

Jordan looked away, pulling at the cuffs of his long sleeve shirt.

I exchanged glances with Franco and Melainey. We made a silent agreement that it was time for me to take on the tougher end of the questioning.

"Jordan," I said, "both you and your dad have told us your mum went through times where she was feeling upset. Can you tell me more about that?"

He didn't answer, still fussing with the cuffs of his shirt.

"Jordan?" I repeated.

He let out a tight, controlled breath. "She, uh, cried a lot. She had a job for a while after we moved there—at a resort. She was happy, then. But then she started getting weird. Crying like she'd never stop. And she gave the job up."

Carlson stared at his son. "Why didn't you tell me that?"

Jordan glanced at the three of us and then hung his head. "I don't know. It was her own business, I guess."

"Can you tell us what it was like for you and your brothers when your mum had those crying spells?" I asked.

Jordan fixed his gaze on me. "Does it matter?"

"I'm just trying to gain a picture of the time leading up to yesterday. Things that don't seem relevant can sometimes prove important later on."

The boy exhaled. "So… when mum was like that, I'd have to get my brothers their breakfast and lunch and get 'em dressed. Sometimes mum took pills. Like, too many. And she'd drink—"

He broke off, as if he'd blurted out more than he'd intended.

"Well, hell." Carlson shook his head, his mouth dropping open. "I didn't know any of *this* was going on."

"Sounds like a rough time, Jordan," I said.

Nervously, he swallowed a mouthful of juice. "I don't wanna talk about that stuff anymore."

"That's okay," I told him. "How about we switch to making sure we've got yesterday's timeline and details correct? Is that okay?"

He nodded reluctantly.

"So, you said earlier you went out for a ride," I stated. "Where were you headed?"

"Nowhere special. Just out. Away from the noise. You know, from Toby and Ollie bickering with each other."

I took care with my next words. "I happened to see you at the town fair."

He blinked at me. "You did?"

"Yes. Can you tell me why you went there?" I asked.

"No reason. Just to see what was goin' on."

I wrote down some notes, just to have a reason to take my eyes off Jordan and give him a breather.

After a few seconds, I asked if he could describe to me what he did after he got to the fair.

"I just hung around for a bit," Jordan answered. "Then I took off. I was goin' home when I had the accident."

I tapped the pen on the desk. "You said the accident was your fault. How did it happen?"

"Don't remember much about it. Like I said, the sun was in my eyes."

"When we drove you home," I said, "you said your mum was sick. But… you didn't seem too sure of that. Was she… actually sick?"

Jordan's left eye twitched. "No. I just didn't want police talking to her."

"Why not?" I asked.

"Because I didn't want to get in trouble."

I took a breath. "Why would you get in trouble?"

His jaw muscles flexed as he shifted about in his seat. "I wasn't allowed out."

Carlson scowled. "Don't get me wrong—I think Angie's a good mother—but… something seems pretty wrong here. A teenage boy shouldn't be kept cooped up…."

I had to agree with Carlson on that one. At the same time, Jordan had told us at least one lie so far, and I had to wonder what else he might be lying about.

Being angry at a parent was one thing. What happened at Witness Mountain was another thing altogether. We needed to get to the truth.

CHAPTER FIFTEEN

At the end of the interview with Jordan Green, I still had big question marks about him. He seemed to flip from being honest to evasive.

After I showed the Greens out of the station, I sat at my computer, typing up notes from the interview. When I was done, I glanced at an online news site. The headlines were all about the event at Witness Mountain. It'd rocked our small town—and the whole of Sydney. No one liked to hear about multiple shooting events that occurred within families. They were always something *other*, something impossible to rationalise—how one member of a family could turn against the others and start slaughtering them.

In the statement I'd given to the media, I hadn't named Gus as the one who'd been the shooter, but I *had* stated that Gus was found with the rifle.

Under one article about the shootings, there were hundreds of comments from people expressing their anger at Gus, including people from our own town. I read those comments with interest, to see if anyone had anything to say that sounded a little suspicious—like they knew too much. But I didn't find anything like that.

I'd lived in the valley for the past twenty-four years, but I hadn't ever noticed the Iversons or Angie. I guessed they were people who'd kept to themselves. The only one I'd noticed about town was the real estate agent—Carlson Green.

The next thing to do was to find out the feasibility of Jordan carrying out the shootings and then getting himself to the fair—by the time I'd seen him there.

I intended staging a re-enactment.

The problem was that Jordan's bike had gotten twisted out of shape in the accident. It'd be difficult to conduct a proper test without a bike that was very similar.

I stepped up to Constable Georgiades' desk. "Thea, would you be able to source a bicycle for me? I want one as close as possible to Jordan's."

She raised her eyes to me, frowning so hard she was squinting. "Not going to be easy, Detective. That bike was old."

"I know. And it had a lot of rust."

"Could we get the actual bike fixed? We've got it at the station, right?"

"Yes, we do. But it's there as evidence of the accident Jordan had."

"Uhhhmmm, well, what if we just have the frame straightened and replace the bent wheel? Would that work? That way, maybe the gears and pedal and frame can stay the same. And we can keep the old, bent wheel as part of the evidence?"

"Good plan. Sounds like the best we can do. Could you organise that?"

"I'll get straight onto it."

"Thanks, Thea. You're amazing."

Melainey, Franco and I spent the next few hours out of the station, interviewing residents near or on Witness Mountain who might have heard the gunshots the morning of the shootings. We split up to get through the interviews faster—people's recollections tended to fade quickly.

As I was heading back to the station, I found myself driving past the grounds of the old carnival.

For a moment, I could almost hear the music of the merry-go-round and smell the popcorn stalls.

I haven't forgotten you. Once this case is over, I'll be back on the trail of everything and everyone associated with you. I'll dig as deep as I need to go. You can count on it.

It seemed ironic that the shootings had occurred on Witness Mountain—so close to the land where the carnival workers had once lived.

I met up with Franco and Melainey back at the station.

We quickly collated all the information we'd gathered from the interviews with the residents. Some people had heard the shots, but no one had seen anything of importance.

"I'm still getting used to this country stuff," Melainey remarked. "It's not like in the city. If there's a murder there, you're almost guaranteed someone will have seen something. Not *here*. Everyone's so spread out on those properties on Witness Mountain."

"Yes," I agreed. "It definitely poses a problem. Well, it's going to take some time before we know the results of the forensic testing on Gus Iverson's body. We need to know for certain that he killed himself."

Melainey rubbed his chin. "Yup, we can't take that for granted. I've got a guy who's an expert on suspicious suicides and multiple shooting scenes. John Farrina. I'll get him straight onto this."

"That's a name I haven't heard in a long time," I mused. "Detective John Farrina."

Melainey nodded. "He's from the old days. He's damned good at what he does."

"I'll be very interested to hear his views," I said. "Because right now, I think we're looking at a case of either two shooters or one shooter—but if it's just one shooter, it can't have been Gus. I've been over and over it in my mind, and I just can't figure out how he'd be capable of it—physically."

"So, the shooter could have been Jordan all on his own, is that what you're thinking?" Melainey asked.

Franco ran his teeth sideways over his bottom lip, looking dubious. "He's a kid. He'd have trouble setting up a suicide scene and rushing away from the scene of the crime."

I nodded. "He'd have to be damned lucky to get it believable enough."

"He was a bit sketchy during the interview," Melainey said. "Can't put a finger on it. But something wasn't quite right."

"Oh yeah?" Franco shrugged. "He just seemed like a scared kid to me."

"He *was* scared," I agreed. "But is there something behind that?"

"What if it's a shooter from outside the family?" Franco suggested. "Could be someone from that island where Angie was living."

Leaning back, Melainey stretched his neck. "Sounds reasonable to me. Should we make a few calls around the island, then? See what we can dig up?"

Rubbing my eyes, I sighed heavily. "It'd be hard to get any useful information out of people over the phone."

Franco eyed Melainey and me. "We need to make a trip out there."

Melainey sighed. "Eh, I would, but I just dug my own grave. I'll have to help John Farrina get started on the case."

"Okay, then it's you and me, Franco," I said. "But what about your little kitty? He's too young to leave in a boarding facility."

"I'd take him," Melainey said. "But I got a dog that's fond of cats. Too fond, if you know what I mean."

Franco nodded. "My next-door neighbour gushes over my kitten. Mrs McNulty. I could ask her, maybe?"

"Got a name for that kitten, yet?" I asked Franco.

"Can't rush these things," he replied. "I don't wanna give him a name he'll hate."

I laughed. "By the sounds of it, his name is going to be *cat* for his whole life."

"Yeah, anyway," Franco was quick to say, "we'd better see about some flights." He opened his laptop. "Hmmm, some Sydney flights have been cancelled due to the bushfires. But we're in luck. There's a flight from Sydney to Hervey Bay. No stops."

"Okay, book it," I said.

Heading off to the island was a good idea, but at the same time, I worried about taking my finger off the pulse here in the valley.

I walked across to Constable Georgiades' desk. "Thea, could I get you to do something for me over the next couple of days—I mean, besides the bicycle?"

"I'm up for anything."

"Could you look into Carlson Green's movements on Saturday morning? And also any trips he's taken to Queensland within the past year, especially to Fraser Island?"

"Done. Oh, and I forgot to tell you, I found out earlier that Gus had poor eyesight. I've been making calls to the places he frequented—the bowling club and places like that."

I smiled. "You're a star."

Returning to my own desk, I sat and began sketching out a rough aerial picture of the Witness Mountain crime scenes. No matter which way I tried to work it—I couldn't figure how Gus could have acted alone that morning.

CHAPTER SIXTEEN

Franco loped into Sydney airport, an overstuffed backpack perched on his shoulder, dressed in a loud red shirt decorated with a pattern of frangipani flowers.

We'd stayed overnight in a budget hotel at the airport precinct. We had a very early flight to catch.

Franco was late. Our plane was due to leave in just a few minutes.

"Hawaiian shirt, Franco? Really?" I said.

He tucked his shirt in with one hand. "It's the tropics where we're going."

"I didn't even know you owned a floral shirt."

"It's not so much floral as *festive*, don't you think?"

"I'll take your word for it. Let's go."

We hurried to the airport gate, where passengers were already lining up, and joined the end of the line.

"Just so you know," I told Franco, "I'll be wearing my usual. Business shirt and trousers."

"You didn't even pack a pair of shorts or a muumuu—in case you feel like cutting loose?"

"No."

"You do you, Wakeland. Mum's fond of her muumuu dresses. One year, when I was a kid, she and my dad had matching clothing designed for our family trip to Fiji. I mean, she wore the dresses, he wore the shirts. Us kids got matching shirts, too."

"That's almost criminal."

"Ah, well, our family didn't take ourselves too seriously."

"I was joking. It's cute as pie. And I adore your mum. You know that. How is she anyway?"

"Not doing so good. Bad knees. Doctor says she needs to lose weight. She told him, eh, I like my wine and pizza."

"I can picture her saying that."

"The good thing is, she's otherwise healthy. It's all good food that she cooks. My dad—he was another story. He'd load up on Mum's cooking at night, but then he'd go for the junk food afterwards."

I shot him a sympathetic glance. Whenever Franco spoke about his father, it was to complain about the lifestyle choices that preceded his death. As if he hadn't forgiven him yet for dying.

"Did you get someone to look after your kitten?" I asked.

"Yeah. The next-door-neighbour came through. Mrs McNulty was only too happy to take him. Mum would have, but she's staying with my sister up at the Central Coast. She's putting her feet up for a while my sis' looks after her."

"Well, I hope her knees improve. And I'm glad little no-name kitty has somewhere to stay."

The gates opened and we boarded the plane. The plane was much smaller than the usual jet. And when it took off, the ascent was ricketier than the usual, too. I wasn't fond of flying at the best of times. But at almost 1000 kilometres away, Hervey Bay was too far to drive for a two-day trip.

Franco seemed unconcerned, almost in holiday mode, with his headphones already on and his eyes closed.

I tried to relax and read a book. I'd been trying to read it all year, but so far, life kept interrupting.

Two hours later, Franco and I stepped out into a small, modern airport, surrounded by flat green fields.

Hopping straight into a taxi, we directed the driver to take us to River Heads—the Hervey Bay suburb where the ferry was docked. The ferry was leaving at 9 a.m. We didn't have much time up our sleeves.

The roads our taxi drove along were bathed in sunlight. Summer was in full swing, with impressive displays of red flowers everywhere—flame trees, poinciana and red bottle brush. Fruit was ripening on the mango trees growing on the roadside.

Fire didn't seem to have touched the area, the sky a clear, brilliant blue.

As the taxi swung into a parking lot, a wide bay came into view. And far beyond that, the island. A bulky ferry sat at the dock.

We'd made it in time. We were in luck—there were a dozen or more vehicles waiting to be driven onto the ferry.

Franco and I boarded on foot. I'd arranged to hire an SUV on the island itself.

We stayed out on the deck during the journey, enjoying the breeze after being cooped up on the plane.

Franco devoured an ice-cream he'd bought from the kiosk, while reading a tourist brochure. "Hey, Wakeland, if we'd come a couple of months earlier, we might have seen whales."

"Shame. We'll come back here for a holiday," I quipped. "Bigley would pay for that, right?"

Franco laughed, pocketing the brochure.

In the distance, Fraser Island loomed larger and larger. At over 120 kilometres in length, it was the largest sand island in the world.

It took a full hour to reach shore. We picked up our rental SUV and drove to the rooms I'd booked at the nearby Kingfisher Bay Resort.

After showers and a change of clothing, we strolled around the resort, getting our bearings.

Inside the resort grounds, narrow wooden boardwalks ran between numerous free-standing cabins. A large restaurant stood open to an expansive swimming pool. A beach ran along one edge of the resort.

None of the restaurant staff who we spoke to knew Angie Green.

Franco and I had an early lunch in the restaurant. Straight after eating, Franco went for a swim in the pool. I returned to my room for a short nap. I was craving sleep. I felt as if I'd scarcely taken time to breathe over the past couple of days.

I woke twenty minutes later.

As I stepped outside the hotel room, I noticed a girl pushing a cart of white towels and bathroom supplies.

"Hello," I said, "do you mind if I ask a question about someone who used to work here?"

She flashed a friendly smile. "I only just started here."

"Oh. Well, maybe you won't know her." I brought up a picture of Angie on my phone. "Her name is Angie Green. She has three children—a teenage boy named Jordan and two—"

"I know her. I mean, I know Jordan, and I've seen his mum around."

"You know Jordan? Are you two friends?"

"Sort of. All the kids on this end of the island are friends."

"Can you tell me about Jordan?"

An impish grin came over her face. "He's really cute. He's sixteen, like me. I asked him if he has a girlfriend… but I think he's one of those boys who are just more interested in their hobbies than girls." She chewed her lip, a suspicious look entering her eyes. "Who are you anyway?"

I showed her my ID, thinking that she really should have asked me for that before. She'd been overly trusting so far. "I'm Detective Kate Wakeland, from Sydney. I'm here to find out a bit about the Green family."

"Oh. Why?"

"Have you seen the news lately?"

"I never watch the news. Did something happen?"

"Yes. There was an incident with Jordan's mum and grandparents. His mother is currently in a coma. Jordan and his brothers are okay, thankfully."

"Sooo, they'll be coming back when Jordan's mother gets better?" She sounded so much younger than her age.

"Do you… know what a coma is?"

"Yeah, that thing where people stay asleep for a while?"

"That's right. She could be in the coma for some time. Would you happen to know of any friends of the Green family? I'd really like to talk with them."

"Um, yeah. Jordan's mum is friends with one of the cleaning staff who works here. I don't know her name."

"Would you know where I can find her?"

"Saw her about fifteen minutes ago."

"I should be able to catch her, then. Can you tell me what she looks like?"

"She's short. Short hair, too. Blonde, kind of."

"Thank you. Can I ask your name?"

"It's Lucy."

"Thanks for your help, Lucy. I'll head off now."

"Tell Jordan I hope I see him again," she called as I stepped away.

I strode along the boardwalk, keeping a keen eye out for the woman that

Lucy had described. Her description wasn't much to go on, but it was better than nothing. If I didn't find her soon, I'd call management and ask.

I found Franco sitting at the bar.

He raised his glass to me. "Buy you a drink?"

"Uh, no. I was just talking with a young staff member. She said that Angie is friends with one of the cleaning staff, but—"

"Roslyn."

"Excuse me?"

"Her name's Roslyn. She's meeting me here after she finishes her shift."

"Right. How did you manage that?"

"By making like a local. Hanging at the bar, cracking a few jokes and asking questions."

"Real smooth, Franco."

He grinned. "So, about that drink?"

"Sure. Order me a lime soda."

When Roslyn arrived, half an hour later, she was indeed small, with closely clipped blonde hair—just as Lucy had said. Roslyn was wearing colourful parrot earrings and a parrot pendant—something that Lucy hadn't thought to include in her description.

"I've got a few minutes," Roslyn told us. Her face and eyes were set in a tired, pinched expression, belying the bright parrot jewellery that she wore.

"Thanks for talking with us." Franco pointed to a table in a corner that was fairly private. "How about we go sit over there?"

"I'm okay here," Roslyn responded in a tight voice. "You said you just had a couple of questions? About Angie? I've got to run home after this. I've got things to do."

She seemed on edge. I wasn't sure that she actually needed to rush home. It wasn't ideal for us to remain standing at the bar. We were unlikely to find out much from her this way. Perhaps she didn't trust us, or she didn't trust the police in general.

"I like your parrots," I said as an icebreaker.

She touched her pendant. "Oh, these? I make and sell them. Gives me something to do when I'm not working my shifts."

I smiled. "They're lovely. I know a little girl who'd love the necklace—my granddaughter, Ivy. She's just turned seven."

Roslyn dug in her bag and produced a business card. "I have a website. It's pretty basic, but, you know, I don't have much internet time each day. My connection's really slow."

I took the card. "Great."

I'd hoped she might invite us back to her home or studio—wherever it was that she made the jewellery. But she didn't.

Franco sipped his gin and tonic. "Let me get you a drink. What's your poison, Roslyn?"

"Uh, a light beer. Thanks."

Franco turned to get the bartender's attention, and he ordered drinks for the three of us.

He bought himself some kind of cocktail that was blue and yellow, with a tiny umbrella perched on the side. He looked pleased with himself as he took a sip, twirling the umbrella between his fingers. "They do good cocktails here."

Roslyn looked amused. "I'm more of a beer drinker."

I decided to let Franco lead the conversation. He was doing better than me.

"It's my first time on Fraser," Franco told Roslyn. "Beautiful place."

"Yes, it is," she agreed. "You tend to forget how amazing it is when you live here."

Franco took another sip of his luridly coloured alcohol. "So, is Angie living somewhere close to you?"

"Yeah. Over on the other side of the island. Eurong. How's she doing? I only know what I'm hearing on the news."

"She's still in a coma," Franco said. "But she's a fighter to have come as far as she has."

"She's a fighter, all right. I know that much."

"How'd you meet her?" he asked. "While you were both working at the resort?"

"Nah. She only worked here about three months before she quit. She decided she wanted to stay at home with the kids all the time. I met her at the beach at Eurong. The locals tend to gather on that side of the island."

Franco winced. "Ah. Sounds like we're on the wrong side."

"It's just an hour away," she said. "You just have to make sure you don't get bogged on the drive over there."

"Bogged? They didn't teach us this stuff in detective school."

Franco's cheesy joke drew an unexpected laugh from Roslyn. I had to admit that Franco did cut a comical picture, standing there in his mismatched floral shirt and shorts, cocktail in hand, talking about *detective school.*

"People get bogged all the time here," Roslyn told him. "Especially on the beach. I've even seen a car float away a couple of times."

"Crikey." He shook his head, a helpless expression on his face.

"Look," Roslyn said in a relenting tone, "is it important that you get over to Eurong—I mean, for Angie's sake?"

"Yeah," Franco said. "It really is. We need to talk to her friends. The case isn't cut and dry. There might have been a second shooter. We need to gain as much info as we can about the Green family. It could help us—"

"A *second* shooter?"

"That isn't public knowledge, so we need you to keep that quiet," he said.

She toyed with the parrot pendant, seeming to wrestle with her thoughts. "Okay. *Okay*. I'm about to head home. You can follow me if you want, and we'll have a chat."

Franco rewarded her with a wide smile. "We'll take you up on that offer, Roslyn."

As Roslyn went to get her car, Franco drank the last of his cocktail. "And *that's* how you do it, Wakeland."

CHAPTER SEVENTEEN

Roslyn hadn't been making it up about the prospect of our car getting bogged. The road across the island was all sand, as she'd said.

She drove just ahead of us, in a huge old SUV that was rusting around the taillights.

Franco drove our hire car, seeming to relish the dips and bumps.

"Take it easy, cowboy," I said after he took the car over a rise that Roslyn had avoided.

"Sorry. Got carried away." He didn't sound sorry at all.

Franco followed Roslyn as she veered off the main road. We had no choice but to follow her, but I wasn't sure where she was taking us.

She stopped at a point where a track led off into bushland.

When she parked, Franco and I pulled up behind her and got out.

"You said you wanted to know about the Green family," Roslyn said. "So, I want to show you something."

Franco and I exchanged uncertain glances, then trailed behind her.

As we descended a short set of steps, a curve of brilliantly white sand greeted us, beyond which sat a clear aqua-coloured lake. A few families were splashing in the water.

"This is halfway across the island," Roslyn said. "The Green family spent a lot of their time here. Angie loves it."

"It's stunning," I said. "What's the name of it?"

"Lake McKenzie. Or, as the original indigenous people called it, *Booran-goora.* If you want to know what life was like for Angie and the kids, then you've got to see the island as they did."

I was starting to understand Roslyn a little. She saw us as two Sydney cops who'd barely stepped onto the island before expecting quick answers.

When Franco pulled off his shirt and waded into the lake for a swim, Roslyn watched on approvingly. I wasn't certain if that was because she liked the look of him or she liked that he was trying to experience the island. I ended up deciding it was both.

We arrived at Eurong half an hour later. The sandy thoroughfares gave way to paved streets. Eurong consisted of a mix of holiday accommodation and private housing along a beach.

Roslyn pointed into the distance, up the wide, endless stretch of sand. "This is the island's highway. It's called the 75 Mile Beach. If you want to drive anywhere, this is the way you go. But you've got to be careful not to get caught out by the tides." She glanced at Franco. "Don't swim here. Unless you like sharks and stingers."

I was relieved when she invited us to her house for a drink. She could have changed her mind and just dumped us on the beach.

Roslyn's home was an aged, two-storey Queenslander, perched high on a grassy hill, a wide sweep of ocean behind it.

Franco and I sat at a well-used wooden bench in Roslyn's kitchen while she served us sparkling water with fresh lemon. A set of French doors were open to a balcony, where the distant ocean sparkled through the foliage of tropical pot plants.

"Wow, lovely view," I began.

Roslyn sliced a lemon on a cutting board. "It's a great position. I talked my parents into retiring here, about six years back. They rent the bottom half of the house out to holidaymakers. Between that and my job at the resort, it gets us by."

A flock of king parrots descended on the balcony railing outside. The birds were a riot of colour with their bright red chests and emerald-green backs and wings.

"You can see where I get the inspiration for my jewellery." A grin lit up Roslyn's face. "But I don't make much from it. It's just for fun."

Franco peeled some rind from a slice of lemon. "So, Angie lives close by your house, you said?"

She nodded. "Couple of streets away. Just big enough for her and the kids."

"I might go take a look around," he said. "It'll give me a chance to dry off. I'm still a bit damp from the swim."

"Yeah, sure." Roslyn sounded uncertain again. She stepped out to her balcony and watched Franco as he wandered away on the hillside.

"Look," she said, turning to me. "It feels kind of strange, to be honest, to talk to you about Angie. She was pretty private."

I joined her on the balcony. "Angie is in a very serious condition. She might never wake up from the coma. She might die without ever seeing her kids again. If there *was* a second shooter, they shouldn't get away with it. Angie can't tell us anything, though. I'm sure she'd want her friends to help us."

Roslyn went quiet for a moment, looking out at the water views. "I heard on the news that the police saved her life. And they found little Ollie and Toby. Was that you and Mr Flower Pants?"

I smiled at her calling Franco *Mr Flower Pants*. "Yes. We got there just in time."

Wordlessly, she picked up a watering can and began sprinkling water on her pot plants. "Angie was scared," she said finally.

I took a breath. "Scared?"

"In the weeks before she left, yeah, she was… pretty unsettled. But look, I love Angie—she's a good friend—but it's true to say that she was like that from the very first day she arrived on Fraser. I had the feeling she wanted to get away… from her old life."

"Did she ever say why?"

"No. And it all escalated, from maybe September onward. She became… kind of erratic."

"In what way was she erratic?"

Roslyn sighed, putting down her watering can. "Drinking more than usual. Saying strange stuff. And… maybe taking more of her antidepressants than she should."

"Okay. That sounds concerning."

"It gets worse. She kept thinking someone was *there*… hanging around, watching her."

"Did you ever—?"

"No. I never saw anyone. I'm telling you, it was all in her mind."

"How can you be sure of that?"

"The thing is, she'd swear there was someone in a certain spot… but then I'd look, and there was no one. I tried to get her to tell the police, but she refused. That was when I started thinking that maybe even Angie wasn't sure if the stalker actually existed."

"Did she ever describe this person?"

"It was a man. Wearing a mask. That's all she said." Roslyn crushed her eyes shut. "When I first heard about the shooting, of course, I thought about Angie's stalker. But then they reported that the shooter was Angie's father." Roslyn gazed at me directly. "And so, I put that thought right out of my mind."

"Did Angie ever talk about her father?"

"A lot. She was close to him. That's why this is so hard to understand."

"Did she ever speak of any problems in the family? Any arguments or issues?"

Roslyn shook her head. "Nope. Nothing."

"Roslyn, do you think it's possible that Angie left the island because of the stalker?"

"She didn't tell me that, but thinking about it now… yes, she might have. There was something else a little odd."

"Oh?"

"She was on the phone a lot in the weeks before she left. She was sort of secretive about the calls. If the phone rang while I was there, she'd walk right out of earshot before answering it."

"Did she seem to be having arguments during those calls?"

"No. She just looked anxious."

"What about her ex-husband—Carlson—did you ever happen to see him here on the island?"

"Angie's ex? If he was ever here, Angie didn't tell me. She never spoke about him at all. Couldn't even tell you what he looks like."

"Okay, thanks."

Below the balcony, a couple who looked in their eighties made their way along the path, the man leaning heavily on a walking stick. The woman carried a picnic basket, looking hot and tired.

Roslyn scowled, peering down at them. "I don't know how many times I've told them not to go down to the beach with food. They could attract the dingoes."

"They're your parents?"

She expelled an exasperated sigh. "Yes. They just do as they please—there's no stopping them. Drives me mental."

I handed her my card. "I'm very grateful for all you've told me today. If you think of anything else, give me a call—anytime."

She nodded. "I really hope Angie recovers and comes home. I miss her."

"I hope so, too. I'll see myself out. Oh… I'd still like to buy some of your jewellery for my granddaughter, if you have any here."

"Sure. I've got a little studio downstairs."

Roslyn took me down to her studio, where I chose a sea turtle pendant and a starfish bracelet.

Just before I left, Roslyn touched me on the arm. "Are you going to put it out to the news—about the stalker?"

"No, not unless some further information presents itself."

"Good. I wouldn't want to alarm my parents. Or the other residents. We're a close-knit bunch, here. We look out for each other. No one noticed a stranger hanging about. It's safe, really."

She gave a firm nod as she packaged up the jewellery.

CHAPTER EIGHTEEN

I greeted Roslyn's parents and then went to look for Franco.

I found him a number of streets away. He was on the other side of a stand of coconut palms, engaged in a heated conversation on the phone.

He spoke the name *Martina* a couple of times.

He ended the conversation abruptly as I approached.

"Everything okay?" I asked.

"Yeah, no problem," he said, but he looked rattled.

"Was that Martina you were speaking with?"

"You overheard?"

"Couldn't help it. Sorry."

"It's nothing. Things went bad between her and Elliot Calladine, apparently. And now she wants to get back with me. Not gonna happen."

"Okay. I'll back right out of this one."

He grinned. "Good. Anyway, did you find out anything?"

"Quite a bit more than I expected. You?"

"Uh huh. I broke into Angie's house and took a good look around."

"How'd you work out which one was hers?"

"Wasn't hard. Found a house with kayaks and a boy's bike and toys in the yard. Got inside easily. There was an unlatched window. I think Angie must have left in a hurry."

"What did you find?"

"Some unusual things—a balaclava hidden at the back of Jordan's wardrobe, for one. I mean, it's not like it ever gets cold enough here for one of *those* things."

"Oh no. That's not good."

"Yup. The other thing was, I found three pairs of binoculars, all kept near the windows of different rooms. Crazy, right?"

"I think I might be able to explain that."

He raised a puzzled eyebrow.

"Angie thought she had a stalker on the island."

"A stalker?"

"That's what she told Roslyn."

"Okay, yep, that explains the binoculars."

"What if the stalker was Jordan? It fits with the balaclava, right? I mean, maybe he was trying to scare his mother… for some reason. Maybe to make her want to leave the island?"

"Hate to say it… but that's what *I'm* thinking. Did Roslyn see the stalker, too?"

"No. She sounded very sceptical. But, you know, I got a strong impression that Roslyn is heavily invested in the idea of everything here being safe and secure. From what she told us earlier, she talked her elderly parents into moving to the island. She also said her parents rent out their house to holidaymakers, so I'm going to assume it's they who own the house, and not Roslyn. What I'm thinking is that Roslyn's worried one of her parents is going to get injured or something, and then they'll want to move back to the mainland. And then Roslyn loses her island lifestyle."

"Not a bad analysis, Wakeland."

"It was kind of obvious, to be honest. This place is Roslyn's little cocoon. To me, she even sounded a bit annoyed that Angie interrupted the peace. Don't get me wrong—she seems to care about Angie, but she doesn't want any trouble."

He grinned. "And here I was thinking it was my charm that got Roslyn to help us. Maybe it wasn't that. She just doesn't want us blundering about."

"She referred to you as *Mr Flower Pants*."

"She *what*?"

"Uh huh."

Franco laughed.

"Well," I said, "I think we should ignore Roslyn's doubts about the stalker. She's got a vested interest in there not being one."

He nodded. "The stalker might not be relevant, though. He's unlikely to be involved in the shootings. Unless the stalker was actually Jordan. What I wouldn't give for a window into that kid's head."

"Yes. I'd lay bets he's hiding things from us."

"Hey, we should head off—go hang out at the local bars and see if we can learn anything else."

"Sounds like you're very interested in hanging out in the bars."

"You read my mind, Wakeland. I could use a drink."

Franco and I spent the rest of the day chatting with anyone we could find. At one point, Roslyn came to find us. She showed us around the local landmarks and kept repeating her theme of the island being safe.

The island *was* safe. One possible stalker didn't make it unsafe. But Roslyn was at pains to ensure we didn't go away with any negative impressions.

She exhausted me.

Franco and I returned to the resort before nightfall. Sitting on the little deck outside my unit, I could hear rustles in the bushes made by small nocturnal animals. This was the kind of place you could easily imagine someone being out there… watching. It seemed alive with movement. At the same time, the night was so quiet I could hear the distant howls and whines of dingoes.

I called Pete and chatted until I felt waves of sleep overtaking me. He was sitting out on our deck at home, on the swing seat. It was nice, the thought of watching the moon at the same time as him.

Franco and I stayed for a second day and night before boarding a flight back to Sydney.

During the flight, we had a bird's-eye view of Australia's east coast, just as the sun was rising. It was nothing but sobering. Thick pillars of dark smoke bloomed from the land. So many fires. Hundreds and hundreds of fires.

Later, as we flew over Sydney Harbour, I could see nothing but a blanket of smoke. Everything had vanished. It seemed as if we were all being eaten alive by a relentless dragon.

I arrived home to a darkened mood in the Blue Mountains. Everywhere I went—the streets and the shops—people had a look of worry set deep into their faces. There was talk of evacuations. Talk of packing up and getting ready to flee at any moment. People were stressed they'd be trapped, or that they'd have nowhere to take their pets to safety.

I found Pete outside our house, preparing the grounds in the event that fire swept in. He'd donned gloves and a bandanna, his shirt soaked in sweat.

"How'd the trip go?" he asked.

"Worth it but tiring." I paused. "I missed you."

I went to hug him, but he stood back. "Honey, I stink like an old shoe."

"Don't care." Smiling, I gave him a bear hug. "How's Abby and the kids?"

"They're good. The baby's sleeping better. And… Logan joined the RFS."

"Oh… How did that go down with Abby?"

I couldn't see Abby dealing well with her partner becoming a volunteer firefighter. She was a worrier. It was already hard for her having a father in the RFS and a mother in the police force.

"She made me promise I wouldn't leave his side whenever we head out," Pete said. "I can try, but to be dead honest, that's not always gonna be possible. Anyway, he seems keen. I was showing him the ropes yesterday."

"I couldn't believe the number of fires I saw on the way home. They're everywhere. I mean, you hear it on the news, but it's another thing to see it for yourself."

"Showing no signs of slowing down, either. I don't know if you've heard—we're losing rainforest in the Blue Mountains that has never burned before. It was supposed to be too wet to ever catch on fire. Well, not anymore."

I gazed back at Pete in disbelief. The rainforests here were our favourite place to go for walks and runs. They were the deep heart of the mountains.

I closed my eyes. "And what about the…?"

Pete knew exactly what I meant. There was a tiny, secret valley in the mountains. A type of pine grew there that dated back to the time of the dinosaurs—the Wollemi Pine. It was the only place left in the world where the pine had survived.

"They were saved," he assured me. "We pulled out all stops."

It was a spot of good news among all the stories of devastation.

"Hey," he said, "I hope you'll take it easy the rest of today. It's a lot of running around going up to Fraser Island and back."

"I know. And I will."

"Good. Because you need that. You haven't been sleeping well for a long time."

"I slept well on the island. Might have been the sea air."

"Glad to hear it."

I headed inside for a shower, and then sat down with Abby and the kids, eating bowls of cut fruit together. I gave Ivy the jewellery I'd bought from Roslyn. She was as excited as I thought she'd be, asking all about the island. I promised I'd take her there one day.

A small collection of boxes and suitcases were stacked against the living room wall. Pete and Abby had been busy packing up our most important possessions, ready to throw them into our cars and leave should an evacuation order come through.

That was our life now. A life on the edge.

CHAPTER NINETEEN

I called a meeting of our homicide team in the afternoon.

Franco was dressed in his usual short sleeve business shirt—the colourful floral shirts nowhere in sight.

Thea handed around a photocopied report of Carlson Green's movements over the past year, including the day of the shootings.

I read through it quickly.

Going by the signals Carlson's phone had given on the day Angie and her parents were shot, he'd been at home—until about 11:15 a.m. In the past six months, he'd taken several trips in which he'd landed at the Sunshine Coast Airport in the state of Queensland.

I raised my eyes to Thea. "This is great work."

"Thanks, Detective," she said with a pleased smile.

Franco sipped his coffee. "So, according to this, Carlson was at his house in Double Bay all morning. You know, it seems a bit unusual to me that an agent would be at home on a Saturday. That's the day they do all their wheeling and dealing."

Thea nodded. "I thought it was unusual, too. Carlson manages high-profile clients and their multi-million-dollar houses."

"Yes," I agreed. "Sales agents are run off their feet on Saturdays, showing houses to buyers. And the thing is, he didn't answer his phone until a bit after eleven that morning. He's running a business. Strange not to look at your phone all morning."

"He could have left his phone at home, but he was actually driving about," Melainey put forward.

"Yeah, he could have been driving back from Tallman's Valley when Shintani called to tell him about the shootings," Franco said. "Shintani was unable to get him on the phone—he had to leave a message."

"So," I said, "it's looking like we have a space of time in which it's feasible Carlson could have travelled to the valley and back on Saturday morning."

"But did he have any experience with rifles?" Melainey asked. "The shooter had a bit of experience. They knew their way around a rifle."

Thea nodded. "I looked into that. Carlson is a member of a shooting range. He's been shooting rifles and pistols since his early twenties."

"Well," Melainey replied. "That answers that one. Nicely done, Thea."

I studied Thea's report in closer detail, taking note of Carlson's frequent trips to the Sunshine Coast, then looking up maps on my phone. "Hmmm, the Sunshine Coast Airport is only two and a half hours away from Hervey Bay. And Hervey Bay is the gateway to Fraser Island, where Angie was living. Could Carlson have been making secret trips to the island, without Angie knowing?"

Franco passed around A4-sized photographs of Angie's house and of the binoculars and balaclava he'd found in Angie's house.

"This is the house Angie Green was renting on Fraser Island," Franco told everyone. "I found a balaclava in Jordan's bedroom, and I found three binoculars inside the house."

"A balaclava? And *three* binoculars?" Thea questioned.

I nodded. "I'm pretty sure the binoculars were Angie's. I spoke with a friend of hers—Roslyn. Roslyn told me that Angie had been terrified of a stalker on the island. She never saw his face because he wore a balaclava."

"Scary." Thea shuddered.

"Thinking about it now," Franco said, "the balaclava could have been planted. It wasn't hard to find."

Melainey winced. "That'd mean Carlson was trying to pin the blame on his own son."

"I couldn't help but notice there seemed to be no real relationship between them," I said. "Jordan treated his father like he was a stranger."

Franco drum rolled his hands on the table. “I think we need to get Carlson Green down here to answer some questions.”

“Right,” I said, “we’ll do that.” I turned to Melainey. “How are things progressing with Detective John Farrina?”

“I supplied him with the police photos and video from Saturday,” Melainey told me. “We’ve been running various scenarios, to see how the day might have played out. He wants to take a trip out to the site.”

“Okay,” I said, “we’ll have to arrange that.” I glanced across the table at Constable Georgiades then. “Thea, have you been able to source someone who can repair Jordan’s bike?”

Thea grinned, nodding. “I picked up Jordan’s bike from the repair shop this morning. It’s ready to go.”

“Already? Wonderful. Well, now we just need to find someone about Jordan’s size and fitness level, and we can run the test.”

Franco lifted his chin. “I’d volunteer, but I haven’t been Jordan’s weight since I was about twelve. I was a chubby kid.”

“How about me?” Thea suggested. “I ride my bike to and from work every day. And I think I might be close to Jordan’s weight and height.”

I cast an eye over the young constable. She was tall and slender.

“Okay, sorted,” I said. “Thanks for volunteering.”

As good as it was to have the test organised, a sick feeling started up in my stomach. So far, small pieces of evidence concerning Jordan were piling up. As a detective, I had to stay impartial. But on a personal level, I didn’t want him to be guilty of any of the shootings.

Franco, Thea and I headed over to Witness Mountain. I stationed Melainey and four others from our team in locations from the base of the mountain to Valley Square. They’d be there to film and verify the test. Thea would be riding through fields and over the creek bridge—the same as Jordan had.

All was quiet at Angie’s property when we arrived, apart from the wind bearing down on the treetops. The forensic team that had been onsite for the past days wasn’t there this afternoon. We had the property to ourselves.

Thea pulled on her helmet, ready for the ride from here down to Valley Square. Franco checked that her sports video recorder was working.

“Ready to roll?” I asked her.

“Ready,” she answered.

“Take care on the road down, okay?” I instructed her to go at a steady pace.

She rode away, out of the gate and onto the dirt road.

I remained at the property with Franco, waiting out the minutes as we watched her on a computer tablet.

Melainey, standing at the gates of Valley Square, radioed us. "Thea's here. That's twenty-six minutes, kids."

Franco and I eyed each other with a quiet dread.

"Thanks, Melainey," I said.

"It's not proof Jordan did anything," Franco said, "but it's not good. I admit I was hoping it'd take Thea the best part of an hour to get there."

"Me, too. We could have counted Jordan out of the running."

I radioed the whole team. "Well done, everyone. Great job, Thea. We'll meet you all back at the station."

I looked up as a single leaf spiralled down from the sky.

Within the next second, a clutch of dark, smoky leaves fell a few metres in front of me.

I shoved my radio back onto my belt. "Franco, did you see that?"

"See what?"

"Those leaves. They're burnt."

"Probably blown in on the wind?"

"Yes. But it means a fire could be close."

Frowning, Franco scanned his surrounds, a hand shielding his eyes from the sun. "Don't see smoke or anything."

"I think I'll give Pete a call and check it out."

Pete answered from an RFS truck. "I'll get eyes on this. Who's there at the site?"

"It's just Franco and me. Pete… if there *is* a fire nearby, I need this land to stay intact. It's a crime site—we can't lose it."

"I'll do what I can. But you know—"

"Yes, of course. You have priorities."

"Yep. While I find out what's going on, you and Franco should pack up and leave. Don't delay, okay, honey?"

"Okay. Got it."

I ended the call, gesturing to Franco. We started across the field.

Pete called me back, his voice cracking with urgency. "I asked the RFS helicopter to scan your location—they've found a grass fire racing towards Witness Mountain. We're sending off trucks to get the residents the hell out of there. Don't take Boxbrush Road. You and Franco need to head in the opposite direction. Take the Foxland Pass. Are you clear? *Don't take the road back down the mountain.*"

"I'm clear."

I relayed Pete's information to Franco.

He eyed me with a fixed gaze. "That means my house is in the path of the fire."

"I'm so sorry."

Franco stepped ahead of me through the gate, his back rigid. When he spoke, his voice had grown hoarse. "Let's go, then. Foxland Pass."

We jumped into the car, me in the driver's seat.

I turned to him, suddenly realising something I knew Franco had already. "Oh God… *your kitten*. He's there in your house, isn't he?"

Franco looked away. "Nothing we can do about it."

I hesitated. "If you were here alone, what would you do?"

"Don't ask me that question."

Thoughts crashed in a chaotic pattern in my mind. "The fire's not at the mountain—yet. Let's go get him."

Franco met my eyes with a torn look. "We can't."

"We'll make it."

He gave an uncertain nod. I drove off towards Boxbrush Road.

Neither Franco nor I spoke. I kept second-guessing myself on the way. If I'd had any other members of our team with us—and we'd only had the one car—would I have made the decision to try to save Franco's kitten? No. No, I wouldn't have.

I remembered something, then. Flames went much faster up a hill than on flat land. And the wind must be blowing up the slopes of the mountain to have brought those burned leaves here. If the fire reached the mountain, it'd roar out of all control.

CHAPTER TWENTY

Three fire engines roared past us in a long flash of red, warning lights spinning.

A thin grey veil moved overhead.

Franco and I travelled along in silence for a few minutes.

He turned to me abruptly, a deep frown creasing his face.

"What's wrong?" I switched my gaze back to the road, steering around a sharp corner.

"I'm not jumping to any conclusions here," he said, "but what if the fire was deliberately lit?"

"Deliberate? What are you thinking?"

"I mean, who would have an interest in stopping the test we were doing today?"

"Oh… you mean Jordan?"

"Hate to think it, but yeah."

"But how would he even know about it?"

"What if he was there—hanging around on his mum's land? He could've overheard us. Or maybe he just saw police cars there and got angry."

I exhaled slowly, considering Franco's train of thought. If it were true, it was shocking. But not more shocking than carrying out a shooting. If he was guilty of the first thing, then he could certainly do something like this.

"I really hope not. But you're right, it's a possibility. Franco, he could still be here, and in danger."

"I doubt it. Your husband said the fire started in the field across from my street, right? If someone lit it, then they were down *there* at the time. They're not on the mountain."

"Yes, you're right."

Franco pulled out his phone. "Look, I'll give Jordan a call and find out where he is."

"Good idea. I'd really like to know."

Jordan didn't answer the call. Franco tried Carlson Green next.

The conversation was short.

"He said Jordan's out somewhere," Franco told me with a leaden breath. "He doesn't know where."

"And what about Carlson himself—I mean, where is he?"

"He said he was at home."

"Maybe he is, maybe he isn't."

Sirens sounded in the distance. A helicopter flew low overhead, intensely loud. My heart banged like a drum, jumping against my ribcage.

I gave a small cheer when we reached the bottom of the mountain.

Swinging the car around, I headed towards Franco's street.

"Oh, God," I cried.

The fire had burned through the fields of dry grasses, leap-frogging the road and jumping onto the line of houses. Flames were already bright on the rooftops.

Firefighters in their yellow uniforms sprayed water at what seemed a losing battle. In the trees high above the houses, flames had caught hold. It'd already started—the climb of the fire up the mountain.

There'd be no saving the houses and land that belonged to Angie and the Iversons. I had to let go of wanting them saved. It was too late.

Fire trucks blocked the road ahead. I parked as close as I could get.

Franco unbuckled his seatbelt. "Wish me luck."

"Franco… it looks dangerous."

"I won't do anything stupid." He was gone before I could say anything else.

I sat there watching home after home burning to the ground. I knew from what Franco had told me that most of the people were elderly. I prayed they'd all gotten out.

My phone buzzed. It was Pete.

"Kate, please tell me that's not Franco running out of his house?"

"Are you *here at the fire*?"

"Yes, I'm here," Pete answered. "Logan's here, too."

From the car window, I looked among the flurry of trucks and firefighters, but they were all too far in the distance to make out who was who.

"You and Franco came down the mountain road," Pete stated in a terse voice.

"Pete, he has a cat…."

"I'll see you at home."

The line went dead. I felt awful. Pete spent his life keeping people safe from fires these days. He wouldn't have expected that I'd put Franco and myself in danger. But that was exactly what I'd done.

I spotted a man running towards me, blanket over his head. Franco.

He pulled the blanket away as he reached the car. He had not one, but two cats cradled in his arms. There was his kitten—and a white cat that was covered in soot. The kitten had his eyes closed.

"Oh, Franco. Is he—?"

"He's alive."

"Thank goodness. I can't believe how quickly all the houses are going up in flames."

Franco spluttered and coughed, catching his breath. "I asked if I could stay and help. They said a big, fat nope to that. The house two doors down from mine is a fireball. Give it five minutes, and it'll all be over—every house gone." He gazed back at the flames. "I was there for nine years."

"I remember the day you bought it. I don't know what to say. This is just awful."

Franco slid onto the passenger seat, carefully holding his two treasures.

I stroked the kitten, blinking back a tear. The kitten raised its head and mewed weakly. The white cat sneezed, ash flying from its fur.

"Where did this one come from?" I asked.

"I went to check Mrs McNulty's house—just in case. She wasn't there, but I heard meowing coming from under a bed. This is Molly. I'm betting that Molly must have got startled by all the noise and she ran off to the burned fields across the road. Stupid thing came back to the house."

I dusted flakes of ash from the cat's pink nose. "Glad you're okay, Molly. She's a ragdoll cat by the look of her—they usually don't leave the house. She must have been scared out there." I glanced at Franco. "Pete just called. He saw you."

"Damn. Sorry. If not for the kitten—"

"No, this is on me. *I* made the decision. Anyway, tell me what you want to do? Stay here to the bitter end? Go somewhere else?"

He expelled a heavy breath. "I'd better get the two cats to a vet for a check-up. After that, I don't know."

I nodded. "Got it."

I took one last glance at the inferno before heading away down the street. The blaze had spread across the bottom of the mountain, looking as if it was about to consume the mountain whole.

CHAPTER TWENTY-ONE

The vet checked the kitten and Molly, declaring them each to have used up one of their nine lives. They were fine.

We went looking for Mrs McNulty after that, eventually finding her at a fire shelter in town. She cried in relief when she saw Molly, rushing up to hug her—and Franco.

We headed back out to the street and to our car. Franco settled back into the passenger seat, juggling the kitten while browsing the internet on his phone.

"What're you looking up?" I asked.

"Accommodation."

"You know you can always stay at my house, right? For as long as you need."

"Thanks. You're a good egg. But you're packed to the rafters over there."

"There's a big spare room with a sofa bed downstairs. It's the kids' playroom, but I can clear the toys away."

"I can't kick the kids out of their playroom."

"We don't let the kids play in there all night long. They *do* sleep, you know."

He laughed. "Okay, but just for one night. I'll find somewhere after that."

"What about your kitten? Can't take him to a hotel. Tell you what, Abby was talking about getting a pet for the kids. She might like to have yours for a little while."

"If she says yes, I might take you up on that."

Franco and I returned to the station to hold a brief meeting with our team. My head felt like cotton wool, and I wasn't up for anything more than that. And Franco certainly wasn't in any mood for work, either.

When I arrived home with Franco, Abby was with her children in the living room—Ivy rolling a ball to baby Jasper.

Ivy squealed as she spotted the kitten. "Oooh, can I hold him?"

"Sure," Franco told her. "He's a bit tired from breathing in some smoke earlier, so he'll probably wanna sleep."

Ivy rocked the kitten like a baby. "What's his name?"

"I'm still thinking of a name." Franco rubbed his eyes, which looked red and irritated.

"How did he get in the smoke?" Ivy asked.

"Uh, the houses on my street burned down earlier," he replied. "Your grandmother and I went to get the kitten."

Abby gasped, holding a hand over her mouth. "What? The whole street burned down? Your house, too?"

He nodded, bowing his head.

"Honey," I said to Abby, "the fire's headed up Witness Mountain. Your dad's helping to fight the blaze… with Logan."

"Logan?" Her bottom lip went wobbly with shock. "I didn't know. I thought they were out on a drill."

"They'll be okay. There are lots of trucks there, and more coming." I sounded far more assured than what I felt. Any large fire carried danger. And this was a whole mountain on fire.

I failed to convince Abby. Snatching her phone from her pocket, she hurried from the room. I knew she was going to try to call Logan.

"Does Granddad and Logan have enough water to put out the fire?" Ivy asked.

Ivy had been hearing a lot of talk about the drought and how water supplies were low lately.

"I'm sure they'll have enough water, sweetie," I told her. "And Granddad knows how to keep everyone safe."

I did a better job of settling Ivy than I had with Abby.

Ivy brushed her nose along the kitten's fur as she held him. "He's like one of those koalas that got saved from the fires. Aren't you, kitty? You're a little, tiny koala bear."

Jasper's eyes were huge as he crawled up beside his sister, watching the kitten intently. "Bear," he said. "*Bear bear*."

I laughed. "Jasper just learned a new word. He only knows four or five."

"That makes it pretty special, then," Franco said. "You know what, Ivy? I think that you and Jasper just gave the cat his new name."

"Really?" Ivy gazed at Franco with excitement.

Franco gave her a nod, grinning. "Yep, *Bear* it is."

It was a nice moment, at the end of what had been a day of utter devastation.

Later, after dinner and after the kids were in bed, Abby, Franco and I waited together to hear news about the Witness Mountain fire. Our local TV station had constant updates. The news included a story about the Green and Iverson families. The story showed a video of Angie from when she'd been a teenager, at school at Valley Grammar. She was dancing in a white, floaty dress. She was beautiful, her red hair up in a high ponytail. The reporter presenting the story described her as having been a talented young dancer.

It was after midnight when Pete and Logan came home. The firefighters hadn't been able to stop the blaze until it reached the other side of the mountain. A lot had been lost.

I stepped outside with Pete to the front deck. This had become our place to catch up and talk. With a full house, we'd needed a spot to recharge ourselves.

Franco was already asleep on the sofa bed in the kids' playroom downstairs. I'd loaned him some of Pete's pyjamas. Franco had nothing but the clothes on his back.

Pete's skin was still red from the fierce heat of the fire, indents of his breathing mask on his forehead and cheeks. "Kate… it was a madhouse out there. I don't know about the state of the land you wanted saved. Logan and I were on the outskirts of that area. We'll know more in the morning… but it's unlikely it didn't all burn."

I hugged him. "It doesn't matter. You and Logan came home safely. And I heard on the news that all the residents got evacuated."

"Yep. We got them all out. It's a very good thing you sent out the alert for this fire. That gave us time. It just… came out of nowhere."

"Pete… do you have any idea how the fire started?"

"No, not yet. We put all our resources into stopping it."

"Is it possible it was deliberately lit?"

"Any reason you're asking?"

"Well, Franco was suspicious that someone might want to destroy evidence at the crime scenes. And I'm wondering about that now, too."

"I'll let you know what we find out tomorrow."

"Okay, thanks. Hey, I'm sorry… about going to get Franco's cat."

"It's all right. You thought you could make it… and you did."

Pete was being a lot more accommodating than I thought he would. He sounded exhausted—maybe too exhausted to be upset with me anymore.

One thing about Pete, he didn't hold on to anger for long. Me, I tended to stay angry a lot longer.

Pete and I had a red wine together on the deck, and then we headed upstairs. Both of us fell into bed with heavy heads.

This day had been bookended by fires for me—all the fires I'd seen during the flight, and then the one on Witness Mountain.

As I tried to sleep, images reared up in my mind of the old carnival again, not giving me any rest. I could see the Ferris wheel turning—and this time, every single carriage was in flames.

CHAPTER TWENTY-TWO

Morning sun spiked through my car window, already brutally hot.

I was driving over to Carlson Green's house at CQ Village. I needed to speak with his son, Jordan, and find out exactly what he'd been doing at the time of the Witness Mountain fire. We had an interview set up with Carlson himself in another hour.

A sudden pain seared the centre of my chest, and I had to pull over.

I sat until the pain subsided.

It'd been enough to give me a scare.

Pete was right. I needed to take things easier.

Jordan whizzed by me on his bike.

I drove off again, slowing as I reached Jordan.

"Jordan," I called, "where are you off to?"

He stopped pedalling, shielding his eyes from the sun as he looked across at me. "Went to see Mum at the hospital."

CQ Hospital was just up the road, so that checked out.

"New bike?" I said, nodding towards his bicycle.

"Yeah. Dad just gave it to me."

"Nice."

"It's not bad."

"I have a question about yesterday afternoon. Can you tell me where you were?"

"Why?"

"Just wondering, that's all."

"I was riding around. Tryin' out the new bike."

"Whereabouts?"

"Uh, in town. Went to the bakery to get a pie."

"Which bakery?"

"Uh, I didn't end up getting anything. Forgot to take money with me."

"I see. Were you anywhere near Witness Mountain yesterday afternoon?"

He shook his head.

"Did you know there was a fire there?"

"No?"

"Well, it was a big fire."

His mouth dropped. "Are my mum's and granddad's houses okay?"

"I'm not sure. I'm sorry. I'll call you or your father later, when I find out."

He nodded, turning his head away from me.

Was he turning away to stop me from seeing him shed a tear, maybe? Or to prevent me from seeing a guilty look on his face?

"Thanks for letting me know," he said, and rode off.

I watched him pedal away. Did he really think I'd stopped him just to inform him about the fire? I could not figure out Jordan Green. Every encounter with him confused me.

I continued to the police station.

Inside the station, the air-conditioning was struggling. I felt completely wiped out, like I was walking through molasses. Part of the weight was the knowledge that the crime sites at Witness Mountain had most probably burned to a crisp last night.

Franco sat at his desk, munching on a cupcake. In front of him was a whole box of cupcakes. He was busy perusing the notes from the bicycle test.

"Nice cakes," I said.

"Uh huh." He yawned and stretched. "Want one?"

"No thanks. They look good though."

"Martina brought 'em into the station. She heard about the fire and felt sorry for me."

"Oh. That's nice of her. Hey, I just spoke with Jordan. He claims he was nowhere near Witness Mountain yesterday afternoon. He told me he went to get a pie, then changed his mind because he forgot to bring any money."

"Sounds like a kid sort of thing to do. Then again…?"

"I think we should have him followed for a few days."

"Sounds like a good idea."

"He worries me. Always seems to be hiding things. I'll get Thea to track him." I paused. "Hey, I didn't expect to see you in here today. I thought you'd be sorting out your insurance and things."

"This is a murder investigation. It comes first."

"I can cover everything. And we've got Melainey on the team, too." I cast an eye over to where Melainey was standing and talking with Thea.

"Nah, I'm good," Franco said.

"Have you been back to your house?" I asked gently.

"I went to have a look. There's nothing there. Nothing at all." He shrugged. "What can you do?"

"It's awful. Hey, if you need to talk to someone—"

"I'm okay. Really. Didn't lose anything important. And I've got Bear." He drummed his fingers on the desk. "I tried to go take a look up at Witness Mountain while I was there, too. The RFS wouldn't let me. The road's blocked off."

"Pete might be able to find out more when he wakes up. He worked a long shift last night, and he was still fast asleep when I left home. Hey, can I get you a coffee to go with those cupcakes?"

He gave a wry smile. "I caffeinated myself on the way here. I should lay off."

"I had to have a strong coffee myself. Did you get any sleep last night?"

"Nope. Nothing to do with your sofa bed and everything to do with things running loose in my head."

"I thought that might happen. Hope you catch up on your sleep tonight. Well, I'm going to get myself a cold drink and then get started."

I walked to the staff room and grabbed an orange juice from the fridge. The humid air in the station today wasn't helping me feel any less lethargic. But I needed to focus.

Inspector Shintani approached me. "Kate, I've got news."

"Please, let it be good news."

"Well, it's mostly good, with a little bit of bad news thrown on top."

I drank down a mouthful of juice. "Hit me with the good news first."

He nodded. "I've just heard from a police helicopter. The Green and Iverson properties were spared from last night's fire."

"Oh, what? *Really*? I could hug you."

"Thought you'd like that. The wind changed, apparently, changing the path of the fire. There has been an urgent discussion between Bigley and the fire chief. The *not so good* news is that those properties are now restricted zones. The chief considers them too dangerous to continue any police work there. There are still embers that could flare up again if the wind picks up. And burnt trees could fall at any time. His words."

I pressed my fingers to my temples. "Okay. Makes sense, but it'll make things difficult. They're our crime sites."

"I'll leave it with you, Kate. Oh… I heard that you and Franco went on a little rescue mission yesterday—to fetch his cat from a burning house?"

"The house wasn't burning at the time, sir."

"I see." Not saying anything more, he turned and stepped away. The look on his face had been clear. *Don't take any more risks like that.*

As I stood there, a thought came out of left field. An idea. I'd need Shintani's approval to go ahead with it. It wasn't a good time to approach him, but I'd need to move fast with this.

"Jiro!" I said.

He faced me, eyebrows raised in a questioning glance.

I walked across. "I want to make a request. If it's viable, then I'd need a few hours at the site. With members of the RFS in attendance—to be completely safe."

He breathed out audibly. "Do you have any matters of urgency there? My understanding was that you and the forensics groups had completed your work for the moment."

"This is something different. I'd like to preserve the crime sites. Let me explain. On the day of the fair, they had a presenter from CQ Technology. His name was… *Ben*, I think. He's been designing a 4D map of CQ Village. It was so realistic and detailed. My thought was, what if we can get Ben to create a map like that of the two properties—including the houses?"

"Kate, we've got an intensive number of photographs and videos—even drone footage."

"I know. But they're never quite as good as being there, in the space. A virtual recreation would be the next best thing."

"Fair point. But that kind of mapping is not something that we do here. And I can't give you a *yes* when I don't know the potential costs… or the time involved."

"Well, I don't even know if Ben would be able to do this. But do I have your permission to find out?"

"You do. If it's within possibility, we'll discuss it further."

"Thanks, I appreciate it."

Walking into an empty office, I made a call to the front reception desk at CQ. From there, my call was directed onto the technology sector and then to the person I was looking for.

"Ben Tremayne speaking," came an American accent on the phone.

"Ben, hello. This is Detective Sergeant Kate Wakeland. We were on stage together recently—at the local fair."

"Oh yeah, I remember. Very nice award you received, Detective Wakeland."

"Thank you. I have something to ask. And I think you're possibly the only one who could do this. Do you have a minute?"

"You've got me intrigued. Disturbed… but intrigued."

I laughed. "It's about your presentation. I was quite excited by the possibilities. My question is, could you do something similar… for a crime scene?"

"An actual crime scene? Let me just pick my jaw up from the floor. Can I have, uh, some more information?"

"Certainly, Ben. I have a crime site that was almost wiped out by a fire yesterday. I'd like to preserve the site, as a 4D copy. It consists of two houses on two large properties. I know it'd be a big ask, so I'm not really expecting a *yes*."

"So… what kind of crimes happened there, exactly?"

"Very serious ones. Two murders. And a third person injured. All shootings."

"*Murders*?"

"Yes. On the day of the fair, actually. You didn't hear?"

"I stay away from the news. Whoa, murders, huh?"

"Yes, unfortunately."

"Well, I'm under the pump right now—finishing off a project. But if you like, we can talk more about this tonight. If it suits you, that is."

"Of course. I'll meet you at CQ—at the tech quarter? What time?"

"No, it can't be here. My mother will be expecting me home. I make the dinners… and she likes to eat early. You could come to dinner with us."

"Oh… I feel like I'd be imposing, Ben."

"Not at all. My mother would love the company. She'll, uh, say she prefers her own company, but I know she'll like you. She's been on her own a lot since we moved out here. How does seven-thirty sound?"

"Perfect."

As the call ended, I inhaled deeply. I didn't have a clue if this was a good idea or not. But, if fire did sweep in and destroy the two properties, I'd be cursing myself. Better safe than sorry.

Sipping my drink, I returned to my desk.

Franco and Melainey were talking together. Melainey had swiped one of Franco's cupcakes.

"You look like the cat that got the cream," Melainey remarked to me.

"That's exactly what I am," I said. "Shintani just got word that the crime sites were saved."

Franco turned both his thumbs up.

"Well, that just made my morning." Melainey crossed his arms. "I was planning on going out to the site today with John Farrina."

"I'm afraid you can't go onsite yet," I said. "It's been deemed too dangerous by the RFS."

"Bummer," Melainey said.

I glanced through the window opposite us.

Out in the street, Carlson Green was walking towards the police station.

CHAPTER TWENTY-THREE

Carlson Green had a tense expression on his face as he sat down with Franco, Melainey and me in the interview room. He was dressed in a business suit today, freshly shaved. His cologne was almost overpowering.

"What's going on?" he asked.

"We have a few questions for you," Franco told him. "Just to clear some things up."

Carlson frowned. "What kind of things?"

"We'd like to know where you were on Saturday morning," I said.

Carlson glanced at each one of us. "You want to know where *I* was? I'm confused."

"I'm sure you'd rather us exclude you as a suspect, Carlson," Melainey said.

"What the hell?" Carlson exploded, locking eyes with Melainey. "You already *have* your suspect. And he's *dead*."

"Mr Green," I said, "this is just routine. All we're asking for is some confirmation of where you were that morning. We were unable to get you on the phone. And the Sydney detective we sent to your house didn't find you there—at least, you didn't answer the door."

Carlson leaned back on his chair, taking a breath. "I went out for a walk. I didn't take my phone."

"All right," Franco said. "Bit of a long walk, hey? Two hours?"

Carlson nodded, but it wasn't a certain nod.

"Pretty smoky in Sydney that day," Franco added. "You were out walking in that smoke for two hours? I'd be coughing my lungs up."

Carlson licked his lower lip. "I… probably got coffee."

"Which coffee shop is that, mate?" Melainey asked.

With his eyes darting away, Carlson shook his head. "My mind is blanking. It was a pretty traumatic morning—as you can imagine."

"Very traumatic," I said in a kind voice. "Carlson, so, you don't normally work on a Saturday morning? Aren't real estate agents at their busiest on Saturdays?"

"I own the agency," he said coolly. "I don't need to be there every minute. I trust my team. I take time off when I choose."

"Do you often go for walks on Saturday mornings?" I asked.

"No… I'm usually showing buyers through houses."

"That's what I thought," I said. "But last Saturday, you didn't do that."

"No," he replied in a dull tone.

I nodded. "Were you with anyone or talk to anyone that morning?"

Carlson hesitated. "Can't think right now. I'll get back to you on that one."

"You do that," I said. "Carlson, how often did you visit your boys at Fraser Island?"

He blinked. "I didn't. I never went there. Angie brought the boys to me in Sydney, about three times during the past year."

"Did you take any trips near the island—to South-East Queensland?" I asked.

"For business, yes—a few trips. I advise clients on real estate investments all over Australia. What's this about, anyway? Why do you need to know that?"

Melainey held up the palms of his hands. "Settle down. We're just trying to build a full picture. We don't know you, we don't know Angie. We wouldn't be doing our jobs if we didn't do our best to be thorough."

"Well, have you gotten all you need from me?" Carlson shot back. "I didn't expect to be hauled down here and given the third degree."

"Believe me, mate," Melainey said, "this isn't the third degree. You'd want to hope you don't get the third degree from us. Because then, things would have gotten a lot more serious."

We ended the questions there.

There was definitely something odd about the way Carlson had dodged our questions. The fact that he couldn't name the coffee shop was suspect. He was keeping something from us. But that didn't mean it was anything to do with the case. He could be seeing a married woman or he could be involved in some kind of shady business dealing—something he didn't want anyone to know about. But it was very, very unlikely that he was out walking around in the smoky Sydney air for hours.

It was close to seven at night by the time I finished typing up my notes after the interview with Carlson.

It was time to go have dinner with Ben Tremayne and his mother.

The sun blared down as I drove across to CQ Village. The light wouldn't start to fade until at least nine o'clock.

The lawns in the village were all so green, kept perfect by the water and nutrients fed to them by an automated system. There were some vegetable gardens here and there, kept so tidy they looked ornamental.

I parked outside number 17, Epicurean Circle.

Ben welcomed me in—sounding as awkward in person as he did on the phone.

Cooking smells filled the hallway.

The hallway opened into an area with a gleaming kitchen and dining room, which looked out onto a garden.

A woman entered from another room, gliding in a wheelchair. She looked in her late seventies, streaks of faded red in her white hair. She held her head high, her eyes inquisitive with a direct expression.

"This is my mom, Ada. Mom, this is Detective Wakeland."

I crossed the floor to her, extending my hand to shake hers. "Great to meet you. And please, call me Kate."

"Eh," she said dismissively. "I prefer to call you *Detective*. You've earned it. So, you're the lead homicide cop in town, huh?" She spoke fast, in a sharp, almost gravelly voice. Her American accent was more pronounced than her son's.

"For the Blue Mountains area, yes. Fortunately, homicides are not frequent here. I usually work on cold cases. This past week has proved the exception."

"I've been watching that case with interest—the one in which three people got shot. So, you're handling that one?"

"I am. In fact, that's why I'm here."

Ben looked a little uncomfortable. "Mom's a keen viewer of true crime shows. She's… right into everything *crime*."

Ada shrugged. “I just like things put right.”

“How are you finding living in Tallman’s Valley, Ada?” I asked her.

“Eh, it’s a nice place. Open spaces. I like it. Can’t say the same about the Close Quarters village. Everything shiny new and crammed in together. Not my style.”

“This house came with the job,” Ben explained to me. “Free rent. I wasn’t gonna turn *that* down. And, with all the fires you guys have been having lately, I feel like it’s safer for Mom being here in the village.”

“I never asked for safety,” Ada said.

“Well, *I* want you safe.” Ben raised his eyebrows at me in an exasperated glance.

“How long are you two here in Australia?” I asked.

“The NineOak Corporation contracted me for a year,” Ben explained. “I thought I’d have all kinds of trouble getting Mom over here, but Nancy Upchurch organised the visas and everything. She worked miracles.”

“Ben couldn’t do without me,” Ada declared.

“Yeah, Mom, I think it’s the other way around,” Ben said wryly.

“Dinner smells wonderful.” I indicated towards the kitchen.

“My father’s recipe,” Ada informed me.

I smiled. “Family recipes are the best.”

“You got that straight,” Ada said. “Tried and true.”

Ben nodded. “It’s just about ready. Come and sit at the table.”

I was thankful the dinner was ready. The conflict between Ben and his mother was making me feel a bit uneasy.

The three of us sat at the table to eat. I tried to guide the conversation, asking Ada about the places in which she’d lived in America, and telling her about my childhood here in Australia. She seemed to approve of the fact I’d grown up on a farm.

After dinner, Ben invited me into his office. Ada retired to the living room to watch TV.

Ben’s office was roomy, containing three computers and five screens.

Ben switched on one of the computers. A similar video to the one he’d shown at the fair displayed on the screen—a fly through of CQ village.

He pointed to a silver vest, gloves and headset that were sitting on a desk. “Ready for the full 4D experience, Detective?”

“Oh, wow, yes. I didn’t realise you’d be able to show me any of that tonight.”

"I don't have anywhere near the computer power here that I have at work, but I can show you a little."

He gave me the vest and gloves to put on, and then he fitted the headset over my eyes. With the headset on, all I could see at first was just a blank screen right in front of my eyes.

"Hold on to the desk," Ben instructed me. "Else you might find yourself falling over. It can be disorienting."

I felt in front of me until I found the desk. I placed the palms of my hands on it.

An entire world opened before my eyes. An overhead view of CQ village. I was no longer looking at a screen but seeing an entire world around me. It was as if I were flying above the houses. I couldn't help myself from gasping out loud. Ben was right—I would have keeled over had I not had something to support me.

Sun gleamed on the rooftops of the houses. A light breeze rippled through the trees below. I realised I could feel the breeze gently pushing against me. The sensors in the vest and gloves were doing an amazing job of making me feel like I was there.

"So, what you're seeing," Ben said, "is done using digital mapping."

I gazed around, viewing the mountains far beyond the village. "It's absolutely incredible. This new technology… I'm just amazed."

"Well, the technology it's based on—photogrammetry—has actually been around for the past 150 years. It just consists of making precise measurements of three-dimensional objects. These days, we're just riding on the back of that tech. What I do is to fly a drone over and through buildings—the drone takes thousands of overlapping images and builds models from that."

Ben guided me on how to get down to the road and start walking on the path. With the sensation of having my feet planted firmly on the ground, I no longer needed the support of the desk.

A little dog came running to greet me—a King Charles Spaniel. I bent down to pat it. A sensation of waves pulsed beneath my hands, something like the wriggly body of a dog.

"The glove sensors make it feel real, don't they?" Ben remarked.

"They certainly do."

The dog scampered inside the open door of a house. I followed it.

In the living room, a young couple sat watching a child who was playing with toy trains.

The dog sat patiently on the floor, looking back at me.

The scene looked so real, as if I could talk to the people. Every detail of the room had been recreated, down to the fibres in the cushions and specks of dust on the oak floorboards. I touched a vase. It felt smooth. I could even feel a small chip on its fluted edge.

"This is even better than I expected," I told Ben. "It would be incredible to have this kind of thing for crime scenes."

"I can imagine the re-enactments wouldn't be pretty," Ben said with a laugh.

I returned the laugh. "No, not at all."

"Well, I hope this has been enough to grasp the concept of what a virtual world is like."

"Yes, and I'm officially blown away."

"You did well. Some people freak the first time they experience it."

"I'm excited, to be honest. I loved it."

Ben removed the equipment from my face and body. He was beaming. I could tell he'd enjoyed showing off his work.

"So, Ben, would you be able to do something like this for us?"

"I finished up a big project today. There's a gap before I start the next one. I'd be honoured to do it—but it depends on my company. NineOak."

"I understand. Now, I need to get down to brass tacks. What would something like this cost us? I'll have to take a ballpark figure back to the inspector."

"You know what? I'm thinking I might be able to wrangle this for free. As a goodwill gesture from the tech sector to the police department. It's the kind of thing Nancy Upchurch said she wants to do—integrate the tech sector into the community. Well, what's better than this?"

"She was the stage presenter at the fair, right? That sounds fantastic, I mean, if it works out."

"I'll make the approach, if you like. I'll explain the time and resources needed."

"I can't tell you how much I appreciate this."

"To tell you the truth, I'd love the chance to work on something like this. What I do now is like a glorified videographer for a real estate agency."

Ada wheeled herself into the doorframe, a scowl on her face. "Soon everyone will be lost in these artificial worlds. Mark my words. It's all Ben does—I know that much."

Ben turned to his mother. "How about we wait and talk about this later, Mom?"

Ada glanced at me, shaking her head and looking like she had no intention of stopping the conversation there. "I keep telling Ben he needs to get out and stretch his legs—and his mind. Too much time spent hunched over a computer is no good for anyone."

Ben winced. "Mom, it's been kind of smoky out there ever since we arrived. I think I'm better off indoors. Better for my lungs." He indicated towards some asthma puffers on the shelf.

"It's especially tough on asthmatics at the moment," I said to Ada.

"Yeah, he's got asthma," she said. "Got that from his father. But there's always something or other stopping you from getting out there in the world, Benjamin."

"Well," I said. "It's time I headed off. I've taken up enough of your time. Thank you both for your company and dinner tonight."

Ada wheeled herself back to allow me out. "It's a slippery slope, Detective. It's coming, but we can't stop it. Who'd want to live in the real world if you could live in a fantasy world?"

"You might be right," I said. "Personally, I like the real world well enough to stay in it."

She fixed her gaze on me. "Well, good for you. We all have to make the best of it, don't we?"

Ben walked out behind her, a resigned expression on his face. He showed me to the door.

Outside, the world had grown dark.

CHAPTER TWENTY-FOUR

When I arrived at the station in the morning, I could see that Franco and Melainey had news.

"Carlson just called," Melainey told me. "He remembered who saw him near his house on Saturday morning. His neighbour—Gerald Finch."

"Gerald Finch *the MP*?" I exclaimed.

Franco blew out a stream of air, nodding. "We'd have to find some pretty strong evidence against Carlson. I mean, we'd be going up against an alibi given by a member of parliament."

I folded my arms. "I was so sure we had something on him."

"Looks like he's a dead end, right?" Melainey pressed his mouth into a taut line.

I glanced around the station—my head filled for a moment with the low thrum of people talking together and the clatter of computer keyboards.

"I want to be sure. I'm going to take a trip out there to have a chat with Mr Finch," I said finally. "I'll see you both back here for the afternoon meeting."

I didn't know whether this was a good idea. But it seemed to me as if Carlson had pulled Finch out of a hat.

I headed off on the two-hour drive into the city. I bumped up the cold air-conditioning in my car to escape the heat. It was another hot day.

Carlson Green lived in Double Bay, an affluent suburb that overlooked

Sydney Harbour. If I drew a line going east from Tallman's Valley until I hit the coast—at a slight downward slope—that was Double Bay.

I couldn't help but note that Carlson lived in the suburb next to Doug Overmire. Overmire lived in Darling Point. I wondered if the two men knew each other.

I arrived at Gerald Finch's house unannounced. It was often better that way. Giving people advance warning gave them time to rehearse their answers.

But when I knocked on his door, it was a couple of cleaners who answered. Mr Finch and his family had gone away overseas to escape the Sydney bushfire smoke—to the UK.

Deflated, I walked along the street. The street was narrow, lined with large, established trees. When I'd been driving in, I'd glimpsed a small beach and the harbour beyond that. It was certainly a nice spot.

I stopped in front of Carlson's house. It was a white, tri-level building—large, but still modest in size for this suburb. I walked through a side gate and around to the backyard. The yard was tiny and featureless, facing the high brick wall of the house behind it.

Through the windows, two sets of stairs came into view. They led to a mezzanine level.

Something odd hung from the handrail on the mezzanine level, at the midpoint between the two sets of stairs. Stepping back and forth, I tried to find the best vantage point to avoid the outside reflection of the brick wall on the windowpane.

I could see the object clearly now. It was a rope tied into a noose. It hung from the handrail into the void below.

What on earth was Carlson doing with a noose hanging there?

Whatever the reason, the noose was a stroke of luck. I could enter the house if I had reason to believe a suicide was in progress. I'd have no way of getting in here otherwise. With no evidence against Mr Green, a search warrant wouldn't be granted.

After informing the city police and ambulance service of the situation, I switched on my bodycam and went looking for an easy entry point into the house.

Discovering an unlocked door around the side, I ran in.

I jogged straight up the stairs to the landing. Then, after slipping on a pair of plastic gloves, I hauled up the rope.

There was no blood on the rope, and no hairs or clothing fibres—none that I could detect, anyway.

I contacted the emergency services, cancelling the callout.

From here, I had a brief window of time in which I could search the house, supposedly looking for someone who was about to harm themselves.

Rushing from room to room, what I actually looked for was anything that might end up being evidence—perhaps a box of bullets for a .303 rifle or a pair of boots covered in dirt that could be from Witness Mountain.

But I found nothing like that.

There was no one in the house, either.

I stepped into Carlson's office.

Something had gone on in here.

I noted seven holes in the wall, as if the wall had been punched repeatedly. Photographs were spread haphazardly over the desk, dozens of them. Some of Carlson's sons, but mostly of Angie. The pictures of Angie were both old and recent. There were even pictures of her in ballerina outfits from when she was a young teenager.

I was at the end of the time I could reasonably justify looking for a person who was about to use the noose. I had to end the search here.

I called Carlson Green.

"I'm just going to come out with this, Mr Green," I said. "Why do you have a noose hanging from the stair landing of your house?"

A dead silence met my ears.

When he spoke, it sounded to me as if he'd forced a jovial tone into his voice. "You're at my house? In Double Bay?"

"Yes, I'm inside, actually. There was a concern a suicide was in progress. I needed to enter to prevent a possible tragedy."

"You're *inside*? But why are you even at my house, Detective Wakeland?"

"I came to talk with Gerald Finch. But it seems he's gone away."

"Oh, right. Yes, he told me that, last time I spoke with him. He's, uh, got a sister in the UK. She lives in London, I think—"

"Mr Green, back to the noose?"

"Yes, of course. I had a party recently. Just a… small get-together. The noose was a prank."

"And it's still there?"

"I'll get rid of it when I come back. I've got my hands tied with my boys right now."

"I'm in your office. There are holes punched in the wall—what happened here?"

"Ah. The party. Things got a bit out of control."

"I see. Are the photos part of the mayhem—the ones all over your desk?"

"Uh, no. I look at pictures of my boys often. I miss them. You've got grandchildren. I'm sure you understand."

"How do you know I have grandchildren, Mr Green?"

"I just assumed."

"Hmmm. I have to say, there are far more pictures of Angie here than of your boys. Angie at all ages."

"I just… dumped out a box of photographs, that's all."

"Okay, well, I'm leaving your premises now. I'll lock the side door on my way out, will I?"

"I didn't realise I'd left it open. I rushed out when I got the call from Inspector Shintani. Yes, please lock it."

I ended the call there.

To me, he'd sounded as fake on the phone as he had in the interview.

CHAPTER TWENTY-FIVE

I stopped for a quick bite of lunch between driving back from Carlson Green's house to Tallman's Valley. A burger and a ginger beer.

A message came through to my phone from Ben Tremayne. Nancy Upchurch of the NineOak Corp. had given the green light to Ben. He was going to make a virtual recreation of the Witness Mountain crime scenes.

I felt encouraged by that news. The crime sites would be preserved. Fire wouldn't be able to destroy them.

I drove on to the police station.

Our team was already assembled when I walked into the meeting room.

Melainey stood at a whiteboard—writing up all the items of interest we had on Jordan Green so far.

Turning, he grinned at me. "Detective Wakeland, so good of you to join us."

"Funny," I shot back, sliding into a seat.

Quickly, I scanned what Melainey had written.

Jordan Green:

- acted strangely the morning of the shootings

- knows how to load and shoot rifles

- has displayed intense anger against his mother

- had time to have been involved in the shootings—according to the bicycle test

- claims to have been out riding his bike at the time the fire started on Witness Mountain. No alibi

- had a balaclava hidden in his bedroom on the island

"So, what do we think, people?" Melainey asked.

"It's a lot, but it's all circumstantial," Franco replied, with a heavy emphasis on the word *circumstantial*.

"I agree with Franco," I said. "We need to find something solid. Is Thea out tracking Jordan today?"

"Yep," Franco told me. "She's on his tail."

Melainey glanced at me. "Did you find out anything interesting from the MP—what was his name... *Finch*?"

"He's gone overseas," I answered. "I'll try calling him later. But I did find some concerning things in Carlson Green's house."

"What did you do—stage a break-in?" Melainey joked, his blue eyes wide.

"Kind of," I said lightly. "I'll show you all a video once I get it uploaded to the system."

A frown came over Melainey's face. "Anything we need to take action on?"

"Not yet," I said. "But I'll be looking very closely at Mr Green."

Franco hooked his head around to me. "The security footage from the fair came in this morning. They were able to get most of the grain out, they said."

I clapped my hands together. "Great. Let's watch it."

Melainey wheeled a monitor and computer over. "I'll get the popcorn."

He sat at the computer, starting the footage.

We spent the next half hour poring over every minute of it.

Franco leaned forward suddenly. "Wait. Stop it there, Melainey."

Melainey tapped a button, freezing the scene. "What did you spot?"

"That girl." Franco pointed at the screen.

The image currently on the screen was of a girl standing next to the entry to Valley Square. I recognised her. She'd been the worker who'd tried to sell Franco and me one of the village townhouses.

"Why her?" I asked Franco, puzzled.

"You'll see in a minute," he said. "Melainey, could you rewind it about ten seconds?"

Melainey rewound the tape.

In the footage, a group of people entered through the gates, and I quickly lost sight of the girl. But then, in the spaces between the people, I spotted her again—*and Jordan.* The two of them were talking. *No, not just talking.* They were having an argument.

Franco folded his arms. "Interesting, right?"

Melainey gave a low, throaty chuckle. "Lemme guess—he asked her out on a hot date. She turned him down. And he didn't like that. The kid's a fast worker, seeing as he's only in town for the school holidays."

"Well," I said, "we need to have a little chat with that girl. She was working there on the day. The organisers must know who she is."

While the team continued to watch the rest of the footage, I stepped out of the room to call Nancy Upchurch.

Nancy answered in that distinctive voice of hers—bubbly, but with drawn-out vowels. "Detective Wakeland. Good morning."

"Good morning to you, too. Nancy, would you have the records of who was working at the fair? I'd like to know the name of the girl who was handing out brochures at the front entrance."

"Oh. Yes, of course. Is something amiss?"

"The girl's not in any kind of trouble. I just need to ask her about someone she spoke to that morning."

"I see. Well, she wasn't very good at her job. She failed to give out most of the brochures we had printed up." I heard Nancy take a lengthy, slightly annoyed breath. "Anyhoo, I just looked up her application form. Her name is Dakota Macklin. She's fifteen and she lives in Tallman's Valley. She stated here that she's working during the school holidays at the *Sweet Eats Bakery* at CQ Retail."

I wrote down the mobile phone number that Nancy dictated to me. "Great. I appreciate your help. I'll be on my way. Oh, and while I'm here, I'd like to thank you for allowing Ben Tremayne to create a map of the Witness Mountain crime sites. I can't tell you how much of a relief it'll be to have them preserved in this way."

"I was only too happy to do that for you, Detective Wakeland. Ben does marvellous work, doesn't he?"

"Yes, he's extremely talented."

"I was so very shocked by the shootings. Just tragic. And to have it happen on the day of the fair! Goodness me. My job is to sell Tallman's Valley to the best talent overseas, to tempt them to come and work at our wonderful technology facility. The news of the murders isn't helping, I can tell you."

"Yes, it was tragic." She was starting to irritate me. She and Superintendent

Bigley seemed like peas from the same pod. They both spoke as if the shootings were inconvenient.

I was grateful she'd allowed the project with Ben to go ahead, but I couldn't wait to get off the phone with her.

As soon as the call ended, I headed out of the station and over to the *Sweet Eats Bakery* at CQ.

CHAPTER TWENTY-SIX

The *Sweet Eats Bakery* was ultra-modern, with mirrors strategically placed to make it look like there were far more products than there actually were. I'd barely ever been in here. I wasn't a big cake eater. Pete was, although he tried hard not to be.

Dakota was the only one at the counter—there were no customers. I guessed their biggest crowds would come in at lunchtime, for the pies. Through an internal door, I could see wire shelves filled with freshly baked buns and breads.

Dakota frowned as I approached the counter. She had her blonde hair in a messy ponytail, tendrils hanging loose. She wore no makeup today, looking much more like the high school student that she was.

"Hello, Dakota," I said. "We met at the fair."

As soon as a light of recognition entered her eyes, she began tripping over her words. "Oh, right. Yeah. You were there with another detective. A man."

"Yes. That's correct. I'd like to ask you a few questions."

She blinked. "Me? Why?"

I showed her a picture of Jordan. "Do you know this boy?"

She shook her head, shrugging her shoulders. It was overkill when a simple *no* would have done the job.

I showed her another photo of him. "Are you certain? Because you were seen having an argument with him."

"Ohhh, I remember now. It was nothing. He was annoying me, and I got rid of him. I was trying to do my job."

"What did he say to you?"

"He asked if I wanted to go somewhere with him after I finished work. I told him I had a boyfriend. But he just wouldn't accept it. It was awful."

"Hmmm, that's not good. So, you have a boyfriend?"

She nodded, pointing at the back room.

Just then, a boy with a stocky build walked out from there, glancing from Dakota to me, his hair tucked inside a baker's cap. "What's going on? Some boy been bugging ya, Dakka?"

"Yes. At the fair," she told him. "And don't call me *Dakka*." She sighed at me. "This is… Lewis."

Lewis placed his meaty hands on the countertop. "Okay, I wanna know exactly what went down, and why the police are involved."

"I'll let Dakota explain it," I said. "I think I've got the information I needed—thanks Dakota."

I walked out onto the street.

Damn. Melainey had it right. Jordan had been trying out pick-up lines on the girl. I felt burned by that fact alone.

It was typical of a teenage boy to make awkward approaches at girls. But a boy getting angry when a girl turned him down was very worrying. And worse still, if Jordan was responsible for the shootings, then his actions at the fair were even more callous.

I remembered something else, then. Yesterday, when I'd asked Jordan what he was doing at the time of the Witness Mountain fire, he'd said he'd gone to get a pie at a bakery—but then he'd backed right out of that statement. Dakota worked at a bakery. Was he stalking her? Even if he *had* gone to the bakery, he might still have had time to get to Witness Mountain and start the fire.

Did the quiet, nervous boy who I'd first come across even exist? Had that all been an act?

Just who are you, Jordan?

I walked outside the *Sweet Eats Bakery*, making a call to Jordan Green.

My head swam with thoughts of what he was capable of. If he was the shooter, he shouldn't be out on the streets. The evidence we had so far didn't have enough legs on which to make an arrest. But it was time for some formal questioning at the station.

Jordan didn't answer. I called Carlson straight after that, who informed me that his son was helping some family friends clear wood and leaf litter away from their house—getting it ready in case of fire.

Was that true, or was Carlson helping Jordan to avoid me? I told Carlson I needed to see Jordan down at the station this afternoon. 4 p.m. sharp. Carlson agreed, but he sounded wary.

If I discovered that Carlson was making things hard for me, then I'd make things very difficult for *him*. This was a murder case. If he'd realised I had concerns about his son being involved in the murders, then he needed to either allow me to ask Jordan some tough questions or get him a lawyer.

A call came through as soon as I ended the conversation with Carlson.

"Detective Wakeland," I answered.

"Uh… bad time?" came an American accent.

It was Ben Tremayne. I realised I'd practically snarled at him, still caught up in the previous moment.

Taking a breath, I softened my tone. "Ben? Look, no, it's not a bad time. What's happening?"

"I'm all good to go."

"Really? Already? Great news. When's the best time for you?"

"Whenever you can get clearance from your fire department."

"Fantastic. I'll clear my schedule."

"It'd work well to do it tomorrow morning—if that suits you. I'd like to do this as close as possible to the time you found the victims. That way, the patterns of sunlight and shadows would be a close match with those on the day. The time that we're looking for is early morning, correct?"

"Yes. I see you've looked it up."

"My mother already had that information," he said wryly. "She's been following the case closely."

I had a small chuckle. "I can believe that. Okay, I'll see if I can get something organised. Call you back in five."

I phoned Pete first, and then he spoke with the fire chief.

Within the next few minutes, it was all settled. Pete and his crew would escort Ben and me up to Witness Mountain tomorrow, and they'd wait there while Ben carried out his work.

CHAPTER TWENTY-SEVEN

The morning sun sparked off the peak of Witness Mountain.

Ben and I travelled in my police vehicle, following Pete's fire truck up the mountain road.

It was sobering to see the damage the fire had inflicted. Lines of charred trees marched along the road on both sides. At a curve in the road, the fire had torn away to the left. That was all that had saved the land ahead—just a random change in the direction of the wind.

Pete and his crew parked the fire truck just outside the gates of Angie Green's property. I pulled up behind the truck. Pete gave Ben and me instructions on how far we could go and what we were to do if there was a fire alert.

I kissed Pete. "See you soon."

"Good luck," Pete told me. "Hey, before you go—I got word about the investigation into the fire this morning."

"Oh, good. What did they say?"

"It started as a grass fire, as we already knew. It began with a cigarette butt that'd been flicked a long way off the road and into the grass. Might have been deliberate. Might have been a careless act. Can't tell for sure."

"Okay." I sighed. "If it was just someone being careless, they should have known what could happen."

Pete nodded. "Yeah, for sure. It caused a hell of a lot of damage."

Unfortunately, I wasn't any clearer about who had started the fire.

I walked back to Ben, and then we drove through the gates and onto Angie's land.

Everything looked about the same to me as it had on the day of the shootings. Except that it seemed a little less humid today and there were fewer flies.

The flies. I couldn't forget the flies that'd been hovering around Angie that morning, feasting on the smashed eggs and on the blood that'd dried on her clothing and skin.

The house and land seemed so empty today. Murders on these country farms were rare and always eerie. When I worked in inner Sydney, murders were different—they were an unfortunate part of the fabric of a large city. People killed others due to disputes over drug money and double-crossings and longstanding family disputes. And, too often, it was one spouse killing the other.

I gazed around at the land that extended from Angie's property to the Iversons'. If the evidence we needed was still here, at least we'd be making a permanent record of everything today. Fire and rain couldn't burn or wash it away. The only thing that Ben's digital mapping couldn't do was to preserve evidence such as fingerprints and DNA.

Ben was very particular about getting everything right. He'd already gathered information about the smoke particles and wind direction on the day in question.

I walked Ben around the two properties, explaining how and where the events had unfolded, including the locations in which we'd found Angie, the Iversons, and the two children.

Ben took careful notes and sketches along the way. "Okay, I think I got it straight. I'll go plan out the waypoints."

"Waypoints?"

"They're markers to tell the drone which paths to take. I'll be using ground station software to map out the flight paths. And then after I get the external terrain all mapped out, I'll move onto the interiors of the houses."

"Okay. Well, I'll get out of your hair. Let me know if I can help in any way. We've also got lots of helpers back there." I indicated towards the RFS truck in the distance.

Ben gave me a shy grin. "Thanks. I'll let you know. Oh, wait, where should I set the virtual fences?"

"Um, can I have that in English, please, Ben?"

"Sorry. Where do you want the perimeters to be? There's a limit to where I can take the drone. I'm not Harrison Ford. I'm not skilled enough to fly the Millennium Falcon through the forest without crashing it."

I laughed. "That's a *Star Wars* reference, right?"

He looked surprised. "You got it."

"That movie was the one Pete took me to on our first date. Back in the 70s."

A wistful look entered Ben's eyes. "Oh, man, it would have been so cool to see *Star Wars* when it was first released. Anyway, yep, I meant I can't go flying the drone between the trees."

"For sure. Don't go destroying your equipment. Just map as much of the two properties as you can. That'd be brilliant."

Ben pulled on a broad-brimmed hat and got to work.

I walked inside the house and perched on a chair at Angie's dining room table. I'd brought my laptop along this morning, so that I could keep working while Ben did his thing with the drone.

The table was still set with plates and bowls that were never used the morning that Angie was shot. She didn't get to return with the eggs to make the breakfast she'd intended. From Jordan's account, she'd planned on making omelettes.

How had things gone from Angie collecting eggs from her parents' house to three people being shot that morning? There were no clues with which to put a story together. Something must have been brewing a long time before that moment.

Placing my laptop on an empty spot on the table, I opened it up to start some work.

The first thing I intended doing was contacting the politician—Gerald Finch. I looked up his mobile phone number and then called it.

It was night in the UK and Mr Finch was at dinner. He was surprised by my questions, but was able to answer them with certainty. He had seen Carlson the morning of the shootings.

Thanking him, I sat back in my chair.

That all but ruled Carlson out as a suspect.

I wasn't done with him though. I still wanted to know what he was hiding from me. And I wasn't satisfied about his explanation for the noose and the holes in the wall. The thing about the photos of Angie all over his desk seemed odd as well.

Returning to my computer keyboard, I began typing out questions I planned to ask Jordan later today.

But as I sat there in Angie's kitchen, my thoughts kept turning to Angie herself. I could almost feel her presence here.

Was there something we'd missed about Angie? If the stalker was real, could he be someone who Angie had known from since before she moved to Fraser Island—perhaps someone even from Tallman's Valley?

I still wasn't clear on why Angie had moved so far away from here, or why she'd moved at all. Had she just wanted a change of scenery, or was there a deeper reason lurking behind it?

Angie was no social butterfly. I'd been unable to discover who her friends were when she lived here. There was nothing of her on social media. That matched with what Roslyn had said—Angie was fiercely private.

Outside the window, Ben's drone flew past at a steady pace.

Returning to my computer screen, I began conducting more intense research on Angie Green than any I'd carried out so far.

I found that she'd been a volunteer at an animal shelter a couple of years ago. Going back much further, I saw that she'd studied art and dance at university. Before university, she'd graduated from the same school that my own daughter had attended—Valley Grammar.

I looked up her parents, then—Gus and Perdita Iverson. Perdita had owned several businesses in the city. Gus had been a delivery driver.

An item of interest popped up in my search. Gus had been in a vehicle accident in 1990, in which he'd fallen asleep in his delivery van and hit a tree. He'd been lucky to survive it. The article mentioned he'd had one child—a daughter, Bridget—who'd died at age twenty-four of a brain tumour.

Frowning, I read through the paragraph again, looking for mention of Angie. Angie wasn't mentioned at all.

It was odd, but perhaps it'd just been an omission.

I decided to take a plunge into the records not available to the public.

Within the next five minutes, I'd found something.

Angie's birth certificate had a permanent seal on it. I knew that seals on birth certificates usually meant an adoption. The Iversons might not be Angie's biological parents.

But… if they'd adopted her, how old had she been at that time? Angie hadn't rated a mention in that 1990 article about Gus Iverson's vehicle accident, and she would have been thirteen, then.

Had she been adopted at age thirteen?

Did it matter? Probably not. But still, curiosity got the better of me. Leaving Angie's house, I walked outside and across to the Iversons' land.

The sun bore down with a fierce intensity. Ben was way across the field, flying his drone. Pete and the fire crew had set up a pavilion outside Angie's front gates, and they were seated on fold-out chairs in the shade.

A sickening, overripe odour met me as I stepped inside the Iverson house. A bowl of oranges in the kitchen was gathering green mould. A blowfly had gotten in, buzzing around in the air.

Apart from the smell of the overripe fruit—and the removal of Mrs Iverson's body—everything was the same as last time I'd been in here. Furniture and belongings were stuffed into every conceivable space. Along the hallway, the photographs of Angie and her parents still hung in place.

I inspected the photos closely. There were no pictures of Angie that were younger than when she was a teenager. Next, I searched for any photograph albums. I found two albums in a cupboard in the main bedroom. Again, there were no photos of Angie in which she was a toddler or young child.

If Angie had been adopted as a teenager in 1990, then where had she come from?

As I stood in the stuffy air of the bedroom, a thought circled my mind.

I sucked in a breath.

Surely, what I was thinking couldn't be true. I was making connections that didn't exist.

But still, like the damned Ferris wheel, the thought kept turning, refusing to lie down.

1990 was just the next year after 1989—when the raid on the Tallman's Valley carnival happened. After the raid, many of the children were taken from their parents and sent off into foster care.

Had Angie been one of those children?

CHAPTER TWENTY-EIGHT

The idea gathered steam in my mind. Angie could have been a child of workers from the carnival.

But did it mean anything important? Probably not. 1990 was almost thirty years in the past.

Still, the idea of it rattled me. Angie and her parents had just been shot in broad daylight. If there was any thread that connected to the carnival—no matter how loose—I intended finding it.

By two in the afternoon, Ben was done with his digital mapping.

I drove him back to CQ and then headed to Carlson's house, which was just a minute away, at CQ Village.

I didn't know whether Carlson would be able to give me an answer to the questions that were weighing on me. But I didn't want to wait.

Carlson answered the door when I knocked, phone in hand, talking to someone. "Yes, Toby, I'll bring ice-cream tonight. Daddy's got to go now—there's a police lady at the door." He shot me an exasperated glance. "That's the fifth time Toby's called me this afternoon. My aunt's been looking after the boys while I get some work done."

I smiled. "Kids are like that."

His eyes lit up as he laughed. "Especially Toby. I make it worse. I hadn't seen them for so long because of the overseas job, and now I'm giving into their every request. Missed them like crazy."

He seemed in a very different mood than when I'd spoken with him on the phone earlier.

"Your boys are out of the hospital?" I asked.

"Yes. The doctor said they'd completely recovered and were ready to leave."

"Good to hear."

"Sure is." He pushed the phone into his pocket. "Uh, anyway, so, the interview with Jordan isn't until four in the afternoon, right? Or… is it me you wanted to talk to?"

"It's you, actually."

His eyes clouded. "Did you manage to contact my neighbour—Gerald?"

"Yes, I did. He said he saw you that morning."

"Great. I'm glad that's sorted. And I'm sorry about the thing with the noose. Must have given you a fright."

"I don't scare that easily. Anyway, I wanted to ask you something about Angie."

"Angie? Okay. If I can help… I'll help."

"Thanks. I'll be blunt. Were the Iversons Angie's biological parents?"

He eyed me with a fixed gaze, the muscles of his face growing lax. "What?"

"I'm asking if Angie was adopted."

"I don't understand. She never told me she was."

"It's not certain, but I have reason to believe that might be the case."

"How did you find that out?"

"Just general research."

His expression grew distant, as if he were internally examining pieces of his past. "It'd explain so many things."

"What kind of things?"

"Well, I've never seen any baby photos of Angie. You know, when we had Jordan, I wanted to compare baby photos and see if he looked like either of us—you know, just the usual thing new parents do. Angie said her baby photos got damaged in a flood… but then wouldn't explain. And she… well, she'd just never talk about her childhood. It was always off-limits."

"I see. How old was Angie when you met her?"

"She was just fifteen. I was twenty-three, and I was running a real estate business back then. She started working there on weekends. She was… really clingy, like Velcro. Far too young for me, of course. So, I kept her at arm's length. When she was eighteen, we started dating."

He ran a hand through hair that had some silver among the blond. He was a handsome guy. He and Angie must have made an attractive couple when they were together. But I wondered if Angie, at the tender age of eighteen, hadn't been anywhere near ready to start a committed relationship—especially with someone who would have been twenty-six? The relationship might have been doomed from the start.

"And you don't know anything about Angie from before she started working for you?"

He shook his head. "I figured that her childhood must have been painful, so I just quit asking her about it."

"Okay. Thanks for talking with me. Like I said, I'm unsure about the adoption thing—I just thought that if anyone would know, you would."

"I'd like to know if it's true or not. I wish Angie had let me in more. Maybe it's my fault. I should have given her the space to do that. It might have helped."

I nodded silently, a little unsettled by his frank admission. I wasn't sure why. Maybe I was feeling guilty about having opened a door to his past.

"Well," I said, "I'll see you this afternoon."

A line deepened in his forehead. "I'm sorry Jordan's been hard to catch—he's pretty restless. He's like his mother in a lot of ways. And in his own way, he's trying to deal with what's happened."

"I realise that it's a lot of trauma."

"You betcha. He's lost his grandparents, and his mum's in a coma. He did well to answer all your questions last time. Would he really know anything more than what he's already told you? As a father, I want to protect him."

"I understand. But I hope you understand I've got a job to do."

"I'm trying to. I'll make sure he's there on time."

"Thanks. I'd appreciate that."

I headed back onto the road. I did understand Carlson trying to protect his son. It was a terrible situation. I couldn't be a hundred percent certain that Jordan had done anything wrong. At the same time, the sense that he was hiding things from me dug deep into my bones. There was every possibility that he'd shot three people, or at least one or two of them, and I had to proceed with that in mind.

I found myself driving out to the site of the old carnival yet again. Parking,

I sat there and gazed at the empty land. Somehow, even with all the buildings and fixtures now gone, it was still eerie.

I could picture the Ferris wheel as if it were there, slowly rotating on its endless journey. When I was small, I used to look up at the swaying cars of the wheel, fearful but fascinated. My parents had to coax me onto it the first time. But once I was on board, and the car had risen all the way to the top, the view had taken my breath away. I could see my town in every direction. I could see the hidden things… the tops of the trees and the shapes the hills formed and the boys kissing girls behind the stalls.

It'd been a revelation.

Sometimes, as a detective, I'd had that same feeling when I could see all the hidden pieces of a crime—when a view suddenly opened up.

I couldn't be certain if it was at all important if a thirteen-year-old Angie had been living with the carnival people at the time of the 1989 raid.

But I wanted a better view.

Constable Georgiades called me.

"Yes, Thea?" I answered.

"I lost sight of Jordan. I was following him, but then he vanished around a bend. I think he knew I was following him. I'm sorry."

"That's okay. Where are you?"

"Kirk Road."

"I'm not far from there at all. I'm on Lancaster, near the site of the old carnival. You keep watch at your end, and I'll take a look around here."

I headed off.

CHAPTER TWENTY-NINE

A boy sped out of the thick bushland on a bike, wearing jeans and a thin, long-sleeve shirt. A helmet obscured his face.

He was fast, but I'd caught enough of a glimpse to know that he was Jordan. The same lanky body and bony shoulders.

I was about to follow him, then had a quick change of mind. Around the next bend, he could take his bike off-road and then across the creek. I'd lose him within minutes.

Maybe it was better to go check the spot where he'd exited the forest. What had he been doing in there, exactly? Had he just been trying to shake Constable Georgiades from tracking him, or did he have a specific reason to go in there?

I parked and then brought up a map of the area on my phone. There was nothing of interest in the particular place where Jordan had been. No walking trails, no caves, no creek.

I sent a quick message to Thea: *I sighted Jordan. He's headed towards town. You can finish for today. Good work.*

Heat and flies hit me square in the face as I left the car and walked into the forest.

After a five-minute trek, I was stopped by a wire fence. Beyond the fence spanned a wide field, cows feeding on the dry grass. A roughly built wooden shed stood on the other side of the fence.

There was a fresh cigarette stub on the ground. Had Jordan walked all this way just to dodge the police? Or to have a cigarette in private? Either option seemed like overkill.

It worried me that Jordan was a smoker. Someone had lit the Witness Mountain fire with a cigarette.

I needed to look at that shed. The fence had some nasty-looking barbed wire running along the top of it, but it was sagging low to the ground.

I made a bit of a run and jumped across. Pain radiated through my right leg. It was the leg I'd hurt when I'd had to kick in a door a few months ago. I used to heal from such injuries quickly. Not anymore.

I rubbed my calf and ankle, then limped to the shed. There wasn't much inside there. Mostly, it was just tools and wire that I guessed were used to fix the fence when it needed it.

There was another cigarette stub, but that was all.

Why did you bother to come into the shed to have a second cigarette, Jordan?

There was nothing to do except leave.

I returned to my car and continued onto the station.

As soon as I walked in, I went to grab a coffee. My energy was flagging, and I had to get ready for the interview with Jordan.

Franco, sitting at his desk, screwed up his eyes at me. "You look like you've been in the wars."

"Say what?"

With a smirk, he gestured at my knee.

Glancing down, I noticed a small tear in my trousers. "Oh, dammit. Thea told me she'd lost sight of Jordan on Kirk Road. I sighted him on Lancaster, coming out of a spot in the forest. I went to take a looksie."

"Find anything?"

"Nope. Except that he'd been smoking in there."

"He's a smoker? So, he could be the one who started the fire?"

"It's ringing alarm bells in my head."

"It's not proof though."

"Admit it, Franco—you've got a soft spot for Jordan."

He shrugged. "He reminds me of myself at the same age."

"Well, he's not you. Remember that."

"Yeah."

"Hey, have you heard back from your insurer?"

"Yep. Sounds like I'm getting a spanking new house built. Only thing is, I can't imagine myself in one of those. The house I had was comfortable. It was sort of like an old log cabin."

"I get it. Pete and I prefer the old country-style homes. Maybe you can sell yours once it's built, and then buy something else?"

"I might do that."

"And you're welcome to stay with us as long as you want. You can even bring in a mobile home or something. We have lots of land, and—"

"Uh, I've got it sorted. Melainey came up to me earlier—said he's got a cabin out the back of the new place he just bought. He caught me off-guard with that offer. I mean, I barely know the guy."

"Oh… okay. That was nice of him."

He shrugged. "At least I won't be under anyone's feet at Melainey's cabin—or kicking any kids outta their playroom. I thought my insurance might cough up for temporary accommodation, but I obviously didn't read the fine print. I needed to pay extra for that."

I exhaled slowly. I knew Franco had money troubles. He'd loaned his father a large sum of money for the family business. But the business kept going downhill, and then his father died suddenly of heart failure. Franco was still getting back on his feet.

I nodded. "Well, I'm glad you've found a place to stay. What about your kitten?"

"If it's okay, could Bear stay with you guys a little longer? Melainey's dog is a cat chaser."

"Of course. My grandchildren will be delighted with that."

I sipped my coffee. "Franco, there's something I want to talk to you about—concerning Angie."

"Shoot."

"I did a bit of research while Ben was out with the drone. I don't think Angie is the Iversons' biological child."

"Oh yeah?"

"Can I show you something?"

"Go for it."

I stepped around to Franco's computer and browsed to the article about Gus Iverson's car crash.

"I see what you mean," Franco said. "No mention of Angie in that article. No mention of Perdita, either."

"Yep. Seems that maybe Gus and Perdita married in 1990—and also adopted Angie that year."

He scratched his chin. "But where are you going with this? An adoption isn't going to change things."

"I'm curious about something. What if Angie had been living at the carnival at the time of the 1989 raid? It'd explain the timing of her adoption—just the year after."

"That's a bit of a reach."

"Maybe. But I think it's worth pursuing."

Expelling a heavy breath, he rapped his knuckles on the desk. "Why?"

I went to reply, but the words stuck in my throat. I didn't have any clear answers.

"Wakeland," Franco said, pausing to soften his tone, "are you sure this isn't turning into a kind of vendetta? Everything that happens in this town can't be about the Mulden family and the carnival."

"It's not a vendetta."

"Forget it. That's not the word I meant."

"Yes, you did."

He lifted his eyebrows in a weary glance. "Do you realise that you haven't checked in here all day? You're the one leading this investigation. I don't even know what the rest of the team is meant to be working on. And shouldn't we be prepping the questions for Jordan?"

"I'm sorry. You're right. I've been caught up. I'll do better."

He checked his watch. "We should get ready for the interview. It's in twenty minutes."

"Absolutely."

I headed for the interview room with Franco, where we discussed the things we needed to talk to Jordan about. It was painfully obvious I hadn't written up the questions I'd said I would. But Franco didn't make a point of it.

4 p.m. came and went. Jordan and his father didn't show. Franco and I sat twiddling our thumbs.

At ten past four, Franco contacted Carlson.

Carlson told us that his son hadn't returned home and he'd been unable to find him.

As Franco ended the call, he threw back his head and groaned. "Well, that's annoying."

"He assured me he'd be bringing Jordan in."

Franco eyed me curiously. "When did you last talk to Carlson?"

"This afternoon. I dropped in after I took Ben Tremayne back to CQ. I… I wanted to ask if he knew anything about Angie and a possible adoption."

"You went there with *that*… just before we were about to interview Jordan?"

"I was just a minute away from Carlson's house at the time."

"Did you consider that maybe Carlson is gonna think we're crackpots, diving into things that may or may not have happened thirty years ago?"

"It's up to us to decide what's relevant or not. Not Carlson."

"Yeah, and maybe he thinks we're just spinning our wheels questioning Jordan—and Carlson himself—because we don't have any other directions with this case. And for all we know, he might be telling his kid to dodge us."

I remained quiet for a moment, not wanting to snap back with a reply I'd regret. In all the eleven years I'd been partners with Franco, he'd never spoken to me about my decisions with this kind of anger. We'd been a good, solid team, with a lot of respect between us.

But as I sat there letting his words percolate, I could see the truth in what he was saying.

"Okay," I said finally. "I might have messed up."

"Don't sweat it. Trouble is, we can't force Jordan to come into the station. Not yet anyway."

"True."

"So, what now?"

"I'm going to look into this thing about Angie. I have to."

He frowned. "No, you don't. You might want to, but you don't have to."

A silence stretched between us before he spoke again. "This case is headed a long way away from the event of a family shooting event at Witness Mountain. That's the case at hand. I don't know what you're seeing, but it doesn't look anything like that."

Franco got up and walked from the room.

PART III

CHAPTER THIRTY

I woke with a tight feeling in my stomach. My last conversation with Franco had been tense. I needed to fix things with him. Only, I wasn't sure how to do that. Because, right now, he and I were on different paths.

After a quick shower, I called the hospital, asking about Angie. I'd been calling every morning, hoping for an improvement in her condition. But she remained in a coma, her condition unchanged.

Thoughts of what her early life might have been like were on my mind. Her childhood must have been terrible for her not to have even told her husband about it.

There was no one else I could ask about Angie's childhood.

No, there *was* someone. Not a relative of Angie's, but someone who was actually from the carnival. *Penny*, the youngest of the Mulden children. She was the youngest sibling of Doug Overmire.

Both Penny and her sister Polly were currently in the remand section of a women's prison, awaiting sentencing for a crime they committed together.

Penny might talk to me. Then again, she might not.

Picking up my phone, I called the women's prison. I was put through to the prison manager.

"This is Detective Kate Wakeland. I'd like to speak with Penny Foster."

"I'm afraid it'll have to wait," he told me. "Penny had an episode about a week ago—a psychiatric episode. She's been moved to another facility and is under the orders of her doctor for complete rest."

"Oh… I see."

I was about to end the call when I decided to make a last-ditch try at something else. There was Penny's sister, *Polly*. But unlike Penny, Polly had refused to talk with anyone but her lawyer so far, so my chances were slim.

"Is it possible then to speak with Penny's sister, Polly?" I asked.

"Highly unlikely. We can't get a boo out of her. I can give you the name of her lawyer—you could make a request through him. I imagine he'd have to attend any session."

"This isn't about the upcoming case. It's to do with something else altogether. If it's okay, could you ask Polly if she'd see me?"

"Hold the line."

A few minutes later, I was surprised when he told me Polly had agreed to my request.

Hopping into my car, I headed straight for the prison. I didn't want to give Polly time in which to change her mind.

The prison was located in a rural location not far from the Blue Mountains. I parked outside and walked to the gates.

On the other side of the fencing, small children ran and played on the lawn. I knew that some of the women were mothers who had their children residing with them at the prison.

The prison manager met me at the gates.

"Polly's over on the other side of the prison—away from the kids," he said.

"Is she considered a risk?"

"To be honest, I don't think she is. But there'd be mutiny if we put her anywhere over there. And I suppose there's still an element of doubt. She was involved in the kidnapping of five children, after all." He paused, glancing at me. "You're the grandmother of one of the children, aren't you?"

"Yes. But as I said on the phone, this isn't about that case."

"Well, I hope not, for Polly's sake. She's decided to wing this without her lawyer."

The manager showed me inside the prison and through to a small, basic room with a barred window.

A guard brought Polly in. She'd lost quite a bit of weight, looking a good five years older. Her blonde hair was back in a simple ponytail. Once she'd seated herself, the guard left the room.

"Hello, Polly," I started.

"Hello."

"How are you?"

"How am I? Well, how do I answer that? I've got a small garden that I keep. I read books to pass the time. That's it, really."

"I'm sorry to hear about Penny. I heard she's under psychiatric care."

Polly's forehead rippled in a frown. "She's been having a very hard time of it. I should have looked out for her more when we were children."

Polly already seemed very different to Penny. The last time I'd spoken to Penny, she'd had a tight bitterness in her voice and expression. But Polly spoke in an earnest sort of manner, her eyes as round as a child's.

"I hope she'll be okay," I said.

"*Okay* is a relative term."

"Yes, it is. Polly, thank you for agreeing to talk with me."

"I wasn't going to… but when they told me the first person you'd asked to speak to was Penny, I changed my mind. I wanted to save her from having to see you. Because when she gets better, you'll be back, won't you? My sister has had enough."

"So, you thought you'd answer my questions in place of your sister?"

"Yes. Look, it was wrong of her to steal the children. She knows that, and she's paying for it. It was wrong of me to go along with Penny's plan, too. It's more my fault than hers."

"Polly… I didn't come here today to talk about the children."

She shot me a look of wide-eyed confusion. "You didn't?"

"No—didn't the manager tell you that?"

"Yes… but I thought you must be telling a lie, just to get one of us to agree to talk to you."

"It wasn't a lie. This is about something else entirely."

"Then… what?"

"It's about the Tallman's Valley carnival."

"Oh." Her face blanched. "I don't like to talk about that, Detective."

"Polly, I really need some help to clear up a few things."

"I don't think I can help you."

"I know you grew up in the carnival. I know you were put into foster care after the police raid."

Polly began twisting her hands together, almost as if she were wringing out a wet rag. "All of that will come out in the court case. I don't want to go over it now."

"It's not your childhood I want to talk about today, Polly," I said in a soft tone.

"It isn't?"

"No. Did you hear about the recent shootings in the valley—the older couple and their daughter, Angie Green?"

She frowned in confusion. "Yes… I heard."

"Do you happen to know Angie?"

"I know *of* her. I didn't know she was back in town though."

"Well, what I'd like to know, Polly, is if she or her family ever worked at the carnival… and if she ever lived on Mulden Farm?"

Polly flinched as if I'd burned her. She obviously *did* know something.

"Polly?"

Her voice was stiff when she answered. "Why? Why are you asking these questions?"

"I'm curious."

"What has it got to do with the shootings of Angie and her family? You know who the shooter was—Angie's father. Case closed, correct?"

"We have concerns there may have been a second shooter."

"Oh… who?"

"We don't have clear information on that."

"Okay. But why were you asking about the carnival? I don't mean to throw so many questions at you… but this isn't making sense to me."

"I'm just trying to understand more about Angie's background. She's in a coma at the moment. She can't tell me herself."

Polly just stared back at me silently, twisting her hands again.

"Polly, please. Was Angie ever with the carnival?" My words flew out sterner than I'd intended. I should have held back. Polly didn't have to agree to this interview, and she could end it at any time.

I waited in the deep quiet that had opened up between us.

Finally, Polly nodded.

I breathed out slowly. "Okay… so Angie *was* part of the carnival. Did she also live at Mulden Farm?"

"Yes. She did live there."

"Was she taken away with the other children after the police raid?"

"No."

"Can you tell me why that didn't happen?"

"Because she left just before the raid. That very morning."

"Oh. Who did she leave with?"

"No one. She was all alone. Her parents had gone away… weeks before."

"They left her by herself? She was thirteen then, correct?"

"Yes."

"What can you tell me about her parents?"

"You mean… her birth parents?"

"Yes, that's who I mean."

Polly had just confirmed for me that Angie had been adopted by the Iversons.

"Not a lot," Polly said. "Her parents were dancers. They did shows on stage at the carnival. I can't remember any more than that."

"Can you tell me their names?"

"I don't remember them. Please, I—"

I gave her a moment. These seemed to be difficult memories for her.

"Polly, I need all the help I can get… for Angie's sake."

"It's all so long ago. How can this possibly help her now? It's too late… for help."

Were there hidden meanings in what Polly was saying?

"I don't know if finding out about Angie's past is going to help," I said gently. "But I don't like leaving stones unturned."

She glanced away from me. "I know you don't leave stones unturned. That's how you found the house where Penny and I were keeping the children. You looked where none of the other police were looking."

I sucked in my lips, trying to figure out how best to proceed. I needed to steer her right away from thinking about the case of the five children.

"Polly… do you have any idea where Angie's birth parents are?"

She began doing the hand-wringing thing again. "No. I don't know."

"Okay. Can you tell me why Angie left the carnival the morning of the raid?"

"She went looking for her parents. As I said, they'd left her all alone weeks before. Unfortunately, the carnival workers were flighty sorts."

"How old were you at the time of the raid?"

"I was nine."

"So young. It must have been frightening."

She didn't answer.

"So, Angie's about four years older than you," I said. "Were the two of you friends at all?"

Her expression tightened. "I thought of her as a friend… but I don't think I was hers. Anyway, we haven't spoken since those days."

"Polly… a few minutes ago, you expressed surprise about Angie being back in town. If you haven't kept in contact… how would you know whether she's in town or not?"

She inhaled deeply. "I sort of keep track of her."

"Help me understand that, Polly," I said carefully. "Why would you keep track of a woman who you haven't spoken to in decades?"

"I care about her. That's all."

"Okay. You sound like a good friend to have."

I wasn't being honest. Polly's explanation for keeping tabs on Angie was a little chilling.

"Can you tell me what you know about her life after the carnival?" I continued.

"I know she attended dance lessons. I'd slip in and watch her practice, and sometimes I'd even go see her recitals."

"Did she know you were there?"

"No. She never noticed me. She was so beautiful, and she had so much attention on her… all the time. She had a big career ahead."

"But she didn't become a professional dancer, did she?"

Polly shook her head. "That sort of ended sometime after she got married."

"To Carlson Green."

"Yes, him."

"What did you think about Angie getting married to Carlson?"

"Well, I thought that Angie should have kept going with her dancing. She would have had it all. A handsome husband with his own business, and a shiny, exciting career as a dancer…."

"In other words, a full life?"

"Unlike mine, yes. Goodness, I sound like a… *creeper*. I'm not a creeper. I'm really not."

"I'm not thinking anything like that, Polly. I'm just happy to have found someone who knew Angie."

That was a brazen lie. I was indeed getting the impression that Polly had been some kind of stalker.

But Polly couldn't have been the stalker that Angie had been afraid of on

Fraser Island. Angie had described her stalker as being male—and besides, Polly had been in the remand centre for the past six months. But I was getting an uneasy feeling about her. Her intense interest in Angie didn't seem right at all. I decided to push a little further.

"So," I said, "you were saying you found it disappointing Angie gave up on a dancing career?"

"I was disappointed *for her*. But then she had a baby—Jordan—and I guess he made up for it in her eyes. I was happy for her. Jordan's always been the apple of her eye. And it was easy to see he loved her back."

"Your impression of Jordan is that he's very fond of Angie?"

"Oh, yes. Last year, before they left the valley, I'd see them out grocery shopping and things. Jordan was always helping her—helping to carry the bags, helping with the two little ones."

It was a glowing view of Jordan that didn't match at all with what I'd seen of him so far. Perhaps Angie's life represented Polly's fantasy life, and she was seeing it through rose-coloured glasses.

She shook her head. "Hard to believe what's happened with that family now."

"The shootings were very tragic for Angie's family," I agreed.

I dusted lint from my trousers, thinking. I'd found out what I wanted to know—Angie had lived with the carnival people. But now that I knew Polly had been keeping watch on Angie all these years, I was desperate to find out what else she might know.

"Polly, do you know why Angie left Tallman's Valley a year ago?"

She stood abruptly. "I should go visit my garden before they lock me away in my room again."

I took a breath, trying not to show my disappointment. "Can I come back and see you again?"

"I really don't have anything else I can tell you. It's mostly all a fog anyway. Goodbye, Detective."

I remained seated as the guard escorted her away. I was left with the distinct impression that Polly knew more than what she'd told me—far more.

And why on earth had she been watching Angie for the past thirty years?

CHAPTER THIRTY-ONE

Ben called me first thing in the morning, sounding as excited as a child on Christmas Eve. "I've put something together, Detective. It's not finished—a lot yet to do—but it's looking good."

"Wow, Ben, I wasn't expecting you to get anything at all done yet. When can I see it?"

"In half an hour, if that suits. Over at CQ Tech. I don't have enough computer processing power at home for this."

"Now sounds good to me."

When I arrived at the CQ technology department, it was buzzing with activity. Groups of high school students were being led through the building. Different accents echoed across the marble foyer—Scottish, American, Asian, and others. The students were the children of the foreign workers at CQ Tech.

My skin prickled at the sight of the tall, silver-haired man who was leading them.

Doug Overmire.

I never saw him about town much at all. The last time had been onstage at the town fair. He lived in a wealthy suburb of the city—Darling Point. But perhaps he visited CQ more than I realised. He and his company had been the biggest financiers of the CQ development, after all.

Overmire stopped the students in the middle of the foyer.

"Okay, students," Overmire said. "Quiet down. You're about to venture to the bottom floor to take a look at our newest supercomputers. Each of these computers is taller and larger than a refrigerator. Together, these walls of computers fill the entire floor. There are only a few hundred of them in the world, and we have a room of them right here at CQ Tech."

As Overmire noticed me, his expression changed. "Students, our computer programmer Anaya Malik will take you down to the bottom floor on the lifts—or elevators, whichever you happen to call them in your country. I'll meet you there."

He strode in my direction. "Detective Wakeland, nice to see you."

"Hello, Mr Overmire. The students seemed very interested in your talk."

"It's a tech-based school holiday camp. They get to try their hand at computer programming, and we show them what career paths are available."

"Sounds really good."

"Yes, it is. We need to encourage as many kids as possible to become interested in technology. It's the future." He paused. "I was devastated to hear about what happened on Witness Mountain. Absolutely horrific. Are you drawing close to any conclusions?"

"Not as yet. We want to be sure before making any announcements."

"Of course."

"Well, I have to go. Have a good day with the students."

I stepped past him. I wondered if he'd discovered that I spoke with his sister, Polly, yesterday. I didn't think they were on speaking terms, but then, there was a lot about that family I didn't know.

Cool air enveloped me as I took the stairs to the third floor. I found Ben in the corridor outside his office, talking with two men I recognised from the day of the fair—they'd given talks on stage with Ben. I remembered that Elliot was from England and Leo from France.

"Detective Wakeland," Ben greeted me. "We've just been showing schoolkids through our floor, showing them what we do."

I smiled. "I saw a group of them in the foyer."

"Do you remember Elliot Calladine and Leo Dubois?" Ben asked, indicating towards the two men.

"Better known as gluttons for punishment," Elliot said in his clipped British accent. "Squirrels hoarding data in our gloomy little tree hollow."

"We work with the supercomputers on the basement floor," Leo offered with a shrug. "And it is not gloomy. It is beautiful. One day, we might even have computers capable of matching the human brain."

"Hello again, Elliot and Leo," I said. "Don't computers already match us—and more?"

Leo shook his head. "In some things. Like a math equation. And human brains tire easily—whereas computers can run all day long. But in other ways, a human brain is far more complex and more flexible, able to rewire itself continuously."

"Well, I'm glad to hear that, Leo," I said with a laugh.

Elliot blew out a groaning breath. "We'd better go help Anaya supervise the kiddies in the computer room—lest they do some damage while poking around."

Elliot and Leo strode away together.

I followed Ben into his office.

His mother Ada sat in the adjoining room, playing a brightly coloured game on a computer. She turned as I entered the office. "Ben makes me play these damned games. He insists they're good for the mind." She rolled her eyes like a teenager.

I grinned. Neither Ada nor Doug Overmire could dampen my mood this morning. "Good morning, Ada."

Ben swivelled around in his chair. "There you are! Can't wait to show you this. Thanks for coming down here so quick."

"Oh no, all the thanks go to you, Ben. I can't tell you how much I appreciate the work you're putting in."

Ben jumped up and began fitting me with the sensor vest and gloves. It was easy to see he was in his element.

"Ready?" he asked.

"More than ready."

Ben placed the headset over my forehead. Like last time, all I had before my eyes was a blank screen.

A login prompt appeared: *Crime Scene—Iverson-Green. Enter?*

Ben typed in a username and password, speaking them out loud. "You can change these later on to something you'll remember," he told me.

Within seconds, the screen switched to a scene of open gates and a field beyond, with a blue sky slightly dulled by a layer of smoke. I instantly recognised the gates as the entry to Angie's property.

The virtual world encased me. It was just as incredible as the last world Ben had shown me. I turned my head every which way, marvelling at the views. The gravel road stretched behind me. A flock of cockatoos shook loose from the gum trees. They screeched overhead.

"Detective Wakeland," Ben said, "The gates are the entry point. I've set up the system so that you need to identify yourself before walking through the gates. It's a security measure."

A carousel of images popped up before me. They were all of birds, except for two human images—one of Ben and one of me.

"What are the birds for, Ben?" I asked.

"For when you want a bird's-eye view," he explained. "For now, select the avatar of yourself."

Reaching out to the screen, I touched the avatar of myself.

"*Detective Sergeant Kate Wakeland, verified*," an electronic voice said.

"Okay, you're ready to go," Ben instructed.

Nodding, I walked in through the gates.

Everything was exactly the same as it was at Angie's property. As if I were actually there.

A twinge of anxiety hit me between my shoulder blades as I walked through the grevillea bushes and towards the grass where I'd found Angie.

"Will Angie be here?" I asked.

"No," Ben said. "No people here, yet. I'll do the modelling for them next."

"Okay." Turning, I walked towards Angie's house.

"You can go faster," Ben told me. "You can even run if you want. Or, if you want to go to a specific location, you can just go straight there."

He gave me instructions on how to do all of that.

Within the next second, I was inside Angie's house.

Everything seemed so real. Folded towels on the sofa. A pan on the stove-top, ready for the omelettes Angie had been about to make. Smudges of tooth-paste on the bathroom vanity. I almost expected to see myself in the mirror above the vanity. But there was no reflection. This property was Angie's world, exactly as it had been on the morning she was shot. I was just a silent, formless visitor into that world.

"Do you want the bird's-eye view, now, Detective?" Ben asked me.

"I would very much like that."

Ben told me how to switch the view.

A wedge-tailed eagle flew past me just as I switched, surprising me at first.

I was now far above the land. I was prepared this time for the soaring feeling of weightlessness. I used tiny movements of my fingers to fly, the same as Ben had taught me before.

I could see dried moss on the tiled roof of the Iverson's house, a tiny willie wagtail bird sitting on the tiles. Chickens pecked the ground inside their enclosure.

"You can get a good grasp of just how close the fire came to wiping out the two properties," Ben said. "Take a look at the far end of the Iversons' land. The neighbouring land got hit hard."

"Oh, gosh. Yes. I didn't realise it came so close."

At the other end of the Iversons' property, I spotted an old cabin that had almost completely burned down.

I felt a tight reel of tension unwinding in my chest. Everything was here, preserved. If fire came again to Witness Mountain, at least I had this.

CHAPTER THIRTY-TWO

Things were quiet in the homicide department when I arrived at the station.

I found Franco in the lunchroom, making himself a coffee.

Instantly, I felt awkward. My last discussion with Franco had ended in him walking out of the room.

"How are things going in the cabin at Melainey's?" I ventured.

Franco turned, shrugging coolly. "It's okay. Melainey's wife insists on me having dinner with them every night. Saves me from cooking, I guess. How's my little Bear?"

"Bear's doing really well. Loves his food."

Franco mixed milk and three sugars into his coffee, a deep line appearing between his eyebrows. "Where were you earlier? I tried calling…."

"Oh… sorry, I forgot to take my phone off *silent*." I poured myself a coffee. "I just came from CQ. Ben's finished the first stage of the virtual world, and he invited me to go experience it." I shook my head slowly. "It's incredible. You should come over next time and see it."

"Eh, I don't really need to. It's just backup, right?"

"Well, yeah. But it's more than that. It's—"

"You seemed to be gone most of yesterday, too. Was that more stuff to do with Ben?"

"No… I drove over to the women's prison yesterday. Polly agreed to speak with me."

"Polly? You mean Penny Foster's sister?" Franco's eyebrows shot up. "Lemme guess. The *carnival.*"

"Yes. Look, I'm sorry that I've been a bit… absent. But I did find out from Polly that Angie *was* with the carnival. Polly was strange during the interview, but I don't know if that means anything. I'll talk to you about it once I get my notes in order."

"Look," he said, "bring me in on this if you've got something that's important in terms of the Witness Mountain case. Otherwise…."

"Okay," I said quietly. "I get where you're coming from. I'm sorry I missed your call—what was it about?"

"It's about Jordan."

"Okay. Shoot."

"Right, well the thing about Jordan is that we keep getting stuck on his alibi—his reason for leaving home on Saturday morning. He can't give us a clear reason, and it makes him look bad. But what if there *is* a clear reason?"

"I'm not following."

"I watched the tapes from the fair again. Something was bugging me."

"Okay?"

"This is what was bugging me—why would a teenage boy haul his butt out of bed that early in the morning, just to go to a boring family fair by himself?"

"All right, I'm with you so far."

"And I started thinking, what if he didn't just meet the girl—Dakota—that morning? What if he already knew her?"

"Hmmm. That's a new way of looking at it."

"If you watch the tape carefully, you'll see that Dakota even touches Jordan on the arm at one point."

"So, are you thinking they had some sort of teenage romance between them?"

"Yeah, I am."

"When I went to talk to Dakota," I said, "she told me that the boy who worked in the bakery was her boyfriend. I think his name was Lewis."

"Maybe Jordan and Dakota had a relationship before he left town, and then he expected her to still have feelings for him when he returned? But she's got another boyfriend now, and maybe that's what they were arguing about at the fair?"

"Sounds reasonable. Okay. If this is true, it means both of them lied to us. Which begs the question—*why*?"

"A couple of days ago, you said you saw Jordan coming out of a certain spot in the forest, right? Maybe we should go have another look?"

I nodded. "Let's go for it. You might find something that I didn't."

I drove with Franco to the place where I'd last seen Jordan. The air was sticky as we made our way through the bushland.

We jumped the collapsed barbed-wire fencing. I made sure to land a little more elegantly this time, careful not to hurt my foot.

As before, the shed on the other side of the fence was empty. The cigarette stub remained on the floor.

"Looks like the only reason he came in here was to have a smoke." Franco gave a sigh that sounded disappointed.

"Wish I'd kept Thea on his tail. He seemed to have noticed her following him around, and so I called that off."

Franco looked past me, at the field that sat beyond the fence. "Maybe the answer lies out there."

"What do you mean?"

"I mean, who owns that land?"

I nodded, exhaling. "I should have thought of that. You're thinking it might be owned by Dakota's family, right?"

Taking out his phone, Franco browsed to a map of the area, zeroing in on our location.

He looked up the address and then the owner.

The result came back as *Sean Macklin.*

"Bingo," I said. "Dakota's last name is Macklin. You were right."

"Yup. You can't say *that's* not interesting." Franco sounded just a little smug. "Jordan's been coming here to see Dakota… or to spy on her."

"You're dead right. Too much of a coincidence otherwise."

Franco and I drove around the block to the front of the house that belonged to Sean Macklin. It was a log cabin style home, built low and wide, with a porch spanning the entire width.

No answer came to our knock on the front door.

We decided to head over to the *Sweet Eats Bakery* at CQ.

When we arrived, Dakota was nowhere in sight. The young baker I'd met last time—Lewis—seemed flustered as he met the rush of orders coming from customers.

Once the last person had been served, Lewis huffed in relief. Turning to us, he placed both hands on the countertop. A smirk crossed his face. "I'm guessing you two didn't come for the doughnuts."

"We want to talk to Dakota," Franco told him.

"Good luck with that. She didn't bother turning up to work."

"Oh," I said, "is she sick?"

Lewis shrugged. "Didn't tell me and didn't answer my calls."

"Your girlfriend left you in the lurch, huh?" Franco said.

"*Girlfriend*?" Lewis tilted his head as though Franco had just spoken a foreign word. "Did she say that? Because last time I asked her out, she said *no*. Maybe she's just shy. Do you think she's too shy to go out with me?"

"Mate," Franco said in reply, "I think I'll take one of these apple Danishes." Franco dropped five dollars on the counter and then picked up one of the Danishes from the basket there. "We'll let you know if we have any more questions."

We walked out of the shop.

Franco bit into the Danish. "Okay, so, was I right, or was I right?"

"You picked it. Dakota duped me. Lewis was never even her boyfriend."

"We've got two possibilities. Jordan has been stalking Dakota, and she's afraid of him, so she lied about knowing him—and now he's kidnapped her. Or, the two of them have a little romance happening, and they've run away together. I'd pick scenario two."

I stared at Franco. "We need to go find out which scenario is the right one."

CHAPTER THIRTY-THREE

Franco and I went looking for Dakota Macklin's father, Sean.

We discovered that Sean owned a motorcycle dealership in Katoomba. We spoke with one of his employees at the dealership. She told us that Sean had been there for an hour in the morning, but he'd left soon after and hadn't returned.

That meant that Sean, Dakota and Jordan were all gone—somewhere.

Were the three of them together? What was actually going on here?

Out of ideas, Franco and I returned to Sean Macklin's house.

Franco banged on his door. "Police. Mr Macklin?"

As before, no answer came.

I sighed. "We'll have to go see if we can rustle up a search warrant."

As we walked back to the car, Franco's phone buzzed, and he stopped to answer it.

"You looking for Sean?" came a voice from across the road. The accent was British.

An older man stood there, holding a wheelbarrow. He'd been clearing away twigs and leaves from the front yard of his house, possibly getting his land prepared in case of fire.

I jogged across to him.

"Yes, we're looking for Sean," I said. "Know where he is?"

The man set his barrow down. Sweat trickled between the deep creases of his face. Fetching a handkerchief from his pocket, he dabbed at his forehead and chin. “Well, I can’t give you an exact location, but he asked to borrow my tent, so I’ve got half an idea.”

This was definitely odd. The saleswoman we’d spoken to at Sean’s dealership had expected him back there. But instead, Sean had suddenly decided to go *camping*?

“Do you know where Sean was intending to camp?” I asked.

The man squinted at me in the harsh sunlight. “Is someone in trouble?”

“We have some… safety concerns,” I answered. It was the best I could think of.

“Oh no.” The man shook his head, dabbing at his face with the handkerchief again. “I did notice Sean looked a bit anxious and all. But then, I don’t like to ask too many questions, you know? It’s not my business.”

“Was his daughter with him?”

“No. Well, I didn’t see her. I saw him throwing some climbing gear in the back of his jeep, and I thought maybe he was taking Dakota for a school holiday trip. The two of them used to go climbing a lot. Mustn’t be easy for a single father to find things to do with his teen daughter.”

“Climbing? Do you know where they used to go?”

“Usually to Butterbox. But Sean mentioned Claustral Canyon this time around. I don’t think he’d take Dakota there. If you’re fit enough, you can have a fair shake at Butterbox Canyon. But Claustral?” The man blew out a long breath. “You’ll come unstuck quick if anything goes wrong. I’ve been, myself, but that was thirty-odd years ago. It’s a young person’s game, and I’ve got bad knees now.”

“I appreciate your help.” I handed him my card. “Please call me if you see either Sean or Dakota.”

I crossed the road back to Franco and filled him in on all the information that the man had given me.

“That sounds like a father racing after his teenage daughter,” Franco remarked. “Sounds like maybe Jordan and Dakota took Sean’s tent, and so Sean had to borrow another one from his neighbour? And Sean’s plan was to camp out near the canyon and go looking for Dakota.”

“You’re right. And if you are, both Jordan and Dakota could be in danger. Going into a canyon like Claustral by themselves is all kinds of risky. Especially if Jordan has become unhinged and he’s somehow forcing Dakota to go with him.”

Franco looked up Claustral Canyon on his phone. "It's at Mount Tomah, about an hour away from here. And the canyon's closed, due to risk of bush fire."

"If the kids are in there, we might have to call in search and rescue."

"But we don't know for sure. It was just a guess. For all we know, neither Sean, Dakota, or Jordan are in the same place right now. We don't have a situation... yet."

"Okay... let's just head out to the canyon, then, and check it out."

"Yup. Let's go."

Franco took the driver's seat, while I jumped into the passenger's side.

I browsed the canyon on my phone as Franco drove. Images of Claustral popped up—they were nothing but magical. Layers of lush ferns and lime-green moss lined a plunging canyon, beams of sunlight stopping short of the watery bottom. It reminded me of the interior of a cathedral at night, its beauty exposed only by the glow of candles.

I turned on speakerphone so Franco could listen to the information about the canyon.

Claustral Canyon was locked away in time for over a million years, untouched by humans, until it was accessed for the first time in the 1960s. You will be abseiling down vertical tunnels, through waterfalls, and swimming through cold streams. You will be rewarded with views of one of the most spectacular canyons in the world. But be warned, this canyon is only for the experienced, extremely fit canyoner. People have lost their lives in this and nearby canyons.

"Sounds like danger central," Franco remarked. "But, you know, I should do some stuff like that before I get any older. Ehhh, maybe it's too late for me already. I haven't even had my lazy butt back on my mountain bike in years."

"Time gets away," I agreed. "You don't notice it running under your feet. Everything just looks... still."

I made a phone call to my husband. "Pete, Franco and I are making a trip over to Mount Tomah. What's the fire situation over that way?"

"There's no immediate risk, but I'd feel better if you didn't go anywhere near there. Is it necessary, Kate?"

"We're looking for a couple of people. Teenagers. It's pretty important that we find them."

"Are they on foot?"

"We think they might be camping there."

"If you don't find them quickly, call me, okay? We don't want anyone camping at Mount Tomah right now."

"I will."

Franco pulled off the highway at Mount Victoria and drove along the causeway. We'd reached the long, winding stretch called Bells Line of Road, which was the original way across the Blue Mountains.

A police vehicle appeared at a distance behind us.

"Who's that?" I asked.

"Melainey. I spoke to him while you were talking with Macklin's neighbour. He asked if we needed help with anything. He was over this way, so…."

"Oh, good. With the three of us, we'll have more chance of finding the kids quickly."

"Uh huh, that's why I told him to meet us there. Have to admit I'd prefer it was just you and me today, Wakeland. Like the old days. Melainey's got his own ways of doing things. We're just not in step with each other."

I glanced at Franco. "Won't be long before it's just you and him though. You've got to find a way to make it work."

"Yeah, I don't have a choice."

"Sorry. I was being a bit of a jerk."

"Yep, you were being a jerk, Wakeland."

"I'll pull up my socks. If it's any consolation, remember that I had to work with Grimshaw earlier this year?"

Detective Sergeant Reagan Grimshaw had led Strikeforce FlyingFox—the team that'd searched for my granddaughter and the other four children during the years they were missing. I'd found her impossible to deal with. It was only in the very last week of the case that I'd glimpsed a surprisingly softer, compassionate side to the woman.

Franco's face broke out in a grin. "She's one damned scary unit."

I laughed. "She'd probably enjoy that description of her."

Melainey followed us all the way to Mount Tomah. It was an area I knew well. The Blue Mountains Botanical Gardens and The Cathedral of Ferns picnic area were here. Pete and I had often brought Abby to both of those when she was little. When Pete and I were in our twenties, we'd done a little canyoning in this area. But I hadn't ever tackled Claustral Canyon.

Studying the map, I guided Franco off the road and to a parking area. There were no other cars here. That wasn't a good sign. Did that mean that Sean Macklin wasn't here?

We exited the car and met up with Melainey, who pulled into the carpark just after us.

Melainey had a barely controlled energy showing in his face and posture. He always used to come alive when there was any action afoot. The thing he used to dodge the most was the paperwork that was part-and-parcel of policing.

"So," he said, "we're off for a bit of canyoning adventure, ay?"

I gave a wide smile. "My hope is that we find these kids without any adventuring."

Melainey shrugged. "Where's the fun in that?" He tugged out a paper map from his pocket, then traced a path with his finger. "Looks like we can head along the creek."

I nodded. "Yep—if you want to get wet, you can. Then you've got to get down a fifteen metre drop when you reach the keyhole into the canyon itself."

He narrowed his eyes at me, the sun in his face. "Well, if we can't go that way, what's the point in being here, then?"

"Finding a campsite," I replied.

"Okay, well, let's go scout the area," Melainey said in a disappointed tone. "Time's-a-wastin'."

The three of us spread out as we began the search.

The sun was hot as a toaster on my forehead. The thought of getting wet in the creek began to seem enticing.

A call came through on my radio. Melainey had found something.

I met up again with him and Franco.

The discovery was a dome-shaped tent. Inside, there were some ropes and a frayed harness, and various carabiners. There was also a faded flannelette shirt and pair of utility pants—both medium size. There was nothing here to tell us who owned the clothing or equipment.

The air was boiling and suffocating in the tent, especially with the three of us in there.

"No telling how long this stuff has been here," Melainey remarked. Crouching, he examined the harness. "Look. M-A-C-K-L-I-N. Macklin. It's faded, but you can still read it."

"Good find," I said.

We stepped outside again.

Melainey exhaled, scanning the grounds and wiping his sweaty brow. "Okay, Macklin, where'd you stash your damned car?"

"I'm not so sure he's hidden his car at all," I said. "It doesn't fit. He hasn't tried to hide any of his tracks so far."

Melainey nodded. "You know, you're right. He hasn't. Maybe the car got stolen, then?"

I thought for a moment, then took out my phone, browsing the map of the canyon. "Or… maybe he parked it somewhere else. So… if you follow the journey through the canyon, you go through a section called Rainbow Ravine, then onto the Camel's Hump and then an exit gully." Raising my eyes to Franco and Melainey, I gestured at the map. "What if Macklin drove to where we are now, set up the tent, but then changed his mind? He could be parked at the other end."

Franco nodded. "He might have thought the kids had made it to that side of the canyon."

"Right," Melainey said. "Let's go, then. Better than standing around here like a pack of gooses."

We walked back to the cars and drove on a little further, heading down Rainbow Ravine Road.

I pointed. "There's a jeep there." I conducted a scan on the licence plate number of the vehicle.

The car belonged to Sean Macklin.

CHAPTER THIRTY-FOUR

Melainey, Franco and I parked at the exit point of Claustral Canyon.

Sean Macklin's jeep was parked in front of us. He had to be around here somewhere.

Melainey got his wish for adventure—we soon found no other way forward but to wade through a creek. The rainforest lining either side of the creek was too thick to pass through. Fortunately for us, the water level was low. The drought had lowered water levels everywhere.

My feet were cool, but my head was boiling. I should have thought to grab a hat before heading out here.

Climbing over rocks, we made our way around a bend.

Three people sat just up ahead, perched on a rock platform in the stream.

I recognised Jordan and Dakota straight away. The third person—a man—had to be Sean.

"Well, look at that," Melainey said with a chuckle. "Bet they weren't expecting *us*."

Jordan and Dakota scrambled to their feet.

"Stay where you are," Melainey boomed. "Sit yourselves down!"

The teenagers didn't move, but they didn't sit, either. Jordan placed an arm around Dakota's shoulders.

Sean Macklin pulled himself to his feet. He was shirtless, wearing only utility pants and a backpack.

Harnesses and climbing gear were piled up nearby.

The teenagers started backing away as we advanced.

"Let me go first," I cautioned Melainey and Franco. "The kids look nervous. I don't want them trying to run off."

"Good thought," Melainey replied. "We'll hang back until you give us the word." He stripped off his sweat-soaked shirt and plunged it into the creek.

I made my way forward, slipping and splashing awkwardly over the rocks and through the water. My trousers were soaked up to my thighs now.

Sean walked out protectively in front of Jordan and Dakota, blocking my view of them. "What's going on?"

"For one thing, you're not allowed to be here," I started. "The entire area is closed due to the bushfires."

"Ah, okay. Sorry. We'll leave. Thanks for letting us know." He pushed his wet hair back from his face. He had fresh abrasions along his arms and shoulders.

"Sean," I said, "why are you here?"

"You know my name?" He stared at me for a moment, then exhaled, shaking his head. "You were looking for us, specifically, weren't you?"

"Yes."

His forehead creased. "But you lot aren't rescue or the RFS. You're... cops."

"That's right, Mr Macklin. We're cops. Can you please explain what you're doing here?"

"I came looking for my daughter. I found some of our canyoning gear gone this morning, and I guessed that she and Jordan were gonna come here. Stupid damned kids."

"Where'd you find them?"

"In the canyon. There's a glow worm cave down there. That's where they were. It used to be one of Dakota's favourite places to go."

"I'm very glad they're safe."

"Yeah. Me too. Jordan hurt his arm though. I had to haul him out of the canyon—just ten minutes ago."

I glanced over Sean's shoulder at Jordan. Jordan had a makeshift sling around his left arm—it'd been fashioned from a long-sleeved shirt. I guessed that explained why Sean was without a shirt—and it also explained the scrapes on Sean's torso. It can't have been easy to lift a teenage boy out of the canyon.

The two teenagers had their gaze fixed on each other. They certainly seemed in love.

Thoughts charged through my mind. Had Jordan tried to kill his mother so he could stay here with Dakota—so he didn't have to return to the island?

I stepped around Mr Macklin and over to the teenagers.

Dakota bowed her head to avoid meeting my eyes.

I noticed a thin, rectangular-shaped box in the pocket of Jordan's jeans. I guessed that was either a packet of condoms or a very soggy packet of cigarettes.

Jordan followed my gaze. He pulled out a squashed packet of cigarettes.

I decided not to comment on that now. But I'd be questioning him very intently about the Witness Mountain blaze at a later point.

"What did you do to your arm, Jordan?" I asked.

"Slipped while try'na climb down the canyon," he mumbled.

"You're lucky you didn't do anything worse. You know we've been looking for you, right?"

"Yeah. I just… needed some time alone."

"Time alone *with Dakota*," I said pointedly.

"She said she knew a place where no-one would bother us. But don't blame her—it was all my idea to come here."

I eyed his arm. "Is it broken?"

Jordan chewed the side of his mouth. "Think so."

"We need to get you to a hospital, pronto," I told him.

I turned back to Sean. "And we really need to talk with you and Dakota down at the station."

A call came through on my radio.

It was Pete.

"Kate, are you still on Mount Tomah?"

"Yes, we are. We've just found the people we were looking for."

"What's your present location?" Pete asked.

"We're in a creek—leading to Claustral Canyon, off Rainbow Ravine Road."

"You need to get them—and yourselves—out now. There's a fire ripping along Bells Line of Road, headed your way. It's not close—you've got time. But don't delay."

I raised my eyes to Sean.

“I heard.” Sean shook his head. “It’s been one thing after the other with these two kids. Okay, Dakota and Jordan—we’ve got to move out.”

Sean grabbed the climbing gear and handed it to his daughter. Sean and I helped Jordan navigate the rocky creek bed. The last thing Jordan needed was to fall on his broken arm again.

Once we were clear of the creek, we all headed for the cars.

Thick grey smoke billowed in the distance.

Franco and I took Jordan in our car, Sean took his daughter in his jeep.

We escorted Jordan to the hospital—staying with him until his father got there. He’d remained quiet for the whole trip—and Franco and I hadn’t questioned him. It wasn’t the time for it. I suspected he was in a great deal of pain with his broken arm, but he was hiding it well.

CHAPTER THIRTY-FIVE

Franco and I walked into the police station together, our shirts and trousers still damp and flecked with dirt.

"Don't ask," Franco said to Inspector Shintani as we passed him.

Shintani didn't attempt to hide a grin.

We had a short break for some lunch and cold drinks while we waited for Sean Macklin and his daughter to arrive for their interview. Jordan was in the hospital, waiting to have an operation on his broken bone.

Detective Reagan Grimshaw walked up to us, munching on an apple. "You two look the worse for wear."

"All in the name of duty," I quipped.

She wiped at her forehead with the back of her sleeve. "Air-con's on the blink again. If I see that scrawny little mechanic about who swore blind he fixed it, I might just strangle his neck."

Franco winced. "I'd believe it."

She bit into her apple again. "Franco, a new case just came in. I was hoping I might be able to pick your brain."

Franco chewed his curried-egg sandwich. "Oh yeah? Missing person, I assume?"

"You got it," said Grimshaw. "She's an old girlfriend of yours."

A deep frown appeared on Franco's forehead. "Who?"

"Martina Bianchi."

"Martina?" Franco put down his sandwich. "I spoke with her the other day. She's *missing*?"

"Her parents reported it," Grimshaw said. "Missing for at least twenty-four hours. Seems there's been a kind of stalker situation happening. Did she say anything about that?"

"A stalker? What? Whoa, no, she didn't mention anything like that," Franco told Grimshaw.

"Right," Grimshaw replied. "Well, if you think of anything that might give me a leg up in the case, give me a shout."

Grimshaw tossed her apple core in the rubbish bin and then walked out of the lunchroom.

Franco shook his head. "That's the strangest. Martina had a *stalker*? She sounded pretty happy every time I talked to her."

I bit down on my lip. "Except maybe for that phone conversation with her on Fraser Island?"

"Oh yeah. That. She was going over old ground. Talking about when we broke up. Hell, her parents must be going out of their minds right now."

"Maybe you should go talk with them? Sounds like a dangerous situation for Martina. I can handle the interview with the Macklins."

"You sure?"

"Of course I'm sure."

Franco looked distracted as he tipped the rest of his sandwich in the bin and jogged from the lunchroom.

It was certainly a worry Martina was missing. A missing woman who'd been the victim of a stalker could end up being found murdered. This was the fine line between the missing persons unit and the homicide unit. Grimshaw and I had found ourselves in heated discussions on this issue in the past. I preferred that the homicide unit be brought in early on many missing person cases. Grimshaw often didn't agree.

Sean and Dakota walked into the station just as I was finishing up my lunch.

They'd both showered and changed clothing.

"Come through," I said. I motioned towards my desk, where I'd set up two chairs.

"If you don't mind," Sean said, "I'd prefer to be interviewed first, then bring in Dakota after that."

It was a surprising request.

"Okay, well, certainly. Dakota, I'll get Constable Georgiades to show you where you can wait."

Thea walked Dakota to the waiting area.

I took Sean over to my desk.

He sat heavily, exhaling and stretching his neck. He was a good-looking man, with waves of dark hair, dark eyes and olive skin. His colouring was nothing like his daughter's, with her pale skin and hair—but they did share very similar facial features.

"Okay, Sean," I began, "what's the reason you wanted to talk with me on your own?"

"Because I'm not silly, that's why. I mean, two kids did a stupid thing and went into a canyon by themselves. But that shouldn't warrant three homicide detectives coming after them. Nor should it warrant a police interview."

I sat back in my chair, surprised yet again by Sean Macklin. "Okay, so, why *do* you think I asked you in here?"

"Because you think Jordan had something to do with the shootings on Witness Mountain."

Sean had certainly captured my full attention now. "Can you explain that to me?"

"It's obvious. If I read between the lines in the media stories, the police haven't named Angie's father as the shooter. Which means they're not sure. Jordan was there that morning, which makes him a suspect—am I right? He's a good kid, and no one's here to defend him. So, I'm stepping in."

"I assure you, Sean, we're not jumping to any assumptions."

"Then why the questions? And why were you looking for Jordan?"

"I'd just like to clarify some things. Anyway, Jordan does have his father for support."

"Carlson's been overseas for a year. He barely knows his kids."

"Do you know Carlson?"

"I know *of* him."

"How about we just… start with what happened today, and go from there?"

"Okay. Go for it."

"What tipped you off that the kids had gone to the canyon?"

"This morning, Dakota said she felt sick, so she stayed home from her job at the bakery. But something felt off. I went to work, but I couldn't get it out of my head. I decided to drive back home and check on her. She was gone. I checked her computer—found a message from her to Jordan. Talking about

Claustral Canyon. I put two and two together—and looked in the garage. She'd taken the canyoning gear."

"How did they even get all the way over there?"

"Bus."

"Well, I'm glad it all ended without anything more serious than a broken arm. It came close to disaster."

"Don't worry—I've been reminding Dakota of that. Such a damned stupid thing to do."

"They took a big risk. How long have Jordan and your daughter been together as boyfriend and girlfriend?"

"They, ah, used to like each other… before Angie left Tallman's Valley. I didn't know they'd stayed in touch."

An alert went off in my mind at the way his tone softened as he spoke Angie's name.

"How well do you know Angie, Sean?"

He looked disturbed by my question. "We were… friends."

"More than friends, perhaps?"

"Just… good friends."

"Any dinners, long conversations, walks together…?"

"I guess so."

"Any intimacy?"

He glanced away. "Yes."

"Call me old-fashioned, but do you mind if I call that a romantic relationship?"

He leaned his head back, sighing. "Angie didn't want anyone to know. And now she's lying in the hospital, in a coma. She wouldn't want this to come out."

This was certainly interesting. Sean had been Angie's boyfriend. That was a relationship of Angie's we hadn't known about.

"Why did she want your romance kept secret?" I asked him.

"Angie's just very private. It's the way she is."

That was a word I'd heard before in relation to Angie—*private*. Why did she hold things so close to her chest?

"How long ago did this start?" I asked.

"Eighteen months ago. About six months before she left town."

"Did Jordan and Dakota know?"

"No. No, they don't know."

"If you were keeping your relationship with Angie secret from the kids, how did they first meet?"

"Angie hired me to make some dog kennels for her. She was fostering dogs at the time—Australian Shepherds. She was taking on ones that'd outlived their usefulness as herding dogs. Angie told the kids I was a handyman. Stupidly, I brought Dakota with me one day. She and Jordan took one look at each other, and that was it. They fell in love. She was thirteen, then."

"Okay. And can I assume your relationship with Angie ended before she moved away to Fraser Island?"

"Yeah. It did."

A thought rolled in, quickly gathering steam. Could Sean have been Angie's stalker on the island? Perhaps he could have gone back and forth, passing the journeys off as business trips.

"Sean, have you been to Fraser Island within the past year?"

"No. I actually didn't even know where she'd gone. She wouldn't tell me."

"Did you part on bad terms?"

He shook his head. "Not at all."

"If you were on such good terms… why do you think she didn't tell you where she went?"

He seemed jittery all of a sudden, a tremor in his hands.

"Are you okay, Sean?"

"Yeah… it's just been a big day. If you don't mind, I think I'm done. I hope I answered all you wanted to know."

"All right. Yes, it was quite a day. If I have further questions, can I contact you?"

"Sure," he answered.

I guessed that was the best I was going to get for now.

The interview had confused me. He didn't have to admit to having been in a relationship with Angie—he could easily have lied. He'd really gone out of his way to save Jordan's skin. I didn't know what that meant. He was correct about Jordan being a suspect, and he hadn't been afraid to tell me that.

With the interview with Sean at an end, I phoned Thea and asked her to bring Dakota over.

Dakota sank into the seat beside her father, her eyes darting nervously around the station.

"Dakota," I said, "all I want from you is the truth. Jordan has been gone from the valley for a whole year. I'd like to know how you're still in a relationship with him. I'll just be sitting here, listening. How does that sound?"

She gave a rigid nod, fiddling with the bracelet she wore on her wrist.

"So…" she began, "after Jordan left the valley, we kept talking to each other. Using online chat. He kept saying he'd come back one day. I didn't know if I believed him. But then… a couple of weeks ago, he told me to meet him at the shed at the back of my dad's land. Just like that. And we started meeting up there…."

"And what happened the day of the fair?" I asked. "Why were you having an argument with Jordan?"

"Jordan came and wanted to hang out with me. I got upset because I was working and trying to do a good job. And… also because my dad was at the fair. I didn't want him to see me talking to Jordan."

"Why didn't you want your dad to see you with Jordan?"

Dakota flicked her gaze towards her dad. "Because Dad didn't want me to be Jordan's girlfriend. He says I'm too young to date. He's strict. Like, *really* strict."

Sean nodded, shrugging. "She *is* too young."

"Okay," I said to Dakota, "you've been meeting up with Jordan over the past few days, right? What has he been like?"

"He's been angry. Like—really, really angry. I understand why. I mean, his granddad shot his family. So scary."

"Thank you, Dakota, you're doing well," I told her. "Can you explain how you two ended up at the canyon?"

Dakota squeezed her eyes shut. "Jordan thought the cops were following him around. He said it felt like the whole town was watching him—the cops, my dad, the reporters, and everyone else. I said I knew somewhere that no one would be. The canyon. I didn't think Dad would find out."

Dakota's eyes were wet and glistening. I got the impression she was telling the truth this time. And the police really *had* been following Jordan around, so he hadn't been lying about that.

I finished up the questioning there, and then walked them both out of the station.

Sean was right about this being a big day. I wondered if, later, he'd realise he'd just added himself to my list of suspects in terms of the shootings on Witness Mountain.

CHAPTER THIRTY-SIX

That night, I sat with Abby, Logan, and the kids in the living room, anxiously following the news of the fires on the TV.

Pete was at the fire that had sped towards Mount Tomah. It had gotten worse—much worse. The residents had been told it was too late to leave. They had to seek shelter where they were.

The images were terrifying—walls of flames higher than the trees, burning red against the night sky.

It wasn't until the early hours that Pete finally returned. It was just me staying up and waiting now.

His firefighting gear was covered in black soot.

I greeted him with a glass of fresh orange juice. "Pete, I was so worried."

"It was intense. Unbelievable."

He drank down the juice in a couple of gulps. He looked and sounded drained, his voice hoarse. His voice often got like that after the hours spent shouting to other firefighters over the roar of a large blaze.

After a shower, he got into bed.

I laid myself next to him. "It's only the first month of summer. What's going to happen in January—and February?"

"The way it's going, there won't be much left to burn by then." He put an arm around me. "No, look, it's going to stop. It has to."

"I hope so."

"You're lucky you and those people got out when you did. I can tell you that much. Who were the people and what were they doing there?"

"It was Jordan… and his girlfriend, Dakota."

"You mean the kid whose family was shot?"

"Yes, that kid."

"And you found them at Claustral? Did they actually go into the canyon?"

"Uh huh. Dakota's father, Sean, went racing after them earlier. Jordan broke his arm—and Sean had to lift him out."

"Dangerous stuff. I had my heart in my mouth the whole time, until I knew you'd all made it out of there safely."

"I was like that all night, waiting for you to come home."

He kissed my forehead.

After a minute, Pete began softly snoring. I knew it wouldn't be long until that snore was so loud I could barely hear myself think. It was how Pete went to sleep—he'd quieten again later in the night.

Sometimes it drove me crazy, but it was one of the constants in my life, and also somehow calming. I'd been very, very glad to see Pete walk through our door. Not every firefighter got to come home to their families.

I felt myself slipping into sleep, too.

On my way to the station in the morning, I decided to turn around and head over to the hospital.

I wanted to see Angie Green. So far, I'd heard from different people who knew her—Sean, Carlson, Jordan and Roslyn—but she hadn't had a chance to speak for herself. That was the maddening part of this. She couldn't speak.

I just wanted to sit with her for a little while.

When I walked into her hospital room, Carlson was there with Toby and Oliver.

I smiled at the two boys. "How are you, Toby… Ollie?"

They stared up at me with round, unblinking eyes. An unwelcome image rose in my mind of when we'd found them in the dog kennel.

"We're good," Toby said in his squeaky, little boy voice.

"I'm happy to hear that," I told him.

Carlson indicated that he wanted to speak with me alone. I walked with him over to the window.

"I want to apologise about Jordan. I don't know what got into him." He sighed. "I'm guessing you don't think much of me as a parent, do you?"

"Teenagers can be pretty impulsive. I'm not blaming you. How *is* he this morning?"

"Still recovering from his operation."

"I hope it went well?"

"Yes, but he has an infection from a cut that happened when he fell. So, recovery is going to take a while."

"Oh no, that's the last thing he needs right now."

"Yeah, poor kid."

Carlson gave an appreciative smile. He was far more relaxed around me than he had been in previous encounters. I could tell he thought he was completely off the hook. But in truth, I still held suspicions about him. I was suspicious about both him and Sean—the two men who'd been in romantic relationships with Angie.

"Carlson, can I ask you something?"

"Yeah, of course."

"How well do you know Sean Macklin—Dakota's father?"

"I don't know much about him. Seems like a decent guy—except he's got something against Jordan. Won't let him anywhere near his daughter."

"Hmmm, okay. Thanks."

He half-turned back to Angie and the boys. "This is really rough on Toby and Ollie. Their mother's in a coma, and now their brother's just had an operation." He sighed. "I hope Angie comes out of it soon. The kids are missing her."

Carlson gathered up his kids and left the room, leaving me alone with Angie.

I stepped over to her and sat.

Her long red hair had been brushed and was draping her shoulders. The nurses were taking good care of her.

"Angie," I said, "this is Kate Wakeland again. You look beautiful this morning. I don't know if you know, but I went looking for your son, Jordan, yesterday. It's okay—everything's fine—we found him with his girlfriend, Dakota."

A flicker of a frown crossed her forehead.

"Angie? If you heard any of that, I hope you heard that Jordan is okay."

Again, there was the briefest of frowns.

Could she hear me? Was she disturbed by the mention of Jordan's name? Or was it just an involuntary muscle movement?

I decided to try something else. "I met a friend of yours the other day. Sean Macklin."

Did Angie's heart rate just jump on the monitor? It certainly seemed to.

"Sean seems to think a lot of Jordan," I said.

A slight moan came from deep in her throat. Her eyelids twitched.

I let a minute pass, allowing her to settle again.

"Angie," I said gently, "I looked at some old photographs of yours. You were so lovely in your dance outfits. Your father looked so proud, standing beside you."

I heard the merest of gasps, and her heart rate increased again.

A nurse entered the room, and she went straight to check the displays on Angie's cardiac monitor.

"I'm sorry," I said. "I think she might have been responding to what I was saying to her."

The nurse gave me a quick smile. "This happens all on its own from time to time. Nothing to worry about. She's fine."

I smiled back, but it had seemed that Angie could hear and understand me.

But even if she *was* reacting, it wasn't going to tell me what she was thinking.

I reached for her hand. "We're all looking forward to you waking, Angie. Everyone's thinking of you."

CHAPTER THIRTY-SEVEN

When I walked into the station, Franco and Melainey were at Melainey's desk, their heads together, poring over a set of documents.

"What's this?" I asked, stepping up.

Franco raised his eyes to me, blowing out a stream of air. "It's the reports from the weapons experts. They give a high likelihood of Gus Iverson being our guy."

My mind reeled. "Just Gus—acting on his own? How is that possible?"

Picking up the stack of papers, I scanned the information. There was a lot of mathematics—about angles, velocity and probabilities. I raced through to the end results.

The forensic weapons report had concluded that the gunpowder burn on Gus's throat proved the rifle had been shot at very close range. And the gunpowder residue on Gus's hands showed he'd held the rifle as it'd been shot.

There was a second report from Detective John Farrina—the multiple-shootings specialist who Melainey had engaged. He'd determined that Gus had shot Angie first, then returned to shoot his wife, finally heading outside to shoot himself.

I released a slow, tight breath, considering the information in both reports. "I need to sit down with all of this and get my head clear."

Melainey frowned, nodding. "I found it hard to come to grips with, too. Maybe we'll just never know how things happened exactly on the day."

"By the looks of it, luck just wasn't on the side of Angie and Perdita," Franco agreed.

A twinge of anger fired inside my throat. "So, that's it? We're just going to close the case? Yes, we have two reports from weapons experts here, but we still have to use our own judgement. Angie was shot in the middle of the field. By an old man on bad legs, with poor eyesight. How does that add up? If Perdita was in the field with Angie, why didn't Gus shoot her there? And the little boys—Toby and Oliver—they didn't mention seeing their grandmother in the field. They only saw their mother—and the shooter."

"Maybe there are viable explanations for all that?" Melainey offered.

"I have serious doubts," I said. "And if it happened in that sequence, why did Gus go outside to shoot himself after killing Perdita? Why didn't he do it right where he was, in the kitchen?"

Franco gave an uneasy shrug. "Couldn't bear to look at his dead wife?"

"Perhaps," I conceded. "Believe me, I want it to be Gus rather than Jordan. But I'm not ready to sign off on it. Not yet."

"Eh, well, you two work it out among yourselves," Melainey said. "My head's gone to jelly after looking through those reports. I've got some things to check on."

Melainey walked out of the station, whistling.

Franco turned to me. "Okay. I get it. You've got doubts. So, where do we take it from here?"

"I want second opinions on the evidence we have. From people other than John Farrina and the current forensics weapons expert."

Franco sighed heavily. "You sure that isn't taking this investigation where it doesn't need to go?"

"It's just being thorough."

"Don't take this the wrong way, Wakeland. But I think you might have needed a longer break before coming back to work."

"Really?"

"Look, I take it back. Emotions are running high, I guess."

"Apology accepted. Look, it's not too much to get a second opinion. It's normal. It's what we do. Why should this case be any different?"

"Because, in this case there was a dead guy holding a gun."

"Are you sure you're not just worried about suspicion pointing Jordan's way? I know you like the kid."

"Yeah, I do. But I'm not playing favourites."

"Hey, I had a message from Ben Tremayne earlier. He's finished the virtual crime scenes. He's got the figures modelled—of Angie, Gus and Perdita. You're welcome to join me."

"I've got a lot to do here. Including the whole thing about Martina going missing."

"Of course. Sorry, I forgot to ask. How did things go when you spoke with her parents?"

"They're upset, naturally. What made it harder is that they're also upset with *me*... for not marrying their daughter years ago. They see it as *my* fault that she dumped me, if you can believe it. Ever since, she's been going for one bad choice in men after the other—that Elliot guy included."

"Does Elliot have any clue as to where Martina could be?"

"Grimshaw's already been to see him. He said Martina wanted some time alone and she hasn't been in contact."

"Hmmm. Well, I hope she's found soon—or she contacts someone."

"Me, too. I've been looking at every avenue I can think of."

"Keep working on it. I'll see you later on."

I walked from the station.

I was glad the conversation with Franco had ended on a more positive note. These conflicts with Franco lately were the last thing I wanted.

Maybe it was the dynamics that were wrong now. Franco and I had been a solid team. But with Melainey joining us, we were having situations where it was two against one.

And I didn't know how to smooth the waters.

CHAPTER THIRTY-EIGHT

Leaving the station, I drove across to meet with Ben Tremayne.

At CQ Technology, I took the stairs up to the third floor and walked out into the pin-drop silence of a corridor. Even though there must be hundreds of people at work here, all of them were currently sequestered in their offices.

Ben greeted me with a huge grin as I stepped into his office. "You look like you fell asleep by the pool, Detective. You're a little, uh, sunburned?"

I laughed. "I *am* sunburnt. And I *did* find myself wading through water yesterday, but it was a creek unfortunately and not a pool."

The smile dropped from his face. "Were you looking for a dead body in the creek?"

"No, nothing like that. I went looking for people who were very much alive, thank goodness."

"Awesome. Speaking of bodies, forgive me if I get a little excited here, but I think the modelling worked out really well."

"I can't wait to see what you've done."

Ada wheeled herself into the room. "A virtual world can't replace seeing things for yourself though, can it?"

"Forgive my mom," Ben said. "I don't think she slept well."

But when Ada lifted her chin to me, her eyes seemed clear and alert.

It was hard to figure out why she was so opposed to virtual worlds. They were the way her son made his income, after all.

Ben shrugged at me apologetically.

Ada made her way into the adjoining room, switching on the computer and starting up a game.

Looking back to me, Ben sighed. "I'm afraid I don't have long, today. Elliot's called a snap meeting, so I'll have to run."

"That's quite all right, Ben," I said.

"Look, I don't wanna rush you. I can leave you with it. You'll just need to log yourself out."

"I can do that."

"Great. I feel better now. I didn't want to have to kick you out."

Once more, Ben handed me the sensor vest and headset.

As before, a carousel menu popped up, with avatars of Ben, me, and various birds. I chose the avatar of myself.

Within a second, I was drawn back in time to the morning of the shootings. I could hear the birds and see the light breeze rippling through the trees.

I walked up to Angie. She was lying on the grass, looking exactly the same as when I'd first found her. Flies were gathering thickly, landing on the dried blood on her shirt and the smashed eggs on the ground.

A feeling of desperation washed through me, as if I still needed to save her.

I forced myself to keep walking. Pressure pushed at my fingers through the sensor gloves as I opened the gate that led to the Iverson property.

There was the frail-looking Gus Iverson, with his cracked watch and the rifle lying across his body. I walked around him, studying his body from all angles.

A chill embedded itself in my spine. The angle of his body looked wrong. Here in the quiet of the virtual world, I could clearly see that he'd fallen too far away from the stone wall to have cracked his watch face on it. And the rifle placement on his body looked too neat. A .303 rifle had a fair amount of kick. I'd shot from them myself.

Something I hadn't noticed before was a scrape on his right arm—the opposite arm to which he wore his watch. The scrape looked as if it had been fresh at the time.

With the scrape on one arm and the cracked wristwatch on the other, it looked as if Gus had been involved in some sort of fight right here next to the garden wall.

Had Gus wrestled with Perdita before she fled into the kitchen?

But Perdita didn't have any cuts or scrapes on her body.

Was it Jordan that Gus had wrestled with?

I hadn't expected to form any new conclusions while looking at Ben's virtual world. This world was only meant for preserving the crime sites. I stilled my breathing, not wanting Ben to realise that I was disturbed by the scene.

I had no answers for the questions forming in my mind.

Unsettled, I walked inside the Iversons' house and into the kitchen. There was Perdita Iverson, her blood pooled on the linoleum.

I studied the kitchen. Every little detail had been recreated. Instinctively, I picked up the phone on the kitchen counter—the phone that Perdita had been unable to reach.

"Oh, I shouldn't have done that," I gasped. "I'll put the phone back where it should be."

"Don't worry," Ben told me. "The virtual world resets each time. You can do whatever you like, and—next time you visit—it will be exactly the same as the original."

"Great, because I've been a bit clumsy. This is all really incredible, Ben. Like walking straight into a crime scene."

"I hoped you'd like it. It's lucky I had some really good police photos and videos to work with. Well, time's up for me. I've gotta run. I'll see you next time, Detective Wakeland."

"Thanks so much, Ben."

After Ben left the room, I poked around for a while, examining things here and there in the Iversons' kitchen. It really struck me how focused I was in this world, in the deep quiet where it was only me observing the scenes.

A willie wagtail bird hopped onto the kitchen windowsill, its head tilted as it viewed the awful scene below. The bird gave me a moment of light relief. This virtual world was all too real.

If you were there on the day, little wagtail, then I wish you could talk.

I wandered out of the kitchen to the yard, examining Gus's body again. He was at the centre of all of this, between the two women who'd been shot.

A willie wagtail was perched on the stone wall nearby.

Ben certainly liked wagtails.

A line of prickles crawled down my back as I kept my gaze on the bird.

The wagtail had been *everywhere* I'd been so far. Like it was watching me.

Was the bird actually… *Ben*? Was he watching me? Was he logged into his laptop while he was in the meeting, following along with everything I was doing?

No, that was ridiculous. Why would Ben do that?

It had to be just a fluke that this tiny bird had been around so much. Perhaps Ben was fond of wagtails, and he'd programmed a few of them in.

To prove that to myself, I decided to test the wagtail.

I crossed the field of holly grevillea and grass to Angie's house.

Entering the kitchen, I stared out through the window. Angie was hidden from my sight here. It just looked like a pleasant country scene, with nothing to tell that three people were lying dead and dying in those fields.

From the corner of my eye, I spotted a bird on Angie's kitchen windowsill. I half-turned. It was the *wagtail.* Again.

No, the bird wasn't random. I marched up to it. The bird flew away.

My mind spun as I logged out of the program and removed the sensor gear from my head and body.

I sank into Ben's office chair.

A sense of fatigue and confusion kept me sitting there as moments ticked away, my eyes unfocused.

Not one thing was going right in this investigation. Not even this. Everything was moving in directions I didn't understand.

No one but Ben could have programmed the bird into the software, right?

It could compromise the investigation if my steps in the virtual reality world were not secure.

So, Ben, who is the bird? Who is watching me?

CHAPTER THIRTY-NINE

A headache pulsed at my temples.

There was no point waiting here in Ben's office for him to return. I'd have to deal with this later.

I rose from the chair heavily.

In the back room, Ada Tremayne was sleeping, her chin resting on her shoulder. It looked uncomfortable. Poor woman. It must bore her to tears being here with Ben all day.

Stepping quietly over, I decided to try to slip a cushion under her head.

I scooped up a cushion that'd fallen to the floor and gently tried to position it without waking her. I glanced at the computer screen in front of Ada. It was blank, apart from a tiny login prompt, with a cursor blinking beside it.

The login prompt said: *Crime Scene—Iverson-Green.*

That was the login for the Witness Mountain virtual world.

Why was the program being accessed from a second computer? And, more to the point, why was it on *Ada's* computer?

Taking care not to disturb Ada further, I leaned across and typed in my password at the login prompt.

It worked. A scene of the field and front gates of Angie's property opened up.

A dialogue box asked a question: *Open Wagtail*? *Yes? No?*

What on earth?

I selected *yes* on the dialogue box.

A tiny wagtail bird appeared on the screen, flying in and settling atop Angie's fence.

Holding in a gasp, I stumbled back.

Ada stretched and yawned.

"You're awake," I said in a dull tone. I now didn't believe she'd actually been asleep at all.

Her head snapped around to me, eyes opening wide.

She coughed. "My throat's a bit dry. I think I'll grab a water from Ben's fridge."

"I'll get you the drink. But first, tell me something. What is with the wagtail bird?"

"Oh, it's nothing. Just a backup program."

"Ben told me the only copy of the program was on his computer."

She looked away.

I noticed something on her desk, then. A virtual reality headset.

"Humour me for a moment, Ada," I said sharply. "You're the wagtail, aren't you?"

She sighed audibly. "Guilty as charged."

"I don't understand this. Why did Ben give you access to the program?"

"It, ah… it wasn't Ben."

"It wasn't? Then… *who*?"

"It was me, Detective."

"You're going to have to explain that. Take all the time you need." I went to fetch Ada a bottle of water from Ben's bar fridge, which he kept under his desk.

She took the water from me. "Can I have a glass?" She pointed at a shelf where four glasses sat, upturned.

"Of course." I picked up a glass for her and set it down on her desk. Impatience was starting to burn a hole in the centre of my chest.

She poured herself a drink. "You have to understand, Detective, that Ben programmed in the capacity for different people to access the software at once. Because you might have a group of police all wanting to be in there looking at the same thing."

"Yes, I know. But *you* weren't supposed to be in there. And how is it Ben doesn't know?"

"I just added a bit of code to hide my tracks."

"You added… *code*?"

"Don't look so surprised. I was a computer programmer for most of my adult years."

"I had no idea."

"It was how the NineOak Corporation got me over to Australia with Ben so easily. On a work visa. Even though I'm not actually doing any work. NineOak wanted Ben, and Ben wouldn't come without me, so, here I am."

"Ben didn't mention your previous job to me, either."

"Eh, kids don't tend to talk about their mother's jobs. It's not cool. He wouldn't like to tell you that he gets his brains from his mother, either. Didn't get 'em from his father, God rest his soul."

"So, what you're saying is that you inserted yourself into *my* program." I brought over a small wooden chair from a corner of the room. Perching on the chair the wrong way around, I folded my arms on its backrest. "Let's just say I'm very, very confused right now. I need you to talk to me. Why on earth did you want to be in a crime scene simulation?"

"Well, for one thing, I get to be a bird. When you're stuck in a wheelchair all day, it's kind of nice to imagine yourself flying."

"Ada, you've been following me around in there."

"I won't lie. I *have* been doing that."

"Why?"

"It wasn't a plan. In the first place, I just wanted to have a look around. Ben left the program open one day when he went out to get lunch. Well, in the space of half an hour, I became more than a little addicted. I guess I began fancying myself as an armchair detective… only, I'm not in an armchair." She glanced down at her wheelchair.

"So… that's it?"

"Yes, ma'am. Scout's honour."

"And, just to be clear, Ben has no idea you've been going in there?"

"Nope. No idea. Zilch."

"So, every time I've been in the virtual world, you've been logged in—on your computer, as the bird? I have to say, that seems a big security breach."

"Ben just didn't expect to have to safeguard his program against his own mother. I think he's forgotten who his mother used to be. It's kind of funny, you know, young people of thirty or forty years old think they practically invented computers and the internet. But they didn't."

She sipped her water.

"Ada, you need to stay out of the program. I'm sorry, but I have to tell Ben. I'm sure you understand that I need it secure."

"It was fun while it lasted." She went quiet for a moment. "I need to ask you something, Detective."

"Yes?"

"Was I the only intruder you noticed in the virtual world?"

I frowned at her. "Yes. Just the wagtail. Don't tell me you have *other* avatars you're using in there?"

"No, I'm just the wagtail. I picked the wagtail because it's so tiny. I didn't think anyone would notice me. But *you* did." She drew her eyebrows in tight. "There's a strange bird I saw a few times—an eagle."

"I noticed the eagle. But isn't it just one of the birds that Ben programmed in to make the world look more real?"

"Its behaviour seemed a little odd. I don't trust it."

"You don't trust an animated eagle?"

"Bear with me. It was circling certain areas. Eagles do that kind of thing. But that's when they're up high, before they come in for the kill. Not close to ground level."

"So, you think there is a person using an avatar of an eagle?"

"You got it."

"Well, I don't know what to think. It's all very unsettling. I'm starting to think this virtual world was a bad idea."

"Now, don't feel defeated. Every program has bugs. Maybe Ben just got something wrong when he programmed the eagle in."

"Ada, since you were a programmer—is that what you think has happened?"

"I was hoping you wouldn't ask me that. I think someone got around Ben's code, the same as I did."

"You think someone is in there as the eagle, watching everything?"

"I do."

"Look… I just can't see anyone having any interest in following me around in there. There is nothing different to the photos and videos that the police and forensics collected at the crime scenes."

"You sure about that?"

"What do you mean?"

"I noticed something in the first edition of the virtual world that's different now."

"Are you playing games with me, Ada?"

"I would never do that. This is too serious. People died on that mountain."

"All right. What did you notice that was different?"

"There was a cabin that burned down at the back of the Iversons' property."

"Yes. I remember seeing that."

"I know. I saw you there."

"Of course you did," I said dryly.

"Well, it looks different now."

"No, that's not possible. It has to look exactly the same as on the day Ben did the digital mapping. Things can't change in the virtual world, Ada."

"Well, *this* has. The burned cabin has been covered up."

"Covered up how?"

"Get the sensor gear back on, Detective, and I'll show you."

I stared back at Ada for a moment, trying to decide what to do. Was she just a lonely, bored woman who was wasting my time?

"All right," I said. "Show me."

Ada remained at her computer, pulling on the headset. I walked back to Ben's computer. With the sensors and headset on again, I switched on the virtual world.

The usual array of avatars appeared onscreen.

As I had last time, I chose the avatar of myself.

"No, wrong choice," came Ada's voice over my headset speakers. "In case someone's watching, you can't be yourself. You need to be a bird. To avoid arousing suspicion… pretend to go look at something, and then log out."

A wedge-tail eagle flew overhead.

"Right on cue," came Ada's voice.

"Is that the eagle you saw before, Ada?"

"Yup. Something seems off about the way it's flying."

"If the eagle is someone's avatar, can that person hear us talking?"

"No. Not unless we select that option. Our conversation is private."

I was out of my depth with this whole thing. I didn't know whether to trust Ada or whether she'd just been concocting some kind of fantasy.

But I did as she asked. I walked a short distance and knelt to the ground, pretending to study the tyre tracks in the dirt that'd been made by Jordan's bicycle. All the while, the eagle circled overhead.

I then exited the program. I was back at the entry screen, with the avatar carousel. This time, I chose a kookaburra as my avatar. I was fond of those birds. The kookaburra that Ben had designed had a cute, roundish body and beady eyes above its protruding beak.

I flew onto Angie's fence and sat on the railing. A little wagtail was already perched there—*Ada.*

"There you are," Ada said. "Now, we have to make sure we don't arouse suspicion. We have to act like birds, not like humans. So, we have to fly all the way to the cabin."

"That's a long way for two little birds."

"Just follow me."

"Right."

I proceeded to fly over Angie's land, keeping sight of the wagtail. I had to keep slowing my pace in order to keep well behind.

The wagtail flew across to the Iversons' land and made its way through the trees.

I lost my way several times and needed to wait on a branch for Ada to come back and find me.

"I'm sorry," I said. "You keep getting away from me. You're kind of hard to see."

"Well, stay alert, Detective."

It was a surreal moment. I was sitting on a branch, as a bird, speaking to another bird. I'd been on a lot of wild goose chases in my working life, but this would have to rank as the most bizarre of them all.

"Hello, there's the eagle again," she said. The wagtail looked upward to the sky.

The wedge-tail eagle zoomed overhead. It looked like the same one as before.

"What do you think it's doing?" I asked.

"I think it's making a final round to check that you're gone. Don't worry, it doesn't know you've logged back in as the bird."

The eagle kept flying—until it vanished from sight.

"Ada, which way now?"

"See that huge tree over to the right?" she said, "the one that looks something like a monkey puzzle tree?"

"I'm afraid I don't know what a monkey puzzle tree is."

"Oh, right. Well, it looks like a pine. But unlike that tree, this one's got pinecones the size of basketballs."

"I see the one you mean. That's a bunya pine. And those *basketballs* are actually nuts."

"Nuts, eh? They look like killers."

"They're ripe. Up to ten kilos each. You certainly have to be careful when they start dropping. Should we head off?"

"Ready when you are."

We flew on, coming to rest on the branches of the bunya tree.

"Look down," Ada told me, "Over in the clearing."

I scanned the grounds below. All I could see was a stack of burned logs.

"Where's the cabin?" I asked.

"Right there."

"*Under the logs*?"

"Yup."

I flew from the branch and over to the log pile. When I circled it, I spotted tiny sections of a burned cabin through the logs.

Ada was right. This had been changed.

I couldn't think of a single logical reason for Ben to have done this.

I flew back to the branch, where the wagtail still perched. "Ada… I need to ask this question—did you program the image of the logs into the virtual world?"

"Still don't trust me, huh? Well, I don't blame you. No, it wasn't me. I wouldn't change a blade of grass in here—apart from adding in the wagtail. I'm damned proud of Ben's work."

"All right, I'm going to have to believe you. Thank you for showing me this. I don't know what it means, but I'm going to find out."

CHAPTER FORTY

I drove up the mountain road to the Iversons' land.

The whole way, I still wasn't sure what I was going to find when I got there. If Ada was playing some kind of game, then I'd find a half-burned cabin near the bunya pine.

I had half a thought to call Franco and ask him to join me, but this expedition would be a tricky one to explain. And I wasn't his favourite person at the moment.

It was best I manage this trip on my own.

I parked outside the front gate. The Iversons' house was close to the road. Unfortunately, there was no way of driving straight to where I needed to go—unless I took the fire trail, and I'd need a four-wheel drive to take that.

I started out under the hot sun on foot, wishing I could magically turn myself into a little bird and fly all the way there.

The quickest path was straight through the middle of the bushland. I kept a close watch on the compass app on my phone as I made my way past the Iversons' house and across the cleared stretch of their land. Then I headed into the forest.

Stupidly, I half-expected to see Ada's little wagtail bird up on a nearby branch, or a wedge-tail eagle circling me. The virtual world felt that real.

It was the best part of an hour before I spotted the bunya pine. Its distinctive, cone-shaped top soared above the treetops of its neighbours.

Dry bark cracked beneath my shoes as I walked on, giving the bunya tree a wide berth. The giant bunya nuts shouldn't start falling until at least February next year, but I didn't want to chance it.

I stopped as I sighted a pile of logs.

There they were. As in the virtual world, they were burnt, and they'd been roughly chopped.

I stepped around the logs, my feet scuffing up the ashes. Bending to peer through gaps in the logs, I glimpsed small snatches of the cabin—what was left of it.

The boards of the cabin were aged and split, with dried moss that had been scorched by the fire. There was some old, rusted farm machinery on the floor of the cabin, all coated in a layer of ash.

Standing back, I snapped a few pictures with my phone.

The first time I'd viewed the virtual world, this spot had most definitely been the site of a burned-down cabin. But then it'd switched to an image of a pile of logs. Just as it was here in the real world.

I wasn't prepared to wait for answers.

I called Ben.

"I'm on a break from my meeting," he told me. "Did you manage the program okay on your own?"

"Yes, I did."

"Awesome."

"But I have a small problem."

"Technical issue?"

"Are you okay to talk right now, Ben?"

"Uh, it's a little noisy. I'll move out into the corridor. Just grabbing myself a coffee on the way… All right… I'm walking out of the room now. So, what's the issue?"

"Okay… the first time I viewed the virtual world, I saw a cabin on the Iversons' land. It was right at the back, near the fence line of the neighbouring property. The cabin had almost burnt to the ground. But now, there's a pile of logs on top of it."

"Um… let me think. That would have been at one of my perimeter points. I haven't looked closely at those areas—I thought they'd be too far away from the crime scenes to be of interest."

"Ben, could someone else have gotten into the virtual world?"

"Wait… what?"

"I mean, could someone else have accessed the program and changed things around?"

"I was afraid you meant that. The only way someone could get into my office is with a key code. It's always locked when I'm not there. And no one but you and me know the username and password to that program."

"And your mother. She knows the password."

I didn't like exposing Ada, but I had no choice.

"My mother?" he spluttered. "Sorry, gulped my coffee too fast."

"She's been going into the virtual world. She's a… willie wagtail bird."

"Ahhh, I don't believe this. No, wait. Yes, I do believe it. I don't know why I didn't consider that she might stick her nose in."

"But, Ben, she swears she didn't change anything about the burnt cabin."

He sighed. "Thinking about it, she could if she wanted to. She's got the programming experience behind her. My mom's got a sharp, analytical kind of mind. Not a good thing for a mind that's got nothing to do. You know, she's always finding faults with me. I'm guessing she did something to make it look like I messed up."

"You really think she'd do that?"

"I wouldn't have thought so. But, who else?"

"I'm here at the actual site of the burnt cabin, Ben. In real life. It has a pile of logs on it, same as in the virtual world. How would your mother know that? And how would she get an image of it?"

"Well, now you've stumped me."

"There's something else. Ada thinks there's an eagle flying around whenever I go into the program—and she thinks the eagle doesn't look right. Like, there is someone else accessing the program."

"Detective… *I* programmed in the eagle. It's supposed to be there. Please, don't listen to my mother. She's… I don't know… I can't believe she's doing this. I'll sort it out."

Did I have Ada all wrong? She'd had me convinced she was an innocent. Was this some kind of elaborate trick, after all? Whatever this was, it was highly annoying. But the last thing I wanted to do was to get between a mother and son. I had to let it go.

"Okay," I said. "I'll forget this, then. As if it never happened."

"I can't apologise enough. I'll put down a layer of security so tough, it'll make it impossible for her to log back in—ever."

"Thanks, Ben. I appreciate it."

I stood in the ashes of the cabin, sweat trickling down the back of my neck. Then I turned to begin the long trek back through the forest.

CHAPTER FORTY-ONE

Ivy stood in our kitchen, wearing a child-size apron and holding a tray of lopsided pies. She'd just made them, with a little help from Abby.

Pete, Abby, Logan and I were sitting on the kitchen stools—Logan bouncing baby Jasper on his lap.

"Nan," Ivy said to me, "do you want an apple, apricot, or blueberry pie?" She was barely able to contain a beaming smile.

I made a careful inspection of the pies. "Hmmm, tough choice. They all look so yummy. I think I'll choose… blueberry."

"Good choice," Ivy replied. "But I'll tell you that there's some apple and raisins mixed in with those, because the chef made a mistake."

I smiled. "Well, tell the chef they did a very good job, because I know I'll love that combination."

Ivy giggled. "Nan, *I'm* the chef."

Laughing, I tickled her under the chin.

Ivy offered her wares around to the rest of us after that.

Logan took a hearty bite of his pie and then sipped his coffee. I guessed that the coffee had already gone cold after Logan had gone to pick up the grumbly Jasper from his playpen. Jasper kept trying to snatch the cup, getting upset as Logan juggled him out of reach.

Franco's kitten began mewing from its little bed underneath the dining room table. It'd just woken up, its patchwork fur slicked down on one side and sticking up on the other.

Ivy quickly abandoned her chef's post in the kitchen. She ran to pick up the kitten, walking away with it in her arms and singing to it.

"She loves Bear," Abby remarked. "She's going to find it hard to give him back to Franco."

"I think you're right. He's such a cutie." I chewed on a piece of Ivy's flavourful pie.

Jasper began tugging on his father's lower lip.

Abby held out her arms to Jasper. "Come here, I think you need a sleep."

I gave Jasper a kiss on his head before Abby scooped him up and took him away upstairs.

"Hey," I said to Logan, "how're you finding being a firefighting volunteer?"

"It's tougher than I thought it'd be," Logan admitted.

"I hope Pete hasn't been barking orders at you." I winked at Pete.

"Hey," Pete protested. "This old dog only barks when he has to."

"Nah, Pete's cool," Logan said with a laugh.

Pete gestured at a spot on the side of my neck. "You look like you've been out fighting fires yourself."

I rubbed at the spot and found ash on my fingers. "Oh… I was at Witness Mountain earlier."

Sipping his coffee, Pete raised his eyebrows. "Again? I thought you were finished there."

"I just needed to check on something." Taking out my phone, I showed Pete and Logan the pictures I'd taken of the stack of logs.

Pete frowned. "Where'd you take these?"

"At the back of the Iversons' land," I told him. "The burned logs are stacked on top of an old cabin—the cabin is half burned down itself."

Pete folded his arms as he turned to Logan. "Did you see who did that?"

Logan shook his head. He swiped at my phone's screen, scrolling through the photos. "I remember the cabin. It was on fire, and we put it out. There's the bunya tree in the background, too. I remember joking with the other guys that if the bunya caught on fire, we'd be bombed with roasted nuts."

"What knucklehead did this?" Pete groaned. "It's damned stupid to stack all that stuff up. There could be live embers inside. It's like someone was trying to make a bonfire. A big one. This could start a blaze all over again. I'm going to have to take a team out there to shift this."

"Pete," I said, "are you saying that you guys—the RFS—wouldn't have done this?"

"No," he said in a definite tone.

I exhaled softly, trying to determine if this mattered. Perhaps some family of the Iversons had come out to the land, trying to clean it up. Except… no one was allowed in there yet. Not without clearance from the RFS and the police. And we hadn't even been able to find any family of the Iverson couple.

A curious look visited Pete's eyes. "Kate, what was your interest in this part of the property? I know it's not easy to access. Must have been something pretty compelling?"

I breathed a silent sigh. "Forgive me if I don't want to explain it just yet. But… if you're going to move those trees, I want to be there."

CHAPTER FORTY-TWO

Stepping from my kitchen, I contacted Franco and Melainey, setting up a three-way call. They were both at the station.

"What's doing?" Melainey asked.

"Most probably nothing," I answered. "Look, there's a cabin on the Iverson land that burned down, and now it's got a big stack of chopped trees on it. Pete thinks it's a fire risk."

Franco spoke up. "And what's that got to do with us, exactly?"

"Well," I said, "I'm wondering if someone was trying to cover up the site. Seems a bit suspicious, that's all. I'm heading out with Pete to take a look."

"I might skip it." Franco's tone was edged with bone-dry irritation. "Sounds like a job for the RFS. I'm here chasing up that second opinion you wanted—on Gus's suicide. Shintani wants to know why it's necessary. You know, lots of extra paperwork to fill in."

It wasn't hard to figure that he thought I was doing things for no good reason.

"Fair crack of the whip, Franco," Melainey said. "Wakeland's just being careful. It's typical Wakeland style. It's a good thing, all told."

I was pleased to have the backup from Melainey, but I felt bad for Franco. I could see things from his point of view.

I made a last-ditch attempt to plead my case. "Pete says that none of the RFS people did this. He asked around."

"I'll be there with bells on," Melainey said. "C'mon, Franco. Chance to stretch your legs if nothing else."

"Yeah, okay. I'm outvoted," Franco drawled. "Still doesn't seem like something we should get involved in."

"See you both there," I said.

I drove to Witness Mountain alone. I blasted myself with loud music to block out the crippling doubts playing on my mind. Someone could be playing tricks on me—perhaps with Ada's help. I might arrive at the site only to find the felled trees gone again.

And Franco had made his opinion clear—the police had no real business in checking this out.

I was the first one on the mountain. The air was still suffocatingly hot, late afternoon sun sparking off the trees.

Pete pulled up in his RFS truck minutes after me. He had Logan with him, and another firefighter volunteer—named Amar, who was a CQ tech professional from India.

We waited for Franco and Melainey. Franco had stopped off for coffee. He wasn't taking this seriously at all.

The six of us piled into the truck, and Pete drove up a steep, rocky fire trail that took us much closer to our destination.

Pete, Logan, Amar and Melainey carried the chains and gear.

Franco ambled through the forest, hands in pockets and barely speaking.

When we walked up to the site of the cabin, the clearing was deep in shadows.

The pile of logs was still there, to my relief.

Pete screwed up his face as he surveyed the logs. "This is idiotic."

"Someone must have come up the fire trail in a truck, and then chopped the trees down, right?" I asked him.

"Yup." Pete kicked up ashes as he walked closer, stooping to look between the logs. "And there you go—live embers. These logs have been there smouldering for who knows how many days."

"Let's get cracking," Melainey said.

Pete, Logan and Amar began attaching chains to the logs. Melainey pitched in where he could.

Franco hung back, watching on with something close to disinterest. He didn't seem like the same person who'd worked at a frantic pace to rescue two children just days ago.

The flies swarmed in, bothering everyone.

The men soon had the site cleared. The logs had all been pulled away to one side—their embers safely put out.

Now, there was just the bottom portion of the cabin and some farm machinery sitting there.

Melainey dabbed at the beads of sweat on his forehead. "Is it a wrap, then?"

Franco rolled his shoulders. "Looks like it. Danger's gone, right? No fire risk now."

What he said was true. The fire risk was gone. But that wasn't why I was here. This cabin was almost on Mulden land. And someone had covered it up —for no good reason that I could see. And they'd tried to cover their tracks in the virtual program, too. Someone hadn't wanted anyone looking around here at the site of the cabin. It seemed almost… arrogant, as if that person felt secure that it'd go unnoticed.

"I'd like to remove the machinery," I said quietly.

"All of it?" Pete questioned.

I nodded.

"Done," Pete said.

Fifteen minutes later, even the largest pieces of machinery had been hauled off the site.

All that remained was a wooden floor—covered in dirt and ash.

We'd found nothing of interest. If there *had* been anything, perhaps it'd already burned to a crisp.

The sun had dropped low while we'd all been at work. The smell of ash saturated everything. The air was only growing more humid as night approached. A headache buzzed through my temples—not painful, but nagging.

Logan and Amar began packing up the chains.

Something my mother used to say floated among my murky thoughts.

In for a penny, in for a pound.

Mum was gone now, but her voice was often still clear to me. And I was only just starting to understand that although she'd been quietly spoken, she'd had a tough inner core. I should have expected that from someone who'd been through World War II as a child.

In for a penny, in for a pound, Mum.

"Pete…" I said. "Can the floor go, too?"

Pete's face was red and slicked with perspiration. "The *floor*?"

Logan scratched his neck, looking tired, as if he just wanted to get home to Abby and the kids.

I nodded firmly to Pete.

He looked uncertain. "It's reinforced hardwood. Probably made strong to hold the weight of the machinery. It'd be murder to get that up."

The other men glanced from Pete to me and then turned away.

I sensed that some or all of them thought I was just standing around giving frivolous orders. In my younger years in the police force, I'd felt the pressure of being the only woman in a team—as too often happened back then.

But I was well past those days now. I no longer carried that same sense of intimidation.

Pete motioned in the direction of the truck. "Logan, Amar—go grab a chainsaw and crowbars."

The flies seemed glad of our extended stay at the site, redoubling their efforts to land on our backs and faces. Mosquitoes had joined in the fun, too.

Amar made short work of a small section of the floor. Pete jumped in with a crowbar, lifting out the square of floor that Amar had cut.

Pete raised his head to me. "Looks like it's just dirt under there."

"Try another couple of sections," I said.

In for a penny, in for a pound.

"What on earth are you expecting to find?" Franco asked me.

"I want to know for sure there's nothing under there," I said quietly.

Melainey grabbed one of the crowbars. "We're losing light. Better get this done, lads."

Pete used the chainsaw on another section.

He jerked back suddenly, cursing.

"Pete?" I queried. "Are you all right?"

"Chain broke," he spluttered.

For the first time today, Franco's interest seemed piqued. He walked across and crouched beside my husband, examining the hole in the cabin floor.

Pete yanked up the broken chain from the chainsaw and set it down.

Grabbing a nearby crowbar, Franco prodded the ground. A sharp, clanking sound echoed.

Franco swivelled around to me, his eyes crinkling in a stray, reddish beam of sunlight. "There's something metal down there."

CHAPTER FORTY-THREE

Pete and Franco worked at a feverish pace with the crowbars now—trying to upend enough of the timber floor to see what was lying beneath.

We moved the splintered wood safely to one side, and then set about brushing away the dirt and ash that had fallen onto the soil below.

We made the discovery of a flat, round metal object. It was set firmly into the ground—less than two metres in diameter.

"Could be an old well with a cover on it… or an underground water tank?" Logan suggested.

"Well, it's the right shape," Pete said, slapping at a large mosquito that'd landed on his neck.

Amar dug around the edge of the circle. "There's a bolt here, and a handle. I'm going to guess that it is a lid." His eyes were large as he stared up at me.

I sucked in a breath. A lid to what, exactly? Whatever it was, why had a cabin been built on top of it?

"Throw me some bolt cutters, please," Amar said to Logan.

Silence fell as Amar cut through the bolt.

Melainey reached down with his long arms to tug at the handle.

Dirt fell away as the lid was lifted.

A deep circular space plunged into darkness.

What was it? A well?

As my eyes adjusted, I noticed a metal ladder attached to one side of a concrete wall.

"I think it might be a bunker…" I breathed. But I couldn't be sure of that yet.

My mind absented itself of all thought except for what sat below that ladder. Angling myself around, I climbed down and placed a foot on the top rung.

Pete grabbed my arm. "You're not going down *there*."

"I was testing it," I said as I let him help me up again. "Seems strong enough... *maybe*."

"I'll go down and take a look," Logan offered.

"Thanks, Logan," I said, "but I've got the police camera on my vest. Depending on what this is, we might need that film later."

"Then *I'll* go," Melainey said. "My camera's fully charged."

I turned to him. "So's mine. And I want to be the first one to film this."

Pete's jaw tightened. "I'll get a harness and ropes from the truck. Nobody move until I get back."

Minutes later, I was pulling on the harness while Pete secured the ropes.

I stepped back to the ladder and climbed down until my foot connected with the top rung again.

I gazed down. There was just a black tunnel below me.

The further I descended, the darker the tunnel got. The air grew cooler with each step.

"Kate," Pete called. "Everything okay?"

My voice bounced off the concrete walls as I called back. "All fine."

After a minute's climb, the ladder vanished beneath my feet. I fetched a torch from my police vest and shone its light below.

I'd almost reached the bottom. If this was a well, then it was almost dry.

Dropping down from the ladder, my feet splashed into a few centimetres of water.

I shone my light around the space. *No, this is not a well.*

It opened into a large chamber.

Shelves came into view. All stacked with crates. Dozens and dozens of crates.

Cupping my hands around my mouth, I called up the vertical tunnel. "I made it. There's a bit of water down here."

"How's the air?" Pete called.

"Okay, I think," I shouted back. "It's a bunker. There are all kinds of stuff down here."

"I'm coming down." It was Franco's voice this time.

"Count me in." That was Melainey.

It wasn't long before I'd have company.

Releasing myself from the ropes, I made my way into the chamber.

There were crates of ammunition. Crates of guns—rifles and pistols. And crate after crate of cigarette cartons. I hadn't seen that design on a cigarette packet for decades.

No wonder this stuff had been hidden away. It was either stolen or illegal—possibly both. Everything down here looked old, as if it hadn't been touched in a very long time.

I walked along the shelving, taking care to ensure that everything was filmed, exactly as it was. Pulling out a pair of plastic gloves from my pocket, I slipped them on. I'd also brought along some plastic specimen bags, but I doubted I'd be using them. It wasn't like I'd found some tiny piece of evidence that I could take with me. This was an entire bunker.

Who'd built this? It couldn't be the Iversons. They'd bought the land in 1990—and the items in here were much older than that.

Melainey came down the ladder. His boots thudded on the wet ground.

Striding over to me, he inspected a box of guns. "Hoo-boy! What a haul. Tallman's Valley just got a *lot* more interesting."

"It's crazy."

"How'd you guess any of this was here?"

"I didn't."

He pulled an incredulous face. "Then you must have a killer of an instinct. I mean, you were sharp when we used to work together. But this is *next-level*. You should have stayed with the state homicide squad."

"It was time for me to move on." I picked up a box of ammunition, studying it.

Franco landed inside the bunker. He moved across to Melainey and me, gazing at the shelves with a shocked expression. "Hell. We'd better get the forensic group out here. Pronto."

"Yes," I agreed. "They're not going to believe this one when we tell them."

He stepped around the bunker with Melainey, the two of them vanishing from sight. I focused on getting everything filmed, until Franco and Melainey re-emerged a couple of minutes later.

"Okay, we'd better get out of here," Franco said, a shade of urgency in his tone. "At this point, we're just sightseeing."

I frowned. "Sightseeing?" It was a term I'd never heard Franco use before in relation to police work.

Melainey glanced from Franco to me, obviously picking up on the tension between us.

"Yeah, we should leave it to the forensics," Melainey agreed. "It could even be a bit unstable. Let's get out of here, kiddies."

"You two go ahead," I said. "Just… give me a minute."

Franco and Melainey exchanged glances.

"What was *that*?" I asked in annoyance. "Actually… never mind. I'll see you both back on top."

I walked away.

I hadn't yet seen every corner of this place—and I intended to ensure that as much as possible was recorded, exactly as it was when I'd first come down here. I'd been on too many cases in which evidence was moved too early or went missing altogether.

I headed over to the deepest part of the bunker, where I hadn't yet been. It looked like lab paraphernalia for making illegal drugs. These people had certainly covered all bases as far as illegal activities went.

To my left, a long, horizontal box was being kept under tarpaulins. Bending low, I went to pull back the tarps.

A hand reached out of the dark and grasped my arm.

I turned sharply. Franco's face was in front of me, his features cast into shadows by the beam of my torch. He had the light of his torch pointed at the watery floor.

"Wakeland, whatever's down here, it's not worth you risking your life to investigate it right now. We're not saving children or kittens. We'll get a team back here with the proper equipment. Look, I saw big cracks in the concrete wall on the other side, with mud squeezing through. With us disturbing the site, it could all cave in."

"All right," I acknowledged, "that doesn't sound good. I just want to see what this is, and then I'm out of here."

Shaking his head, Franco stepped away, taking his light with him. Everything fell into darkness again, apart from the narrow beam from my torch.

Juggling the torch, I crouched and drew the heavy tarps back from the box.

Underneath sat a vintage metal container, about a metre by two metres in size, with images of clown heads painted on it.

The clown heads looked like those from the Laughing Clown game, in which you'd pop ping-pong balls into the clown's mouth and hope the ball landed on a lucky number.

I guessed that the clowns' heads had once been packaged in this box.

My hands trembled at the discovery. *There it was*—a direct link to our town's carnival. This bunker had most probably belonged to the Mulden family. It wasn't proof positive—*yet*—but I couldn't wait until all the goods in this bunker saw the light of day.

The groundwater had eroded the metal, making rusted holes.

I directed my light over the holes, attempting to see inside.

It seemed there might be objects from the carnival's old haunted-house ride stored in the box—I spotted a skeletal hand.

A cold niggle began tapping at the back of my neck, as if the fingers themselves were doing that to me.

I knew *bones*. And these bones looked about as real as bones could get.

There were two latches on the box. The latches held padlocks, but the latches had rusted away enough that a few knocks made them come loose.

I wrangled with the lid, shoving it up.

Breath pushed from my lungs at what was exposed.

Human ribcages and skulls showed through damp, disintegrating sheets.

Two skeletons were tangled together, adult in size. Their bones darkened and mottled.

I drew back, keenly feeling the darkness surrounding me.

PART IV

CHAPTER FORTY-FOUR

Pete shook me awake. "Kate, you're having another nightmare."

I sat up, breathing hard, my heartbeat erratic. I'd been dreaming about being in a pitch-dark room that was filling up with water, skeletal remains floating all around. The water leaked out of the room, flooding the ground outside. The water kept coming and coming… unstoppable. And bones kept rising from the earth.

"This is the third time tonight," Pete told me, placing a glass of water and two sleeping pills in my hands. "It's just like last night. The dreams. You're crying out, shaking...."

It'd been two nights since the bunker had been uncovered. Two nights of precious little sleep.

I gripped the glass of water so hard that Pete took it away from me, setting it down on the table beside my bed. The pills dropped through my fingers. Tears splashed warm on my cheeks.

"Pete… every murder victim that I've seen… they all made me sad… or angry. Some had me raging at humanity. But those skeletons we found in the bunker, they just… I don't know… they made me feel a kind of *desperation*. As if murder is so commonplace that bodies are hidden everywhere. And what I do—*what I've been doing as a job for most of my life*—is barely a drop in the ocean."

"Honey… listen. You've had a year that no one should have to go through, not even the most hardened homicide cop. It's bound to have consequences. You've needed a break for a long time now. I've tried to tell you. Tried to warn you. You haven't been okay for many months."

"I should be stronger than this." I breathed deeply, forcing my breaths to slow.

"Everyone's got a breaking point."

"I'm not at breaking point. I'll get through it. I have to."

"It doesn't have to be you leading the charge, you know. You're gonna take the whole day off tomorrow. Maybe a couple of days. And you're gonna see your doctor."

"I can't."

Pete wrapped his arms around me. "*Yes*, you can. Honey, the bones in that bunker are *old.* This didn't just happen. It's in the past. You don't need to race and find out who did it. Whoever the culprit was, they might even be dead by now."

"I'll see how I feel tomorrow." It was a compromise with Pete.

I picked up the sleeping pills, about to down them with the water.

But my head swam and a sudden pain hammered in the centre of my chest.

"Pete? I don't feel so good...."

At half-past three in the morning, I found myself sitting in a bed at CQ Hospital.

Pete had called an ambulance an hour ago. He sat beside my bed, eyes closed. He'd just drifted off to sleep. He'd always been quick to sleep.

A doctor walked in—a slim, bespectacled woman who was possibly in her sixties—looking way too bright and awake for this time of the morning. "Detective Wakeland, how are you feeling?"

"Much better than when I came in," I answered.

"That's what we want to hear. The good news is your electrocardiogram isn't showing any damage to your heart muscle. You didn't have a heart attack."

I took a breath. "That's great news."

"Yes, it is. And your tests also didn't detect any previous attacks or enlargement to your heart. That's the good news out of the way. Now for the concerning side of this—there is some weakened heart muscle. That can be caused by stress cardiomyopathy."

"That's a thing?"

"It most definitely is. It's reversible, at this point. But you wouldn't want it to continue. Do you have any situations causing you stress at the moment?"

I pulled my mouth into a tight line. "You'll hear about it on the news in a few hours."

"I see. Well, that level of stress isn't doing you any favours. I'd suggest further testing—and rest."

"Thank you. Sorry about all this fuss. I should have known that it was just stress—"

"I'll stop you there, Detective," the doctor said, putting up her hand. "I didn't mean to give you the impression that it's not dangerous. It is. You'll need follow-up tests. And besides, chest pain is nothing to mess about with. You did the right thing in coming down here. You can't undo a major heart attack."

She recommended I stay overnight, but I asked to be signed out.

I woke Pete up, and we headed from the hospital into its almost empty parking bay. The moon drifted behind a sheer curtain of smoke.

Wordlessly, I sat in the car as Pete drove away, headed for home.

I walked into the police station at eleven in the morning. I'd made a deal with Pete, and I'd gone to see my regular doctor earlier. She'd prescribed me some medication for anxiety.

Avoiding Franco and Melainey's eyes, I slipped behind my desk.

They'd both been busy with the discovery of the bodies in the bunker. There was already a preliminary report on my desk.

Forensics had confirmed that both victims had sustained injuries that were most probably caused by nooses hung around their necks. They'd been a man and a woman, aged between twenty-five and thirty. We didn't have results back yet of the exact number of years since their deaths, but early analysis was telling us that the bunker hadn't been opened for about thirty years.

Constable Thea Georgiades approached me. "The superintendent's here."

"Again?"

"Yeah. He's called a meeting. Thought I'd give you a shout out, in case you wanted to make yourself scarce or something."

"Thanks, Thea. You're a treasure. I'm going to make an educated guess that he's been waiting for me. I'd better head on in."

As I entered the meeting room with Thea, everyone was standing. Bigley and Shintani were leaning against a desk, both with their arms folded.

Everyone turned when I entered.

"Detective Wakeland," Bigley started, "I heard you had some heart trouble last night."

"Who told you—?"

"My wife is friends with the doctor you saw at the hospital."

Great doctor-patient confidentiality, I thought privately. "Right. Well… it didn't end up being anything serious. I'm fine now."

"Brilliant," Bigley replied. "Do you need to pull up a chair?"

"No, I'm good," I said.

He grunted. "Well, we've got an ocean of trouble here in this town right now, don't we?"

"Yes, we do, sir," I answered.

"Utter madness," he muttered. "Two historic murders. On top of the recent murders. On top of the rather unusual crimes of this year." He paused. "We have an international community of workers here, who came to our valley on the promise of green hills and tranquillity. We haven't exactly delivered on that promise."

His eyes came to rest on me.

"Seems to me, sir," I responded, "that these murders and crimes are a reflection of this town. From about fifty years ago to now, by my reckoning."

He stared back, his face recoiling into his neck. "Well, we can only deal with the here and now. We can't travel back in time and change anything."

"Of course," I acknowledged.

"If not for the fire," Bigley said. "That bunker would have remained as it was. Lost to history."

I couldn't believe what I was hearing. He had a subtly exasperated tone underlying his words, as if I were to blame for digging up things that should have stayed buried.

Constable Georgiades shot me a shocked glance. Even Shintani looked rattled, and very little ever rattled him.

"And now the bunker has seen the light of day," said Shintani. "Well done, Detective."

Bigley nodded with a sudden firm rigour that didn't fool me for a second. "Absolutely. Investigative policing at its best. Well done—*well done indeed*—Detective Wakeland." He cleared his throat. "Now, where are we at so far with this case? I'm getting calls about it on the hour, and I'd appreciate being kept up to date."

Melainey half raised a hand in a slow, lazy gesture. "Sir, I can give you a report I've prepared on the preliminary results of the two victims. As far as the bunker goes, we've got a team tasked with retrieving all the items—Franco and I have been busting a gut clearing out a room that it can all go into."

Bigley nodded. "Good work. Have we got the media out at the site, filming all of this? We need to show that we're tackling the case head on."

"Ah, yup," Melainey told him. "I made an address to the media early this morning. They've been camped out there on Witness Mountain ever since. They're not missing a beat."

"That's the way, Detective Melainey." Bigley seemed pleased. "Shows everyone that Tallman's Valley people aren't all outlaws. It's been looking a bit Wild West out here lately."

"Wild West?" I mouthed. We were hardly that.

"Speaking of the Wild West," said Melainey, not missing a beat, "we found relics of the old valley carnival in the bunker. And do you want to know what else is interesting? We've found the title deeds to the land that belonged to the owners of the Tallman's Valley Funfair. Seems that the land Angie Green and the Iverson couple's houses are sitting on used to belong to the Mulden family, too."

I stared at Melainey, impressed. He'd certainly been busy. Busy going above and beyond to find out all he could. It seemed a lot more than what Franco was doing.

It was certainly interesting news about the carnival having originally owned all that land. After finding the bunker, I'd suspected as much—but I hadn't yet found time to do the research. My focus so far had been on the bodies in that bunker.

Superintendent Bigley laced his fingers together, pressing his thumbs into his dimpled chin. "Hmmm. So, someone had a vested interest in keeping that cabin in place."

"I think you got it right, sir," Melainey answered.

I was grateful Melainey had taken the lead. Superintendent Bigley exhausted me. And after the night I'd had, I just couldn't deal with him at all.

Franco was quiet the whole time. Normally, he'd have my back.

Bigley's little meeting drew to an end. Which was a good thing, because I had somewhere else I needed to be.

CHAPTER FORTY-FIVE

The air-conditioned environment of the CQ foyer closed around me as I walked in. Soft, transcendental music met my ears.

I headed for the technology quarter.

Ben was at work at his computer, a coffee and pizza beside him on the desk. Ada was in the back room, as usual, but not at her computer. She had a magazine and pen in her hands—perhaps doing a crossword puzzle.

Ben looked up as I entered, mid-bite of his pizza, his expression apologetic.

"Can't tell you how sorry I am about the unwelcome little bird in your program." He glanced meaningfully in his mother's direction.

"Well, I'm certainly glad our little wagtail noticed what she did," I replied.

Ada lifted her chin a touch, but she didn't look up from her magazine. But did I detect a small smile?

Ben swallowed his bite of pizza. "You're *glad*? Call me confused."

"Have you been watching the news, Ben?" I asked.

He blinked. "Uh, no?"

"There *was* a cabin," I told him. "We went out there and removed the logs. We also found a bunker beneath that cabin. Filled with illegal goods. It'd all been there for decades."

"Mind blown." His mouth fell agape.

"There's more," I said. "There were two bodies in the bunker."

That got Ada's attention. Dropping the magazine on her lap, she wheeled herself out to Ben's office.

"There were bodies, Detective?" Her voice was even huskier today.

I nodded. "Both people are murder victims, sadly."

I'd half-expected Ada to gloat. After all, the details she'd noticed in the virtual world had led to these discoveries. But there was nothing gloating in her eyes.

"I've been following the news items about the bunker," she said, "but I didn't see anything about the bodies."

"That's being announced shortly," I said. "We had some investigations to do before releasing that information. Ada, I have to thank you for alerting me to the alteration in the program."

Ben eyed his mother with a changed expression. "Well, I'll be damned. And you didn't even tell me about what's been on the news?"

Ada shrugged a shoulder. "You've barely been speaking to me, Ben. I get it—I shouldn't have stuck my nose in. Or my beak, as it were."

"Ben and Ada," I said, "I have to make a request. Everything that's been happening here in this office needs to stay under wraps. At the moment, we're not giving any details about the virtual world to the public."

"We'll keep it zipped," Ada assured me. "What you need to figure out now, Detective, is who had their fingers in the cookie jar. Besides me."

Ben drank down a mouthful of coffee. "I'll put this bluntly, it wasn't my mother who made changes to the site where the cabin is."

"Who did, Ben?" I questioned.

"I don't know," he said with a sigh. "I've set up the system software to log everything. The image of the pile of trees was added through my own account, at a time when my mother wasn't in the office. She was in a therapy session over at CQ Hospital. She exercises in the heated pool there, twice a week."

I frowned. "So, someone else has access to the program—the one who's using the eagle avatar?"

Ben nodded. "They must have gotten in and added their own code before I started layering on the security—just like Mom did."

"I'll ask you to lock all access to the program until we figure out what's going on. I'm going to have to arrange some help—an expert who can give us some insights into who hacked your program."

He scratched the back of his head, suddenly looking uncomfortable. "Uh... I'd have to pass that with the company that employs me. It's in my contract with NineOak—I'm not allowed to have any unauthorised persons accessing my work."

"It's my understanding that the program is owned by our police area command?"

"True. But the framework that it runs on is owned by NineOak. I developed the framework, but I don't own it."

"Okay—look, don't do anything at this point. I'll get back to you." I glanced from Ben to Ada, threading my hands together in a gesture of gratitude. "I want to thank you both. The bunker that we found really is a major discovery—I don't want this business about the intruder in the virtual world to cloud that. Once I get on top of things, I'd like to invite you both to my place —for dinner with my family."

I thought Ada might reject that offer, but, instead, a grin lit up her face. "Dinner with the area command's most prominent detective? Can't say no to that."

I returned the smile. "Wonderful. I'll be in touch."

CHAPTER FORTY-SIX

I drove from CQ Technology to an area of Tallman's Valley that was known as *The Ponds*.

On the way, I made a phone call. I couldn't keep the issues that had been happening with the Witness Mountain virtual world to myself anymore—it'd gone well beyond that point.

Parking the car at The Ponds, I gazed out at the grassy hills and lake. Ahead, a creek glistened through the trees—the water level so low that the rocks were prominent. To the far left, the residents of an aged care home sat near the lake, watching the ducks.

I had a deep connection with this place. My parents used to bring me here when I was a child. It was also the place from which five children had been stolen four years ago—one of them my granddaughter, Ivy. I used to come here often after Ivy vanished, to feel her presence, to tell myself not to lose hope. And the aged care home was the place where I spent my mother's last days with her—both of us gazing out at the lake and listening to her favourite music.

I allowed my body to relax—my neck, my spine, my muscles. And I attempted to still my racing thoughts. I couldn't risk having another health episode like I'd just had.

A figure approached. A man in a business shirt and smart, tailored trousers.

I stepped from my car.

"Jiro, we have a problem," I said.

Inspector Shintani gave nothing away in his expression. "I know you wouldn't have called me for a private discussion without due cause, Detective."

I explained the events that had happened within the virtual world as clearly as I was able, including the details about the eagle and the wagtail. I was out of my depth with this, on every possible level.

"This is very serious," he said. "We're going to need to tread carefully."

"But in what direction? The only people with knowledge that this virtual world was being developed were our homicide team and Nancy Upchurch—of the NineOak corporation. And Ben Tremayne and his mother, of course."

"I'll get an AFP cybercrimes unit straight onto it."

I thought for a moment. I knew that the Australian Federal Police handled crimes committed online, but if they took this on, what would be the consequences for Ben and his job? He didn't deserve to lose it.

"Jiro, Ben said he needed to inform his company about any external access."

"I don't think that's wise. Perhaps the AFP can do this without raising any alerts."

"Maybe. But what if we scare away the *eagle*—whoever that is? If they were smart enough to bypass Ben's code, then they're probably smart enough to realise we're following their tracks."

He softened his tone. "I don't think we have a choice. In any case, whoever did this might not have even realised their tracks had been discovered."

"But how do I avoid this person realising they've been discovered? I mean, if not for the eagle and the virtual world, how else will I explain becoming suspicious about a pile of logs?"

"Your cover story is already in place. Your husband and son-in-law are firefighter volunteers who discovered the pile of logs on top of the burned-down cabin. And they needed to attend to it due to the bushfire risk. They mentioned it to you, and that's how you became suspicious. *That's* the story we'll feed to the media."

I turned Shintani's idea over in my mind. Nodding, I exhaled. "That might work."

Shintani returned to his car and drove off.

I was left alone with my thoughts again.

CHAPTER FORTY-SEVEN

Something that I was certain of was that there were people from Tallman's Valley who knew about the bunker.

And right now, they must be shaking in their boots. The bunker was a Pandora's Box.

The most likely people to have a connection with the bunker were the Mulden family.

Opening the glovebox of my car, I took out my notebook.

I looked over my notes about that family.

The people who'd started the funfair in the 1950s were *Harold* and *Beatrix Mulden.*

Harold and *Beatrix* also bought the land on Witness Mountain, to house themselves and all the workers from the carnival.

Harold and Beatrix had one child, *Henrietta.*

Henrietta had five children with a distant cousin—*Mickey Mulden. Mickey* also had children with other women—most of them workers at the carnival.

On all accounts that I'd read, the carnival had been formed and run with honest, hardworking people. The rot had all started with Mickey. He'd taken over the running of the carnival in the 1970s, after *Harold* and *Beatrix* died.

The carnival was finally shut down in 1989, after the police raid.

It was supposed to have been raided because of child neglect and also the illegal activities there—gambling, drugs and stolen goods.

But the police had barely kept any records of what happened the day of the raid.

I had not found a single reference to the finding of any money, either. There *surely* must have been a huge stack of money hidden somewhere in the funfair. People didn't deal in illegal goods for no reason.

On the morning of the raid, many children of the carnival families were taken into the care of the state. Some of the adults scattered like rats, leaving the children behind.

At that time, Henrietta and Mickey had five children together:

Doug, aged 28

Gordon, aged 25

Adele, aged 16

Polly, aged 9

Penny, aged 7

The births of the three girls had never been registered. They'd had other names as children, but they'd all changed those names after the carnival raid. The two older boys changed their last names by deed poll, not wanting to be tainted by the Mulden surname.

Here in the valley, the Mulden name died. And with the carnival long-shut down, people started to forget all about the Muldens and their carnival.

Doug became *Doug Overmire*—a financier and business leader.

Gordon became *Gordon Quinley*—a psychiatrist. He was currently in jail, charged with historic child sexual abuse offences.

Adele became *Adele Hobson*—the mother of one daughter, named *Nola*. *Adele* was currently overseas, on the run from police.

Polly became *Polly Brightwaters*—a drifter who spent her life in and out of psychiatric wards. She was currently in jail awaiting sentencing for the kidnapping of five children.

Penny became *Penny Foster*—the mother of one son, named Max. Like her sister, she was currently in jail awaiting sentencing for the kidnapping of five children.

With my pen, I put a question mark beside each of the names. Who could I get to talk with me about the bunker?

Polly might not agree to talk with me again—and, besides that, she'd only been nine when the carnival closed down. It was unlikely she'd know much.

Penny had been even younger then. And she was in a psychiatric ward at the moment—unavailable to speak with me.

That left Doug, Gordon and Adele.

There was little chance that Doug—the eldest—would give any information that would further tarnish or implicate his family.

Gordon—the second eldest—was out of the question. He was sure to ask for a plea bargain in return for giving any information. And the last thing I wanted was for Gordon to get a light sentence.

I underlined Adele's name in my notebook. She was my best bet.

Except that getting information from her depended upon finding her. She'd been on the run from police for months now. She was wanted for crimes committed overseas as well as Australia, but we might be able to gain her an extradition back to Australia, if she'd agree to talk to us. An Australian prison would be a picnic compared to some others she might end up in.

To obtain an update on Adele, I called the person responsible for tracking her down.

Detective Sergeant Liz Booth was based in Sydney, leading the child protection squad. She was a hard hitter who dealt with the worst of the perpetrators. She was also a close friend of mine.

"Snap, I was just thinking of you, Kate," came Liz's bright voice over the phone.

"Oh? What have I done now?"

"I'm sitting in a lovely little café in Cebu City—the Philippines. And thinking I'd love to be sharing a coffee and a chat with you. One day, my dear, we'll have to take a trip together somewhere nice."

"Let's make that happen. How are you?"

"I'm all right. Early this morning, I took a walk along one of the most beautiful beaches I think I've ever seen. And then we drove through one of the poorest parts of town. The contrast was heart breaking." She paused. "How are you and your family, Kate? I've been following the news about the fires when I can."

"We're all okay. The fires just don't seem like they're going to end. We've had a fire of a different kind here in the valley the last few days. Have you seen our local news lately?"

"No, I'm afraid I haven't. I've been very caught up here."

"We found an underground bunker—on Witness Mountain."

"Seriously? A *bunker*?"

"Yes. You know the people who were shot recently on that mountain? That's where the bunker was—on the land belonging to the older couple."

"Goodness—what was in it?"

"All kinds of illegal goods. Some things belonging to the carnival. And… the remains of two people. The bunker hasn't been touched in decades—possibly not since the day of the police raid."

"Well, I'm stunned. Your little valley has certainly been rocked by a lot of things this year. And did I hear you mention the carnival?"

"Yes. The carnival just keeps rearing its ugly head."

"I'll take a wild guess that you'd like to talk with Adele Hobson?"

"Very much. The minute you find her, I'd like to know."

"I wish I could deliver her to you—I really do. After *I'm* through with her, of course." She sighed. "We're close, but not close enough."

"Have you had any sightings?"

"A couple. But she was too far away. Across a river and the other side of a busy street. We tracked her from Ho Chi Minh City, Vietnam, last week. She arrived in the Philippines a few days ago, and she's been island hopping ever since."

"Surely she's got to run out of money, sooner or later."

"I think she's got people helping her—people with a vested interest in the kind of material she's been supplying them with. But she can't get out of the Philippines—not by air anyway. I've made sure of that."

"I wish you luck. She'll slip up sooner or later."

"The sooner, the better. She doesn't deserve to be free."

"No. No, she doesn't."

I chatted with Liz about other things for a while, before saying goodbye.

I had to cross Adele off my list for now. Liz wasn't closing in on her—yet.

CHAPTER FORTY-EIGHT

Fast running out of options, I made a call to Doug Overmire. I knew he'd do anything to avoid meeting with me. I'd have to go in strong and not accept *no* for an answer.

"Mr Overmire," I began, "I know you will have heard about the discovery of the bunker. I need to talk about that with you."

A short silence followed before Doug replied. "The bunker? What a strange find that was. To think that was hiding away on Witness Mountain all this time."

"On land that originally belonged to your family."

"Did they own land on that side of the mountain? I'm not sure that they—"

"Yes, they did. We found the title deeds—in the bunker itself."

"Seriously? Ah… well, my grandparents *did* own more land than they knew what to do with. And they were far more generous than they should have been, allowing the carnival workers to build whatever they wanted."

Doug was waffling, trying hard to deflect any possibility of his family being responsible for the bunker.

"I need to speak with you—in person," I said.

"I'm afraid I'm busy this week—"

"So am I. This whole business of the bunker and the two bodies is coming on top of the recent shooting incident. It'd really help me if I could clear up some things—things that you might be able to answer."

"Ah. Well, of course. I'll be at CQ again in a couple of days. I'll pencil in an appointment with you then."

"It has to be today. It'll be me or it'll be other detectives. Might as well be me."

In actual fact, there were no detectives who'd expressed an immediate interest in pursuing the Mulden family. The bunker victims had possibly been killed three decades ago. It was a cold case, and other, more recent cases had to take priority in the short term.

But I didn't mind bending the truth. Doug had started out by not being quite truthful with me. If I had to play his game, I would.

"I see. Well, I'll be at the office after four in the afternoon."

"That's a bit late for my schedule. Where will you be before then?"

"I'm at home. I've got some renovations happening, and I need to be there. The carpenters have been messing up my instructions."

"Fine. I'll see you there. Address?"

Reluctantly, Doug gave me his address. Of course, I already had it. I'd been writing up extensive notes on all of the Mulden family for weeks now. But I wasn't about to let him know that.

It'd take me at least two hours to get there. I hoped it'd be worth the effort.

I ended the call and then made the long drive into the city.

Darling Point was just four kilometres away from the central business district of Sydney. But there were pockets where the high-rises vanished from view and the houses were a mix of stately federation and Victorian, surrounded by palm trees and lush, cool greenery.

I turned into a narrow street and onto Overmire's property. I couldn't see much from the front—just a high gate. Leaning out from my car window, I pressed the buzzer on a stone pillar beside the gate.

The gate slid across and I drove inside. Overmire's property was huge in terms of the inner city. I couldn't even take a guess at how many millions this place was worth.

I parked on an asphalt area that was surrounded by a perfect lawn and shrubbery.

Overmire didn't greet me at the door. From what I knew of him so far, that didn't surprise me.

A woman ushered me inside. She introduced herself as Pinkie—Doug's wife. I knew from my notes that she was forty, over fifteen years younger than Doug. She had an oddly preserved look. Her facial skin was stretched tight over cheek implants, and her puffy lips didn't match with the rest of her features.

Pinkie's dress floated around her thin legs as I followed her through the house to an expansive living room.

The living room was beautiful, but it was the view that had me stunned.

Glass bifold doors spanned a good thirty metres across the room, beyond which sprawled a glistening view of Sydney Harbour. Yachts streamed across the water, in front of the distant Opera House. Immediately below the living room, steps led down to a pool and tennis court, then more steps led directly down to the water, where a luxury yacht was moored.

Pinkie gazed at me knowingly. "People are always knocked out by that view. Best in Sydney. Can I fetch you a cold drink… or a freshly brewed cup of coffee?"

"No, thank you," I said politely.

"I'll leave you to it, then. I have to take the dog to the vet. It's too fat, apparently, and the vet's going to design a diet."

On cue, a cute, rotund dachshund waddled down the elaborate stairway. Pinkie scooped it up and walked to the front door.

"Detective Wakeland." A man waved me over.

It was Doug Overmire. I hadn't even noticed him yet. He was standing by a sofa setting in a corner, close to the glass bifolds.

"Hope you don't mind meeting with me in this spot," he said in a gracious tone. "But it gives me a bird's-eye view of the builders. They're putting in a new pergola. The one they built last week had to be torn down. It wasn't at all what we requested."

I walked across the massive floor to Doug. Glancing out through the glass doors, I could indeed see builders at work from this vantage point. The pergola being built was very large and elaborate.

"Impressive pergola," I told Doug.

"My daughter's getting married in a month's time. We're holding the reception here. So, we're hard at work getting everything ready. The ceremony will be at St Mary's Cathedral."

"I didn't realise you were Catholic, Mr Overmire."

"I'm not. That's Pinkie's side of the family."

"I see."

He turned to look out at the builders.

This was the first time I'd seen Doug with natural light on his face. Like his wife, he seemed to have had quite a bit of construction work done to his face. Too much to look natural. I wondered if he was forever paying out for upgrades to his face, just as he was for his house.

"Well." I smiled. "Shall we get started?"

"Yes. Have a seat, Detective."

I positioned myself on the sofa across from him. "Mind if I record this? Saves me writing notes."

"Uh, no. That's fine."

"Great. Well, I'll begin by asking if you know the exact location where we found the bunker?"

"No, I can't say that I do."

"It was right at the back of the Iversons' land, near the boundary line. The next property is owned by the Mulden Family Trust."

"Right. I inherited that land, but really, I don't want it."

"Is there a reason you haven't sold it?"

"There is family history there. My grandparents bought it and started the carnival. It seems as if I should keep it in the family. Only, none of my siblings wanted to live on the land. So, it's just been sitting there, like a dusty old skeleton in the closet."

"There definitely were skeletons there, in the bunker."

His gaze shifted out to the harbour view. "And that's horrific. As I said on the phone, my grandparents were far too lenient with who they allowed to build on their land—same goes for my parents. We had lots of seasonal workers, and also some very shady characters."

"Shady characters? Can you give me names?"

"Far too long ago." He looked back at me, giving a lazy sort of shrug.

"Hmmm. See, my problem is that it's not an easy thing to build a bunker. I looked it up. It's quite involved. I'm trying to picture how all of this work went on—day after day—on your family's land, without you or your parents noticing."

"I was away more than I was there. At boarding school, then university, and then I started up a business in Sydney. As for my parents, they were at the carnival during the days—and many of the nights."

"Right. But, bear with me, I'm imagining excavator machinery and bags and bags of concrete—all sitting right there for weeks while the bunker was being built. As well as specialised boring equipment—trenchers. And, oh, the noise! Trenchers are very noisy, I'm told."

"Looks like you've really been researching your bunkers."

"Yes, it's quite fascinating. And the more I find out, the harder it is to figure how no one saw or heard any of this. I mean, it's nothing like building a cabin out of wood. You could bang one of those up in a day or two, if you were handy. But not a bunker. And the Witness Mountain one is fairly well built, too. Lasted over thirty years. We think it was maybe built in 1984."

"Sounds like the people who built it were very motivated."

"Oh, I agree. They had a lot to hide. They don't just sound like blow-ins who came to work at a funfair, wouldn't you agree?"

He arched his manicured eyebrows. "I guess not. They had a plan."

"A plan? What sort of plan are you thinking?"

"To hide stolen goods, obviously."

"But why on *your* family's land? That's where I'm hitting a wall. Why not get their own land, where they wouldn't be disturbed. Especially as it was intended to be an ongoing thing. A lot of goods were to be shifted in and out of that bunker."

"Perhaps if the bunker were to be discovered, the culprits wouldn't be held accountable." He tossed me a shrewd glance. "You know… this could absolve my father of any wrongdoing. The illegal goods were the doing of other people, all along. I think you should pursue that line of investigation."

"I'll be looking to uncover every stone—don't worry about that."

He scratched his ear, giving me a smile that seemed forced. "Do keep me updated."

"Do you have any idea of the identity of the two bodies from the bunker, Mr Overmire?"

"No. I would have said."

"Ever notice that a couple of workers from the carnival suddenly vanished, perhaps on the same day, perhaps not?"

He shook his head. "Nope. As I said, I was barely there. I didn't even know most of their names." A frown crept onto his forehead. "Who's to say they're from the carnival?"

"The bodies were found in a metal box—something that clown heads had once been in."

"I had no idea."

"It was reported in the media."

"I admit I haven't focused on it. It's disturbing… awful." He turned to view the harbour again. "The whole episode with the bunker—it's not a good look for the valley."

"No, not a good look at all. I, ah, I have a question about your sister—Adele. We're looking for her, as I'm sure you're aware. Have you happened to hear from her?"

"Adele? I haven't spoken to any of my sisters in years. As for Adele, I gave up on her a long time ago. And, of course, I didn't even know what she was involved in. Very nasty stuff indeed."

"Did you know she fled overseas?"

"I did read that in the news. I know as much as anyone else. I hope you find her. She certainly chose the wrong path in life."

An expression of annoyance crossed his face as his gaze switched once more to the builders in the garden below. "Ah, I don't believe it. They're getting it wrong again. I'm going to have to go down there." He stood. "Is there anything else, Detective?"

"Just one very broad question. Do you know anything at all that could help us with our enquiries into the bunker?"

He sighed. "It's a complete mystery to me."

"All right. Thanks for your time."

"Pleasure."

"I'll see myself out."

The abundant greenery of Doug Overmire's front garden enveloped me as I stepped out through the front door.

The evasive expression Doug had worn on his face the whole time told me he knew exactly who the bunker victims were.

But he hadn't divulged anything.

I was down to my very last option—Polly.

As I walked to my car, I decided to try calling her again. There was a chance—however slim—that she might be able to give me a morsel of knowledge about the bunker victims.

That was if I could convince her to talk with me one more time.

I drove away from Doug Overmire's house and parked at a spot where I had a view of Sydney Harbour.

I called the remand centre at the prison for the second time in a week.

But Polly refused to see me. It was what I'd expected, but still, it was a blow.

I watched a ferry cutting across the water, a burning sensation expanding across the centre of my chest. I had no idea where to take this case next and the hopelessness of that was eating me up inside.

CHAPTER FORTY-NINE

The next morning, I woke once more caught in a dream of the carnival's Ferris wheel in my mind. Again, its carriages were on fire. Except this time, fire hadn't reached the very top carriage.

Angie—*a young, teenage Angie*—was sitting in that top carriage. But she wasn't screaming or terrified. Instead, she just looked sad.

Shuddering, I headed off for a shower.

I needed to focus.

There must be someone else who I could contact about the bunker—and its victims.

But I'd already tried talking with every worker from the old carnival that I could find.

Months ago, during a time when I was supposed to be on leave, I'd started my investigation into the carnival. I'd made a database of workers and I'd tracked them down, one by one. A few of the people had died—they'd been in their forties, fifties or sixties at the time the carnival closed in 1989. Some of them were now affected by dementia. The few people who agreed to talk with me had known nothing of interest.

I'd also tried to find out the names of every police officer who'd taken part in the 1989 raid. There'd only been one name documented, and that detective had died many years ago.

My attempts to investigate the carnival and the subsequent raid had failed pretty miserably.

I stood in the shower, scrubbing my scalp with shampoo, then letting the warm water pour down over my head and shoulders.

The image from my dream of Angie sitting forlornly in the Ferris wheel carriage returned to me.

I remembered where I'd seen a photo of her looking sad like that. It was in a photograph I'd seen on a wall in the Iversons' house. Angie had been wearing a ballerina costume, her red hair up in a knot, her eyes almost haunted.

Her parents had recently left her all alone, and she'd quickly been adopted. It was kind of the Iversons to adopt a teenager and move all the way to Tallman's Valley for her—but Angie surely would have been pining for her birth parents.

I frowned, inhaling a quick snatch of air.

Angie's birth parents—what if they never left the carnival? What if *they* were the murder victims in the bunker?

They could be. They really could be.

I turned off the shower and gathered up a towel around me.

Thoughts spun faster in my mind now.

Some of the workers had fled the carnival after getting wind of the coming police raid—leaving their children behind. I had just accepted the idea that Angie's parents had done the same.

But the more that I considered the fate of Angie's parents, the more likely it seemed they were the bunker victims. From the sounds of it, they had never resurfaced—not since the day they vanished.

The initial forensic testing of the victims had shown that they were aged close to 30. The two of them would have been very young to have had a daughter Angie's age—but it was still in the realm of possibility.

I dressed quickly and then called the women's prison again.

This time, I told the manager that I knew the identities of the bunker victims and needed to speak with Polly urgently.

It was a big leap to make—and it could backfire on me.

Ten minutes later, the reply came back. Polly had agreed to see me.

When I arrived at the remand centre, Polly was on an exercise break.

She had her hair out this time, and it hid half her face.

"I hate the daily walks," she muttered. "I have a little vegetable patch I'd rather be working on, but they say I need to walk. So here I am."

On the other side of the wire fencing, prisoners were taunting her, calling her names.

Polly turned her head away. "They're not bad women. They just don't understand. They think I'm some sort of child abuser. That's not me at all. I didn't harm a single hair on those kids' heads."

It wasn't the time to tell her what I was thinking—it was true she hadn't physically harmed the five children, but it'd certainly been harmful to keep them away from their families for years.

"Polly," I said, "should we go sit somewhere else—near the garden you just told me about, perhaps?"

"I'm supposed to be walking. You know, getting my daily exercise."

"The officers will be fine with you sitting this one out."

"Good. I feel like I'm on show out here. Like a zoo animal."

The jeers continued as she led me around to her garden patch, in which there were neat rows of flowers and vegetables.

We sat together on the bench.

"So, you know who the bodies are… in the bunker," she said tightly.

I nodded, inhaling the summery smell of the flowers, hoping she'd just come out and say the names of the victims.

But she didn't. Instead, she moved from the bench to sit on the grass, legs tucked under her like a child. She plucked flowers from her garden, one by one—all of them delicate shades of pink and white. Roses, proteas and baby's breath.

"Polly… it's time to just say what you know."

She stayed silent, picking flowers almost mechanically. She bent herself over, hair draped around her face and knees.

What she said next chilled me, spoken in a broken, whispery voice. "I saw them...."

"Who did you see?" I asked her gently.

"I saw *them*… hanging from the tree."

Shock rose inside me. She'd actually seen the murder victims?

She still hadn't spoken any names. But I couldn't rush her. If this had all been folded up a long time inside her, then she needed to unfold it at her own pace.

"Tell me, Polly… where did this happen?"

"At the carnival. It was night-time. I'd stolen a toy for Penny's birthday. We… we rarely got presents. I almost got caught, and I had to hide in the forest. Where I wasn't supposed to be. That's where they were."

"I want to ask you something. I want you to tell me your story… and I'd like to record it. You can take it as slow as you want, and you can tell it in exactly the way you want you tell it. Would you do that?"

I sensed a struggle playing out within her, in each rise and fall of her shoulders as she breathed.

She let the flowers drop through her fingers to the ground… and she nodded.

CHAPTER FIFTY

POLLY, 1989

Tallman's Valley Funfair

I'm not supposed to be here. I'll have my bottom whipped if I'm caught. I'll have to be quick as a wink.

The ink-dark forest stretches out so wide and deep it could swallow me without a second thought. Scents of burnt popcorn and butter waft on the warm air, all the way from the carnival's food stalls.

Digging out a peppermint bullseye from my pocket, I jeer at myself.

You're nine, Polly. You should be braver than this.

I pop the bullseye in my mouth without bothering to wipe the lint off. If I'm brave, I shouldn't care about lint.

Just keep going. Don't stop.

But something makes my stride falter. A strange, raw odour. The popcorn smell has faded away to nothing. There is just this sickening, overpowering stench all around me.

It smells like rust and decay.

My stomach rolls, and I spit out the bullseye.

Keep going, stupid.

As I round a stand of pine trees, my whole body recoils. Like I've been sucker punched.

Two figures are hanging by their necks from a low branch.

A man and a woman.

The distant spotlights of the carnival cast just enough of a glow for me to see awful details that I don't want to see.

The eyes of the hanging people look all wrong, bulging and staring. Their faces are disfigured and bruised from ropes knotted tight around their necks. Streaks of blood are drying beneath their noses, dirt caked in their hair.

I discover two things at once:

That dried blood smells metallic.

That death looks like this.

I know both people. They're carnival workers.

The woman is small and thin boned, with long, black hair and Asian features. She wears her Snow-White stage costume, the white stockings on her legs torn and one shoe off.

The man has a mop of red hair and pale skin. A dark mess spreads at the bottom of his white shirt. I realise that it's blood. As if he's been stabbed in the guts.

The two people are Tiên and Anthony Kowalski—the parents of my friend, Angelina. I want to be mistaken, but I know I'm not.

Rain begins to fall. I barely feel it wetting my face. Terror whips up inside me, taller than the trees.

A scream forms in the deepest part of me.

But I don't dare let the scream out, don't dare let it tumble into my throat.

I don't dare make a single sound.

CHAPTER FIFTY-ONE

POLLY, 1989

FIFTEEN MINUTES EARLIER

The carnival has just closed.

The adults are busy locking up and tying everything down—so we can all get home and have dinner.

My family owns the Tallman's Valley Funfair. It's our whole life.

I hate it.

It's like being hooked up to a machine that constantly pumps your veins with blood that's not your own. My blood is made of grease and sugar and popcorn butter.

I finish polishing the last of the glass in the Hall of Mirrors. It's been my job to do that ever since I turned eight. The mirror hall is an eerie place to be after closing time, but it's the only part of the carnival I like.

The mirrors are old, from when my grandparents used to own the carnival. Made of real glass, they're beautiful. A few of them broke and had to be replaced by lucite or plastic sheeting. I have to be extra-careful when cleaning those ones, or they'll quickly go cloudy—and I'll be in a heap of trouble.

Climbing down from the stepladder, I study my handiwork. I've done a good job. The mirrors gleam. During the day, kids with greasy, sticky fingers constantly smear the mirrors. Earlier tonight, a group of silly teen girls left lipstick smooches. Why, I don't know.

I stand and stare at myself.

For a second, I pucker up like the teen girls that I saw. Then slap my face hard. It's silly to be interested in kissing.

But I like looking into the mirrors and pretending I'm someone else. With my feet flat on the ground, my head doesn't reach very high on the mirror in front of me. I'm small for a nine-year-old. The inward curve of the mirror squashes my face, making it teeny-tiny on my shoulders.

My big sister, Adele, marches up behind me.

Her head looms large in the mirror, way above mine.

I spin around.

Her eyes have a mean glint as she stands there in her spangly halter top and her jeans tucked into combat boots. Her blue eyeshadow is as bright as a clown's. Her lipstick's smudged on one side. At age sixteen, Adele isn't quite grown-up yet—but for years now, she's seemed like a short, angry adult.

"Polly, I'm gonna tell Dad you're just standing around and not helping." Adele sticks her hands on her hips to show she means business. The bunches of keys that she wears on her belt jingle. Adele keeps copies of keys from every lock in the whole carnival. She doesn't need to. I think she just likes striding about with all those keys, as if she owns everything here.

"I *am* helping," I tell her. "I just finished cleaning the mirrors."

"Well, I walked past the bumper cars a minute ago, and they stunk like vomit. Go clean 'em."

"That's *your* job."

"I just promoted you. Go get a bucket and get started."

I catch sight of another figure. He's wearing some kind of dark blue uniform. His tall frame is reflected in the line of mirrors. With one hand, he buttons up his shirt, and with the other, he smooths his messy hair. Before I can see his face clearly, he swings his head away. Whistling, he walks out into the night.

Adele stares after him, biting her bottom lip in a way that looks strangely nervous.

"Is that your boyfriend?" I ask in a hushed tone.

"None of your beeswax," she snaps back.

Adele was often off with teenage boys instead of doing her chores, but I've never seen her with a boy who is old enough to have a job.

Adele seems distressed, scrunching up her forehead. Then she runs off in the man's direction, briefly turning her head back to me. "What are you waiting for, you idiot? Get the cars cleaned up!"

With a huffing sigh, I head down into the corridor where the buckets are. I rarely argue with Adele. It's easier not to.

There are framed photos of our family along the walls. Most of the glass is cracked, but no one ever bothers to replace it. There are my grandparents in a sepia photograph—Harold and Beatrice Mulden, standing outside the carnival they built. And there is a photo of my parents and my siblings—Doug, Gordon, Adele, Penny and me. We all have thin, straight blond hair and look very similar to each other.

I continue to the old bathroom at the end of the corridor. The bathroom had been built fifty years ago or so. Most of the wall tiles have fallen off, and the floor is always damp from leaks. I hate coming in here.

The pipes screech as I fill a bucket with water. On the way out, I grab some detergent and a sponge. I return along the corridor. The bucket sloshes water and wets the floorboards.

One of the doors to the supply rooms is ajar. I can't help but peek. The supply rooms are often stocked with toys. My father would buy big lots of goods that were going for a discount, and then he'd sell them at the funfair.

I'd overheard talk a few times that the goods had been stolen, but I tried not to think on it too hard. I don't want to hear bad things. I don't know what to do with *bad things* inside my head.

Putting the bucket down, I step inside the supply room door.

A sharp breath sucks from my lungs. There are shelves upon shelves of dolls, all looking out at me from the transparent plastic windows of their boxes.

I'd seen the doll in a Kmart catalogue. She was the brand-new, 1989 *Happy Holidays Barbie*. And now, there she was in her sparkly white dress, with a fur wrap around her shoulders. Looking like a princess dressed for a magical winter ball.

I know someone who would love her to bits. My little sister, Penny. She's fond of dolls in pretty dresses.

It's Penny's birthday in a couple of weeks, but she knows better than to ask our parents for toys. Dad thinks toys are useless lumps of plastic for pampered brats. In those exact words. *Us carnival people are smarter than that*, he says.

Standing here, a terrible idea sneaks into my brain. I'll snatch one of the dolls and hide it away. Then I'll surprise Penny with it on her birthday.

The idea came in like a surprise attack from a ninja. But I can't make it go away.

No one's here. No one will know I've taken a doll. Penny will just have to keep the doll a big secret.

My stomach clenches hard as I run and lift down a box.

I get bold and grab a Halloween showbag, too.

I've stolen two things now. But I can't stop myself. Penny is going to love her presents, and I'd do anything to make her happy.

My heart hammers like tap shoes as I race out. I need to hide the doll and showbag away somewhere. Tomorrow, I'll bring a backpack with me and find a way to bring the stash home.

I head down to a room that I know is full of old office equipment. Boxy-looking computers and floppy disks and printers. None of it works anymore. No one comes in here.

Opening the drawer of a filing cabinet, I place the doll inside. Before dropping the Halloween showbag on top, I stop and admire the images on the outside of it. Witches and monsters.

It'd been Halloween last month, and we still had some leftover stock. The bags were now being sold off at half-price. The idea of Halloween both puzzles and thrills me. I can't imagine why people would give out treats to strange children. We didn't celebrate Halloween in Australia. Only Americans went *trick or treating*. But us carnival kids always know when it's Halloween, because that's when we get the stocks of creepy showbags in from America.

I rifle through the showbag, inspecting the haul.

There's a plastic bat on a string, vampire teeth, and a coffin-shaped money box. There's also peppermint bullseyes, candy cigarettes, and a kit to make marshmallow ghosts. Best of all is a box of *Sea Monkeys*.

They are the kind of treasures right under my nose every day at the carnival, treasures I am never allowed to touch.

A mix of excitement, fear and guilt stirs up inside me, growing as thick as marshmallows.

I've got to get out of here.

Stuffing the bulleyes in my pocket, I push the drawer shut. Then I creep from the room like I'm a marionette on a string.

Voices travel down the corridor.

One of the voices is my father's. "Lock it all up. We're getting out of here. Right now. No stragglers."

I freeze, knowing that the most hated thing in my father's universe is *stragglers*. He expects everyone to work hard and fast. If I appear out of nowhere now with a bucket and sponge, I'm just going to look like a *straggler* who hasn't finished her jobs yet.

It's not just that. There's a fierceness undercutting Dad's voice. It almost sounds like a snarl, like that of an animal getting ready to pounce.

The air is dark as anything in the corridor. That's a good thing.

Carefully, I pick up the bucket and then step backwards all the way to the bathroom.

Don't drop the bucket. Don't you drop it, stupid.

There's no way out of the funhouse, except past Dad or through a back door that leads to the forest. The forest scares me, but I can't think of a better plan.

Taking the deepest breath I've ever taken, I slip out the back door.

The forest seems dangerous in a way it's never seemed before. Maybe because, tonight, I'm a bad girl. I'm a thief. And bad things happen to bad people, don't they?

I have to race behind the funhouse and then behind a long line of outbuildings and then the food and amusement stalls.

I can make it without being seen. But I have to go through the forest.

I begin weaving my way through. Back at the carnival, the popcorn stands are being cleaned out—and the smell reassures me that I haven't wandered too far away.

But then I see something.

Objects hanging from a tree.

At first, the objects seem like a Halloween trick. Like human-sized bats hanging upside down.

But it's not a trick. They are not bats.

They are people. People who I know.

I stumble away on legs that no longer seem to support me. I need to get out of here, back to the carnival.

My mind pushes at the sight I just saw.

It's not something I was supposed to see. I have to pretend I didn't. Pretend like I never went into the forest at all.

A man fills the space before me.

My father.

An instinct tells me to clamp my lips tight and not say a word.

His face wears a hard and strange look. "What're you doing back here, Polly?"

I struggle to think up a reason.

"Thought I heard Milo barking," I stammer. "Kept gettin' out of his collar and running off earlier. Stupid damned dog."

"Milo's already in the truck."

"Oh… is he? Must've been a stray?"

"Guess what, Polly? If you think it's fine and dandy to be chasin' after a dog when you're meant to be in the truck, you can sleep with the dogs tonight."

I stare back at him, unblinking. "But the dogs sleep under the house."

"That's right."

I swallow a gasp. Fear bleaches my mind of all thought except for an image of the cobwebbed space where Milo and the other dogs sleep.

"Get in the truck." He stomps away, in the direction from which I'd just come.

Any second now, he'd see them. *The dead people.*

But no sound comes. No shouts of shock and horror.

I understand something right there and then.

My father already knows about the people hanging in the tree.

He knows.

CHAPTER FIFTY-TWO

POLLY, 1989

I sit in the truck, wedged between Adele and Angelina. Adele is puffing cigarette smoke out the window.

I'm terrified of Angelina's shoulder touching mine, as if what I know about her parents can pass between us. And then she'll start screaming, just like the scream I feel inside.

Penny sits on my lap, her bony backside and elbows sticking into me with every pothole in the road. My two brothers are in front—Doug and Gordon. Doug—my eldest brother—is driving.

The carnival trucks drive single file up the bumpy mountain road that leads home. The top of Witness Mountain is a black shape against the night sky.

Dread claws at my insides.

Angelina looks pale in the moonlight, her long red hair spilling over her shoulders. She keeps turning her head to look back. "I don't see my parents' van. Has anyone seen it?"

I stiffen, but stay silent.

"No one's seen it," Adele says with a yawn. "They probably snuck out for a beer in town."

"They'd tell me," Angelina replies in a tight voice.

Doug glances at her from the front seat. "Give it a rest, Angie. They'll turn up. Speaking of beer, I had to fire one of the clowns today. The drunk bastard fell off the stage. Bloody useless."

Adele turns to me, blowing smoke in my ear. "Where'd you sneak off to earlier, Polly? I came back, and you were gone. I was worried we'd be locking you up inside the House of Fun."

A smile curls on her lips. I can tell she'd love nothing better than to lock me in the fun house overnight.

"So, where *were* ya?" she repeats.

"Nowhere," I tell her.

"Don't smart-mouth me. I'm telling Dad you snuck off."

"He already knows. I went looking for Milo. I thought I heard him behind the stands."

"Yeah, right," she says. "You can clean the dodgem cars *and* the hotdog steamer tomorrow."

I shrug. "I don't mind."

Penny wriggles around. "Those are *your* jobs, Adele."

"I'm in charge of you two pipsqueaks," Adele retorts. "What I say goes."

She's been saying that ever since I can remember. The truth is, I really don't mind cleaning the dodgem cars all by myself—if it means I don't have to work anywhere near Adele. Besides, there are always coins dropped inside the cars. Whenever I spot them, I secretly scoop them up. I've been hiding a stash of coins for a while now, in the hope that one day, I can pay for Penny and me to run away from the carnival.

For a minute or two, I let myself dream about that. But then the sick feeling swoops back in. I'm going to vomit.

In the nick of time, the truck drives onto the farm and parks.

I bolt from the truck. Then throw up a watery fluid that burns my throat.

Wiping my mouth with the collar of my jacket, I head off quick. I don't want Dad to see me like this, because then he might wonder why I'm feeling so sick.

Angelina runs between the vehicles, asking over and over if anyone has seen her parents.

I know where they are. I know *exactly* where they are.

I need to vomit again.

As I step foot inside my house, Mum herds me into the kitchen. "We're running late tonight. Need to get the dinner on."

"I need to—"

"You don't need to nothin'. Come and help."

Her voice is sharp. Usually, she just sounds tired and beaten down.

Obeying her, I walk to the kitchen, swallowing down the bile that enters my mouth.

I start peeling potatoes at the sink, staring out at the farm through the dusty windowpanes. Mulden Farm has cabins and sheds all over the place. Higgledy-piggledy. Almost all the workers live here. I remember Mum saying that's so we don't have to pay them as much, because they get their food and board.

All the girls and women are dashing off to their kitchens. The men begin setting up outdoors at the wooden tables and bench seats. I know they'll start drinking next, and then Dad and a couple of the older men will count the money. There'll be loud jingles as the coins are dropped into the coin counting machine. My father will curse the loudest when a coin inevitably gets stuck.

I can only hope that Dad will forget my punishment in the middle of all of that.

Dinner tonight is shepherd's pie. Penny washes the potatoes in a bucket while I peel them.

My fingers refuse to work properly, and I nick them twice with the peeler.

Mum makes an irritated sound between her teeth. "You're going at it like a bat out of hell."

I try to focus, but I can't.

The image of the two *hanging people* rears up in my mind, clear in every detail.

Are they still there, hanging by ropes on the branch? Will they still be there in the morning?

"Are you listening to me?" Mum cuts in. "You're dripping blood."

Numbly, I glance at the trickle of red on the white flesh of the sliced potatoes. My hands start trembling.

Mum bandages up my fingers. That was something she rarely did. Usually, cuts and scrapes on the farm went untreated. Unless you got a cut that wouldn't stop bleeding. Only then did you win yourself a trip to the hospital.

Tonight, Mum seems on edge, her face drawn tight.

With the dinner cooked, all the daughters, mothers and other women carry it out to the tables. We always eat together at the farm.

I don't look at Dad while I fork the pie into my mouth. I pretend to be absorbed in my food, even though I can't even taste it.

Dinner is always noisy—and fast. Mum says food is to be devoured, not savoured. Food is too expensive for fancy meals.

Tonight, dinner sounds a hundred times louder. Scrapes and clangs of knives and forks on plates. Loud voices and loud chewing.

The dogs pace restlessly between the tables, whining and hoping for scraps to be thrown their way.

Once dinner is done, it's time for the women to clear it all away again. I balance a load of dirty plates in my hands and carry them away. I work as quick as I can, so I can get away from Dad. He usually goes and drinks with the men outside and doesn't come back until very late. I've heard Adele say he's got other wives he goes to see, too. I don't like to think about that.

The rain returns—just a light sprinkle, but it makes everyone head for the cabins.

Penny tugs at my sleeve. "Wanna play poker?" A raindrop tracks down her forehead.

"Okay. Sure. We'll play in our bedroom."

The only card game we know is poker. I don't feel like playing games. But I never say no to Penny.

A deep voice comes from behind us. My father's voice. "No, not you, Polly."

My spine stiffens as I turn around. "I have to help inside." I glance down at the stack of plates in my arms.

His eyes look like dark spaces in the glow of the lanterns. "You're spending the night under the house. Just like I told you. You didn't follow the rules."

Penny glares at Dad. "People don't sleep under houses!"

But Dad barely glances her way. "Go help your mother, Penny. If you backchat again, I'll make you sorry."

I expect her to run away. Instead, she charges forward, pushing him in the belly.

With his big hands, Dad grabs her by the shoulders. "Okay, you've made your choice. You're staying with your sister tonight. Under the house."

Letting go of Penny, he snatches the plates from me. Then slams them down on the table. The plates clink and shatter. "Okay, the two of you can go right now. To where the dogs sleep on the rugs. And don't move from that spot." He grabs an old blanket that's draped over a bench seat. "Here."

My throat seizes up tight as I turn to stare at the space beneath the underside of our cottage.

Dad stomps away.

I notice then that Mum and Adele are looking on from the kitchen window. Mum shakes her head and walks away. She's not going to help us. Adele winks at me and tosses her hair to one side. Then she laughs, pointing at me.

My knees feel so weak I can barely stand. "Penny… you go into the house. Dad won't notice. It's *me* he's angry with."

"No. I'm staying with you."

She's almost impossible to sway when she has made up her mind. The rain starts coming down harder. Grabbing her by the hand, I run for the cottage.

I'm the first to crawl under the house. The damp dirt stinks. I'm certain that a cobweb is about to wrap itself around my face. But I have to be brave for Penny.

I head for the collection of old blankets a short way in. The dogs sleep on those, but they're not here yet. They're being fed on the other side of the grounds.

Penny follows, and then clings to my arm. Only the lanterns light the grounds. Soon, they'll burn out.

I touch my head to Penny's. "Are you scared?"

"No."

She's lying.

"You shouldn't have gotten yourself into trouble," I tell her.

"Don't care."

"Hey, guess what I've got in my pocket?"

"Coins? I always nick some coins that are lying about after the count."

"No, not coins. Peppermint bullseyes."

"You do not."

I dig into my pocket and then hand her a bullseye. "You gotta get the lint off."

"Who gave you that?"

"I gave it to myself."

Penny doesn't ask any more questions, for which I'm grateful.

On the dark side of the cottage, a dog runs up and crawls underneath. Instantly I know which dog it is. *Milo*. His fur is so white that it catches the faint glow of the lanterns. He comes straight to us, his large, fluffy body making me feel safe as I hug him. Even though he smells of wet fur.

Milo noses us, trying to shift Penny and me out from under the house. My father once told me that Milo is a Maremma herding dog, and Milo wants all the animals and people on the farm to be exactly where he thinks they should be.

When Penny and I fail to move, he soon leaves, going off to patrol the grounds.

The other three dogs come sniffing under the house now. These ones, I don't like so much.

In the dark light, they terrify me. Each of the dogs has dead chickens tied to their collars. At night, I've been seeing them running around on the hills through my bedroom window, looking like freakish monsters. They got into the chicken pen two nights ago and killed all the chickens. To teach them not to do it again, Dad is making them wear their horrible necklaces of dead chickens. He says that if it was good enough for his father and grandfather to do the dead chicken punishment, then it's good enough for him.

A year ago, when the same thing happened, Mum tried to cut the dead chickens off the dogs. But my dad stopped her, shoving her away so hard that she cracked her head on the side of the cottage. Her cut bled everywhere, but she refused to go to the hospital, saying it was her own fault.

The dogs bring a smell of rotting death with them as they come near us.

My world has turned fierce and terrifying. I need to wait out this night with Penny… any way I can.

CHAPTER FIFTY-THREE

POLLY, 1989

"The dogs stink like hell." Penny holds the bottom of her cardigan over her nose.

I hiss at the dogs. "Go away. *Get.*"

But the dogs, with their horrible necklaces of rotting chickens, refuse to move away. They settle in on the rug beside us.

I want to push them off the rug, push them right out from under the house. But the truth is, I'm afraid of them. They growl at me all the time.

Penny starts crawling away. "I'm not sleeping with *them*."

"Okay, you go inside."

"You, too, Polly."

"I can't."

She stops and turns her face back to me. "Why?"

"You know why. This is a punishment. I have to be good."

"Being good gets you dead."

I suck in a breath. "What?"

"I heard one of the men say that earlier."

"It's not true. Don't repeat everything you hear."

"It *is* true. You don't have to be good. You just have to be smart."

"Penny… go inside."

"What if you die out here?"

"I'm not going to die."

"I'm scared that you will."

Somehow, it makes me feel a little lighter than Penny seems more worried about me dying than about staying out here in the dark. She might be the only one who cares about me. I know that she's the only one in my family who I love.

I sigh so that I don't risk sounding soppy. "Look… let's just… get away from the dogs. If we go over to the other side, maybe they won't follow us. They like sleeping on their rugs."

She blows out a big, huffing breath. "Fine." Then she hesitates. "What about spiders?"

"I'll go first. Okay?"

Picking up a stick, I wave it in front of my face, even before I start crawling. It's a warning to any spiders to run away.

With my heart bouncing like a tennis ball, I start off across the rocky ground and soil. I try not to think that some of those rocks will be old bones that the dogs have left under here.

Penny follows me between the rickety brick supports of the cottage. I know that Doug and Gordon often come under here to jack up the house with whatever they can find. Mum often says it's a wonder the house doesn't fall down. Now, being right under it, it seems all too real that the supports could give way.

I don't know why we can't build a better house. We seem to have lots of money. I've seen Dad counting it—tall stacks of money all over our kitchen table.

The musty stench of earth makes my head spin. It stinks of soil and what I imagine being worms.

"I don't like this," Penny said in a voice that sounds as if it's been crushed small and thin.

"Almost there. Don't worry." My voice doesn't sound right, either.

I crawl quicker. Once I poke my head out on the other side, I can smell fresh rain and eucalypt leaves.

But there are no lights here. And no cabins or cottages in sight.

Taking off my jacket, I spread it out on the ground for us both to lie on. It's not big enough, but it's better than nothing. Then I pull the old blanket across us that Dad had thrown at me.

Penny shivers under the blanket.

It'd been a warm day, but the air is quickly growing cool now.

Slowly, the shapes of the trees become clearer in the moonlight. It should feel better to see trees instead of just the inky dark. But somehow, it just makes me feel as if monsters had been lurking there all along… just unseen.

Milo comes and lies next to us, which calms me.

But Penny can't settle.

"Will spiders come and bite us during the night?" Penny asks.

"No."

"Snakes?"

"No. We'll be okay. You know, like, when the people here get too drunk, and they end up sleeping on the ground—they don't get bit, do they?"

"Doug got bit by a snake."

"He was stupid. Tried to kill it, and he missed."

"But—"

"Shhh!"

Dots of lights have appeared in the forest. Torchlight. Close to us.

For mere seconds, I catch sight of Dad and other men carrying two objects as long as themselves. The objects are wrapped up in sheets. The men puff and wheeze as if the objects are weighing them down. Dad is the only one whose face is captured in the light. I can't see who the others are.

Penny grabs my arm. "What're they carrying?"

"I don't know." My voice squeezes down into a whisper.

I do know.

They're carrying Angie's parents. Angie's *dead* parents.

Fingers of ice run along my back.

"Let's cuddle up and stay warmer," I tell her.

She falls asleep quick.

Sometime later—I don't know how long—a sound of metal slamming on metal echoes in the forest. I don't know what it is except that it came from the direction in which Dad went.

It's a strange sound I've heard many times before, late at night when I've been in my bedroom. There's nothing in that part of the forest, except for a cabin in which Dad keeps farm machinery. I always thought it odd Dad went to use the machinery in the dark.

But I never ask questions.

When sleep finally comes for me, it feels like I'm being pulled deep, deep underground.

CHAPTER FIFTY-FOUR

POLLY, 1989

I wake spitting dirt.

There's dirt in my mouth, in my eyes, in my hair.

Penny's still curled up beside me, hanging onto my arm. The jacket we'd gone to sleep on had somehow slid out from under me during the night, and I'd slept with my face on the damp ground.

Milo is gone.

Slapping the dirt from my hair and face, I wriggle into a sitting position. It's a grey morning and I can't tell what time it is. We have to move before Dad finds out that we didn't sleep exactly where he told us to.

Shaking Penny's shoulder, I lean close to her ear. "Wake up!"

Penny doesn't stir.

Grabbing both of her shoulders, I start dragging her out.

But I stall as a girl walks out of the forest. She's wearing a bomber jacket with the hood drawn and her red hair hanging like a curtain.

Angelina.

Instinctively, I slink back.

A man jogs up to her. It's Dad.

Penny blinks her eyes open. As she goes to speak, I jam a hand over her mouth and shake my head. Penny frowns, but she quits squirming. I guess that my expression must be scary.

"Where've you been?" Dad says to Angelina.

"My parents didn't come home last night."

"You went looking for them? Why'd you think they're in the forest?"

She crosses her arms tightly. "I don't. I just don't know where to look. I thought maybe they came back late and went for a walk and then got lost… or something. They like going for walks. They say it's healthy."

"I'm afraid I got some bad news for ya, honey."

I hold my breath. He's going to tell Angelina what happened to her parents?

A dull hope flickers in my chest—a hope that some kind of explanation will come, something that'll make sense of the terrible things I've seen.

Angelina's arms fall by her side. "What do you mean? Where are my parents?"

"Your parents decided to move on," Dad tells her.

"*Move on*?"

"It happens," he says with a shrug. "Carnival people come and go. I'm sorry, kid. They'll return one day when they're ready."

She shakes her head wildly. "No. You're wrong. They wouldn't do that. They wouldn't just… *leave me*."

"Angie." He sounds frustrated, drawing out the last syllable of her name. "I can only tell you what they told me. They said they left you a note and some money. It's in your caravan. Not sure where. You'll have to find it. They asked us to look after you until they get back."

"Tell me where they went. *Tell me*."

"Honey, I don't know. They didn't say. It's not like this hasn't happened before. Ricky's dad left us last year. But Ricky's still here."

"Ricky's dad was a drunk who didn't even care about Ricky. My parents aren't like that. We were going to leave the carnival just after Christmas." She paused. "I wasn't supposed to tell you that."

"Don't sweat it. Maybe they went off early, to look for work before coming back to get you. Tell you what, kid, you can take on your mother's birdcage gig if you like. You've turned thirteen, right? Old enough."

Sticking his hands in his pockets, he walks away.

He's told no end of lies to her. Her parents are never coming back.

Angelina runs off in the opposite direction, sobbing.

Penny splutters as I take my hand away from her face. "Your fingers taste like mud."

"Sorry. I didn't want them to know we were here."

"Angelina shouldn't cry like a baby just 'cos her parents went away for a while. *I* wouldn't."

"Listen to me. Don't tell anyone you heard Dad talking to her. And… what you saw last night in the forest, you don't say nuthin' to anyone about that, either, okay?"

"When Dad and the others were carrying stuff in the forest—you mean that?"

"Yes. *That*."

"Why?"

"Because I say so. If you do, we'll be punished again."

She picks a leaf from her long pale hair. "I don't ever wanna sleep under here again."

"Then do what I told you. Keep it zipped."

I sound like Adele. Harsh and horrible. But if Dad finds out we know anything, I'm positive his punishment will be a lot worse than just being made to sleep under the house.

I don't even want to think what that punishment would be.

CHAPTER FIFTY-FIVE

POLLY, 1989

People flood in through the gates of the carnival.

It's Saturday today, and the crowds have swollen.

To me, their voices are as loud as church bells. They screech like flocks of cockatoos on the rollercoasters. When they buy their food at the stalls, they constantly yell out things like, *Bradley asked for mayo on his hotdog. Where's the damned mayo?* As if the world will stop because little Bradley didn't get his mayonnaise.

Everything is far too noisy and far too colourful. The rides spin and clatter on their tracks. Children lose hold of their balloons and sob like their dog just died. People shove ping-pong balls in the laughing clown heads and then grab their stupid prizes. Popcorn spills on the ground like confetti.

I stay well out of Dad's sight all day. I clean vomit and mustard and greasy patches from the seats of the dodgem cars. I keep busy, busy, busy.

But when I close my eyes, all I can see are the dark shapes of two people hanging lifelessly from a tree.

Adele has her eyeliner on extra-thick today, and she's making googly eyes at every male customer over the age of fifteen. She says flirting is good for business.

After making a pimply teenage boy blush and stammer, she turns to wink at me. "See? That's how it's done. You should take tips from me."

She adjusts her cowboy vest and tugs her top down to show more of her boobs. Then she fixes her ponytail.

I cringe. "I'm nine years old. I'm not gonna *flirt*."

"Everyone has to pull their weight. Hmmm, you probably wouldn't be any good at it anyway. You're a shrinking violet, Polly. And your face looks like a squashed turnip. Oh, well."

Adele's walkie-talkie crackles. She whips it out of her leather cowboy holster like it's a gun. She answers it quickly, then shuts it off again.

"Okay, turnip-face. You gotta get over to the gondola ride. Quick smart. Some kid spilled his chicken nuggets in the water."

I'm glad to get away from her. Wordlessly, I'm off and running—dodging and ducking my way through the crowds.

The crowd thickens near the stage. Most of the carnival's shows are pantomimes. Every hour, they have fairy tale and comedy skits, with lots of singing and dancing.

The pantomimes are really popular. The stars of the shows were Angelina, her parents, and the man that Doug fired last night.

But now, they've almost got no one.

Up on the stage, our carnival mechanic guy struggles to perform magic tricks. Lida—the woman who usually runs a popcorn stand—is his assistant. She looks awkward and confused in her ill-fitting leotard.

A man throws his hotdog on the ground. "I've seen classier shows in a strip joint."

I don't know what he means, but he sure gets a strong reaction from the crowd. Some of them clap and cheer him. He grabs the hands of his two small children and marches away.

I catch sight of my father in the crowd. He's staring at the magic act on stage and looking worried. Or angry. I'm not sure which.

Keeping my head down, I keep running.

At the gondola ride, impatient people are standing in a long line, waiting for the spill to be cleaned up so they can have their turn.

Gordon's sitting on his stool, all relaxed. He never cleans anything. Neither Mum nor Dad ever make him. All he does is park himself there on that stool and take the tickets. Occasionally, I see him with a book. He's studying psychology at university and thinks he's some kind of big shot.

"About time someone showed up," Gordon says. "Get the chunks outta there. You've got two minutes." He checks his watch, admiring it as he does so. He has a fancy watch that shows the inner gears through the glass face. Dad gave him that.

Eyeing the soggy, bloated chicken nuggets floating in the water, I instantly know it's going to take much longer than two minutes.

Juggling a bucket and prawn net, I trudge through the water.

On either side of the river are fake palm trees, fake toucans, and treasure chests. It's supposed to look like some kind of pirate adventure. I used to think it looked magical when I was small. Now, it all looks faded and cheesy to me.

I walk around the bend of the river. A huge, golden birdcage hangs from a stand on the left-hand side. Inside the cage, a girl sits listlessly on the swing, dressed in a blue leotard with a gold, feathery headdress and tail feathers. She wears a beak over her nose and mouth.

Angelina.

She's supposed to be swinging in and out of the birdcage—the front side of it is all open and meant for the swing to move freely. But she just sits there. The layers of makeup she's put on have failed to hide her red, swollen eyes.

I try to hide my shock at seeing her. I'd forgotten I'd overheard my father telling Angelina that she should do the birdcage gig now. This was always Angelina's mother's gig—before yesterday.

I pretend to be so caught up in scooping chicken chunks that I don't notice her. But that doesn't work for long.

"Polly," she calls.

I turn. "Oh… Angelina. Hi."

She's removed the beak from her face. "Hi. Have you seen either of my parents around?"

"Sorry… I haven't."

"Your father… he said they've gone travelling. But they wouldn't do that."

I don't answer, because I have no words.

She sniffles and starts crying, yanking off the headdress. Red strands of hair stick to the thick stage makeup on her forehead. "I just want them to come back."

"They will." My voice comes out in squeaks. I turn back to the water. "I have to get this cleaned up."

Each of her sobs feels like a punch to the middle of my back.

Jeers and angry shouts come from the line of people waiting at the entry to the river ride.

Gordon strides towards us on the narrow path at the side, hands in his pockets. “I had to close the ride down. It’s out for the next hour.”

I spin around so fast that chicken nuggets fly from my bucket. “Dad never lets us close rides for that long.”

A lazy smile slides across Gordon’s face. “Well, he’s not here running it. *I am*. Between the mess in the water and Angelina bawling her eyes out, it’s a damned dog’s breakfast.”

“But it wasn’t me being too slow,” I stammer. “Don’t tell Dad I was too slow.”

“I won’t tell him if you finish up here and then get lost.” Gordon jerks his chin up towards Angelina. “What’s up, buttercup?”

“I don’t want to do the birdcage anymore,” she tells him from her swing. “Some of the guys made rude comments about me as they went past on the gondolas. My mum warned me about that. That’s why she never wanted me to do this gig.”

“I’m giving you the afternoon off,” he says, helping her down out of the birdcage.

She stares at him with watery eyes, like he’s some kind of saviour. “But… who’ll do it?”

“I’ll find someone.” He slides a length of her red hair between his fingers. “Another girl won’t look as good as you, but it’ll be okay. Come on, I’ll walk you to the changing rooms so I can grab your costume from you.”

Angelina glances back at me as she walks away with him. She looks scared.

I know where the changing rooms are—they’re on the floor above the funfair building, up a rickety set of stairs next to the Hall of Mirrors. The whole upstairs area is dimly lit—and deserted in between the performers’ costume changes.

My stomach feels hard and wrong, as if I’ve swallowed a large, cold stone. I want to do something, but I don’t know what.

CHAPTER FIFTY-SIX

POLLY, 1989

It's Penny's birthday today.

Often, no one remembers the birthdays of the kids at Mulden Farm. They only seem to remember the men's birthdays, and I think the only reason they remember *them* is so they can have big drinking nights to celebrate.

It's just on dawn when I wake Penny. She's sleepy and doesn't want to get out of bed. But I have to give her the gifts in secret.

I snuck the doll and Halloween show bag back to the farm days ago and have them hidden away. I can't rustle up the same nervous excitement I felt when I took them. I feel horrible when I think about that night. But Penny doesn't know about any of that. I still want her birthday to be special.

I lead her down to an old shed that no one uses anymore.

Her face lights up like Christmas when she sees what I got for her.

She squeals happily and lets out two swear words I didn't even know she knew. Then she surprises me with a hug around my middle. Penny's not big on hugs.

"How'd you get this stuff?" she demands.

"Don't worry about that. D'ya like the doll?"

"She's a beauty. But how'd you get 'er?"

"Not saying. Penny, the important thing is that you've gotta keep it a secret, okay?"

"You stole her, didn't you?"

"She fell off the back of a truck. I just… picked her up."

For a split second, Penny looks dubious. But then her expression goes blank, as if she's decided to accept my explanation.

Tearing open the box, she's nothing but happy again. "I love her. I want a dress just like the one she has. I'd look pretty, wouldn't I?"

"You sure would."

"It's just like a marriage dress."

I frown. "You mean, a *wedding dress*? Guess so. It's white."

"A girl could wear a dress like this and look all pretty, and then hook a rich hubby."

"Huh? You don't get the dress before the husband. Anyway, where'd you hear that? *Wait*. Don't tell me. Adele, right?"

"Uh huh. She says you gotta dress nice if you want a boy that'll buy you stuff."

"I don't think that's the kind of dress she means."

Penny screws up her face. "How do *you* know anything? You haven't even had a boyfriend yet."

"Let's look at the show bag, Penny. Just wait until you see."

We dig through the Halloween show bag together, picking out lollies to eat and playing with the toys. I realise I've actually been having fun for a few minutes and forgetting all the bad stuff.

Penny picks up the doll again. "I'm gonna call her… *Penny*."

"I thought you might." Penny isn't my sister's real name. Her name used to be *Maisie*. But she's insisted we call her Penny ever since she saw an episode of an old TV series called *Lost In Space*.

It's not unusual for people to change their names at the carnival. People do that a lot. Adele used to be named Maude. But she didn't like it, so she changed it. Adele says it doesn't matter because our births aren't registered anyway. Whatever that means.

"I'm gonna keep the doll on my bed," Penny says.

"You can't. I told you. You can't let anyone see your presents."

She shrugs. "Okay, I'll keep her with the others."

"What *others*?"

"My dolls."

"You don't have any."

"Do so. I'll show you."

I follow Penny in confusion as she leads me through the forest. We end up at one of the cabins. My parents let the workers build their cabins wherever they want on our land. There are cabins everywhere, most of them half falling down.

Penny knew the way exactly, as if she came here all the time.

"Whose cabin is this?" I whisper as we sneak inside.

"J.L. That's what Adele calls him. He's her special friend."

"We shouldn't be here."

"S'ok. He hardly ever comes here. And *no one* is gonna try breaking in here and taking his stuff. So, no one's gonna even come here."

"What makes you think no one's gonna do that? Dad's had to fire lotsa workers who ended up being thieves."

"Because he's not a worker. He's a cop."

"Oh."

"And he's mean. I heard him talkin'. He sounds really mean."

"Well, you need to stay away from him."

I realise he must be the man in the blue uniform I saw walk past the Hall of Mirrors last week. Adele had run after him, her lipstick all smudged. I knew she'd been kissing him.

Humming, Penny takes a key from under a boot and unlocks a door. "The cop doesn't come into this room. There's always cobwebs over the door."

I peer into a small, dark room. There's nothing at all in here apart from some shelves, on which a ragged collection of dolls stand. There are Kewpie dolls, Strawberry Shortcake dolls and Star Wars figurines.

"Where did you get all these?" I breathe.

"When kids drop 'em at the carnival, I pick 'em up."

"What if someone sees you? Be careful."

"I *am* careful."

I don't know whether to be proud of her. No wonder she'd instantly guessed that I'd stolen the Barbie doll. She'd been stealing dolls for quite a while now.

"Why didn't you tell me?" I ask.

"Because you'd think it was bad. You're always telling me I have to be *good*."

Penny places the Barbie doll on the shelf. She looks like a shining princess among all the older, grubbier dolls that Penny has.

We sit on the floorboards and make marshmallow ghosts with the kit from the Halloween show bag. Then we play with the dolls.

Penny has an odd way of playing with the dolls.

She places a boy doll on a shelf and then puts five girl dolls around him, and then she marries them, like she's a priest.

"You can't have five brides for one man," I protest.

"Can so. Dad's got lots of girlfriends. Maybe he'll marry 'em all one day."

"No, he doesn't."

In truth, I knew he did. There was lots of talk about our father's various girlfriends around the camp. Sometimes, people called them the *other wives*. We had a few half-brothers and half-sisters here, too. Even our mother and father were some sort of cousins.

"Don't talk about that, Penny," I scold.

"Can if I want. Sometimes, when I'm cranky with our mum, I go to the house of one of Dad's girlfriends. I ask for cakes and sweets—and I get 'em, too. I pretend that she's my mother for the day."

"That's a bad thing to do."

"Why?"

I can't come up with a reason why that's bad, so I don't answer.

Penny seems to be finished playing her marriage game. She begins lining all her toys up on the shelves, and then she gives each of them punishments. She yells the punishments out at the top of her lungs.

Penny really doesn't know how to play with toys.

"Shhh," I warn. "Someone will hear you."

"Who's gonna hear me in the forest? No one, that's who. You can do what you like here, and no one will ever know."

Penny spoke those words in such a sing song way that it gave me chills. She sounded so much like Adele, or like Gordon.

I don't want her to grow up like them.

I realise that as well as stealing dolls, she must be breaking into the cabins. How else would she have known about this room?

Am I any better? I'd just stolen from the carnival, from my own parents.

My happy day is turning grey yet again.

CHAPTER FIFTY-SEVEN

POLLY, 1989

Mum gave Penny a gift for her eighth birthday just before we left for the carnival. It was a Goldilocks outfit. I didn't think it was much of a gift, because it was just a pantomime costume—Penny was about to play Goldilocks in a new show for the carnival. But Penny was over the moon, wanting to wear the outfit straight away.

Today, Adele's mascara is smudged below her eyes, looking like black tears. She just keeps applying more makeup over the smudges, which looks weird.

She screams at the kids in the dodgem car rink every time they even look like trying to crash their car into someone else's.

"You have to stop that," I warn. "Their parents will complain to the carnival management. And that's *Dad*."

"Shut your face," she hisses.

"Did ya have a big fight with your boyfriend or something?" The words slipped out.

She yells at me so loud everyone can hear. "I don't have to answer to an irritating, po-faced little bitch."

I can tell I was right about her boyfriend.

"Make yourself useful and go clean the mirrors," she adds.

"The mirrors? It's not time to clean them yet."

She twists my arm so hard it hurts, and then she shoves me. "Well, I say it is. There's hardly anyone in there right now. Just some old fart who won't leave. Clean the damned toilets, too."

Every head turns my way, mouths open. All the kids and their parents, watching Adele and me. Humiliated, I slink away towards the Hall of Mirrors.

What do people think of us—the carnival family? Do they talk about us? Pity us? With every passing year, I feel it more and more.

I don't belong here. I don't know where I belong.

I grab a spray bottle of cleaner and a cloth and walk into the Hall of Mirrors.

As Adele said, there's an old man wandering around. I've seen him here before. Everyone says he's crazy, but he always seems nice—and kind. Besides Penny, he's the only person who ever smiles at me.

The man stops and stares into a mirror like there's a secret world he can see in there.

I wish that were true. I could just step into a mirror and go to a magical place. I'd take Penny with me. And never come back.

Raising the cleaning bottle, I shoot a stream of solution at a dirty spot on the glass. The solution splutters out and dribbles. The bottle's empty. I need a refill.

But the supply room is upstairs. The dark, stuffy upstairs area always stinks of sickly perfume and greasy makeup. And it's eerie. I don't know if I believe in ghosts, but I always run in and out as quick as I can—just in case.

Leaving the man in his secret mirror world, I head upstairs.

The first room is where they keep the dust-covered prizes for the amusement stalls. Stuffed toy lions and giraffes that teenage boys win for their girlfriends.

The next two rooms are for the carnival performers to change into their costumes. All the costumes are kept here, too.

Right at the end of the corridor is the room where the cleaning supplies are stored.

Voices come from one of the dressing rooms. I feel better, because people are here—until I figure out that one of those voices is Gordon's. I don't know who the other person is. I can just barely hear the small voice of a girl.

The door is open a crack. I can look, if I'm careful. Stepping just close enough to see in, I peer around the door frame.

The girl is Angelina.

What I see instantly feels wrong.

Gordon's helping her into her Cinderella dance costume, zipping up the back of it. His face is almost buried in her long, red hair.

As soon as the zip is up, Angelina spins and retreats from him. "I'd better go. The show starts in a few minutes."

"It's in half an hour," Gordon replies in a crooning tone. "Why don't you do your warm-up in here?"

Her voice is rigid when she speaks again. "I normally do that with the other dancers, to make sure we're all in sync."

"You're the best dancer we've got, now. You don't even need the others. I want to see what you can do… without all the others around."

She pulls clumsily at the elastic of her costume. "I don't want to… if that's okay."

"An-gel-ee-na." He draws out the syllables of her name in a way that makes my skin crawl. "You're being difficult. I said I want to see what you can do."

"I… okay. Just for a minute."

She begins her routine.

I've seen the routine many times, but it's never looked as awkward as it does now. There's no music, no crowds, no rumble of carnival rides in the background. There's just the shuffle and tap of dance shoes on an old wooden floor.

"Your hair doesn't look right," Gordon tells her. "Come here."

She steps across the floorboards to him, her head dropping low.

Taking out a comb from his pocket, he runs it slowly through the locks of her hair. "You look a little messy, Angelina." With his hands on her shoulders, he turns her around so that her back is to him. He continues to comb her hair, watching her and himself in the narrow mirror in front of them.

Her eyes squeeze shut, hands curled tight at her sides.

I want to say something, but I don't know what. I'm just… *Polly*.

The empty bottle of cleaner falls through my fingers and makes a dull clatter on the floor.

Both Gordon and Angelina whirl around.

Angelina's eyes are wide, relieved. Gordon's expression instantly turns to anger.

"What are you doing, Polly?" he demands.

Scooping up the bottle, I hold it out as evidence. "*This*. I need more cleaning fluid."

His teeth are set together. "The cleaning supply cupboards aren't in this room."

Angelina's already running to get the masquerade mask for her Cinderella costume. "Time for me to go."

Gordon's eyes are still fixed on me.

He storms out.

Angelina turns to me. "I'm glad you came up here, Polly."

"Are you… okay?"

"No, I'm not okay. I want my parents to come back. I don't want Gordon helping me anymore. He's… getting weirder and weirder."

Her shoulders crumple, as if she's scared of what she's just said.

"He'll be back at university soon—after summer. You won't have to see him at all, then."

"But that's months away."

I stare at Angelina in the mirror in front of us, seeing what Gordon sees for perhaps the first time. Angelina is beautiful. She's tall like her father, Anthony, and she has his red hair. She has the olive skin and large, upturned eyes of her mother, Tiên. Tiên is a beauty, too. Angie told me once that her mother is Vietnamese, and her name means *angel* in the Vietnamese language.

With a start, I remember all over again that Tiên and Anthony are dead.

Frowning, Angelina runs an eye over me. "Are you all right, Polly?"

"Yes… sorry."

"You know, maybe you could become a dancer, too. I can teach you. Then we can stick together, and I won't be so alone."

"Me? I can't be a dancer. I'm not… *pretty*."

"You could be, with a few changes. A bit of stage makeup. A different hairstyle."

"Adele says I'll never be a performer. Penny's different. She loves the stage. Not me." I shrugged. "Adele doesn't want to do the stage either. She says there are better ways of making money."

Angelina's eyes are glistening now, her eyelashes wet. "Be careful of Adele."

"I know. She says weird stuff. Like, girls have to snag a rich boyfriend."

"No, it's not that. Polly, can you keep a secret?"

I nod, but inside, I'm squirming. I don't want to know any more secrets. My head is already stuffed full of secrets that I never wanted to know.

Angelina crosses her thin arms across her body. "Adele's trying to convince me to do some… *photographs*. Like… without my clothes on."

My mind blanks with horror. I can't speak.

"Adele says it's no different to being a performer on stage," Angelina tells me. "She does it with her boyfriend, and then they sell the pictures."

"She can't make you do *that*."

Angelina bursts into tears. "I want my mum. I feel so… alone."

Tears prick my own eyes.

I have to tell her about her parents. I have to.

But I can't. The adults are in charge. I'm just a stupid little kid.

"I'm sorry," I tell her. "I hope you see your mum again… soon. I better get back to my job. Adele will be on the warpath if I'm gone too long."

I turn and dash out, then run up the hall to the supply cupboard. I haven't refilled the bottle yet. I don't even worry about ghosts now. There are worse things than ghosts.

I return downstairs to the Hall of Mirrors.

My spine runs cold to find Gordon there. He's standing in front of a mirror and gazing at himself.

His head looks big and shapeless in the mirror.

When he notices me, his expression changes. "What did you say to Angelina? She ran out of here like the devil was chasing her."

"She was worried about being late for her Cinderella show."

"She wasn't late. She should be listening to *me*, anyway, not worrying about her performances. *I'm* her boss."

"No, you're not. Dad is." I suck in a breath at speaking to Gordon so boldly.

He turns to face me. "Doug and I are in charge when Dad's not around. Don't ever forget that. Oh, and I got rid of the batshit crazy guy who was hanging around in here. I told him he'd get his face kicked in if he ever steps foot in the carnival again. That's what happens to people who don't do what we say."

I don't trust myself to speak to him again. Taking my spray bottle and cloth, I walk around to the next hall in the mirror maze, and I start cleaning.

The idea crawls into my head that Gordon might have been one of the men who were carrying Angelina's dead parents through the woods. Maybe Doug, too.

Did Angelina's parents do something wrong, and then they were punished?

I hadn't let myself think too hard on why they'd been strung up in the tree. I'd tried to push the images of that night out.

But now, thoughts wind around and around in my mind, sharp and twisting.

CHAPTER FIFTY-EIGHT

POLLY, 1989

For weeks, Gordon chased after Angelina, hanging about the changing rooms. Things got worse. He began making her dance for him between costume changes, when she was barely wearing anything at all.

Angelina grew quieter and quieter. So quiet, she barely spoke to me anymore.

Dad was away a lot. He'd brought shipments of things in on his truck—shipments I never saw. I'd just hear the clang of metal-on-metal late at night. I knew he was storing the stuff some place where there was a metal door.

When Penny wasn't doing her Goldilocks pantomime or her chores, she kept sneaking off into the forest, to play with her dolls and break into people's cabins.

And Adele grew meaner.

It's just a week away from Christmas now. But there are no Christmas decorations on Mulden Farm, apart from the pinecones that Penny and I painted and strung up with fishing line. I know that the only indication that it's even Christmas is that there'll be cherries and ham and prawns.

But, this morning, I'm not even thinking about Christmas.

I'm lying in bed, trying to muster up the courage to approach my mother about what Gordon is doing to Angelina. My heart feels like a drum. *Boom… boom… boom.* I could get in big trouble for telling on Gordon. Or get Angelina in trouble.

The sun is just coming up. The air in our cottage is so muggy that I woke feeling sticky. It's going to be a hot day.

I find Mum in the kitchen, making a big pot of porridge. She wears one of her faded, floral dresses. Her face and hands look even redder than usual in the light of the intense, crimson sunrise. The skin on her face is rough and lined, her blonde hair hanging in dry wisps.

I'm struck by how different Mum is to Adele. Mum never wears makeup—she says makeup is for showgirls and show ponies. She's never mean like Adele is. She's just kind of… absent. It feels like she just drifts about the house, doing what she has to, not connected to anyone.

She reminds of the spider that used to live above our front door—all by itself, making the exact same web day after day, never seeming to catch anything. Until one day, I found it hanging by a single thread—dead and shrivelled.

"Mum?"

She nods without turning around.

"I need to tell you something."

"What do you need to tell me, Polly?"

I blurt it out. "Gordon's been going into the changing rooms when Angelina's in there. He's… he's making her dance for him in her underwear."

She half-turns, mouth agape with horror.

But then she shakes her head with an exasperated sigh and returns to stirring the pot. "I caught him doing something like that years ago. I whipped his legs 'til they bled. Can't change him now. He's all growed up."

"But he can't do that to her… right?"

"He shouldn't."

"He's making her scared."

"Did she say that?"

"Yes."

"She's sixteen though—"

"Thirteen."

"Really? Such a tall girl—looks older. Anyway, she's not a child anymore. She's got to learn to keep men at bay, like all us women do."

"Mum, you have to make Gordon stop."

"And how would I do that…?"

I'm struck silent by her reply. I can't even make sense of it. I draw a deep breath and tell her, "I… I don't know. I'm not an adult."

"Go get me some milk for the porridge, Polly."

I stand there for a moment, stunned that the discussion seems to have ended already. I fetch her the milk, trying to think how I can convince her that Gordon is a problem that needs fixing.

As she pours the milk into the pot, she looks up for a moment and stares through the kitchen window.

She freezes.

The milk drains out, splashing everywhere, until the whole bottle is emptied into the porridge.

At first, I think what I just told her must finally be sinking in. But then I realise it's something outside the window that's disturbing her.

I hope it's Gordon out there. And I hope she's about to march out and yell at him.

I peek out the window.

It's not Gordon.

In the distance, police are sneaking across the grounds. They have guns—big black rifles.

Mum's voice is coarse when she speaks. "Polly, get your father. *Get him now.*"

"What's happening?"

"Trouble, that's what."

I tear inside, but instead of going to get Dad, I rush into my bedroom and shake Penny awake. I don't know why the police are here, but Penny's the only one I care about.

No, I also care about Angelina. And that's why I have to go and make sure that she's okay.

Taking my sleepy sister by the hand, I help her climb out our window. Staying well out of the way of the police, we run to Angelina's caravan.

Angelina's already up and dressed, in jeans, an old T-shirt and hooded denim jacket. Her thick hair is back in a ponytail. At first, I barely recognise her. It's one of the handful of times I've ever seen her without heavy makeup. She and her parents didn't use to mix with the rest of us—they'd stay in their caravan after the working day was done and eat their own food.

Yawning, Penny throws herself down on Angelina's bed and curls up into a ball.

"Why are you two here, Polly?" Angelina asks.

"Have you seen what's happening out there?"

She frowns at me, shaking her head.

"There are cops with guns everywhere," I tell her. "Something's really, *really* wrong."

Taking a step across to the window, she draws the curtain back.

Our dogs are circling one of the cops, barking and jumping at him. He shoots at one of them, and the dogs run away, yelping.

Angelina and I gasp and draw back.

Angelina turns to me, catching her breath. "I'm not surprised the police are here, to be honest. I overheard my parents talking a month or so ago—about drugs and stolen stuff being sold here."

I swallow. "I don't want to know about that."

"Of course you don't, Polly. You're a Mulden."

Her sharp retort stings me.

But I have no reply. I hadn't exactly defended the carnival, but I hadn't sounded horrified, either. And I know why. It's because I'd already heard about the stolen goods and the drugs. And I'd seen worse. I'd seen dead people.

"Don't be scared," Angelina tells me, scooping up a backpack from the floor. "It's not your fault. The police won't hurt you and Penny."

"I'll kick them if they try to hurt me," Penny says, still curled up on the bed.

"Don't do that," Angelina warns her. "The police aren't bad people. Not all of them anyway. If you want to kick anyone, kick Gordon or Adele."

She stuffs clothes into the backpack—jackets and jeans and underwear.

As I watch her, my heart twists into a knot. "You're running away… *aren't you*?"

She squashes two books into her bag and then slides money into a zippered compartment. "No. I'm not running away, because I have no one to run away from. I'm just… leaving."

"I don't want you to go. You're like a big sister to Penny and me."

She pauses for a moment. "I think your carnival is finished. Everyone's going to go."

Penny screws up her face. "Does that mean I don't get to be Goldilocks anymore?"

Angelina bends to ruffle Penny's hair. Then she loops the straps of her backpack over her shoulders.

I grab hold of Angelina's arm. "Please stay."

"I need to find my parents."

"Angelina…."

"Yes?"

I can scarcely breathe. "What if… what if you don't ever find them?"

She stares at me like I've gone crazy. "That's a horrible thing to say."

"I'm sorry—I didn't mean it like that."

"I know you didn't." She gives Penny and me quick hugs. "You two are the only people I'm going to miss from this place."

Tucking her bright hair into the hood of her jacket, she steps out the door.

And heads straight into the forest.

PART V

CHAPTER FIFTY-NINE

DETECTIVE KATE WAKELAND

DECEMBER 2019

I sat there stunned as Polly ended her story.

As she'd shared her memories, the surrounding environment of the women's prison yard had fallen away, replaced by the world of the 1989 Tallman's Valley carnival.

I could almost see the nine-year-old Polly in the woman she was now.

My thoughts scattered. There'd been so many revelations in what she'd said, it'd taken my breath away.

"I… don't know where to start," I told her. "I can't tell you how much I appreciate you telling me all of this. Your sister told me a little before—but just fragments."

Leaning down, Polly stretched to pluck a rose from her garden. "Penny doesn't remember a lot. I think she's shutting it out. But *I* remember everything."

"I had little idea of the whole picture, how life was for you both back then."

She arranged and rearranged her picked flowers into a bunch, with the baby's breath on the bottom and the roses and proteas on top. "What I just told you was only the last month or so of the carnival. There was so much more."

"I can only imagine."

She continued arranging her flowers. "My father ended up shot by the police during that raid. He died in hospital months later. I was in foster care when he died. They asked if I wanted to go to his funeral. I didn't. Then my mother died—three months later, of heart failure—just before she was due to attend court."

"I've seen the court documentation. With your parents both dead, the prosecutors had lost their key defendants. And the police didn't find much evidence of illegal and stolen goods. They did find evidence of child neglect, including a boy that was tied up."

"That was Ricky. They found lots of kids that were being neglected—left on the farm while their parents went to work at the carnival." Polly kept her head down. "When I was a kid, I didn't understand why Angie's parents were murdered. But I do now."

"Because of what they knew," I said softly.

Polly's shoulders shuddered as she exhaled. "Yes. Us Muldens were bad people. Like I said, just before Angie left the carnival, she threw it in my face that I was a *Mulden*. It hurt so badly. I was from a family who murdered people. I don't even know how to reconcile that."

"You were a child, Polly."

"I could have at least done the right thing by Angelina. I could have told the police about what happened to her parents. I could have told them what my brother was doing to her. But… I didn't." She shook her head, her face creased in anguish. "I heard it in the news a few months back—Gordon called himself *The Lullaby Man,* and he did horrible things to young girls."

"Yes, he was *The Lullaby Man.* But you're not to blame. *He* is."

A tear splashed on her cheek. "I kept watch on Angie all this time, trying to look out for her. But I kept my distance… because of the guilt I felt inside."

I inhaled a long, steady breath. That explained why Polly had been keeping track of Angie. She hadn't had any bad intent.

"Polly…" I said, "we've recently discovered that Angie had a stalker during the past few months that she lived on Fraser Island."

She raised her face to me, shocked. "A *stalker*?"

"Do you have any idea who that could have been?"

She shook her head. "I'd have said Gordon. But… he's been in prison.

Besides that, he'd only have been interested in Angie when she was a kid. It could have been Adele—she hated Angie. But, of course, Adele's been overseas. So, it can't be her."

"Why did Adele hate Angie?"

"Because she thinks it was Angie's parents who ratted out the carnival to the police—and caused it to be shut down."

"Oh, okay."

Polly shivered. "You need to find her—Adele. She's... *bad.* As bad as Gordon. Maybe worse. She'd know a lot more than me about the carnival, too. She was older."

"Believe me, we're trying. She's running from us in the Philippines right now."

"One thing about Adele—she'll keep going 'til the bitter end. She'll never, ever give in. I know her. You'll have to corner her like a rat in a cage."

"I'm hoping that happens very soon."

There was something else about Adele pressing on my mind.

Her boyfriend from when she was sixteen.

There'd been lots of things to unpack in Polly's story, but this was something that stood out in bright, flashing, warning lights. Polly had said he was a cop. I wanted to know exactly who that cop was.

"Polly, you said Adele had a boyfriend back in the carnival days—the police officer. You said his name was J.L?"

Polly nodded.

"Do you know his full name—or at least *one* of his names?"

"I'm afraid I don't."

"Did you ever get a look at his face?"

"No, I didn't see his face. I only ever saw him once. The night that I found Angelina's parents dead."

"Do you have any other memory of him? Body shape or whatever?"

"Oh, yes—as I said, I remember everything clearly. He was tall, broad shouldered... short dark hair. Walked with a swagger. As for his age, I'm unsure. At the time, he seemed so much older to me. But, looking back, he might have been anywhere from eighteen up."

I exhaled. "Okay. And... you said he had a cabin at Mulden Farm—the cabin where Penny was keeping her dolls?"

"Yes."

"I wonder if the cabin is still there...?"

"It might be. The land that my family owned has been abandoned all these years. I mean, it passed onto Doug, but he hasn't done anything with it."

I felt gears spinning inside my head. I needed to track down J.L. Where was he now? And was he still in the police force?

"I'll go and leave you in peace now," I said to Polly. "Thank you so much for all you've told me today. It's been eye-opening."

Polly bundled up the flowers into two bunches. "I want to give one of these to you, as a token for all the pain I caused to you and your family. I know it's nothing, but I do mean it sincerely."

I took the flowers. "Thank you, Polly."

I never would have pictured myself thanking the woman who'd helped the abductor of my granddaughter. But this was the place in which I'd found myself.

She handed me the second bunch, then. "Please… would you give these to Angie? I know she won't be able to see them, but could you tell her they're from me?"

"Of course. I don't know if they'll be allowed into her hospital room, but I'll be sure to describe them to her if I can't."

A tear ran down Polly's face. "I appreciate it."

CHAPTER SIXTY

DETECTIVE KATE WAKELAND

I walked into the police station with the two flower bunches Polly had given me.

Melainey, sitting at his desk, nodded towards the flowers. "For me?" he quipped.

"Nope," I said.

Franco looked over from his desk. "Not for me, thanks. Flowers make me sneeze."

I grinned. "Well, aren't you two a pair of comedians?"

I placed the flowers on my desk. "I need to talk with you two."

Franco and Melainey walked across to me.

"What's up?" asked Franco.

"I've just been to see Polly," I said.

"Prison Polly?" asked Franco.

"Yes, that one," I said. "I realised something this morning, and I went to check it out with her. It's about Angie's parents—her birth parents." I paused, taking a breath. "They are the bunker victims."

Melainey whistled. "How can you be sure?"

"Polly saw them. Hung from nooses on a tree. Back when she was nine years old."

Franco shook his head, frowning. "What if she's just making things up?"

"I don't think she is," I said. "It makes sense. Those two people have never been heard from since the day they left the carnival. I'm going to assume they are the ones who went to the police with information about the carnival's criminal activities. But they were murdered before they could leave."

"If they went to the police," Franco said, "then wouldn't the police have been suspicious when they vanished?"

"You'd think so," I replied. "But hardly anything was documented by the police who carried out the raid. They don't seem to have investigated properly. And there's only one name given of the police involved. He died a few years after the raid."

Melainey nodded. "Are you thinking some dirty business went on?"

"Yes," I said. "Exactly that. Polly even thinks there was a cop who lived at the carnival back then."

"Wouldn't surprise me at all," Melainey told me. "You and me, Wakeland, we were about during the days of dirty cops. Brought a few of them to justice, too." He eyed Franco. "You missed all that excitement—you would have been too young."

Franco crossed his arms, turning to me. "Anyway, you'd better let forensics know you might have an ID on the victims."

"Yes," I agreed. "I'll do that."

"Well, speaking of the bunker," Franco said, "Melainey and I were just about to head out there. There are still lots more items to be brought out."

"Want to come along, Wakeland?" Melainey asked me. "This is your parade, after all."

I shook my head. "I've got some things to go ahead with here."

Melainey shrugged. "Okay. Well, we'll let you know if we find anything juicy."

After he and Franco left, I called the forensics team, and talked with them about the identity of the bunker victims.

It was time to look into who J.L was.

My first port of call was Detective Liz Booth.

"I've got a question for you," I said when Liz answered the phone.

"Sounds interesting," she said. "Shoot."

"Liz, I know you've looked much deeper into Adele's past than I have. Did you happen to find anything about her having a cop for a boyfriend—back when she was a teenager?"

"A *cop*? Can't say that I have. You've got me intrigued now."

"It was Polly who told me. She ended up agreeing to talk with me again.

She divulged a *lot*. And, apparently, Adele was seeing a cop when she was sixteen. I want to know who he is."

"Way to go, Polly. Well, damn, I want to know who he is, too."

"Apparently, he kept a cabin on the Mulden family farm. He had to be doing a lot more there than just hanging out with Adele."

"I'd place bets on it. We'll drag that information out of Adele once we get our hands on her. Do you have a name for him?"

"Unfortunately not. Polly only knew of him as J.L."

"J.L? Pity. A name would go a long way."

"Yes, it would. How's things going for you over there?"

"I think we're getting closer, but it's two steps forward, one step back."

"You sound exhausted, poor thing."

"I admit I haven't been sleeping. Because Adele's certainly not. She's as slippery as a damned eel."

"You'll get her."

"When that day comes, I'll be ready with a glass of champers. My Filipino police partner—Rosa Alonto— recommends Bollinger. We're planning on toasting together once we've got hold of Adele."

Liz was trying hard to sound upbeat, but she had a quality to her voice that sounded bone-tired and intensely focused at the same time. It was a dangerous mix. I knew that the months Liz had spent engaged in the international chase for Adele must be taking its toll.

"I'll be cheering you both on from here," I said. "But… promise me you'll take care of yourself, Liz. Okay? Take time out. And get some decent sleep."

Liz assured me she'd do those things, but I didn't know if I believed her. I worried for her.

After the call ended, I began planning out my next steps.

I needed to contact Adele's only child—*Nola*.

If I could avoid it, I wouldn't bother Nola at all. But this was too important.

It was only this year Nola had told me about the terrible things her mother did to her—from the time she was just twelve years old. Forcing her to pose for photographs and videos. As soon as Adele had gotten wind of her daughter's revelations, that was when she'd skipped out of Australia and gone on the run.

Nola was twenty-four now. She'd never even known that her mother had grown up in a carnival—until a few months ago.

I called her on the phone.

She was out of breath when she answered.

"Oh… Kate. Hi. I'm on a run at the park."

"Sorry to interrupt. How are you, Nola?"

"Trying to keep busy. Trying not to think too much."

"Going for a run always helps. It helps *me* anyway."

"I never was a runner. But I'm giving it a go. What's on your mind?"

"Is it okay if I ask a question—about Adele?"

Her voice immediately clouded. "Yes, of course."

"I've been looking into her past, and I've discovered a boyfriend named J.L. It was during the carnival years. It seems he lived on Mulden Farm, in his own cabin. I was wondering—did she ever mention him?"

"Not that I remember. She was pretty close-lipped about her past."

"I know. And I'm so sorry to call you about this. It was just a wild thought, really. Your mother had, uh—"

"Don't call her *my mother*. I don't want to think of her as that *ever again*. Because she never was."

"God, I'm sorry. That was thoughtless of me."

"I didn't mean to bite your head off. I've been doing really well, but then I saw the news about the bunker, and I'm feeling raw all over again. It's horrible—two people *murdered*. And you know, I'm part of that family. I'm one of *them*."

"By blood only. You're a good person, Nola. You're doing good things."

"Thank you. I try. Most of the time, though, I feel like I don't have a clue. Especially with Max."

Max was Penny's son—in Nola's care while Penny was in the remand centre. In all likelihood, Penny would go to prison, and she would never get Max back.

"How is he?" I asked.

"He's good," she replied. "But he's so quiet. I wish I knew how to draw him out of his shell."

"It'll take time… and love. He's been through a lot."

"Yes, he really has." She went silent for a moment. "Kate, I just thought of something. It's just a small thing and probably not important. Adele used to collect keys and keyrings. They're still in her house. The police took some items of hers for evidence, but I don't think they took those."

"What made you think of the keys and keyrings?"

"Because they go way back. I mean, I never knew about her past—I thought her carnival keyrings were just retro items she'd bought at flea markets or something. Anyway, maybe one of them used to belong to the boyfriend you mentioned?"

"Sounds good enough for me to go have a look, Nola."

She'd certainly piqued my interest. The old carnival was gone—razed to the ground—but many of the cabins that'd belonged to the carnival workers still stood. They were dotted across the land next to the Iversons' property—the land that Polly had told me still belonged to the Mulden family.

"Whereabouts did she keep the keyrings?" I asked Nola.

"Last I saw, they were in the top drawer of her dressing table. Are you going there now?"

"Yes, I might as well. I spoke with Polly earlier—she told me Adele liked to walk around with lots of keys on her belt as a teenager. Sounds fitting she has a drawer full of keys."

"Oh, I really like Aunt Polly. I've been getting to know her when I take Max to the prison to see his mother. I didn't even know Aunt Polly existed until this year. And Aunt Penny, well, I only ever saw her once when I was a child. Except, my mother told me she was just a friend. I always thought my mother was an only child."

"That's a big shame. I think Polly and Penny would have loved you as a niece when you were growing up."

"Adele completely cut me off from anyone who might have shown me love." She hesitated, inhaling an audible breath. "Kate, I'm coming down to the house."

"*You are*? Are you sure you want to?"

"Yes. I've only been back to the house once since I left as a teenager. That was a few months ago, when I opened it up for the police. I think it's time for me to go cast out some demons."

CHAPTER SIXTY-ONE

Adele's house was close to Coldwater Lake.

It was an ordinary two-storey building, with vines criss-crossing the exterior. Extensive paving kept the grounds fairly neat, but the long grass growing along the side fence showed that the house had stood empty for months. A birdbath held a bowl of foul-looking water and weeds.

It was awful to contemplate what'd gone on behind closed doors here at this house.

Nola pulled up behind me in her small hatchback car.

When she stepped up to me, I drew her into a hug. I'd grown very fond of this young woman. Her nervous way of speaking belied the core of inner strength she had.

We walked up the front stairs together. The police had gained permanent access to Adele's property the day after she'd gone on the run from the law. She'd lost the right to any kind of privacy.

Nola straightened herself, shooting me a quick, determined glance.

I unlocked the door and we stepped inside.

The interior smelled like stale cigarette smoke. The carpet was the colour of moss. Yellowed wallpaper ran along the hallway.

As I walked through to the living room, the first thing I noticed were the paintings of young, half-nude women adorning the walls. I was no prude, but the paintings seemed obscene in this setting.

Nola winced. "I hated those pictures when I was a kid. It was like they were speaking to me: *This is all you'll ever be. Just a body, to be leered at.*"

"You know what? Let's get them off the walls. Get rid of them. If you want, that is."

For a second, Nola held back, staring around as if she were still a child and under her mother's rule.

Then she marched up to a painting and tore it off the wall. Throwing it down, she kicked it over and over. I helped take down the rest of them, stacking them behind a sofa.

"Better?" I asked her.

"Not yet." She continued through the house. I could hear crashing sounds as painting after painting came down. Nola screamed as she ripped each picture from the wall.

I didn't go try to calm her down—I sensed that this was what she needed to do.

Adele and Nola's bedrooms were almost the only rooms in the house where the paintings were absent. Now that the paintings were gone, there was... *nothing*. Just two framed photographs of Adele above the fireplace, from the days when she must have been in her twenties.

But there was absolutely nothing at all of Nola. No photos of her anywhere. Nothing to say that a young girl had once lived here.

Nola reached for the photos of Adele and tossed them across the room. They crashed into the wall opposite, cracking it inward.

She looked at me, and then she tore away to a room at the back of the house. It was the only room she hadn't yet entered.

I followed her.

Inside the room, there was a single four poster bed, with a sheer canopy and a pink, frilly coverlet. Toy stuffed animals sat against the pillow, staring blankly at us with their painted eyes. Jewelled hairbrushes and hair clips sat on a bedside table.

It wasn't Nola's bedroom—I'd already seen that. Her room had been fairly plain.

I made a guess that this was where Adele had made Nola pose for the nude photos and videos when she was a child. The second eldest of the Mulden children—Gordon—had been one of the customers that Adele had brought into this house. He must have spent time right here in this room. The thought was sickening.

Nola swept the brushes and hair clips off the table and then snatched the coverlet and pillows from the bed—until everything was strewn across the floor.

She stood in front of a shelf now. A single framed photograph occupied the shelf. Her back crumpled and her expression went numb.

The photo was of Nola, my daughter, Abby, and a friend of theirs—Layla Maddox—all in bikinis down at the lake. They were twelve or thirteen years old.

Breath left my lungs to see my daughter in *that* photo, in *this* room. And poor little Layla. She hadn't gotten much older than she was in this picture before she died.

The ceramic frame had bluebirds painted on it. It was an innocent photo, but it hadn't been put there for innocent reasons.

Abby had known Layla well, but she'd barely known Nola in those days. Adele had kept Nola locked up in the house, except to go to school.

"You want this photo gone?" I asked her.

"I just want it out of *here*. Cooper Tecklenburg took this photo of us. It's special. My mother insisted on putting it on the shelf, but it was never *hers*."

Cooper Tecklenburg and his brother Davey had been friends with Abby, Nola and Layla back in those days. They'd been nice young boys, unlike Gordon—who'd been a middle-aged man preying upon young girls.

"Done." I scooped up the picture.

She nodded. "I'll take you to see the collection of keys now."

I followed her to Adele's bedroom. Nola opened up the top drawer of her mother's dressing table. The deep drawer contained hundreds of keys and even more keyrings.

I picked up a keyring. "She was certainly fond of these things."

Nola twisted her mouth. "I never did figure out what the big attraction was."

"Your aunt Polly said Adele used to keep bunches of keys on her belt that she didn't need. Maybe they made her feel a sense of power."

"That'd describe Adele to a tee. She loved holding power over people."

Nola and I cleared off the dressing table and then began the task of placing all the keyrings in rows on top of it. As Nola had said, Adele had kept lots of keyrings from the carnival. Some of them even had the carnival logo on them. There were also keyrings that must have been from trips Adele took to places like Bali and the Bahamas and New York City.

I picked up a keyring from Cebu City, the Philippines. It seemed that Adele had been to the Philippines before. No wonder she knew her way around there now.

"Did she ever take you holidaying to these places?" I asked Nola curiously.

"Nope. She always just left me here. She'd stock the pantry with food, and then off she'd go. I'd have to get myself off to school and make my own dinners."

"My goodness—she left you all alone?"

"Yes. I was about seven the first time she went away for a weekend. The trips started getting longer and longer. I was happy when she went, though. I felt… free."

"I really wish I'd known about you back then."

Nola gave me a tight smile in reply. "I wish I'd known to tell someone. I didn't know."

"Kids often don't." I rubbed her arm. "I'm proud of how far you've come—this was such a terrible start for a child."

"Thank you. Means a lot that someone's proud of me. No one's ever been *that.*"

Turning, she continued sorting through the keyrings.

She snatched up a dull brass keyring. "Bingo. It's got J.L scratched into the back of it."

"Oh, fantastic! Well done, you."

Her eyes were serious as she faced me. "I hope it helps. And I hope Detective Booth finds Adele. She doesn't deserve to be free even one more day."

I put an arm around Nola. "No, she doesn't. Hey, how about we grab a coffee? Just for some downtime. Coming here can't have been easy for you."

She nodded. "Coffee sounds perfect."

As we made our way out of the house, Nola took one last glance around.

I locked up the house, and we walked back into the broad sunshine.

CHAPTER SIXTY-TWO

After coffee with Nola, I headed home. I was bone-tired, my head buzzing with Polly's revelations.

I tried to hide my exhaustion from Pete, heading straight upstairs for a shower. I'd promised him I'd take it easy today, but in truth, I'd done nothing but run about.

Pete and I had our usual wine out on the deck that night.

I ended up sleeping well. No more disturbing dreams—none that woke me up anyway.

I headed to the station at eight in the morning, feeling renewed.

Franco and Melainey were at the bunker on Witness Mountain, cataloguing the items as they were extracted.

I grabbed a cold can of soda and headed into the homicide study room.

After hearing Polly's recollections about the young police officer named J.L, I was very motivated to find out exactly who he was.

I switched on a computer and ran a search, looking for the names of any male officers who'd worked out of the Tallman's Valley police station in 1989. My own knowledge was sketchy. I'd worked in the city back then, not here.

I searched through the list, looking for any officers with the initials J.L.

There were no perfect matches. Just two half-matches:

Jiro Shintani

Joshua Lee Parker

Inspector Jiro Shintani had been a constable in 1989. He started the year at Tallman's Valley, but he'd moved to Sydney a few months later. All he had in common with J.L was a first name that began with J. He had no middle name. Anyway, I discounted Shintani as a possibility. There was no way he could be J.L.

The second name was Joshua Lee Parker. He'd been a constable in 1989, too. He'd left the force in 1998, after an injury. His hair was blond, and he was short in stature. Polly had been sure that J.L's hair was dark and that he'd been tall. Joshua wasn't the mysterious J.L.

I ran another search, this time looking for probationary constables from 1989. Perhaps J.L had only just joined the police force.

The name that popped up gave me a jolt.

Jace Luciano Franco.

This wasn't possible. In 1989, Franco would only have been eighteen. And Franco had told me he joined the police force in his late twenties.

A cold thread of worry tugged at my insides.

Franco's first two names started with a J and an L. Jace Luciano.

But Franco could not have had anything to do with the carnival—or with Adele. Because that would mean he'd been lying to me all along.

No, I *knew* Franco. I did, didn't I?

I couldn't deny that this discovery had rattled me to my core.

I sat there in silence, digging deep into the past years I'd spent as Franco's police partner, replaying everything.

It was one of the worst things I'd ever had to do in my time as a detective.

At the end of it, I drew a steady breath. No, Franco was not J.L. Of that I was certain. I knew enough about Franco to know he'd never be involved in anything shady.

There had to be some other explanation for a Tallman's Valley cop to have used the initials J.L.

I just had to find out what that explanation was.

Meanwhile, I had J.L's cabin key burning a hole in my pocket.

Leaving the station, I began the trip over to Witness Mountain.

A small truck seemed to take the same roads as me. Was I being followed?

The truck was too far away for my police vehicle to detect its licence plate number. When I pulled off the road, the truck slowed and then veered off down a side street.

It might have been co-incidence that the truck had taken the same route as me. But still, I was wary.

Fifteen minutes later, I set foot on the land owned by Doug Overmire.

Wild grasses covered the open land as far as I could see. The forest was hidden from my view by the hills.

This was where Polly, Penny, Adele, Doug and Gordon had grown up. Thirty years ago, it had been a very different place.

With Polly's stories of Mulden Farm thick in my mind, I began walking.

I didn't have a clear direction in which to head. Polly had tried to give me an idea of where J.L's cabin might be, but the problem was that many of the landmarks she remembered were now gone.

Someone—perhaps either Polly's mother or father—had set fire to their cottage just before the police took them away. So, that was gone. And trees and shrubs would now be occupying a lot of the land that used to be cleared.

The sun burned the back of my neck as I walked to the crest of the nearest hill. There was a collection of cabins and cottages in a loose ring on the land below. That must have been the main hub and where Polly's house had been.

Slapping away flies, I headed down to the circle. The buildings were all sagging; the wood bleached grey and the windows cracked.

One thing Polly had told me was that J.L's cabin sat between her house and where she used to hear the bunker being opened and closed.

I knew where the bunker was located. I guessed if I walked in that direction, I'd find J.L's cabin.

Using a map on my phone to orientate myself, I began walking.

I found cabins along the way, but none that fit with Adele's key. Some of them were unlocked—they'd never even had locks fitted.

In the thick of the forest, a cabin stood completely on its own. Grass grew on its roof. A small canopy over a porch protected the front door. Using a stick, I poked dirt from the lock and then tried the key.

A perfect fit.

I'd found J.L's cabin.

I pushed the door open. Apart from a pair of boots and an oilskin jacket hanging from a hook, the interior was empty.

I searched the pockets of the jacket and emptied out the boots. There was nothing in either except for spiders.

Two doors led to other rooms.

The door on the right was locked, and the keys I had wouldn't open it. A swift kick cracked it inward.

Inside the room, a mattress was decaying through the springs of a rusted bed. Dust swirled in a stray beam of light coming through a hole in the roof. A wooden cabinet had been nailed to the wall—its doors hanging open and exposing its empty shelves. A lacy bra was tangled on the floorboards, covered in dirt. Had that been Adele's? Polly said Adele had posed for photographs in this cabin.

Returning to the main room, I tried the other door.

This was it. Where Penny's secret stash of dolls had been. There were only a handful of figurines left.

What Polly had told me was all lining up… but there was nothing here that would identify who'd owned this cabin.

A deep breath of disappointment entered my lungs. The only thing I could do now was to get forensics in here to search for any DNA. Slim chance of finding anything useful. Wind had swept rain and dirt through most of the cabin.

I entered the bedroom again, hoping to spot something I'd missed before.

I peered under the bed. Nothing except for dead moths.

Climbing on top of the bed's frame, I had a good look at the cabinet. I still couldn't see on top of it. Reaching on tiptoes, I felt around.

There was something thin and plastic here. Gently, I tugged at it.

I lost my balance, managing to jump to the floor just in time to save myself from an undignified landing.

In my hand, I held a plastic sleeve full of photographic negatives. I hadn't seen old-style negatives like these for at least fifteen years.

As I held them up to the light of the window, I could see they were all of a young woman. I guessed she was Adele, though I couldn't be certain. She wore jeans with cowboy chaps, and she was topless.

Slipping the negatives into my pocket to protect them, I headed back out into the forest.

CHAPTER SIXTY-THREE

On my way back from Mulden Farm, I stopped to organise a courier—I wanted the photography negatives to go straight to a police processing facility. I hoped there would be something—even the smallest clue—as to the identity of J.L.

As I headed into a café for a coffee and a sandwich, a news report blared from a radio. An expert was speaking about the fire situation. Everyone in the café went quiet, listening:

"*The fires at Gospers Mountain have joined to become one mega-blaze. It has destroyed an area seven times the size of Singapore. When fires get to this size, they can create their own weather patterns. The technical term is a pyrocumulonimbus. With a fire creating its own wind patterns, fire can be sent racing in any number of directions. It may even create its own lightning strikes, starting yet more spot fires. Please, have your fire evacuation plan ready. Download the fire app on your phone and be ready for any alerts*."

Around the café, a quiet terror made people's expressions pinched.

When I walked into the station, the story was the same. Worry was chewing on everyone's nerves.

Bigley was the only one with an expression as weightless as a child's. He was here again, walking across the floor as if he were going on a Sunday stroll.

He caught sight of me, raising his chin in greeting. I hoped he'd continue on his way. He didn't.

"Kate," he said on his approach, "I was pleased to hear about your team's progress on the Witness Mountain case."

"Our progress? What exactly are you referring to?"

"All the good work on ferreting out a motive."

"A motive? I'm not sure—?"

"Detectives Franco and Melainey filled me in."

I glanced over at Franco, who was sitting at his desk—head down and engaged in paperwork. Melainey was at his desk, too, looking apologetic.

"Well, Andrew," I said, "I don't believe I've been updated yet."

Bigley nodded like it was all completely normal for the homicide team's lead detective not to be kept informed.

Bigley clucked his tongue. "From what I've been told by your detectives, it seems that Perdita Iverson had a terminal illness. Brain tumours. Nasty business. It's a fair guess that her husband went out of his mind with grief. He didn't want her to suffer, but he couldn't live without her, either. And, perhaps, his daughter Angie just got caught in the middle of the mayhem."

Stunned, I locked eyes with him, trying to find words but failing.

"Kate," he said. "Don't mind me—it looks like I've stepped in too soon. I was just so surprised by this finding and how all the pieces of the puzzle are finally falling together. But, of course, you need to discuss this with your team."

"Your office, *now*, Andrew."

I marched ahead of him.

Bigley closed the door after he stepped inside his office, turning to me with a regretful expression plastered on his face. I knew he was regretful I'd reacted negatively, rather than being regretful about his own actions.

"Kate, look," he said. "We should really bring Melainey and Franco in here. They were the pair who worked together on this."

"It's *you* I want to talk to. I've known you way before Franco—and even before Melainey."

"Very true. But, as you know, my role is very limited these days as far as the day-to-day operations go."

"That's not where I'm going with this. I don't want to discuss the case with you. My point is that I knew you before you were a superintendent, before you were an inspector. I knew you when you were just Sergeant Bigley of the Tallman's Valley police station. You've known me all that time. Yet, you stood out there telling me how my own homicide case is going."

"I already said that I shouldn't have—"

"No, you shouldn't have. But you did. It might be true that Perdita had a terminal illness, but it's *not* evidence that her husband went ahead and started shooting at his family."

"Take a step back, Kate. I'm just relying on the experience of two of your expert homicide detectives. This finding, they tell me, is coming on top of the fact that Gus is proven to have been the one who shot the rifle."

"This case has not been closed yet," I snapped.

"Of course. Settle down. I just thought you'd be close to throwing out the anchor, now."

"Stop. Please. Stop trying to placate me. And quit with the damned nautical references."

Sighing, he laced his fingers together. "I can see you're upset."

"Oh, can you?"

"Look, let's just—"

"I have some questions for you, Andrew."

"Oh?"

"It's about the carnival."

"The *carnival*?"

"Yes, I want to talk about the 1989 raid of the carnival. You were the sergeant here at the time, and you sanctioned the raid. Correct?"

He sighed again. "Yes. I did."

"The documentation leading up to the raid is very sketchy. Who came to you with the request to conduct the raid?"

"Well… that would have been my officers. There would have been good reason. And… even though we didn't find enough evidence at the time, what's now been found in the bunker demonstrates they were right to be concerned."

"Did you attend the raid?"

"No, I didn't attend."

"Why not?"

"I had a station to run."

"Why didn't the police find the bunker on the morning of the raid? It shouldn't have been hard to find it at that stage. It'd been last used the night before."

He pursed his lips. "How do you know it was last used then?"

"I have a witness statement."

"Hmmm. Well, unfortunately, the bunker was missed."

"Seems a lot of things were missed. Not much evidence was found. But you gained a fat promotion out of that raid, Andrew."

"What is all this about? The carnival was closed down. That was a pretty good result, wouldn't you say?"

"It was closed down, but the main order of business went on. Which was, the production of illegal drugs, the buying and selling of illegal weapons, and the laundering of money. Just not at Mulden Farm anymore."

"Those are rather bold statements."

"Are they untrue?"

"I'm not sure what you're talking about. Everyone can see that the bunker hasn't been touched in decades. As far as I'm concerned, all the bad dealings ended the day of the raid."

"Did they? Well, my research says they continued. I wasn't here during those years, but I've been putting a picture together. And it's not pretty."

"Our police force did what they could with the resources they had available to them at the time."

"What happened to the money?"

"What money?"

"The money from all those illegal businesses that Mickey Mulden was running. I've been through the files many times, page by page. No money was found. It's not in the bunker, either. It seems that the money went up in smoke."

"I don't have any information about that."

"Because the money went into the pockets of the police conducting the raids?"

He puffed up his chest. "Those are some hefty accusations."

"Andrew, I'll ask again—why is there no money listed among the evidence found on the morning of the raids? And what are the names of all the police involved?"

"I… look, is this what you've been investigating? Franco and Melainey indicated to me that you've been off on your own a lot recently. It's not my place to say this, but you're in homicide, Kate. Chasing up missing money from thirty years ago is surely—"

"It's all part of a larger theme—one that I'm starting to suspect is behind everything that went on at Witness Mountain, now and in the past."

"A *theme*? This is all starting to sound quite… hazy. I'd even suggest you didn't give yourself quite enough rest before returning to work."

"Excuse me? I hardly think it's your place to—"

I stopped mid-sentence as a sharp, urgent knock came at the door.

Only too happy to end our talk, Bigley made quick steps across the room. He opened the door to Constable Thea Georgiades.

Thea's gaze skated nervously between Bigley and me. She must have overheard the raised voices in this office.

"Yes, Constable?" Bigley calmly lifted his eyebrows as if everything were normal.

Thea took a breath. "Detective Franco just took a call from the hospital. Angie Green is awake."

CHAPTER SIXTY-FOUR

Franco, Melainey and I drove over to CQ Hospital in the one police vehicle.

Everything other than Angie was forgotten for the moment. She'd woken from her coma. This was what I'd been praying for—for the sake of Angie, for her kids—and for the Witness Mountain case.

Would she be able to tell us anything?

When we arrived, Dr Castile stopped us in the hall. She told us Angie had begun coming out of her coma early this morning, but they'd given her time to orient herself before calling us. Her family had been informed, but they'd been asked to wait until after the police had spoken to her.

I had a quick word with Samuel—the security guard that stood in the hall outside Angie's room. I asked him to keep watching any visitors carefully, even now that Angie was awake.

I then entered Angie's hospital room with Franco and Melainey.

Angie was lying in her bed, as always, but this time, her eyes were open. Her eyes tracked us as we crossed the floor. Her red hair was spread in messy skeins on her pillow, as if she'd thrashed about in her effort to wake up. The freckles on her forehead and cheeks floated on her pale, waxy skin.

My mind flashed back to when I'd first found her, a hair's breadth away from dying. To see her now, like this, tugged at my heart.

On the way here, Franco, Melainey and I had agreed that I would be the one to speak with Angie. We didn't want to overwhelm her, and my voice was the one she knew.

I sat at her bedside, while Franco and Melainey stood at a short distance behind me.

Touching her hand, I gave her a warm smile. "I can't tell you how good it is to see you awake."

"I know you," Angie said softly, her voice weak and wavering.

"I'm Detective Kate Wakeland."

"Yes… that's the name…."

"How are you feeling?" I asked.

She pressed her lips together grimly. "Not myself, that's for sure."

"You've been through an awful lot. We've all been hoping you'd wake."

"I heard your voice… when I was asleep. You helped me find my way. And the doctors and nurses... especially the Irish nurse. You were all so very kind."

"I know that your medical team has been giving you the very best of care," I said. "Are you okay to talk to us?"

"I think so."

"First… do you understand what happened to you?"

She shook her head. "I don't understand… anything."

"It's normal for your memory to be hazy. It's okay."

"No… I do remember what happened. I just don't understand… *why*."

I held a breath. "Are you saying you remember the day you were brought into the hospital—I mean, the events that occurred just before?"

She nodded, her eyes filling with terror.

I ached for her, knowing the shocking things that must be in her mind right now. But at least she could finally tell us what happened that morning.

"Angie," I said, "I know these events will be very upsetting for you to tell us about. But we'd very much like to know what you know."

Her gaze drifted and her lower lip began to tremble. "He had a gun… a rifle…."

"Who had a gun, Angie?"

She didn't seem to hear me, eyes fixed on the ceiling now. "How could he do that to us? How could he? We're his own family."

I waited, my stomach clenching.

Which one was she talking about?

Gus Iverson?

Or *Jordan?*

I squeezed her hand in support.

She licked her lips anxiously. "But he… he came after me with a rifle. Shooting. He… shot me."

"Can you give me a name, Angie?" I asked softly.

"My father… Gus."

She'd just confirmed that the shooter had been Gus Iverson.

Swallowing hard, I turned to face Franco and Melainey. To Melainey's credit, there was no victory in his eyes. He lifted his shoulders as he exhaled. Franco's expression was stony.

I'd been wrong to doubt the evidence. I'd twisted things out of all proportion. But all along, the answer had been simple.

Gathering myself, I turned back to Angie. "Angie… if you can, could you tell us what happened just before your father came after you with the rifle?"

"He taunted me. He said… *better run, Angie… run.* Like it was just a game to him."

An image of what that moment must have been like flashed through my mind. Gus had taunted Angie?

"Where was your mother at this point?" I asked.

"My mother was screaming… screaming." Angie's eyes squeezed shut. "I can't bear it. I can't. I want to see my children. Where are they? Why can't I see them?"

"They'll be brought in to see you very soon," I assured her.

But my assurances weren't enough. She began to fret, crying out for a doctor and demanding to see her boys.

I stood, turning to Franco and Melainey. "We should go."

"Are you sure?" Melainey whispered. "We didn't get very far with the questions."

I shook my head. "We got what we needed the most."

A nurse came running in.

Saying goodbye to Angie, I left the room.

Angie's cries echoed down the corridor as she called her children's names over and over.

Jordan! *Toby*! *Ollie*!

When she called for Jordan, there was nothing fearful in her tone. And she hadn't spoken of Jordan doing anything wrong the day of the shootings. She'd only named her father. The reaction I thought I'd detected when I'd mentioned Jordan's name to Angie had been coincidental.

The shooter had been Gus—*just Gus.*

I walked alone along the cool hospital corridors and out into the heat of the day.

CHAPTER SIXTY-FIVE

I met up again with Franco and Mclainey in the parking bay of the hospital.

Melainey drew his eyebrows down in a serious expression. "Perhaps we should have a quick chat before holding a meeting with the team back at the station? This way, we'll show a united front. What're everyone's thoughts?"

Franco's tone was dark. "It's pretty clear. She saw him with the rifle. She saw him shooting at her. The evidence that we've got lines up—almost. Close enough."

My stomach was clenching as I spoke. "Angie did sound very certain. And she's the one who knows what happened."

Melainey nodded. "Even though I was leaning that way—towards Gus being the only culprit—I wasn't a hundred percent. But, you know, to me, if it looks like a duck and quacks like a duck, then it's a duck."

"Well, you were right," I admitted. "Gus was the duck."

But I couldn't stop my mind from whirling, from replaying everything from the crime scenes. I'd never been so completely wrong about a case before. It had wiped the floor with me. Had my judgement been clouded by my refusal to believe that an elderly man could have been the sole shooter? Had the motive been there all along? Perdita's illness could have posed some sort of tipping point for Gus from which he couldn't return.

Struggling to keep composure, I nodded at Melainey. "How did you find out his wife was ill?"

Melainey shrugged. “Just a bit of the old Melainey leg work. I found out about a church she used to attend years ago. Spoke to a few of the ladies there and discovered that Perdita had kept in contact. So, I gave them a bit of chat. Found out what I could.”

“Good work,” I told him.

“So, are we together on this?” Melainey asked. “Any doubts?”

Franco shook his head. “No doubts. All in.”

“Count me in on a united front,” I said, trying to sound like I was throwing weight behind my words.

In truth though, I was feeling knocked off my feet. I’d been wrong to question the crime scene as it had presented itself at Witness Mountain. But I couldn’t shake the unsettled feeling in my stomach.

My phone buzzed. The name, *Detective Sergeant Liz Booth,* flashed up on my screen.

“Would you both excuse me?” I said to Franco and Melainey, and I walked away out of their earshot.

“Liz, hello,” I answered.

Liz was breathy and speaking fast. “Hi, Kate. Are you all right? You sound a bit… down?”

“I shouldn’t. The coma patient just woke up—Angie Green. That’s good news. She’s named her father as the shooter. I’m just… well, I’m still processing it. I had my doubts about who the shooter was.”

“Wonderful that she woke up. Well, I guess at least you know now.”

“Yes, true. Anyway, that’s what’s happening here. What’s happening with you?”

“I have an update. Not the kind of update you’d want, unfortunately. Do you have a minute, or are you on the run?”

“I’m all ears.”

“All right. If I sound out of breath, it’s because I am. I’ll explain. We tracked Adele to an apartment in Cebu City. Had to pay off quite a few people to get through all the layers of protection she had around herself. But we were finally certain of her exact location.”

“Sounds good so far.”

“It goes downhill from there. We were about to pounce. Had everything set up. She’d only just gotten home—she’d been to the market, arms full of groceries. But then she left the apartment again, not a minute later. That took us by surprise. Something—or someone—must have tipped her off. She took a route that made it impossible for our team to follow by car. Detective Rosa Alonto and I followed on foot. I could see Adele, not even fifty metres in front, running through a street market. We almost had her. *Almost.*"

I exhaled, feeling the tension in Liz's voice. "Liz, I know you'll get her. You will."

"We *did* find her."

"You did?" I said in confusion.

"Yes. We kept looking. We came across some young boys looking for plastics floating in the river—they sell the plastics, apparently. There was all kinds of rubbish and plastics heaped up high on either side of the river. We couldn't see very far. We asked the boys if they'd seen a white woman running past the river—and, luckily, they had. We gave them some money, and they pointed us to where she went. We found Adele... under a bridge, lying on a pile of rubbish. She... she'd broken a bottle. And she'd used the sharp end to cut her wrists."

My chest tightened. "Polly told me Adele would never give in."

"Polly was right. Adele was laughing at us, if you can believe it. Actually, she was trying to laugh, but she wasn't, really. It was evident she was frightened and in great pain."

"Like a rat in a trap," I muttered, quoting Polly.

"I'm sorry, Kate," Liz told me in a drained voice. "I know you wanted her —*alive*—but there was nothing that could be done. I broke a few of her ribs giving her resuscitation. Tried everything I could to keep her damned heart pumping. But she bled out too quick."

I closed my eyes, almost picturing the scene. I hadn't even considered the possibility that Adele might kill herself. Everything Adele knew would have died with her.

"I wish I were there with you," I said. "You sound exhausted. Rest easy now, okay? You did all you could."

"It certainly doesn't feel that way right now. I'm cursing myself."

"Don't do that. Adele's not out there causing harm to children anymore—remember that."

"Kate... I'm not so sure of that."

"What do you mean?"

"I'm afraid her legacy is going to live on. I'm strongly suspecting she was involved in more than what we know. She was paying for those expensive overseas trips somehow. For all I know, she was a major player."

I pictured all those keyrings Adele had kept from her trips to Paris and California and dozens of other places.

“Promise me one thing?” I asked. “You’ll give yourself some time off. You know you need this, Liz. Or maybe you don’t know. You’ve been doing nothing except tracking Adele for months. Fly home for a while, and we’ll catch up. Please?”

“I understand what you’rc saying, my lovely I do. But *now* is my best chance of catching hold of any loose ends Adele left behind. Before her network steps in and seals everything shut.”

“I understand. But I’m worried for you.”

“I’ll be all right. I’ll have a glass of red with Rosa tonight. It might not be the glass of champagne that she and I had planned—because it’s not a celebration—but it’s an end to the chase for Adele anyway.”

“No, Liz, you two have your champagne. You’ve earned it. Stay safe, okay?”

CHAPTER SIXTY-SIX

Before heading home for the day, I drove across to Nola Hobson's house. I had something to tell her—and I wanted her to know before it hit the news.

She was out in her garden, plucking weeds. Max was playing with a toy truck on the grass.

She tilted her hat up as I approached.

"Did you find out anything?" she asked me with a note of eagerness. "Did the keys help?"

I nodded, sitting down beside her on the grass. "I did find the cabin."

"Oh, wow. So, did you find out who J.L is?"

"Not yet. I didn't find much… just some old photos. They're all of Adele."

"Oh. That's a shame. Looks like my good idea wasn't such a good idea, after all."

"No, it was a *great* idea. It really was." I picked a blade of glass from the lawn. "I have something I need to tell you."

She frowned at me. "Sounds serious?"

"Detective Booth was with a team of police earlier today, and they found Adele. She was underneath a bridge in Cebu City, in the Philippines. She… she died there."

"They shot her?"

"No. She killed herself."

Nola sat back, her jaw gone slack. "I can't say I'm sad. I don't know what to feel."

"Tell me if there's anything you need right now. I've got a counsellor on speed dial who can come by—if you need to let stuff out. If you want to go somewhere, I'll be your driver. If you need a hug, I've got that, too."

"I'll take you up on that third option."

Leaning across, I embraced her. I was fast coming to think of Nola as a daughter. She'd been through the worst in life. I wanted much better things for her in her future.

Nola began crying.

Wiping her eyes with her sleeve, she moved back to face me. "Don't think for one minute these tears are for *her*. They're not."

"Oh, honey... I know."

She sucked in her mouth as if trying to stop herself from sobbing. "I just thought… I thought that one day I'd have the chance to tell her how much I hated her, and how much she hurt me. I wanted to say that to her face. But the minute I told someone what she did to me—the minute I told *you*—she ran."

"I'm sorry she stole that chance away from you."

"No matter what I said, it wouldn't have bothered her, though. Water off a duck's back."

Nola's eyes grew distant now. I sensed that memories of the past were rearing up inside her.

"Nola, would you and Max come to dinner at my place tonight? Ivy would love to see Max. We've got a little kitten Max might like to see, too. It's Detective Franco's kitty. His house burned down in the Witness Mountain fire."

"Oh… that's terrible. I'm glad his kitten was saved. I think I'll accept your invitation to dinner."

"Wonderful."

"Do Aunt Polly and Aunt Penny know?"

"I'm about to call the prison. Penny isn't in a good way at the moment. Her psychiatrist might decide that she shouldn't know."

"Would you mind if it's me who tells Aunt Polly? It's silly, but it feels like it'd give me just a little bit of control over Adele—being the one to give out the news of her death."

I gave her a small smile. "Of course."

I drove home after talking with Nola and headed straight upstairs for a shower.

But the hot water failed to ease the sensation of knots twisting the muscles along my spine.

I changed into light clothing and returned downstairs.

Pete had cold drinks ready inside, and he'd switched the air conditioning on.

"Abby made lemonade with Ivy earlier," he told me.

Briefly, I explained to Pete what I'd been doing today, starting with the trip out to Mulden Farm and ending with the news about Adele's death and about Angie waking from her coma. It was best not to include my conversation with Superintendent Bigley. Pete looked worried enough already.

"Great news about Angie," he said. "But you shouldn't have been charging about Mulden Farm on your own."

"It was a spur-of-the-moment thing."

"You had chest pain just a few nights ago. Running about in the heat on your own isn't smart. If something had happened, who would know?"

"I had my phone at the ready the whole time. I felt fine though."

"Next time, send Franco or someone else to do the grunt work. You don't need to. Right?"

"Right."

Leaning my head back against the sofa, I tried to relax and empty my mind. Everything felt too heavy. My body, my mind, the weight of the Witness Mountain and underground bunker cases.

Pete put on some music.

For the next hour, we sat together, listening to music, our heads touching, falling into a brief nap together. The kind of thing we used to do in the year we first met, when we were young—both of us studying at university and tired all the time.

Nola and Max came over a little later. Nola seemed to have recovered from the news about Adele, which I was glad to see.

Max and Ivy zoomed around in the yard, playing with kites. Logan came home from work and played a ball game with the kids.

The noise and activity took my mind off everything else for a while.

As all of us sat down to dinner, I was grateful for the people at my dinner table. Those faces made my life. They spurred me on. They gave me a reason for everything I did.

CHAPTER SIXTY-SEVEN

In the morning, a round table meeting of our homicide team ended with three initiatives.

Gus Iverson was to be named publicly as the Witness Mountain shooter. A release would be sent to the media about Angie Green waking from her coma. Detectives Melainey and Franco would be the ones to give the briefing about those two items in a press conference.

I'd declined being the spokesperson to make the announcements to the media. I hadn't been as involved as Melainey with the steps leading up to Gus Iverson being confirmed as the shooter and killer.

I knew I should feel relief at this point of the investigation. We were at the end point. But I didn't find relief. The air of unreality had clung to me since yesterday. All I could do was to keep going.

Franco barely spoke during the meeting—only putting in a vote when asked to by Shintani or Melainey.

With the case of the shootings wrapping up, our team would be turning their attention to the bunker murders. But before then, there'd be a ton of paperwork to prepare for the case at hand.

Melainey and Franco gave the media address upstairs in our conference room, with the rest of the team watching on via video link.

Melainey stressed that the naming of Gus as the shooter had been a team effort, with Angie's testimony providing the final piece of evidence we needed. He was a good, clear public speaker. He used to try to hog the limelight a little in his younger, brasher years, but not anymore.

Perhaps Melainey really had mellowed, as he'd said he had. And perhaps country life was helping to further soften his hard edges.

During the conference, Franco was merely present, speaking only once, and only to back up Melainey. I didn't understand what was going on with him. Franco was fast becoming a very different kind of cop—and person—than the one I'd known.

A text message popped up on my phone:

Photo negatives ready, Detective Wakeland. A few damaged and scratched, but most in pretty good shape.

The message was from the photo processing facility. I headed out of the station to meet the courier outside, into yet another hot and smoke-hazed day.

After collecting the photographs, I walked to my car and sat inside. I wasn't yet ready to share my research into the carnival. I wanted some strong evidence before I did that.

I began looking through the A4-sized images.

As I'd thought, the photos were of Adele. She'd certainly been a wild sixteen-year-old. If it'd been any other girl, I might have said she'd been manipulated by the man taking the photographs. But from what Polly told me, the photos were Adele's idea.

I studied her face. She looked exuberant, as if she'd enjoyed having the photos taken. They were all nude shots of her.

She'd been a tall, large-boned sixteen-year-old who looked a good four years older than her age. From what Polly had said, Adele wanted to sell photos of herself to men who liked images of young girls. But Adele had grown to look much closer to a woman than a child. I wondered if that was why she'd been trying to rope in girls that were younger than herself.

Most of the photos had been taken down at a lake—Coldwater Lake, by the looks of them. A man was in a few of those photographs. He had to be J.L.

My excitement waned as I realised he'd been careful not to show his face. His only interesting feature was a tattoo on his left shoulder. Using a magnifying glass, I examined the tattoo. It was a jail cell.

So, a cop with a tattoo of a jail on his shoulder. What a tough guy he must have thought he was.

I sat back in my chair, releasing a breath.

This was proof positive that Franco was not J.L.

I knew Franco had tattoos on his back, chest and upper arm—but he had none on his shoulders.

A voice at the back of my mind reminded me tattoos could be lasered off. But surely there'd be a small scar left behind? I'd never noticed a scar. But then, I'd never looked closely, either.

I shook the thought.

J.L could not be Franco.

I cursed the fact that only a small number of the photographs had been taken in the cabin. I studied those photos carefully, trying to spot any small detail that might give me a clue about J.L.

There was only one cabin photo in which the man had included himself. He and Adele were standing in front of a mirror, back-to-back. They were both smoking cigarettes. Again, he didn't show his face.

Adele was sporting a tattoo, now, too. She hadn't had any tattoos in the lake photos. Adele's right shoulder bore a tattoo of a bait fish on a hook.

It seemed that Adele had copied the style of her boyfriend's tattoo—a simple, black line drawing.

Why had Adele chosen a picture of a bait fish? It seemed a bizarre choice. Could Adele's tattoo somehow match with the jail cell tattoo?

But a jail cell and a bait fish didn't go together.

Until I realised that they did.

Puffing up my cheeks, I blew out a breath. *Okay. I got it.*

Jail and bait. *Jailbait.*

Adele, at age sixteen, saw herself as jailbait. Cute. *Not.*

I began examining the background of the cabin now.

The same oilskin jacket and boots as I'd seen yesterday were there. A full-length mirror was propped against a wall. A calendar hung on a nail, a naked woman posing for the month of December in 1989.

There was something written on the calendar.

Using my magnifying glass, I tried reading it. The scrawled writing said: *spring blossoms.*

Disappointment bled through me.

What was so important about spring blossoms that either Adele or J.L thought to write it down on the calendar? Perhaps they'd wanted to do a photo shoot of Adele among some spring flowers. Except, the calendar was open on the month of December, and so there weren't going to be actual spring blossoms for many months.

I'd hoped for much more from this set of photographs, but these were the cards I'd been dealt.

Sweat trickled down the back of my neck. Even though my car was parked in the shade, the air inside was already starting to cook me. I packed the photographs back into their envelope and returned to the station.

CHAPTER SIXTY-EIGHT

My next step was to run a search on the jail cell tattoo. Tattoos were an identifying mark, and police kept a database of them.

When I re-entered the station, Franco and Melainey were missing from their desks.

"They've gone for a celebratory drink," Thea told me in a dry tone. "Cheers for the end of the Witness Mountain case. Melainey invited us all for beers back at his house, but then Franco said he'd rather it be just the boys. Said he wasn't up for the drama."

I lifted my eyebrows high. "Say *what*?"

"Yup. Franco thought the whole thing with Gus Iverson was a bit of a debacle—just stalling the inevitable."

Heat flamed my chest. Had Franco always been like this when I wasn't around? He was so different to my face.

"Well," I said, "maybe you and I can do lunch together, Thea?"

"I'd like that."

"Great. See you in an hour."

I headed down the hall and into the room that we called the study. It was just a room meant for dedicated research—filled with fast computers capable of running large programs and secure operations.

I still felt burned from what Franco had said. I almost wished I didn't know.

Putting my thoughts about Franco to one side, I ran a search for the jail cell tattoo. The search didn't return any viable results.

I emailed Liz the tattoo images of the fish bait and jail cell, hoping she might know something. I called her straight after that, requesting a video call. I wanted to see her and make certain she was okay. I'd been worried about her last time we'd talked.

"Good to see your face, lovely," Liz said.

Liz sounded like herself again—brisk and efficient. Her tone belied the dark circles under her eyes and the strands of hair falling loose around her face.

"Wonderful to see you, too," I replied. "How are you?"

"Getting there. Mountains of work ahead, so all I can do is take one step at a time."

"I'm glad to hear you're pacing yourself, at least. Don't take on too much at once."

"Hmmm, I'm just looking at the pictures you sent. I've seen one of them before."

"Oh? Which one?"

"The little fish on the hook. I viewed Adele's body at the morgue this morning. She had that exact tattoo."

Viewing bodies—even those of criminals—was never pleasant. And, added to that was the fact that Adele was a criminal that we'd particularly wanted alive. I could clearly see the strain in Liz's expression.

I explained how Adele had gotten a jail bait tattoo to match up with J.L's image of a cell.

Liz hooted, shaking her head. "You'd think that Adele would've inked over her tattoo with something more appropriate. A woman in her mid forties is decades past being jailbait."

I laughed. "I had the same thought."

"Or… perhaps she still held a candle for this man, and so she kept the tatt?"

"An interesting thought."

"Isn't it? Did you run a search on the tattoo?"

"Yep. Nothing."

"Okay, that might mean he's still a cop. If he'd left the force and become a petty criminal, he'd probably have gotten picked up sooner or later. And then his tattoo might be on the system. But if he'd stayed a cop, there's a possibility he'd have been able to hide his crimes."

"You might be right. J.L is still a cop."

"Awful to contemplate."

"The only other thing I found in the photos was a message someone wrote on a calendar."

I sent a picture of the calendar through to Liz's phone.

Liz rubbed her chin back and forth across her knuckle. "Hmmm, *spring blossoms* might have been his pet name for Adele."

"I guess it fits. She was very young, then."

"Back up the bus. It reminds me of something. It wasn't someone's name. It was a business… in the inner city."

"What kind of business?"

"A sex parlour—not well known… except by paedophiles, that is. It was called *Spring Blossoms on Stimson*. Stimson was the name of the street."

"Oh… sounds terrible."

"It was a long way from Tallman's Valley, though. So, it's probably not relevant."

"You know what? Polly did say that Adele approached Angie about a place in the city—where she could go and have photographs taken. I wonder…?"

"Well, that's interesting."

"Do you have any information about the place?"

"Police shut it down a long time ago. Twenty-five years or so ago. Let me log into the Sydney database and have a little look. Back in two shakes."

Within minutes. Liz was back on the line. "Okay, Kate, police shut it down in 1994. They were luring in some very young girls, aged from twelve to fifteen. It was run by a Mr Tran. Prior to that, it was run by a Miss Laurier. Apparently, Miss Laurier married in 1990 and sold the business to Mr Tran."

"Sounds like Miss Laurier is the one we'd want to speak to."

"Yes. But unfortunately, the police were never able to track her down. It was before my time in child protection, so I didn't deal with the case myself. The information here says that a neighbour told police that Miss Laurier married a delivery driver. The driver had recently been in an accident—he'd fallen asleep and crashed his vehicle. He'd been on heavy medication, apparently, after the death of his daughter. He suffered brain damage, and Miss Laurier nursed him back to health."

"Sounds like she raced him off to the altar."

Liz chuckled. "She must have wanted to get out of town in a hurry." Sobering, she gave a sad sigh. "Terrible that a woman like her got away with the things she did."

"*Wait*… oh no, it can't be…."

"Did my story ring a bell, Kate?"

"Yes, it's rung a very, very loud bell. Oh my God. If I'm right, it's absolutely shocking. *Gus Iverson* crashed his van in 1990, soon after the death of his daughter. Let me send the news article to you."

I sent a link through to Liz.

She read it swiftly. "No wonder I never saw this article—the accident happened out in a country area. Well, this is too much coincidence, my dear. I think Miss Laurier might be your Perdita Iverson."

I ran a quick search on the name, *Perdita Laurier*. I found a photograph of her.

Yes, she was Perdita Iverson.

I sent the photo through to Liz.

"That's her," Liz said. "Same squinty little eyes."

"But… how does this fit?" I breathed. "How on earth did a newly married couple like the Iversons—a man recovering from brain damage and the madam of a Sydney sex parlour—suddenly find themselves in Tallman's Valley, adopting a teenage girl?"

I closed my eyes, realising I'd already made the connection. "Oh, my… Perdita must have already known Adele. That means Perdita knew the Muldens and the carnival. It was no random adoption. It was planned."

"You're right," Liz said. "Sounds like the marriage was just a sham, to enable Perdita to adopt Angie."

"But, for the life of me, I can't figure out why. I mean, on the one hand, it would have given Perdita access to a young girl. But why go to so much trouble?"

"I agree," Liz told me. "It makes no sense. Angie was just *one* girl—and she was soon to grow too old for the age range of the girls Perdita was exploiting."

"There has to be something else to this—some reason Perdita was desperate to adopt Angie. Liz… I think I need to go talk to Angie again."

"Go for it," she said quietly. "When you need me, I'll be here."

CHAPTER SIXTY-NINE

When I called the hospital to ask about seeing Angie, I was told I'd need to wait an hour or so—she'd just fallen asleep.

I'd been going to cancel the lunch date with Constable Georgiades, but now I had a whole hour to burn. In any case, I needed to sit and eat. Running about on an empty stomach wasn't going to do me any good.

I stepped into the lunchroom to make a coffee.

Detective Reagan Grimshaw was in there, sipping a cup of tea.

"You look wrecked," she commented.

"Thanks," I said wryly. "I feel like a wreck."

"Anything amiss?"

"My cases lately have been a wild ride, that's all."

She twisted her mouth. "As much as I hate to do this, I'm gonna have to congratulate you on finding the bunker. You shot the lights out, Wakeland."

"Coming from you, that's high praise," I quipped.

"Some interesting items coming out of that bunker," Grimshaw said. "I've been watching as they're bringing them into the station. What a blast from the past."

"Once everything settles down, I'm going to go through every single last thing."

"I bet you will. If you want a hand, give me a shout. I love old stuff. It'd be fun going through it."

"For sure."

I thought to myself that this might just be the first time Grimshaw had ever described anything as being *fun*.

I stirred milk into my coffee. "Hey, anything new happening with the missing woman—Martina Bianchi?"

"Not so far. The fires are making things damned complicated. Can't conduct searches in no-go zones."

I nodded. "Do you have a reason to think Martina might be in a fire zone?"

"The last signal we got from her mobile phone was going towards Iron Bark Crest."

"Oh, dear. I hope she kept going and didn't stop there anywhere."

"Yep. We're doing all we can, but our hands are a bit tied at the moment."

I sipped my coffee. "Thea and I planned to have lunch together. Want in?"

"Yeah, why not?" Grimshaw said. "I don't have a better offer."

I grinned. "Right."

Thea and Grimshaw and I ordered lunch in from the sandwich shop around the corner.

We sat chatting about our pets while we ate. Georgiades had a horse and a couple of parrots that she'd moved to her mother's farm, to keep them safe. Grimshaw had three cats that were still at her house—she lived right on the edge of an evacuation zone and knew that she might have to go grab them at any moment.

The same situation was playing out everywhere in the Blue Mountains. People worrying over arrangements for their animals.

After lunch was done, I drove over to CQ Hospital.

Due to the nature of the questions, a psychologist was assigned to join me during the questioning.

The psychologist—Dr Maybury—met with me outside Angie's room.

"She's still in a fragile state," he told me.

"I'll try to go easy with the questions," I replied. "But I'm afraid the nature of the questions themselves might be a little difficult."

"I'll end the session if I see her getting too upset. I need to confirm something with you—you're not going to speak to Angie about the discovery in the bunker, am I correct?"

"That's right."

"Good. Because I feel that she's not ready to hear about the fate of her birth parents. I've requested that Angie not have access to that news yet. One step at a time."

"I agree. It's going to be awful for her when she finds out."

"All right, then, all ready to begin."

I nodded in acknowledgement at the psychologist and then entered Angie's room.

For the first time, I encountered Angie Green sitting up. It made a difference that took me aback for a moment. She'd lost her fragile look, and she had so much more colour in her cheeks.

I smiled. "Good morning, Angie. Thank you so much for seeing me. I appreciate it."

"I know you need to do your job, Detective."

The psychologist—Dr Maybury—positioned himself on a chair near the wall.

I pulled up a chair and sat next to Angie. "You're looking so much brighter today."

"I feel more together," she said. "And I'm glad you're here."

"You are?"

"You've been an anchor for me. I know you're the one who found my kids… and I know you found *me*. You kept coming to talk to me when I was in the coma and not understanding what on earth was happening. That means a lot."

I smiled. "It must have been wonderful for you to see your children yesterday."

Tears formed in her eyes. "They're so beautiful. They have no idea how beautiful they are."

"They're lovely boys. All three." I paused. "Are you okay to answer my questions now? I'm afraid they could be upsetting…"

"Don't apologise. You've done so much for me, I'll answer anything you want."

This was certainly a good start. After how anxious Angie had become last time, I'd been steeling myself.

"Thank you. I'd like to begin by asking why you returned to Tallman's Valley?"

Her gaze immediately shifted, and her voice went tight. "For the kids to see their grandparents. They hadn't seen them in a year."

"No other reason?"

"No. What other reason could there be? I didn't cause what happened."

"Oh, of course not. I wasn't saying that at all."

"Sorry, I'm just… feeling sensitive."

"Very understandable. Could I ask you about a friend of yours—Sean Macklin?"

"What about Sean?" Again, her voice was tight.

"What was your relationship with him?"

"There was no relationship. I mean, we were just *friends*. He came to do work for me—he built the dog houses and fixed the fences. Things like that."

That was very, very different from what Sean had told me.

"Okay, thank you. Now, I'd like to form a better picture of the relationship between you and your parents. To do that, I'll need to ask about your teenage years."

"Oh…" She touched her forehead, as if my request troubled her. "Is that important?"

"Call me thorough."

"Okay." She swallowed, glancing away to the window.

"What was your relationship like with your parents?"

"This is hard. So very hard. My father was… well, he was always wonderful to me. And then… what he did. I just can't—" She shook her head.

"You're saying he was a good father?"

"Yes. Always. There was nothing he wouldn't do for me."

"And… your mother?"

Her eyes instantly clouded. "I don't like to speak ill of the dead."

The psychologist eyed Angie with interest.

"It's not *ill* if it's the truth," I said to Angie in a soft voice.

Nodding, she gathered the sheets up around her middle, like a child seeking comfort. "She was cold. We never got on."

"Why do you think you didn't get on?"

"It just seemed like she resented me. She spent a lot of time away. She didn't love my father, either. I'm sure of that."

"Did your mother ever ask you to do things that she shouldn't have?"

She frowned. "What do you mean?"

"You said she was cold. I'm just trying to understand that. Did she… do anything bad to you?"

"Not exactly. Despite how cold she was, she looked after me well. She and Dad sent me to the dance school that I wanted."

"This is going to sound strange—but bear with me. Did she ever take photos or videos of you that made you uncomfortable? To be clear, I'm talking about abuse—images of a sexual nature."

Angie stared at me curiously. "I didn't expect the direction that these questions would go in. Nothing like that happened."

I decided to twist the truth. "We had a report from the public. We have to investigate such reports in order to determine whether they're real… or not."

"What did they say?"

"I'm afraid I can't divulge that."

"Oh, okay. I understand."

As far as I could tell, Angie wasn't hiding anything. Perdita hadn't abused her in the way she'd abused other young girls.

"Angie, moving forward to recent times, had you been upset with either your mother or father prior to your return to Tallman's Valley?"

Her lip twitched. "No."

"Are you sure?"

"Yes. I am."

"Okay, thinking about Jordan now—had he been upset with anyone? With his grandparents… or with you?"

"Jordan?" Drawing her mouth in, she shook her head.

There was something she wasn't saying. I glanced at the psychologist, and I could tell by his expression he thought the same as I did.

I tried asking Angie the same question in a different way. "Was anything upsetting Jordan at the time?"

Her shoulders trembled and she gripped the sheets, twisting them in her hands. "I'm not feeling well…."

Turning to look out the window again, she began sobbing.

"What's wrong, Angie?" I asked.

"I just don't understand why he tried to kill me."

"Who tried to kill you?" It was a bold question because she'd already answered it last time. I waited for her answer, my heart bumping my chest wall.

She looked confused, her breaths quickening. Her tone wasn't at all certain when she said, "It was… my father?"

"I'm going to ask you a difficult question. Are you certain it was Gus who shot at you? Could it have been someone else?"

"I… of course it was him. Who else could it be? He… he even killed the chickens… and he loved those chickens."

"Angie… the chickens were fine. I saw them myself."

A deep crease appeared between her eyebrows. "*No*… they were all slaughtered. All dead."

"Angie—"

She was no longer listening, eyes closed and mouth quivering. "And he hunted down Toby and Ollie. He shot at them, over and over…."

I cast a helpless glance at the psychologist. What was going on?

Dr Maybury stood. "That's enough for today. I'm going to stay with Angie for a few minutes, Detective. And then I'll meet with you out in the corridor."

I nodded and then walked from the room.

Sun spilled in through the windows that extended the entire length of the corridor. Far below, cars drove in and out of the parking bay. In the distance, the smoke over the mountains seemed darker than usual.

Ten minutes passed before Dr Maybury emerged. "I've given her a sedative. I sat with her until she drifted off."

"I feel terrible. Things really went off the rails. There were no dead chickens, and there is no evidence that Gus Iverson shot at the children."

"I'd say it's just Angie's mind trying to make sense of a very traumatic event. It possibly feeds into her idea of her father going crazy. She wants to believe he went insane, so her subconscious gives her the story she needs to feel better."

"Is that sort of thing common?"

"Yes, it is. Patients recovering from comas don't snap back to reality overnight. Not usually. I've had recovering coma patients imagine all kinds of scenarios. I had one patient imagine I was a Russian spy. It never occurred to him I have the wrong accent."

"I understand. Thank you. I have one more question."

"Go right ahead."

"If someone has been shot by a family member, might they imagine a different person having shot them? Like, in the scenario that someone's son fired the gun, might that person imagine it was someone else—to protect the son?"

He eyed me with a sudden intense interest. "You think the shooter was possibly her son?"

"Let's just say I'm open to it."

"The only thing I'll commit to saying is that she did have an extreme reaction when you mentioned her eldest son's name."

"Yes, she did. What are your thoughts on that?"

"I'm afraid I can't say. It seems she's experiencing some altered perceptions at the moment."

I thanked the doctor for his time and headed away down the corridor. I needed to unravel all of this, but I was in unfamiliar territory. Angie's memories were chaotic right now and couldn't be trusted.

One thing was clear to me. I was no longer happy to declare Gus Iverson as the shooter.

CHAPTER SEVENTY

I bought a coffee at the café in CQ Hospital and then went to find a seat.

While it'd been a relief to hear Angie say that Perdita hadn't abused her, I wanted to know why Perdita had chosen to adopt Angie in the first place. The answers seemed wrapped up tight in dense layers of the past.

And there was still the puzzle of why Angie had become noticeably agitated when I'd mentioned Jordan to her.

What was the truth in all of this?

I stirred my coffee, deep in thought.

When my phone buzzed, I answered without looking to see who it was. But I instantly recognised the throaty, American accent.

"Thought you might want to come and say goodbye to us, Detective," Ada said.

Startled, I dropped my spoon, making a clatter on the table. "*Goodbye*? You're going away?"

"Ben's employers have told Ben to finish up. So, we're going home. He's a little angry about it. More than a little."

"I'm so sorry. Is this anything to do with me—I mean, with the project Ben's doing for me?"

"They're not saying that. But it sure is confusing."

"I'm coming to see you both—right now. I'm actually at the CQ building, at the hospital."

"Ben's not here. He said he'd be back soon."

"I want to see you, too. I'll come and wait with you until Ben returns."

I gulped the rest of the coffee and exited the café.

This was devastating news. Had someone found out that the federal police were investigating the identity of the person who hacked into the virtual program? And if Ben's contract with the NineOak corporation had been ended because of the AFP involvement, what did that mean?

I found Ada sitting in Ben's office, in the glow of his computer screen. She turned to me with an anxious expression.

"Oh, Ada," I cried. "I'm really sorry about this. Did they give any reasons?"

She drew her mouth down. "Nancy Upchurch told Ben it was due to budgetary constraints. She said they've reconsidered the future of the CQ Virtual Village project, and they've decided they've gone as far with it as it needs to go."

"That's not what Ms Upchurch said on the day of the fair. I recall her saying it was just the beginning."

"Well, that woman has back-tracked her words."

"This is just *wrong*. Doesn't Ben have a contract with NineOak?"

"Yup. But it turns out it's not worth the paper it's written on. It came with clauses that gave them an *out*. So... we're out on our ears."

"I can't believe this."

"It's a damned shame. I like it here. So does Ben. He always says he can't breathe in big cities."

"Unfortunately, you two came here at a time when our air is choked with bushfire smoke," I remarked.

"True. But that won't go on forever. Trust me, Ben's enjoyed his time here. Getting away from home was the best thing for him. He's been different. Far more alive. The project he did for you had a lot to do with that. He was like a pig in mud."

"I'm glad about that, at least."

She went quiet, her chest rising and falling with heavy breaths. "There's another side to Ben that no one sees. He has a thin shell. That worries me. He might decide one day that life is too much to bear. I'm fairly sure he's come close to that point a few times." Her eyes filled with pain.

I touched her arm. "I'm so sorry to hear that. My own daughter struggled with something similar. It was agony to watch it happen. That was just a couple of years ago. Things are very different now, thankfully."

Ada shook her head. "I'm sorry about your kid. I'm glad she made it through. I bet *she's* glad, too."

"Yes, very much so."

"I'd like to show you something, Detective."

"Of course."

She wheeled her chair over to a VR headset and lifted it from the desk. "You'll need to put this on."

"Is this to do with the virtual world? I'm not sure if I should be logging on there right now."

"Nope, this is about Ben. Just Ben."

Puzzled, I fitted myself with the headset. "Do I need the sensor vest and gloves, too?"

"No," she said. "There isn't anything that you can move or change in this world, so they're not needed."

As I turned on the headset, the grey screen changed to a green door.

What was Ada about to show me?

"Open the door, Detective," Ada instructed me.

"I don't have to choose an avatar or something, first?"

"No, Ben didn't program this particular world with avatars."

"Okay." Stepping forward, I turned the brass handle and pushed open the door.

A lush, riverside scene spread out before me. Willows and oaks and cherry trees. It was autumn in this world, and several of the trees displayed brilliant shades of red, orange, and yellow. A rustic log cabin stood to my right.

"Oh, my goodness. It's beautiful," I said. "Is this a project Ben's working on?"

"It's an old project of his," she told me. "Explore, Detective."

If I didn't have so much on my mind right now, this really would have been a place I'd like to explore. It was idyllic.

Humouring Ada, I walked along a path, looking around. The air filled with bird calls.

Down at the river, a man aged somewhere in his sixties fished from a boat in the river. He had an angry rash on his neck—making his pale skin red and sore-looking—but he seemed as happy as Larry sitting there in his boat.

I peered through the window into the cabin. A woman of a similar age to the man worked on a computer—cat on her lap and dog by her feet. The fire was lit. It was a cosy scene.

I turned as someone walked past me. She was a young woman, possibly in her early twenties, with smooth, deep brown skin. She wore her black hair braided in the front and loose at the back. Her yellow cardigan and floral dress looked lovely on her. As she turned to greet the dog that bounded out of the cabin, I could see that she was pregnant.

Who were these people? And why did Ada want to show me this?

I wandered into the house. There seemed to be no one in here but the woman. She looked up from her computer screen, removing her glasses and rubbing her eyes.

"Oh…" I said. "Ada—that's *you*."

"Yeah, that's me," came Ada's voice over the speakers in my headset. "A good ten years ago. When I was in my sixties."

"And that's your husband out on the lake?"

"Yes, that's Stan. He'd blundered into some poison ivy earlier that day, while trying to launch the boat. That's how he got the rash. He liked nothing better than getting out there on the river. As for me, I should've known better than to bring a damned computer away on a family trip. If I had that day over, I'd have been in the boat with Stan. We bought the land and the cabin when Ben was small, and we used to go there every year."

"It's lovely. And the girl I saw outside? Who is—?"

"That's Grace. Ben's girlfriend."

"Oh?" Ben and Grace must have split up. Perhaps Ben had a child back in America, being raised by Grace. I was unsure why Ada was showing me this very personal look into the former lives of her family.

"That yellow outfit is the same outfit Grace wore that day," Ada said. "It was her birthday. She was turning twenty-six."

"She's a beautiful girl."

"Yes, she was. That night, we went out in the car, headed for a restaurant to celebrate Grace's birthday. A truck careened into us on the road. Stan, Grace, and Grace's unborn baby all died." She paused. "Ben and I survived."

"Oh… God, I'm so sorry."

"Ben doesn't like to talk about it. So, I don't."

"He made this virtual world as a memorial, didn't he?"

"Yeah. It's a place he escapes into. He keeps living that last day that Grace and the baby were alive, over and over."

"Ada, I… I shouldn't be here, in this world. It's private—"

"There's no one I can talk to about this. No one understands how real these worlds are. But *you* do. I guess I just wanted someone else to know. I worry constantly about me dying, Detective. Not because I'm scared of death, but because I'm the only family Ben has left. Sometimes, he stays in this world that you see in front of you—*for days*—and he'll barely come out."

I understood now why Ada had expressed so much concern over virtual worlds. It was because of *this*—this memorial of Ben's. A world he couldn't move on from.

I switched off the headset and removed it. "Ada, does Ben know that you've been inside this world of his?"

"No, I don't think so."

"It feels like I've invaded his privacy. I had no idea what I was going into."

"I know, I know, I've overstepped all kinds of lines here." She shrugged. "It is what it is. I'm too old to care about things like that anymore."

I placed the headset back on the desk. "That last day at the river you all had—it was beautiful. I'm so sad for you and Ben."

She sighed. "Ben wants me to sell that land. We haven't been back. I guess I keep hoping that Ben might find love again and take a new girl back there. She won't be the same as our Grace… but you can't quit on life, right?"

I smiled. "No, you can't quit on life."

She nodded, but her eyes held an expression of defeat.

We both turned towards the door as a low alarm sounded from out in the corridor.

"Is that a drill?" Ada asked sharply.

"We'd better go see."

I poked my head out into the corridor. People were filing out of their offices, puzzled looks on their faces, checking their phones.

I took out my own phone and turned it on. I'd switched it off just before I'd entered Ben's virtual world.

Two urgent messages popped up.

One was from my fire alert app: *Low level fire risk at current location. CQ building, Tallman's Valley. Evacuate at your earliest opportunity.*

The other was from Pete: *Honey, check your fire app. The time to evacuate our area is now. I can't get Abby on the phone. Please go check on her. Love you.*

PART VI

CHAPTER SEVENTY-ONE

As I wheeled Ada out into the corridor, the fire alarm continued to sound.

"Where's Ben?" I asked her.

"I'm not sure," she breathed. "He didn't tell me where he'd be."

People were flooding into the lifts. Dodging them, I pushed Ada's wheelchair down the hall, looking for Ben.

Ben came running towards us. "Kate? I didn't know you were with my mom." He took over the wheelchair handles. "I'll take it from here. I, uh. I had some things to do down on the bottom floor."

Ben was breathing fast, his eyes large. He seemed rattled, and I wasn't certain that was to do with the fire alarm.

"Calm down, Ben," Ada told him. "Doesn't seem like there's fire anywhere close."

Ben shot his mother a frazzled look. "They wouldn't be evacuating everyone for no reason."

"There are several evacuation centres in town," I said. "Do you know where to go?"

"I don't think it's a good idea for me to stay in town." He flicked his head around, looking behind him. His expression grew almost fearful.

"What's going on, Ben?" I asked quietly.

"No time to explain." Discreetly, he took a small object from his pocket and passed it into the palm of my hand while giving me a handshake. "Don't look at what I'm giving you. It's a flash drive. I planned to get it to you before I left. But it seems like this might be the last chance I get."

"I understand. Got it."

I didn't actually understand at all. All I understood was that Ben was extremely concerned about something.

"Listen, there's something else," Ben said. "I don't know where Leo Dubois is."

"You mean, the computer programmer? What's going on with him?" I asked, surprised.

"He's been acting weird. And then he didn't come into work today. I want to check on him, but I can't. I gotta go."

"Okay, I'll look into it," I promised him.

"I appreciate it. I enjoyed working with you, Detective Wakeland." Ben glanced down at Ada. "We're gonna grab some things from home, Mom, and then we're off to the airport."

Ada stared at him in surprise, then nodded, sighing. "I know you're doing what's best for us, Ben."

"Stay safe, both of you," I said. Bending, I reached for Ada's hand. "It's been a pleasure knowing you."

"Ha!" she responded. "I'll bet it hasn't been. Goodbye, Detective."

Ben wheeled his mother away.

With the USB that Ben had given me securely into my pocket, I headed back to the main corridor. I'd look at it later, when I was alone. And I'd try to find out where Leo Dubois was when I had a moment, too. Did he have a connection with the USB Ben had given me?

A rush of people had me positioning myself against the windows. As I waited for them to pass by, I called Abby.

"Hi, Mum," she said brightly.

"Abby… have you heard?"

"Heard what?"

"There's an evacuation. Check your app."

"Evacuation? Oh, God. I've been listening to music with Ivy."

"Get Logan to come home from work. I'll be there as soon as I can."

"Logan came home earlier. He went out with Dad in an RFS truck. Mum… I'm here alone with the kids."

"Stay calm, honey. Just—"

"But what do I do? I have to get the dogs and the kitten. And all the boxes and suitcases."

"Remember the plan? You go, with the kids—and the kitten. We've pre-arranged with some friends to get the dogs. I'll come and pick up the luggage and boxes. Don't wait for me. Just *go*, okay?"

"Okay. It's just scary, y'know?"

"I know. But remember, the fire probably won't reach us—they're just being cautious. I love you. And drive safely."

"I will. Love you."

I hurried along the corridor, headed for the stairs. From the long stretch of windows, I could see ribbons of people leaving CQ and heading for their cars.

A boy tore down the road to CQ on his bicycle, one hand on the handle-bars, the other arm in plaster and a sling. The thick lines of departing vehicles held him back as he tried to navigate his way through. Throwing down the bike, he began running.

It was Jordan.

A cold fear gnawed at me. There was something about Jordan that was upsetting Angie. I didn't know what it was, but something was definitely wrong.

What if Jordan were trying to get to his mother in order to harm her? She'd woken from her coma—and there might be things she was about to remember that Jordan didn't want her to remember.

CHAPTER SEVENTY-TWO

I needed to get to Jordan—before he got to his mother. Just in case.

The lifts at CQ Technology had a crowd of people waiting. I rushed to the stairs and headed down the three flights to the foyer. Then I sprinted across to the hospital quarter.

I just missed Jordan as he made it to a lift. I caught the next lift that was going up. I didn't catch up to Jordan until I found him coming out of Angie's room on the fourth floor.

What had he done?

"Jordan!" I gasped, running to him. "What are you doing here?"

His face was coated with oil and sweat, his eyes dark and angry. "Where's my mother?"

Bewildered, I went to look in Angie's room.

It was empty.

"Where is she?" Jordan demanded.

"I'll find out," I told him.

I went from room to room—all empty. Okay, that was good—a lot of patients had been moved, not just Angie.

A nurse stood in an empty room, collecting some equipment. It was Joseph, one of the nurses who'd been looking after Angie.

"Joseph," I said, "Hi. I'm looking for Angie Green. Can you tell me where she is?"

He turned. "The patients from this floor have been moved down a floor. It's just a safety procedure, due to the fire alert. I'm not sure exactly which room she's in. Everything's a bit topsy-turvy right now."

"Okay. Thanks, Joseph."

"I'll let you know that all visitors have to leave the hospital," he added. "It's patients and staff only."

"I understand," I said.

When I returned to the corridor, Jordan was already running for the stairs.

I followed him down to the next floor.

Jordan raced along the corridor, looking in each room, finally vanishing inside a room at the end.

I was totally out of puff by the time I reached the end of the corridor, hauling deep breaths into my lungs.

Inside the room, there were four patients in their beds. Three of them looked over at me, startled. The fourth patient—Angie—was sleeping.

Jordan was sitting beside his mother on her bed, one arm leaning against a trolley. His other arm was encased in plaster and a sling.

I made my way over. "You got away from me, Jordan," I scolded.

"Mum's worried someone's gonna hurt her," he told me. "She called and told me."

Pulling up a chair, I sat down heavily, my chest almost wheezing. "She said that?"

"Yeah. She's scared."

I glanced at Angie, who appeared to be sleeping peacefully.

"What did she say, exactly?" I asked.

"She said a doctor that she didn't know came at her with a syringe. She yelled for help, and the doctor ran off. That was when she was in the other room, up on the next floor."

I softened my tone. "She's still recovering from her coma. She's going to see and feel some things that aren't real. I spoke with a hospital psychologist about your mum recently."

"Well, the psych is wrong," Jordan insisted. "Mum's not scared for no reason."

"Jordan, you can't stay here. There's a fire alert—did you know that?"

He shook his head.

"Well, visitors are not allowed. You need your dad to come and pick you up."

"I'm not leaving Mum."

"I'm afraid you have to. Look, I'm going to find out what happened to the security guard that I had stationed here for your mother. I'll get him back, okay?"

"Why did he leave my mum alone?"

"I don't know. But I'll fix this."

Taking out my phone, I called Samuel, the security guard.

"Hey, Detective," he answered. "I was told my services were no longer needed—that the patient was being moved."

"Who told you that you weren't needed?" I asked.

"I got a phone call to go to another job. Something must have gotten mixed up with the messaging."

"Hmmm, okay. No problem. Could I get you back on *this* job?"

"Yeah, I can do that."

"Great." I explained to Samuel where Angie was currently located in the hospital.

Next, I called Carlson. But he didn't pick up.

Frustrated, I turned back to Jordan. "I'll take you to your dad's house, now, okay? That's if he hasn't evacuated yet. He's probably out looking for you."

"Not until the guard comes back."

I stared at Jordan for a moment. It was clear he wasn't going to budge. And I wasn't about to leave him alone with Angie, either. I waited for fifteen minutes at Angie's bedside with Jordan until the guard arrived.

Jordan seemed so normal—just a son who was worried about his mother. But was he? I was still unable to get my thoughts straight about him.

A text message popped up on my phone. It was from Abby. Her message said the neighbours had come for our two Maremma dogs, and that she'd arrived at the evacuation centre.

Those were two things off my mind.

I left the hospital with Jordan and took him a few streets away to his father's house. No one answered my knock at the door.

Turning the car around, I headed towards the evacuation centre.

After exiting my car, Jordan walked with hesitant steps towards the centre. I asked Abby and the RFS volunteers that were there to keep an eye on him.

Then I finally headed home.

The dark sky was terrifying as I parked outside my house. There was an eerie quiet and lack of movement as I walked up the steps and entered through the front door. No dogs greeted me. No kitten mewed. No child called out to me. And there was no Pete.

I paused for a moment, taking the object out of my pocket that Ben had given me. It was what Ben had called a flash drive—an item that I knew as a USB. This was the first moment I'd had a chance to think about it since he'd given it to me.

Whatever was on it, Ben must consider it to be very important. Was it about the identity of the eagle avatar?

I didn't have time right now to think more on that. I placed the drive in a secure spot in my police vest.

Next, I wheeled out the suitcases and packed them into the back of my car. Then I hauled the boxes out.

That was it. I was ready to go. By the end of this day, our house might still be standing, or it might not. As long as we all made it through, that would be enough.

CHAPTER SEVENTY-THREE

I returned to the strange quiet of a large police station that was on skeleton staff.

Thea had gone to help control the traffic at police roadblocks. Franco and Melainey still weren't back from their lunch break. That was good, because I wanted time alone right now.

My steps echoed along the empty floor as I headed to the study room.

I took the USB from my vest and inserted it into a computer port.

But the information that came up on the screen was encrypted.

I had no idea how to unencrypt a document. I didn't deal with this kind of thing.

I should send it onto the federal police.

But as I sat there with my fingers reaching for my phone, I hesitated.

What if someone at the NineOak corporation had become aware of the AFP involvement? It could explain why Ben Tremayne's contract had been terminated. I didn't want the wrong people alerted to whatever was in this document. Ben had trusted me with it.

There was someone else I could send the document to—someone not directly connected with the AFP. And that was Detective Liz Booth. In her line of work—chasing paedophiles across the dark web—she dealt with a lot of encrypted documents.

I sent Liz a text message, writing a quick line about the document.

Within seconds, she was calling me back. "Kate…" she yawned. "Give me a minute."

"Oh… you were asleep, weren't you? I forgot to check the time difference."

"Don't give it a thought. I told you to call me anytime, and I meant it. I'm sleeping at all kinds of odd hours anyway. Whatever you've got, I want it."

"Okay, I'm sending you the document now."

I sent the contents of the USB through to Liz. And waited.

I heard rustling on the other end of the phone line as Liz moved from her bed and opened her laptop. A few moments of silence followed, apart from the clicking of keys.

Someone was trying to call me. Was it Pete?

While I waited for Liz to come back on the line, I checked the caller's ID.

No, not Pete. It was Jordan Green.

I sighed. What did he want? To tell me wild stories again? I didn't have time for that.

I heard Liz make a few more taps at her keyboard. Then she inhaled a sharp breath.

"Liz?"

"Don't tell me who sent you this," she replied, "but please know they risked a lot to get it."

"What is it?" I breathed.

"I need a little more time to be certain of what I'm seeing here. But if I'm right, this is going to blow sky-high. It's a photograph taken of a web page."

"What kind of website?"

"It's a site on the dark web, where jobs are being posted and fulfilled. The jobs are of the worst kind. Jobs for paid killers, illegal types of pornography…. This is huge. It's a meeting house for criminals."

"I'm stunned. I don't even know how my contact managed to source this file."

"Oh, gosh, there's Adele's fish bait symbol. This was her, just days ago. Asking for assistance. Oh… lovely—she put a price on my head. To get me off her tail—permanently."

"Oh, God."

"Don't worry, it looks like it's been called off. Anyway, I guess I knew what I was letting myself in for in the chase for Adele." She paused. "Kate, there is something more to this website that I can't quite figure out."

"What kind of thing is it?"

"Numbers. Big numbers."

"Money?"

"No, these numbers are too large. There isn't enough money in the world for these kinds of numbers. I have no idea what this is all about."

A text message jumped up on my phone. It was from Jordan. He must have grown impatient when I didn't answer his call.

I quickly read the message: *Just talked to Toby. He's at home with Ollie, but my dad's not there. I need to get them, but the RFS people won't let me out of here.*

Was Jordan just trying to cause trouble? There shouldn't be anyone left at CQ Village—where Jordan's father lived. It'd all been evacuated.

"Liz, I need to go," I said. "I'll call you back soon."

"Be careful, Kate. If anyone knows you have this information, it'll be dangerous for you. Stay safe, okay?"

"I understand. You stay safe, too."

After ending the call with Liz, I attempted to contact Carlson. No answer came. Okay, if Jordan had spoken with Toby, then Toby must have access to a phone. I called Jordan and asked for the number that Toby had called from.

I tapped the number Jordan had given me into my phone—and called it.

A tiny voice answered. "Hello?"

"Hello, is this Toby?"

"Yes."

"This is Detective Kate. You remember me, don't you, Toby? Can I talk with your daddy?"

"He went out."

"Where are you?"

"At home."

"Where's Ollie?"

"With me."

"Is anyone else there with you?"

"No."

"Wait there, Toby. I'm coming."

Taking the USB with me, I left the room.

I couldn't begin to tell what this was all about. What had happened to Carlson? How did the kids get left behind?

It was only when I'd driven halfway to CQ Village that a dark thought lodged in my mind.

Could this be some kind of elaborate trap that Jordan had concocted?

It felt as if the air had changed. Underneath the thick smoke, things seemed to be shifting about.

CHAPTER SEVENTY-FOUR

I pulled up outside Carlson's house and raced to the front door.

Everything was still and quiet, apart from the monotonous sounds of the evacuation alarms in surrounding streets.

Rapping urgently on the front door, I called out. "Open up, please—Carlson! Toby!"

No one came.

If the children were here, why weren't they opening the door?

I ran around to the side of the house, trying to check through the windows. But Carlson had all the shutters closed.

A child's voice came from inside the house: *be quiet*!

Okay, so they *were* here.

I tapped on a window. "Hello?"

Tiny fingers appeared through the shutter, only to be snatched away.

I knocked on the pane of glass again. "Toby! Ollie! It's Detective Kate."

The shutters opened. Toby and Oliver stood in the dark room, staring back at me. I guessed that it'd been the smaller one—Oliver—who'd stuck his fingers through the shutter, before his brother had pulled him back.

"Can you open the front door?" I called to them.

"We're not allowed," Toby called back. "Daddy said to wait."

"Where's your daddy?" I asked.

Toby just shook his head.

"I'm the police, Toby," I said. "It's okay. You can open up."

The boys stood there silently.

As I was weighing up whether to break in through the window or the front door, Oliver turned and sped from the room. I headed back to the front of the house.

Oliver opened the door. Toby stepped up behind him.

"We have to wait for Daddy," Toby explained, but he was no longer sounding as convinced of that.

"Don't worry," I said as softly as I could manage, "your dad will understand. I'll take you somewhere where there are lots of people who can look after you. I can even show you Detective Franco's kitten. Would you like that?"

Toby's nod was hesitant, but Oliver was eager, slipping his hand into mine.

I took them to the car and buckled them in, then drove away, bound for the same evacuation centre as where Abby was.

What had happened to Carlson? A vehicle accident? A victim of foul play?

I drove along the road out of the village. Ahead, the massive CQ building squatted. I needed to drive around the building to get out of here, towards the other side of town.

Hectares of forest surrounded CQ. Dense bushland grew on either side of this road. If the fires reached this area, it'd go up like a tinderbox.

A man raced along the road just up ahead.

From the back, he looked like Sean Macklin. As I drove closer, I became certain that he was Sean.

The loose shirt he wore flew up as he ran. A pistol was jammed into the back waistband of his jeans.

I sucked in a breath.

He was headed for CQ. With a gun.

God. Is he going after Angie?

I had to warn CQ. But by the time they'd have a chance to secure all entry points, Sean would be inside the building.

I've got Angie's little boys right here with me. I can't let Sean get to her. I have to act.

Clicking out of my seatbelt, I put my foot on the accelerator. As soon as I was just in front of Sean, I brought the car in sharp. I parked straight, so that the children would have no view of Sean through the small rear window of my SUV.

"Stay here!" I instructed them, before parking and jumping out of the vehicle. I pressed *lock* on my keyring, ensuring that the kids couldn't get out.

I ran to the back of the car, pulling out my gun and holding it on Sean. "Hands on head. And drop."

Sean's eyes were dazed as he stared at me, gasping as he collected his breath. He had long scratches down his face, blood mingling with the sweat in his three-day-beard.

He shook his head. "You gotta let me go."

"Don't leave me with no choice, Sean. And don't think about touching that gun. You'll lose."

"You can have the gun. If you let me go."

"I can't do that."

"Then we have a problem."

Blood dripped in a thin line down his neck and onto his tee-shirt.

CHAPTER SEVENTY-FIVE

"Make no mistake, I *will* shoot," I told Sean.

I stole a quick glance back at the car. Toby had unbuckled his seatbelt and was standing on the seat, peering out the rear window. He couldn't see me holding my gun from that angle at least.

Sean's jaw went slack. "You've got Angie's kids."

"Not your business. Hands on head and get down on your stomach. Now!"

"Will you talk to me if I do that?"

"Guaranteed."

Sean dropped to his knees and then stretched himself out on the grass.

Stooping, I swept up Sean's gun from the back waistband of his jeans.

"Okay, now listen—" Sean started.

"Wait your turn." I told him and then called the station.

Shintani answered.

"Jiro, I've got an arrest in progress. Just outside CQ, on the hospital side. It's Sean Macklin. He had a pistol and was running towards CQ."

"I'll be there as soon as I can," Shintani said.

I was surprised that Shintani chose to handle this himself. Franco and Melainey might have been off having a beer together, but they were still on duty.

As I ended the call, I looked around at the car. There was no little face at the rear window now.

"Okay, Sean, you've got your chance to talk," I said. "Tell me what you're doing here, *with a gun*."

"The gun's not loaded."

"It's still an offence, Sean. Hey, how'd you hurt your head?"

"I was on my motorbike. The police and fire brigade have a roadblock up, and I couldn't get through. I tried going through the forest. Smashed my bike on a tree. So, I ran the rest of the way."

"Where were you going?"

"Angie's in danger."

"Angie's not in danger. The hospital has an action plan in the event that fire does reach CQ."

"It's not the fire I'm worried about. I'm worried someone's going to hurt her."

"They've placed Angie in a room with other patients. She's in full view of hospital staff."

"I know. She called me."

"Sean, if I have this straight—that would be the first time you and Angie have spoken to each other… in over a year?"

"Yeah, that's right."

"If Angie has a problem… tell me, why would she call *you*?"

"Because no one else will listen to her. She woke up a short while ago to find that a doctor she didn't recognise was about to give her an injection. She cried out, and he left."

It was the same story that Jordan had told me.

"Sean, Angie's a bit hazy at the moment. She's been saying things that aren't quite correct."

"What if she's right? You've had a guard stationed outside her hospital room for a reason. What she needs now is someone by her bedside. Look, I wasn't going to hold the gun on anyone—just if a doctor insisted on injecting Angie with something. Until that doctor can be checked out, I wasn't gonna let that happen."

The story was ludicrous. A doctor trying to inject Angie with something he shouldn't? Either Sean was lying or Angie was still delusional.

But the guard could keep watch at Angie's bedside just as well as he could outside the door. Making a call to the guard, I requested he move to a chair beside Angie.

Sean noticeably relaxed.

Above the trees, grey smoke moved across the sky. I continued to hold my gun on Sean. I didn't know if I could trust anything he'd said.

A new thought gripped me. Had Sean done something to Carlson Green?

I drew in a long breath. "Sean, do you know where Carlson is?"

"Carlson? Why?"

"Just answer my question, please."

"Is that why you've got Toby and Ollie in your car—because Green is missing?"

"When was the last time you saw him?"

"Days ago. And that was only in passing. I saw him in town."

"You sure of that?"

"Yeah, I'm sure."

I chose not to continue questioning Sean. If he'd hurt Carlson, he wasn't going to tell me.

If Carlson *had* been harmed—or killed—then Sean Macklin was going to become my number one suspect.

CHAPTER SEVENTY-SIX

Dressed in his expensive suit and tie, Inspector Shintani didn't look quite the part when he pulled up in a police wagon. But he handcuffed and collected Sean Macklin in the same smooth, efficient manner that he approached everything.

"What happened to Franco and Melainey?" I asked him.

Shintani shook his head. "Can't get hold of either of them."

That wasn't right. Two detectives who were on duty should be contactable.

Shintani left with the sombre, handcuffed Sean Macklin.

I drove Toby and Oliver to the evacuation centre.

Abby took the little boys under her wing without question. She'd teamed up with Nola, and together they were keeping the kids entertained.

Jordan was in a corner, talking with Dakota Macklin. Her eyes were red and swollen. She'd obviously been crying. When the two of them noticed me, they rushed over.

"My father called me," Dakota cried. "He said he's in *jail*. He wouldn't tell me why."

I'd forgotten all about Dakota.

"Your dad is only in a lockup cell," I told her. "That's not jail. How did you get here?"

"I was staying with Grandma Macklin, in town. I'm here with her."

"Okay, good," I said.

I turned to Jordan. "Okay, so you were right about your brothers—they were all alone. Have you heard from your father yet?"

He shook his head, an anxious, tense look in his eyes. "No."

"Look, just stay here. I'll go find him—all right? Help Abby look after your brothers. And don't go anywhere. Do you promise?"

"Will the guard keep watching my mum?" Jordan asked.

"Yes, he definitely will," I replied.

"Okay, promise," he said somewhat reluctantly. "Thanks for getting Tobes and Ollie."

"No problem."

I walked across to hug Abby, Nola, and all the kids, and then headed off again.

When I returned to the station, Franco and Melainey were still gone. That was a very long time to be out having a beer. Shintani was looking peeved, and I didn't blame him.

After lunch, I headed down to our station's holding cell.

Sean Macklin stood as I approached, fists curling around the bars. "Don't think anything bad of me. You don't understand."

"Sean," I said, "Carlson Green still hasn't shown up."

He met my eyes, but in a guarded way. "That's got nothing to do with me."

"My problem is that I found you just streets away from Carlson's house. With a gun. And now he's missing."

"I told you it was unloaded."

"Was it unloaded when you left home with it? Or was it holding a bullet or two?"

"You think I shot Carlson? You can go check that my story's true. You'll find my motorbike in the forest, all banged up. Like I said it was."

"We're on skeleton staff. We can't go searching a forest for a bike right now."

"Trust me—I know nothing about Carlson. All I care about is Angie."

"And that's another problem. *Angie*. There's a huge, missing chunk out of your story about you and Angie. According to you—you and she were an item. But then she suddenly gets up and runs to the other end of Australia. She doesn't tell you where she's going, doesn't communicate with you for the next year. She doesn't even tell you when she comes back to town. Angie herself says you two weren't in a relationship. So… you can understand why I'm having trouble with your story."

Still holding the bars, he hung his head. "I can't..."

"You can't *what*?"

"I can't tell you."

"If you can't fill in the blanks for me, then what do you think is going to happen? I'm going to come up with my own theories, that's what."

He remained quiet, pressing his forehead against a bar.

"Sean?"

Inhaling deeply, he nodded. His eyes were wet as he raised his face. "Jordan... he's not Carlson's biological son. He's mine."

"Jordan is *your* son?"

"Yes."

I exhaled. "I don't understand. If he's yours, then—?"

"Angie and I first met a long time ago."

"Right. Seeing as Jordan is sixteen, then what you're saying is that you and Angie met about seventeen years ago?"

"Yeah, about that. She was married to Carlson at the time, but she was separated from him. At first, I was just a friend who was trying to help her. But, we, uh, we fell in love."

I wasn't at all sure if I believed Sean. This revelation was certainly a shock. But I decided to play along and see what else he had to say.

"And what happened next?" I asked.

"Angie changed her mind about leaving Carlson. She didn't tell me why. She had a baby a few months later. *Jordan*. I just assumed he was Carlson's. Dumb of me, I know. I got on with my life. I got married and had a daughter. My marriage didn't last long. Marie left me when Dakota was only three."

"And how did you find out that Jordan was yours?"

Sean sighed with a heavy fall of his shoulders. "Fifteen years after Jordan was born, Angie divorced Carlson. I was on my own, raising my daughter. I was lonely. I started coming to see Angie. No one was more surprised than me when Angie and I fell in love all over again."

"So, you're saying you rekindled your relationship?"

"Yeah. And at first, things were good. Really good. But then I brought Dakota over. She was thirteen, and I still thought of her as a little girl. But, she became infatuated with Jordan. Do you see the problem?"

"Yes, I definitely do. If what you're saying is true, then Dakota is Jordan's half-sister by blood."

"Exactly. And that was the point at which Angie first told me that Jordan was mine. I couldn't believe it. Jordan looks so much like Angie, it never occurred to me that he could be my son."

"He does look like Angie. A lot."

Sean nodded. "As soon as she told me, I wanted to tell Jordan. I thought he deserved to know. But Angie disagreed. We had a big argument. She left town."

"Why didn't she want Jordan to know—did she say?"

"I assumed it was because she wanted to get back with Carlson—yet again. I thought I was fooling myself that she loved me. But Carlson went to live in the city after that. I didn't know whether Angie was heartbroken over that. She confuses me."

"But you're still in love with her?"

"Yes. I think I *have* been ever since the day I met her. It's probably why my marriage to Marie didn't work, being honest."

"Hmmm. I take it that Jordan still doesn't know he's your biological son?"

"No. I want to tell him—but it didn't feel right while Angie was in a coma. But I did tell Dakota. I ended up telling her the night after I went to get her and Jordan from the canyon. I had to. It blindsided me that Dakota was still interested in Jordan, but I couldn't let that situation go on any longer."

"Of course. How did she take the news?"

"Not well, as you can imagine. Lots of tears, lots of anger. I hated hurting my little girl like that."

I pictured Dakota as I'd seen her at the evacuation centre. Perhaps some of her tears had been about the situation with Jordan and not only about her father being in the holding cell.

"Poor kid. Sean, do you have any idea why Angie came back to Tallman's Valley?"

"No, none. I didn't even know she was here. Until the day she and her parents were shot."

"You're certain you didn't know?"

"Yeah. Dead certain. All I knew was what I saw on the news. Angie's parents were dead, and she was in a coma, and Jordan—*my son*—was now in Carlson's care. And I couldn't do anything about Jordan being with Carlson. Look, I know he raised Jordan—but he's been a pretty absent sort of father."

I looked away, trying to grasp all that Sean had told me. If it was true, it was a startling confession.

"Sean, this is hard to say… but how can you be sure that what Angie told you is real—about Jordan being your son?"

He met my eyes. "Angie has a safe deposit box, at the post office in Tallman's Valley. And I have the key. I initially had a hard time accepting what she told me, so she agreed to have a DNA test done."

"On Jordan?"

"Yes."

"How did you and Angie manage that without telling him why?"

"She told him it was an ancestry test."

"Right."

"Well, the results came back, and there was no doubt."

"Okay. So, where's the key?"

"On my keyring. You've got it, along with my wallet… and gun. The number of the box is E21."

"I'll be back," I told him.

CHAPTER SEVENTY-SEVEN

The Tallman's Valley post office was closed, but the large bank of safety deposit boxes was located along an external wall.

Standing in front of box E21, I unlocked it. There was nothing in it but an envelope.

Quickly, I opened the envelope. It was a paternity test—just as Sean Macklin had told me it would be.

The results were definite. Angie was Jordan's mother. And Sean was Jordan's biological father—with a probability of 99.9999%.

What a terrible situation for everyone involved.

I snapped a photo of the document before replacing it in the envelope and closing the deposit box.

I glanced up at the sky as I walked back to my car. The smoke was still thick, blocking out the sun. I had little idea what was happening on the fire front, apart from the news reports.

Taking out my phone, I called Pete. I just wanted to hear his voice—I wanted to know that he and Logan were okay.

There was no reply. That wasn't unusual. Big fires were noisy, with communication kept to what was necessary. Still, I wished I'd been able to contact them.

Switching on the radio, I listened to the fire report.

Today, in terms of Sydney, everything depended upon whether the fire would jump the mighty Hawkesbury River. So much of Sydney could be wiped out today. And, as for Tallman's Valley, we had fire bearing straight down on us.

I sat in my car, out of the smoky air. Letting my eyes close, I stole a moment to calm and recalibrate myself. This was the kind of day in which mistakes could easily be made. And I couldn't get anything wrong. Too much was at stake.

I believed Sean when he'd said he was trying to protect Angie. I sensed he really did care deeply for her. But taking a gun with him was the wrong way to go about it. He'd left me with no choice but to arrest him.

I still didn't know what had happened to Carlson Green. Until I had more information, I had to consider that Sean might have harmed him.

Sean had told me the truth about some things, but perhaps not all things.

An alert came through on my radio. It was Shintani.

"Kate, a resident just reported a body on the banks of Coldwater Lake."

I took a breath. "Male or female, Jiro?"

"It's a male."

"Heading down there now."

I drove to the part of the lake Jiro instructed. It was just off one of the boat ramps.

All the way, Carlson's name was on repeat in my head, like a low drum beat. Something dire was keeping him from his children.

Was the body Carlson's?

Perhaps Sean had grown angry, thinking that Angie had returned to Tallman's Valley in order to try to reunite with Carlson. Was that enough for Sean to have killed Carlson?

I arrived at a scene of a man face-down in the reedy mud at the lake edge. He wore a red tee-shirt and denim shorts.

His hair was blonde, like Carlson's. But with the muddy residue clumped on his hair and body, I couldn't be certain it was him.

An elderly man stood on the ramp with a walking stick, looking on with a gloomy expression. There was no one else here.

"I was in my house looking out at the smoke with my binoculars," the man told me. "Trying to see if I could spot any fires. But then I saw *him*. Terrible, terrible thing. What a waste of a life."

I nodded at him. "Thank you for calling us, sir."

I stepped across to the body and crouched. Gently, I moved the man's head enough to expose his profile. I caught a glimpse of a face that was much younger than Carlson's.

By the ligature marks around his neck, it seemed likely he'd been strangled.

I recognised him. He was Leo Dubois. The programmer who worked with Ben.

CHAPTER SEVENTY-EIGHT

I waited at the boat ramp for the forensics team to arrive. There were only two of them. No one else could make the trip today.

Leo's body was taken away.

Who had killed him?

Ben had told me he was worried about Leo not showing up for work and that Leo had been acting strangely.

There'd been no clues at the site—it seemed that Leo's body had been dumped in the water and had merely drifted until it had bumped up against the ramp and remained there.

There was nothing here now but a depression in the muddy ground where Leo's body had been.

Carlson Green was still missing.

I contacted Detective Grimshaw, telling her about the discovery of Leo Dubois' body and requesting help with finding Carlson. I was becoming increasingly concerned that Carlson had met a similar fate to Dubois.

Leaving the lakeside, I drove out to Sean Macklin's house. I still had his keys, and I had his permission to enter his property. On the way, I had to stop at three roadblocks and show my ID. I cursed being in my own car and not a police vehicle.

I parked outside and walked up the front steps. The field surrounding his house was empty of the cows and horses I'd seen there last time. I guessed that he'd moved them elsewhere in case of fire.

Sean's large, ranch-style home and sheds took me twenty minutes to search. I even drove down to the small shed right at the back of his property to look inside that.

There was no sign of Carlson.

I tried calling Carlson's phone again. Still nothing.

A minute later, my phone rang. But it wasn't Carlson calling me back.

It was Liz.

"Kate," she said, "there's a new development."

"What is it?"

"Before I proceed, I need to say something. I'm worried for you. This is dangerous information we're dealing with."

"Okay, I understand. I need to take this higher up."

"Yes and no. You need to be careful who you take this to. Kate. This is *my* world, the kind of world I've been dealing with for the past couple of decades. Even so, this document of yours is something new. It's something I haven't seen before. That makes it even more dangerous."

I inhaled the humid air outside Sean Macklin's house. "I'll be careful. Should we talk again tomorrow, when we've had time to figure out our next steps?"

"Kate, we need to figure out those next steps right *now*. I'm sorry. I've opened a gate. My team and I managed to figure out Adele's password and get into that website. If the open gate is discovered, those people will do anything to close it. Do you understand? Your life is in danger." She took a breath. "Where are you now?"

"I'm at a property out of town. I'm looking for a missing father. Carlson Green—Angie's ex-husband."

"On your own?"

"Yes."

"Get out of there. Don't talk to me again until you're in your car. *Run*!"

I did as Liz instructed.

As I pulled on my seatbelt and began driving, I spoke to her again. "I'm on my way."

"Good. I need to ask you something—who, at your level or higher, would you trust with your life?"

"*You*. And Shintani."

"Then go to Shintani. Explain the situation. Then call me back while you're there with him. I'll tell you what I know then."

My search for Carlson Green would have to wait.

A small white truck drove past. The driver peered across at me. The dark window tinting prevented me from seeing their face.

I cursed being in my own car for the second time today—I couldn't run the truck's licence plate number.

As I watched in my rear vision mirror, the truck parked at the roadside near Sean Macklin's house.

Whoever they were, they must have come through the roadblocks. The only people being allowed through to these streets were residents or police or the fire brigade.

There didn't seem to be any point to their coming down this street—especially because the driver had just pulled back onto the road and was driving up behind me.

CHAPTER SEVENTY-NINE

The white truck stayed at a distance behind my car. But I understood that I was being followed.

The truck peeled off just before I reached the police station, vanishing around a corner as I walked inside.

I was okay. I was safe. Whoever was driving that truck, and whatever they intended to do, I didn't need to worry right now.

Franco and Melainey still weren't back at the station. That was getting very concerning. They should have at least seen the fire alerts by now. They should have been in contact.

I headed along the hallway to Shintani's office.

The door was ajar.

I knocked, and when no answer came, I nudged the door open.

Shintani was sitting at his desk, bolt upright—a distant look frozen in his dark eyes.

"Jiro?"

Frowning, he turned to me, his eyes focusing. "Kate. Yes, come in. Close the door."

I sat heavily on the plush armchair next to him. "What's wrong?"

He exhaled. "The investigation into the tampering of the Witness Mountain virtual program has been suspended."

"*Excuse me*? Who gave that order?"

"I wasn't given that information."

"But… the investigation would barely have gotten started. That was a *federal police operation.* Who has the power to stop *that*?"

"Trust me," he said, "I'm going to do my best to find out why that order was given."

"I'm floored."

"I knew you would be. I'm sorry." He shook his head. "How did things go at Coldwater Lake?"

"It was a young man named Leo Dubois. Up until yesterday, he worked at CQ Tech. Ben Tremayne was worried Leo had been acting out of character. Ben's on his way back to the US at the moment."

Shintani bowed his head. "We need a statement from Ben as soon as practical."

"Yes, we certainly do. Jiro, there's another problem."

"Go ahead."

"I was given a document this morning—an encrypted document. I passed it along to Detective Liz Booth for decoding. I… I wasn't certain about sending it on through the usual channels…."

"I understand."

Nodding, I threaded my fingers together. "The document was a photograph taken of a website page—on the dark web. Liz isn't exactly sure what the main business of the website is, but it isn't good. There were big numbers coming up—and she didn't understand what they were about. She also saw jobs being posted on there—of the worst criminal kind."

Shintani's expression hardened. "I see."

"Liz has more information, but she wants me to have a trusted team in place before proceeding. I'm starting that team with *you.*"

He gave me a serious look. "I appreciate your confidence in me."

"Shall we start? I have Liz waiting."

"Yes, let's do that."

I called Liz, and we opened a secure three-way video call on Shintani's computer.

"Hello, Detective Booth," said the inspector.

"Inspector Shintani, good to see you," Liz replied. "It's been a while."

Shintani nodded, the briefest of smiles flickering at the corners of his mouth. "Months."

"Not the best of circumstances at the moment, I'm afraid," she said. "Has Kate filled you in?"

"She gave me a summary," he replied. "So, this document that Kate was given is from a website on the dark web?"

"Yes, it is," she told him. "Did you hear about the recent death of Adele Hobson?"

"I did," he said.

"Well," Liz said, "through the laptop that Adele left behind and the document that Kate just gave me, we have a short window of opportunity. We've found our way into a criminal base on the dark web. The website is worldwide. The UK, America, Asia—everywhere."

I drew in a breath. "It's incredible you found your way in so fast. I meant to tell you that before… but, I was on the run."

"I've got a great team," Liz said, nodding. "Detective Rosa Alonto is especially brilliant with this sort of thing. And, would you believe that Adele's username is *jailbait*?"

"Oh, my stars," I gasped. "After all this time, she was still identifying as *that*?"

Shintani frowned. "I'm not following."

"I'll catch you up quickly," I told him.

Within a minute, I'd explained everything I knew about Adele and J.L and their tattoos.

Shintani stared at me, the muscles beneath his eyes drawing up. "So, we might still have this J.L character in our police force? That's not a pleasant thought."

"No, it isn't," Liz said. "We need to find out who he is, pronto."

"Can you please explain this website you've found?" Shintani asked.

"The website is called *The Quarry*," Liz began.

"*The Quarry*?" Raising his eyebrows, Shintani leaned forward in his chair. "Odd name."

Liz nodded. "Our team think it's called that because they're carrying out mining."

"Mining? What sort of mining?" he asked her.

I listened in carefully.

Liz chewed her upper lip, nodding again. "They're mining information. And it's the kind of information that takes up enormous computing resources. I'll give you an example. A request was put through on *The Quarry* last month to find and kill someone on a witness protection program—Duncan Anderson. The responder to that request used a computer program to find Duncan."

I stared at Liz in shock. "Duncan Anderson? That was the Australian man who died in the UK—he fell from a bridge. And yes, he'd been on a witness protection program, which is why I remember his name. So, it wasn't accidental…."

"No, not an accident." Liz drew in her mouth. "I haven't come across this sort of thing before—not at the level I operate at."

Shintani released a long, deliberate breath. "How did they find Duncan? Using computer programs, you said?"

"Artificial intelligence," Liz answered. "We've worked out that they're running AI programs day and night."

"Sounds like a sophisticated operation," Shintani remarked. "Kate mentioned that you also saw large numbers posted on *The Quarry* website. Do I assume those numbers are to do with the AI programs?"

"Correct," Liz said. "We suspect they're using supercomputers on a network—computers that can perform millions or even billions of calculations per second. These people would be feeding in the known information, and then letting their programs determine the likeliest possibilities."

"And, in Duncan's case, after the calculations were done, a paid killer was sent to murder him?" I asked.

"Yes," Liz said. "Exactly that."

Shintani looked from me to Liz, his brow deeply furrowed. "Do you and your team have any idea why they're posting the calculation numbers on the website, Liz?"

"We think so," she replied. "These supercomputers and the processes they run are very expensive. People are paying for that computing power—for the hours of processing billions of calculations. The numbers are the amount of calculations carried out per job."

I folded my arms in tight. "I'll take a running guess that at least one or more of the supercomputers on this network will be found at CQ Technology."

"Almost certainly," Liz agreed. "We're working to determine who is behind the avatars. We know Adele's, obviously, because we're logged in as her. She uses the image of a bait fish. And… we found J.L. He's using an image of a jail cell as an avatar. It seems he's one of the paid killers."

"This is very shocking news," Shintani said. "If J.L is in the police force, that means we've got an officer that is a hitman."

"That's right," Liz said. "And there's no guarantee that J.L is the one and only cop on *The Quarry*. We don't have the slightest idea who the other identities are. We've caught hold of the tail of a fast-moving animal—and that's all."

Shintani inclined his head, nodding. "Perhaps, at the moment, this shouldn't go any further than us three, and your team, Liz."

"Oh, I agree," Liz said, rubbing her weary-looking eyes. "We need to keep this locked down. We're racing against the clock. Adele being dead poses a distinct problem. Because a dead woman can't have logged into *The Quarry*. It's only a matter of time before someone picks up on the fact they've been infiltrated. Then I'm quite certain that The Quarry website will vanish in a puff of smoke."

A spell of silence followed.

Liz inhaled deeply, her gaze settling on me. "Kate, there's one last thing I need you to know."

I frowned. "What is it?"

"The latest job that J.L has agreed to take on is one of his paid killer jobs. It's local. The Blue Mountains. He's been hired to go after a target there. The trouble is, I can't tell who that target is. The only thing I can tell is that the target… is in the police force. And the person I immediately thought of is *you*, Kate."

I gazed back at Liz. "That's why you urged me to leave Sean Macklin's property, isn't it?"

Her face creased with concern. "Yes. I'm sorry, Kate. I hate to give you this news."

My throat thickened. "There was a truck. The driver followed me all the way from Macklin's house."

Shintani met my eyes with a direct gaze. "You're not to set foot outside this station without me. Do you understand?"

CHAPTER EIGHTY

Shintani and I walked to the lunchroom together, lost in our thoughts.

We didn't speak as we made ourselves cups of tea.

The room was empty. The whole station felt silent. The only officers on duty were two at the front desk and Grimshaw on the other side of the station.

I felt shaken, not myself. I needed to find my sense of balance—quickly. There wasn't time for anything else.

This wasn't the first time in my career that people had threatened to kill me. I worked in homicide. Many of the people I'd dealt with were the worst kind of criminals.

But this was a *paid killer*. It was different. I'd never dealt with anything like this. At this moment, all I could think of was Abby and my grandchildren… and Pete.

It didn't feel so much like a fight for my life as much as a fight to come home… *to them.*

Shintani had made his usual green tea. He held the cup in both hands, steam rising before his serious eyes. "I've thought about… *the situation at hand.* It might be best you go away for a time, Kate. We can't guarantee the safety of an officer on the job."

"I don't want that. There's too much to—"

"I know. But I can't have you risk your life."

Shintani raised his chin, looking across to the entry.

When I turned, Franco was standing in the door frame. He had a questioning look set in his face. "What's going on?"

"A matter that's to do with Kate, personally," Shintani informed him.

"Right." Franco glanced from Shintani to me, his expression turning cool. "I saw Macklin in the holding cell."

I nodded. "I found him running towards CQ Hospital—with a pistol."

"World's gone mad," Franco said.

"No argument there," I replied.

"Kate," Shintani said, "I'll see you back in my office."

He left the room.

"Hey," I said to Franco, "I've called you a couple of times. Guess you were having a long lunch with Melainey?"

"No, that's not what I've been doing. Did you need me?"

"I wanted some help with finding Carlson Green. And… there was a probable homicide victim—down at the lake."

"A homicide? I'm sorry—I didn't…" He sighed deeply. "Who was it?"

"A young IT professional from CQ."

"How'd he die?"

"Possible strangulation with a thin rope."

Franco shook his head. "Poor guy. Look, I know I should have been there."

"It would have helped."

"I'm here now. I'll get started on the case. Any leads on who did it?"

"Not so far. But I have some thoughts on that."

"And what was that about Carlson? He's missing?"

"Yes, he is. I went to pick up his two little boys from his house—they were alone. No one seems to know where he is."

"That's odd. But shouldn't Grimshaw take care of that?"

"I put in a report to her. But she's tied up trying to locate Martina."

"Yeah, me too."

"Is that what you were doing just now—looking for her?"

"No. Something else."

"Right." I waited a beat, but he didn't give any further information. He was sounding incredibly evasive.

I sipped my tea. "Well, I'd better go finish my meeting—with Shintani."

"Uh huh." He blew out a hard breath, giving the impression he wasn't done talking.

I folded my arms, resting my cup of tea against my shoulder. "Franco… it feels like we've been talking past each other lately. I don't want it to be that way."

"In that case, maybe you should start filling me in a bit more. Then we might have a chance of understanding each other."

"For the last hours, no one's been able to get you on the phone."

"Fair enough. But I meant in general, over the past week or so. You've been keeping a lot to yourself."

"There are some things I need to understand better before I—"

"In other words, Wakeland, you're going to continue the lone wolf routine?"

"Lone wolf routine?"

"Yeah."

"If I've been doing that, it wasn't intentional."

"I've been on my own with everything for days now. This isn't how we're meant to run things."

"Franco… you've been off with Melainey, a lot—right? I thought you two were forming a bond, figuring out how to work together. That kind of thing."

"Wrong. You've been out. Melainey's been out. I've been here at the station, stuck on paperwork."

"Okay. Look, I didn't realise. I just assumed. And you're right, I've been away from my desk for much of the time. I can see that you're rankled—"

"That's not the word I'd use."

"Okay," I said quietly. "I accept that I've let things slip. Right now, though, I need to go."

"Yeah. Look… I don't even know if there's a place for me here anymore."

I inhaled a quick breath. Franco was certainly in a dark mood. I wasn't entirely certain what had prompted it.

"I didn't know things had gotten that bad for you," I said. "I care, you know."

"Let me paint you a picture. I was supposed to be walking into the role you were leaving behind, right?"

"Yes. I mean, that's the way I thought it would go. Instead—"

"Yeah, instead, who walks into the role? *Melainey*. So then, I'm stuck trying to fit in with his way of doing things—and I'm lost. Up the creek without a paddle. He barely documents anything. Half the time, I don't even know where he is."

I frowned. "I… I'm sorry. I didn't realise. I really didn't. I thought you two were at the bunker site the last few days."

Franco's expression tightened. "Nope, it's mostly just been me there. Do you have any idea where he is right now?"

I shook my head.

"Me either," he said. "You see the problem? You're still our homicide lead, Wakeland, but new boy Melainey is running his own race."

"Yes, I do see the problem. I haven't been doing my job properly."

"I'm glad you see that. I didn't think you would."

I sighed. "I have to talk with Shintani right now, but we'll get this sorted. I'll step up. And Melainey's got to be accountable. Maybe we can get him to help Grimshaw with finding Carlson and Martina."

"I don't want him anywhere near Martina."

"Franco? That sounds like there's a lot more to this than what you've said."

He gazed back at me for a moment, before taking out his phone and switching it on. He browsed through images on his screen and then turned the phone around to me.

"What's this?" I asked.

"Just… *look*."

CHAPTER EIGHTY-ONE

I studied the image that Franco had just shown me on his phone. He'd snapped a picture of a photograph.

The photograph was of a young couple at a lake—Coldwater Lake, by the looks of it. It had to be an old photo, because the location where the two of them were sitting was where an aged care home had now been built. It was summer. The girl wore an orange bikini. The man wore trunks and a short-sleeved shirt. He had his arm around the girl. The wind was blowing the girl's hair across her face, and she was laughing. The man had his face away from the camera.

Confused, I raised my eyes to Franco. "Who are these people?"

Wordlessly, he scrolled to the next photo. It was almost exactly the same as the last picture. Same angle. I guessed it'd been taken on a camera set up on a tripod.

There was only just enough change in the way the woman held herself for her hair to have whipped away from her eyes. The man had turned just enough to see a quarter of his face.

Those changes were enough—just enough—for me to see who these people were.

The woman was a young Adele Hobson.

And as for the man—he was a young Trevor Melainey.

I felt my lungs squeeze.

What had Melainey been doing here in Tallman's Valley—with *Adele*—of all people?

From his pose with Adele in the photos, it was obvious he'd had some sort of romance with her. He'd never mentioned that.

And he'd claimed never to have set foot in the Blue Mountains. But here he was, at Coldwater Lake in Tallman's Valley.

He'd lied.

My hands trembled, and I had to set my cup of tea down, or I would have dropped both the cup and Franco's phone.

Was it possible that *Melainey* was the mysterious J.L?

Surely not.

My gaze travelled back to the phone screen, to Melainey's arms in the photographs. I searched for the tattoo of the jail cell. But Melainey's sleeves were just long enough to cover his shoulders.

I glanced back at Franco, my jaw almost too rigid to speak. "Where did you get these photographs?"

As Franco was about to answer, Superintendent Bigley entered the station.

He was the last person I wanted to see right now. I was certain he was about to barge into my conversation with Franco, demanding to know how close the Witness Mountain case was to being wrapped up. But, instead, he barely noticed us, striding across the floor and disappearing down the hall. He was either heading down to his office or going to see Shintani.

I turned to Franco again. "These photos… where did you get them?"

"Melainey's house," Franco answered.

"His house? He had these just lying around?"

"Not exactly. They were in his garage. He's got stacks of boxes in there. The boxes are from his move to the valley. He and his wife just haven't put them away yet."

"So, were you out there in the garage with Melainey today?"

"No. He keeps his garage locked up tight. I've been suspicious about that for a while. I'll explain. The first thing is that a couple of boxes from the bunker went missing. And the only person about at the time was Melainey."

"Okay. That's a concern."

"Yeah. I couldn't help but wonder if he'd taken them home and put them in his garage. The cabin he's renting to me gets a bit stuffy at night, and I can't sleep. I've been going outside for some air during the nights. Melainey takes phone calls in his garage at all hours. A few times, I overheard him in there, saying some really weird stuff. When I say weird, I mean concerning. Like, *don't worry about Wakeland, I've got her under control.*"

"Seriously?" I was both horrified and indignant.

"Yeah. At first, I thought it was just him talking big. Shooting the breeze with an old colleague or whatever. But then I started hearing him talk about doing some kind of deals, and then he'd take off in his car—even at two or three in the morning. I ended up thinking, this guy is running drugs. And there was still the thing about the missing bunker boxes. But I wanted evidence."

"So, you decided to look through his garage?"

"Yup. But as I said, he keeps it locked up. Earlier, he asked us all for a beer at his house—to celebrate naming Gus Iverson as the shooter. I told him it'd be better if it was just me and him."

"I heard. Thea told me."

"Okay. So, I said to him there'd be drama if we asked the girls—meaning you and Thea. Because that's the language he understands. That's how he talks to me when no one else is around. But the real reason I wanted it to just be him and me was so I could make a cast of the key to his garage. When he drinks, he usually belts the beers down and then passes out. Instead, after we had a couple of beers, he got a call from someone and said he had to go. And so off he went." Franco shrugged. "I ended up just breaking into his garage. His wife wasn't home, so I was home free."

"And you didn't find any drugs?"

"Nope. Nothing like that. But I did find one box from the bunker. Full of photos of a half-naked teenage girl."

"*Adele.*"

"Yes, Adele. At first, I thought he was just your average, bog-standard creep, taking a box of those kind of photos home with him. But then I found the pictures of him and Adele. I didn't find the second box that he took. He might have destroyed it."

I went silent for a moment, my mind spinning with the darkest of possibilities.

If Melainey is J.L, then he's a paid killer. What has he done in the past and what has he been doing since he's been in Tallman's Valley? And has he been contracted to kill me?

"Franco," I said urgently, "I need to look at your footage from the day we went to the canyon—when we were in the creek at Rainbow Ravine."

"You want that footage? But you'd have exactly same film I do."

"Not exactly. At the time we got to Sean Macklin and the kids, you were behind me. And you were also behind Melainey. He took his shirt off at one point. That's the section of film I want to see."

"You gonna tell me why?"

"I'm looking for a tattoo. On his shoulder. The tattoo in question is a jail cell."

"A jail cell?"

"Yes. There was someone who called himself J.L, and he was a cop, thirty years ago. He was—and is—involved in criminal activities. And he had that tattoo."

"Hell. And you think he might be *Melainey*? He can't be your guy, though. He's got tattoos, but nothing like that. Lemme think. He's got a Celtic dragon on his back… and, uh, a Celtic knot on his shoulder."

"You sure?"

"Yeah, I know my tatts. I'd get way more ink than I've already got if I wasn't a cop."

I inhaled a tight breath. I wanted to be wrong. I didn't want Melainey to be J.L. He'd been a senior homicide detective for decades. The thought of someone in that position being a hired gun was terrifying.

"Okay," I breathed. "I'd still like to see the footage you have."

"Sure thing."

Franco and I went into the study room and logged into one of the computers there.

I watched the film from Franco's camera carefully.

There was Melainey and me trudging through the creek. Sean Macklin, Jordan and Dakota came into view, way off in the distance. In the video, I turned to Melainey and Franco to tell them I was going the rest of the way alone. Melainey shrugged and tore off his shirt, dunking it in the water and then wringing it out.

I kept watching as he rolled his shoulders and stretched, shirtless.

As Franco had said, there was the Celtic dragon design on Melainey's broad back. Melainey twisted around to speak to Franco. When he turned, I had a view of the Celtic knot on his shoulder.

I stopped the footage there and zoomed in. The tattoo design was a geometric pattern of lines that were all interconnected.

I released a relieved breath. "His tattoos are just as you described."

"Told you." Franco shrugged. "I thought maybe Melainey had picked the Celtic designs because he's got an Irish background."

"Yes, possibly. I still want to know why Melainey was with Adele all those years ago, though. I don't have a good feeling about that."

Franco stooped close to the screen, studying the Celtic knot closely. "Send the jail cell tattoo through to this computer."

"Of course," I replied, though I was puzzled as to why he wanted it.

Franco took a screenshot of the Celtic knot tattoo from the police video. Then he opened a graphics program. In the graphics program, he uploaded a picture of the Celtic knot tattoo. Then he placed a half-transparent image of the jail cell design on top of it.

I wasn't certain what he was doing until he rotated the half-transparent jail cell tattoo on top of the Celtic knot.

The lines of the jail cell exactly matched with a section of the Celtic knot. Melainey had simply had the jail cell design tattooed over. It was cleverly done, barely leaving a trace of the original design.

Franco looked back over his shoulder at me, his dark eyes wide.

Clapping a hand over my mouth, I contained a gasp. "It's a match."

There was no doubt remaining.

Melainey was J.L.

CHAPTER EIGHTY-TWO

Franco met my eyes. "Seems I need to play a game of catchup. You obviously know a hell of a lot more than me."

"That's true."

"Well?"

"I'm shocked… reeling. I'm trying to grasp the fact that J.L is Melainey."

"Talk, Wakeland."

"I will. But this feeds into something else—something I was in the middle of with Shintani. I need to get back to him. And then I'll sit down with you. Promise."

"Hang on a red-hot minute." Franco drew his eyebrows down in a dark, incredulous gaze. "So, if I have this straight, you've been trying to find the identity of someone you only knew as J.L. Correct?"

"Yes. Correct."

"And he was a cop thirty years ago, you said?"

"Yes."

"Right. Well, those are *my* initials—my first two. *Jace Luciano*. J.L. And *I* was in the police force thirty years ago. Brief as it was. Tell me something, Wakeland… was I ever under suspicion?"

I hesitated, trying to craft the right words and then editing them furiously in my mind. But there were no right words. And it was time for honesty. "For five minutes or so you were on a list, yes."

"So, you *did* have me on a list."

"Franco…" I stopped for a moment. "Your initials and location matched. I wasn't aware you were a probationary constable back then. You never told me. So, it came as a surprise."

"And… you thought I could be J.L."

"I had no idea how bad he was at that stage. At that point, I thought he was more of a petty criminal."

"So, you thought I might have been a petty crim back then?"

"Like I said, you were on a list for a minute. Before I took you off. I *know* you. I knew J.L wasn't you." I drew a breath. "Why didn't you ever tell me you joined the force back then?"

"Because it was a big embarrassment, that's why. It was just a few months of my life. I was too young and stupid to be a cop when I was eighteen. I needed to go away and grow up."

"And when you came back, years later, you made the best homicide cop I've ever worked with."

"Should I believe that?"

"Yes. Yes, you should. Like I said, you weren't really ever on a list. I've made a lot of mistakes this year. That wasn't one of them."

"All right, I guess I'll have to go with that. Jeez, all this has been going on below the surface, huh? Stupid old Franco was oblivious. Like a mushroom growing under the dirt."

"I'm sorry. I know I haven't been open with you."

"Nup. And this explains why you haven't been. You didn't want to clue me in."

"To be fair, you didn't express any interest in investigating the carnival. In fact, you were opposed to it."

"This has got to do with the carnival?"

"Yes, it does."

"Okay. I messed up. Guess it just seemed like everyone was running their own race. And the carnival was part of that."

"I guess we *were* running our own races—especially Melainey."

"Before you go… tell me just one thing. When it comes to Melainey, what are we talking about? What type of crimes? Remember, I'm living right there on the guy's property. Don't you think it's the kind of information I should have?"

I hesitated before speaking, glancing around to ensure we were still alone. "His crimes are the worst kind. He's been carrying out contract murders."

As hard as the words were to say, they were even more difficult to comprehend.

Franco's jaw slackened. "Melainey?"

"I had no idea," I added quickly.

Franco stared at me with intense eyes. "Hang on. When did Melainey poke his ugly head into Tallman's Valley? The morning of the shootings, that's when."

I stared back, stunned by Franco's suggestion. "He can't have been responsible for the shootings. He wouldn't have had time."

"Do you know that for sure? Maybe we should look into that."

"I remember he had breakfast with Bigley."

"So the two of them say."

"Franco, Bigley is a superintendent. He's not going to lie to cover Melainey…."

But as I spoke the words, I realised I wasn't certain of that.

CHAPTER EIGHTY-THREE

I stepped into Inspector Shintani's office with Franco.

Shintani glanced up from his computer, a frown puckering his forehead as he noticed Franco.

"Jiro," I said, closing the door behind me. "I request Franco be brought in on this. He's just found something—the identity of J.L."

He lifted his chin at Franco in acknowledgement. "I didn't realise you knew about this J.L person?"

"I didn't," Franco told him. "Until a minute ago."

Shintani eyed me in confusion.

"We'll explain it," I said.

Franco and I showed Shintani the images we had on our phones—of Melainey and Adele, and of Melainey's original and current tattoos.

A stunned look came over Shintani's face. "Detective Melainey is a paid killer?"

I nodded. "It appears so. And Franco has raised a concern about where Melainey was at the time of the Witness Mountain shootings."

Shintani crushed his eyes shut for a moment, as if trying to iron out his thoughts. "What is your understanding of where he was at that time? From memory, he was with the superintendent."

"Yes," I said. "But we have no proof of that."

"But why would Detective Melainey be paid to kill those three people? I'm not sure that scenario makes sense," Shintani said.

"I don't know," I replied. "What I do know is that Angie once lived at the carnival. And her adoptive mother—Perdita—had a connection with the carnival, too. And Melainey makes three. In 1989, he had a cabin on Mulden land. And he was Adele Hobson's boyfriend."

"I wasn't aware of all that." Removing his glasses, Shintani rubbed his eyes with the heel of his hand.

A call came through from Liz.

Shintani accepted it, and Liz popped up on the screen of Shintani's computer.

She looked across at Franco. "Oh, we have someone new in our little group?"

"Hey, Liz," Franco said.

"Hello, Franco," she replied with a quick wave.

"Liz," I said, "Franco just made a discovery. We now know who J.L is."

"Don't leave me in suspense," she breathed.

"It's Trevor Melainey," Franco told her.

Her mouth dropped. "What? *Melainey*?"

Franco and I sent her through the same images we'd just shown Shintani.

Liz spent a few seconds looking at them. "I don't believe it. I've had lots of dealings with Melainey over the years. He seemed rough around the edges, but always like someone who wanted to see justice done. This is horrifying."

"We're going to have to work out where we go with this," I said. "He might have others working with him."

"I agree," Liz said. "This is dynamite."

"Liz," I said, "I attended the scene of a probable homicide earlier. Next to a boat ramp at Coldwater Lake. His name is Leo Dubois and he worked at CQ Tech. Was there any mention of his name on *The Quarry*?"

Liz stared back at me. "There seems to be a real theme here. But I didn't notice his name. I'll have a careful look through. They're using code words for some things, as you can imagine, so we haven't been able to work out what most of the jobs are that are being posted. But we will."

The four of us sat in silence for a few moments. We were all struggling with this new reality.

I didn't know how Liz had managed her role for so many years—in her world of the dark web and the people who occupied it.

"I'm sorry, Liz," I said finally. "Did you call with an update, or just to check in with us?"

"It's an update," she said. "We discovered a job that was posted weeks ago. And it was local to the Blue Mountains, so I thought it'd be of immediate interest to you. The job was to do with stalking a woman. Whoever posted the job wanted the woman running scared. A photograph of her was posted on *The Quarry*."

Liz showed us the photograph of a pretty, dark-haired woman.

Gasping, I glanced at Franco.

Franco stared at the screen. "It's Martina."

Liz raised her eyebrows. "I didn't realise you knew her, Franco."

"We dated for quite a while," Franco explained.

"I'm so sorry," Liz said.

"Let me guess," I said, "her new boyfriend is the one who wanted her stalked. Franco, I spoke with Grimshaw earlier. She said they just found the last location at which Martina's phone gave a signal. It was Iron Bark Crest."

Exhaling, Franco leaned his head back. "Martina had a girlfriend with a cabin at Appleby. That's about twenty minutes past Iron Bark Crest, I think."

I folded my arms, gazing at Martina's picture on the screen. "We need to find out where Elliot is right now."

"He's at CQ Tech right now," Franco told me. "I've been keeping a close eye on him. I didn't trust him."

"Is it possible Martina went out to the cabin at Appleby to get away from the stalker—Elliot, or whoever it is?" I asked.

Franco jumped to his feet. "That's what I'm thinking. I'd better go see."

I watched Franco jog out the door, thinking this day could not get any more surreal or more dangerous.

It was as if we'd entered an entirely different world.

The silent town.

PART VII

CHAPTER EIGHTY-FOUR

The room went quiet as Franco left.

The taut, fearful expressions on Liz and Shintani's faces terrified me.

Shintani bent his head. "So, there is a possibility that Detective Melainey came here to establish himself in town as a member of *The Quarry* network. Which means we have to ask a very hard question. We have to ask why he was rushed into the role of lead homicide detective when Franco would have been the perfect candidate for the role."

For a moment, I wished Franco had been here to hear that. He hadn't been feeling good about himself lately—and this was big praise from Shintani.

"And who was the one who rushed Melainey in?" Liz asked in a hushed tone. "Superintendent Bigley."

"Franco and I had the same thought," I said wryly.

"I've made a decision," Shintani told us. "I have a few questions for the superintendent. And the time for that is now."

"Is that wise?" Liz asked in alarm.

"He came into his office here in a great hurry," Shintani said, pulling himself to his feet. "I want to know exactly what he's doing. There are fires raging out there, but the superintendent found something he urgently needs to do at an office he usually only visits once a month."

"I'll go with you," I told Shintani.

"Good luck, you two," Liz told us. She left the conversation.

Shintani switched off his computer, and we stepped out of the room.

I had no idea how this was going to go. Only one thing was certain—Bigley was not going to be impressed.

I walked along the corridor behind Shintani. He rapped on Superintendent Bigley's door.

Unusually, the door was locked.

"Hello?" Shintani called. "Andrew?"

When Bigley cracked open the door, his face was flushed red. "You two look serious. Is there an evacuation order for the station?"

"No," Shintani told him. "We need a few minutes of your time."

Bigley scratched his chin. "Ah. Well, I'm afraid we'll have to postpone whatever it is. Once I'm done here, I have to get home to Clare and Davinia."

"They're still at home?" I asked in concern. They were Bigley's wife and grown daughter. I knew the family lived in a deeply forested area, and it was fairly isolated, too.

Bigley gave me one of his trademark reassuring smiles, but it seemed forced. "Clare needs help to pack up all of Davinia's equipment. She can't do it on her own. It's quite all right. Our house isn't in a danger zone."

Davinia was a lovely young woman of about thirty-five. She had several very challenging physical conditions, and she was confined to a wheelchair.

"Anyway," Bigley said, starting to close the door, "I'd best get on with it."

In a move that surprised me, Shintani stopped him by placing a hand on the door. "We absolutely do need to speak to you."

Bigley recoiled before collecting himself. "I see. Well, of course. But you'll have to be quick."

He moved from the door frame, and Shintani and I walked in.

A screen on Bigley's computer displayed a countdown bar—a number of large files were being deleted. The bar was at 96% complete.

Bigley strode over and switched off the screen.

Why on earth had he chosen to come here and delete all these files —*right now*?

Shintani hadn't missed it either. I noticed him staring at the now blank screen with a curious expression on his face. He lifted his chin as he faced Bigley. "As time is short, I'll get straight to the point. We'd like to know what period of time you were with Detective Melainey on the morning of the Witness Mountain shootings?"

Bigley froze as he packed some folders into his briefcase. "Excuse me?"

"Would you like me to repeat the question, Andrew?" Shintani asked.

Bigley straightened himself, glancing from me to Shintani. To his credit, he looked genuinely perplexed. "It's an odd question, Jiro. Very odd, indeed. Why would you ask such a thing?"

"Kate and I have our reasons," Shintani told him. "What was Melainey doing that morning?"

"Trevor was preparing for his moment on the stage, as I recall," Bigley said. "He'd driven over from Sydney early in the morning so that he could attend the fair."

"Andrew," I said, "did you have a long breakfast with Melainey that morning? That's what he said on stage, at the fair."

Bigley's skin flushed red again, as if his blood pressure were rising. "Well, probably. I can't really recall much. That morning was a frenzy. Due to the heat and bushfire smoke, Nancy Upchurch and I were trying to reschedule the itinerary, and… that's it, really."

I stared at him incredulously. "It'd be quicker to just answer the question."

"I've answered to the best of my ability," Bigley protested.

"Okay," I said boldly, "I'll ask this in another way. Did you see Melainey between the hours of six-thirty and seven-thirty that morning? Which was the time of the shootings on Witness Mountain."

Bigley's blue eyes popped wide open. Agape, he stared at Shintani and me. "You two aren't seriously suggesting foul play on the part of Detective Melainey? I'm astounded. He's a senior detective—with a distinguished career."

Shintani locked eyes with Bigley. "We've come to you with grave concerns, asking simple questions."

Bigley broke eye contact. "Take a look at the news today, Jiro. There are fires bearing down on us. I've got family to take care of. Whatever all this is about, it'll have to wait."

With that, he put his briefcase under his arm and left the room, his head bowed as if against a storm. He hadn't given us a chance to ask anything else.

Rushing to his computer, I switched on the screen. The program he'd been running had ended. The bar was at 100%.

I looked back over my shoulder at Shintani. "Wish I knew what he was deleting."

"We'll get someone onto that," Shintani said.

I filled my lungs with air. Bigley had evaded our questions—completely evaded them. I didn't know what that meant. He was a *superintendent.*

Something had Bigley spooked. He hadn't elected to come in here and delete files for no reason. And the way he'd hurried out of his office, he'd reminded me of a large, white rabbit—one with a red, perspiring face.

A thought began twisting in my mind.

I called Liz.

She answered immediately.

"Liz," I said, "can you tell me something? When your team identified me as a target, what did they find, exactly?"

"I'll be blunt. The instruction is that the target is to be killed—*today.* And the target is someone in the local police force. *The Quarry* people aren't messing around."

"What if I *was* being followed, but the actual target of the killer is someone else? Someone like… *Bigley*. He just ran out of here like the wolves were after him. He was acting really odd, deleting a large number of computer files, while at the same time claiming he had to rush home to his family. Shintani and I confronted him about the whereabouts of Melainey on the morning of the shootings. But he blew us off."

"Oh, that's not good, Kate. But if he's covering up for Melainey, how does it make sense he's in the crosshairs of people from *The Quarry*?"

"In his favour, he did seem confused about the whole situation with Melainey."

"Let me check if my team has any further insights," Liz said.

Shintani looked on with an intent expression as I waited.

Liz came back on the line after a minute, sounding breathy. "In terms of the target, an alert just came through. They're tracking a car that's heading away from the police station. You're right—Bigley's their target."

CHAPTER EIGHTY-FIVE

I eyed Shintani as I ended the phone call with Liz. "Bigley's the target. Not me. If he's going home, he's on his way to Cypress Ridge."

"Whatever his involvement in all this is," Shintani replied, "he's certainly got himself in deep. This is very delicate. I'll need to go meet in person with the federal police officers I know I can trust. They're going to have to move in on everyone involved in this—in one fell swoop. No advance warning."

"What about Bigley? *The Quarry* people will kill him before we can arrange protection for him. And if he dies… he'll take whatever he knows with him. I've been to his house a couple of times. It'd be child's play to run him off the road that leads there. There's a gully on one side and a steep incline on the other. Bigley's house is on the edge of a drop—with views forever. Figures—Bigley *would* pick a house that makes him feel like a king."

"That does sound like him. We'll have to arrange some sort of police escort. Not an easy thing to do though without raising alerts. And I don't want any alerts raised."

"I can go."

He shook his head firmly. "Not on your own, no."

"What choice do we have?"

"I'm not sending you alone."

I understood Shintani's position. But if Bigley died, he couldn't tell us all that he knew. I was also worried for Bigley's family, who would have no idea what was going on.

My phone buzzed.

It was Franco.

"Wakeland, I just talked with Martina," he told me.

"Well, that's a huge relief. How did you manage to contact her?"

"I called Martina's friend—the one who owns the cabin at Appleby. She said Martina had been there the past few days, but she'd gotten scared being all on her own. Martina left yesterday, and she's gone to stay at a hotel in the city. I'm going to go stay with her."

"Good. Sounds like she needs a friend right now."

"What's happening there?"

"Nothing good. We've worked out that *The Quarry* people are after Bigley. They're going to kill him."

"You serious?"

"I'm afraid so."

I hadn't even told Franco that we'd originally thought the target was me.

"What's the plan?" he asked.

"There's no plan. Not so far. Shintani's worried about tipping people off who shouldn't be tipped off yet."

I glanced at the inspector. He was pacing the room, looking deep in thought.

"Tell me you're not going to go save the day, Wakeland?" Franco asked.

"Bigley will have his family with him," I said. "It's a bad situation."

"Meet me at Appleby," Franco told me. "It's on the way to Cypress Ridge. I was driving that way when I decided to call Martina's friend."

"But what about Martina? You were planning on staying with her, right?"

"She doesn't really need me. She didn't want me before, when she had me. I think she was trying to butter me up over the past couple of weeks because she wanted police protection."

"Or maybe she realised she'd lost a good thing."

Franco gave a sad laugh. "Anyway, you can't go giving Bigley an escort all on your own. I'm not gonna let that happen. I'll call Martina's parents and tell them to go stay with her. I'll let Grimshaw know what's happening, too. It's all right, Martina will be safe. She just won't have *me*."

I met up with Franco off the side of the road at Appleby. We decided it was best to take the car that I'd driven here in—an unmarked police SUV.

He wanted to drive, and I said yes to that so fast he shot me a confused glance. I'd become aware of heart palpitations tapping against my ribs, and for the first time in my life, I didn't feel like a completely safe driver.

We drove away.

"So, you've been looking into Elliot Calladine?" I asked. "Do you think *he* posted the job for Martina's stalker?"

"Not sure. Wouldn't put it past him though. He strikes me as an arrogant guy. He wouldn't have taken it well when Martina tried to leave him."

"That's a worry."

"Yeah. So, about Bigley—do we get a police helicopter or something to help us out?"

"That'd raise suspicion. We've got to give Shintani time to organise things with the federal police. We'll be delivering Bigley to them. At the same time, the AFP will be looking into who else is involved and going in for the arrests. Elliot Calladine will be one of them, by the sounds of it."

"Right. Well, I can't wait to get Bigley out of there and then deliver him to the feds. He deserves it."

"If all goes well." I glanced at him, softening my tone. "You didn't have to come along, you know. You had an *out*—Martina."

"I want to see this to the end. I didn't see what you were seeing before—but now I do."

"Thanks. Means a lot for you to say that."

"Sorry I thought you were going all vigilante."

"Don't be sorry. I didn't do the best job of communicating what was going on in my head."

"You've never been great at that."

"Really?"

"Yeah."

"You never told me that before."

"You didn't ask."

"Now I'm wondering what other faults I've got."

"Got a notepad and pencil?"

I grinned. "Yeah, yeah, keep it to yourself."

He shrugged, shooting me a smile.

"Hey," I said. "How'd Martina take the news you weren't coming?"

"Not well. But she'll be okay. She'll be safe."

"Any chance of a replay with you two?"

"I don't know. I don't think so. There's a lot of water under the bridge."

"I remember a time when you and me were sitting on Loft Hill, on a stake-out, waiting to bring in a murder suspect. And you were talking about Martina. You were so sure then you were going to marry her."

"I know. I was. I thought we were on the same page. But then, she changed. Out of the blue. We'd both agreed we didn't want kids. I was forty-four, then. She was thirty-nine. She came to me and said we should have a baby the first year after we married. Don't get me wrong—I love kids—but I just never saw myself having one. I like sleeping in and having weekends to myself too much."

"But Martina wanted a child?"

He sighed. "That's the thing. She was being pressured by her parents and some of her friends. They told her it was now or never, and that she'd regret not having one. But I don't think it was what she wanted."

"Sad story. Sounds like other people got between you two."

"Yeah, that's exactly what happened." He steered the car around a bend. "Anyway, enough about my life. How's Petey-boy doing with the fires today?"

"It's a battle. He didn't sound too confident last time I talked with him."

"What about the direction we're headed in?"

"Hmmm, I'd better call him and check it out."

I messaged Pete on my radio.

A low roar came over the radio. I knew that sound well. It was fire.

"Kate, sorry, can't hear you very well," came Pete's raspy voice. "I'll jump inside the truck. Wait a sec."

"Pete, can you hear me? What's the situation over there?"

"It's not looking good, honey. We might lose this fight."

I shut my eyes. "I know you're doing all you can."

"We're pulling out all stops to hold it back. Never seen anything like it."

"Are you keeping safe? And what about Logan?"

"We're both safe. I'm keeping a close eye on Logan, don't worry."

"Is everything okay? How's Abby and the kids?"

"They're all good. They're at the evacuation centre we agreed on."

"Good to hear."

"Pete, what's the fire situation out at Cypress Ridge?"

"Cypress Ridge? The fires aren't moving in that direction, but we're evacuating everyone—just as a precautionary."

"So, it's okay to head out that way?"

"Honey, I'd rather you didn't."

Franco smirked at Pete's cajoling use of the word *honey*.

"Pete," I said, "I've got Franco listening in on this call. We have a compelling reason to take a drive out there."

Pete immediately deepened his voice. "Hey, Franco. Well, the official advice is we're still allowing people down the roads that lead in and out of Cypress Ridge, but everyone's got to get out of there within the next hour."

"Got it," I said. "We'll be out of there well within that time."

"What are you doing over that way?"

"Just helping Bigley out."

"Bigley? Okay. Be careful. And stay in contact—things can change rapidly."

"We will," I said, and ended the call.

I couldn't tell him the reason we were headed out to Cypress Ridge.

All I could do was to hope my next call to Pete was to tell him we were safely out of there.

CHAPTER EIGHTY-SIX

Bigley's house stood tall and proud among the trees, a neat rose garden lining either side of a stone pathway. It formed a tranquil, picture-perfect image. A yacht stood at the side of the house, covered in a tarpaulin. I wondered how often Bigley actually sailed it, or if it'd just been a toy he wanted to possess.

The road ended here. The house was even more isolated than I remembered. It made me uneasy. I wanted the family out of here as soon as possible.

Bigley himself was walking along the pathway, wheeling two large suitcases. He packed the suitcases into the back of his SUV. Next, he picked up some oxygen tanks and fitted them in. I knew they'd be for his daughter, Davinia.

Davinia came behind her father in her wheelchair, helped along by her mother Clare. Davinia was clutching a violin case. She'd learnt to play it with the use of a physical aid, and she was very skilled at it.

Franco and I drove up and parked. I got out and crossed the road while Franco remained in the car.

All three members of the Bigley family looked over at us in surprise.

The superintendent marched up to us, out of earshot of his family. "Detective Wakeland, why are you here? Of all places?"

"We're here to give you a police escort out," I told him.

He bristled, but there was a quiet look of terror in his eyes. "I hardly require an escort." Turning, he called to his wife, "Everything's all right, Clare. You two get yourselves into the car and I'll be there shortly."

He smoothed back silver hair that was damp with sweat. "You're not intending on escorting me all the way to my destination in Sydney… are you?"

I eyed him with a direct gaze. "Are you asking if we're going to be arresting you at the other end?"

His jaw went slack. "I have no idea what you—?"

"Listen carefully. We have reason to believe you are the target of a contract killer."

He stared at me like a trapped animal, his voice fading. "What?"

"I mean that there's a contract on you on a website named *The Quarry*."

He licked his lips and swallowed. "That's not possible."

"You know the website I'm talking about, don't you?"

He turned his head, looking away. "I've heard of it. I know nothing about it."

"Andrew—why? Why are you involved in any of this?"

Bigley kept his gaze on the forest. "I'm not involved. Over the years, I've granted a few favours here and there. That's all. It's only in the past months that I've begun to understand the impact of those favours. But there hasn't been any personal gain to me. None at all."

"That's all it takes for great harm to be done. You're a superintendent."

"I've always done my best. I might have made a few mistakes—"

"*Mistakes*?" I took a breath, calming myself. "Anyway, now isn't the time to go into all of that. You need to follow my instructions, because this might just save your lives. You need to drive straight to Sydney. No detours. Do not stop for anyone or anything. Do you understand?"

His shoulders collapsed and he nodded at me with haunted eyes. "I've put my wife and daughter in danger, haven't I? They don't deserve to come to any harm."

"Franco and I will do everything in our power to keep the three of you safe. Now, we need to go. Stay in contact over the radio, okay?"

The superintendent turned and walked to his car, where his wife was standing and patiently waiting—his steps heavy and uncertain.

CHAPTER EIGHTY-SEVEN

Franco and I drove away from Superintendent Bigley's house.

"Bigley didn't look happy," Franco remarked.

"No," I said. "Not happy at all."

"Bet he didn't admit to anything."

"Surprisingly, he did. Well, hmmm, it was half an admission. He said he's been granting favours to people over the years—favours he didn't gain anything out of."

"Huh. You know, that makes a terrible kind of sense. It probably puffed up his ego to grant favours."

"He's going to pay a heavy price for that *puffy ego* of his."

"Or not," Franco said. "It's not over, yet. He might wrangle his way out of this and just go live the easy life in retirement—in his mansion in the woods. Same goes for the rest of the people who are involved in this."

I hated the thought of that. But Franco was right.

I tried to release a steady breath, but my chest felt locked up tight.

"You okay, Wakeland?"

"Yeah, fine."

"You don't look fine."

I forced a wry smile. "Is that a nice way of telling me I'm looking haggard?"

He gave a sardonic chuckle. "This job has been ageing all of us fast this year. I can feel it."

"It's been intense."

"My idea of leaving the job is starting to feel more and more concrete."

"I get you."

"And look at us now. Escorting our *superintendent* to the federal police. So… what's it all for?"

"Let's just see this day out, okay?"

"Yeah," he said grimly.

I rested my head back on the seat, taking slow breaths. My chest felt better. But I could still feel the patter of my heart. Something I'd taken for granted was not being aware of my heartbeat. It wasn't like that for me now.

I glanced in the rear vision mirror. Bigley was still following us at the same steady pace.

The forest zipped by us, the late afternoon sun glinting on the soaring trees. If I wasn't feeling so tense, I'd have enjoyed the scenery. As lovely as it was, I wanted to be well away from here. It was far too isolated, far too hemmed in.

I drank some water from a bottle, continually scanning the road ahead.

A message came over the radio.

It was Pete.

"Kate, what's your current location?"

"Driving on Blackwood Road, heading away from Cypress Ridge."

A moment of silence followed.

"Kate," came Pete's voice again. "I was hoping you'd be out of there by now. There's a new development. It was picked up just two minutes ago. There's a fire."

"A *fire*?"

I switched the call onto speakerphone so that Franco could hear.

"It's coming up from a gully, towards Blackwood Road," Pete said.

The piercing staccato of a helicopter cut through the air, coming closer, up over the ridge and hovering above the road.

Pete's voice came in again. "Wait a sec. I need to contact Hugh in the RFS helicopter."

I watched dark smoke move overhead in the seconds before Pete came back on the radio.

"Okay, Hugh can see you," he said.

"Where's the fire?" I breathed, meeting eyes with Franco. "Behind us, or—?"

"Honey, it's in front of you," Pete told me.

"What do we do?" I asked him urgently. "Should we keep driving?"

Another moment of hesitation came.

"You can't continue in your present direction," Pete replied in a heavy tone.

I inhaled sharply. "Pete… it's the only road out. Should we return to Bigley's house?"

His voice was rigid as he replied. "You can't return to the house. The projection is… the fire will rip along the gully and up to the ridge. The house is going to burn."

"Then… *what*?" My voice squeezed down to a whisper as Franco eased the car around a hairpin turn.

Franco glanced at me with a frozen look in his eyes, then turned back to the road. The road descended around a series of bends.

As Franco steered around the next sharp turn, the fire came into view.

A wall of flames rose on one side of the forest. In the near distance, fire was leaping along the trees and right across the road. Embers rained down on us, shooting everywhere like millions of tiny firecrackers.

With terrifying speed, the sky turned from grey to black. As if day had turned to night.

Bigley was breathless as he joined us on the radio. "I'm being advised from the RFS that we are essentially trapped."

"Yes, sir," I answered, "we are."

"Kate and Superintendent Bigley," came Pete's voice over the radio, "keep driving."

I stared at the leaping flames. "Pete, we can't."

"I'm not taking my family into that," Bigley called. "We'll all burn."

I could hear Clare and Davinia cry out over the radio.

"I'm afraid there's no choice," Pete responded. "There are two fire fronts headed your way. From ahead of you… and coming up fast behind."

"Does that mean our house is gone, Pete?" asked Clare.

"Yes, Clare," Pete answered bluntly.

Clare went silent.

My breaths were quick and shallow. "Pete, there's no way out… is there?"

"Keep driving," he said in a tight, hard voice that I'd never heard from him before. "I'll guide you. You won't be able to see. Just… keep going."

Surely no one could survive this. No one was coming out of this alive.

"Keep talking to us, Pete," I breathed. "Please."

"I'm here," he said. "I'll be with you all the way."

CHAPTER EIGHTY-EIGHT

I caught Franco's eye and then turned my head. I couldn't bear the look on his face.

A dark, terrifying world of smoke enclosed us. Above was nothing but a fiery ceiling of black and an intense, bright red. Embers zipped and skittered through the air, sizzling on our car's windscreen.

All the while, the fire screamed and crackled like demons in my ears.

"I'm on my way there," Pete called out over the radio, his voice gone hoarse. "I'm thirteen minutes away."

I gasped. "No. Don't come here. You won't get through."

"Let me worry about that," Pete said.

"Is Logan with you?" I asked, hoping that he wasn't.

"No," Pete told me. "I insisted he stay behind."

"Pete, if we don't make it through to each other..." I began, aware that everyone else was listening in, but I didn't care.

"No talk like that allowed. *Okay*?" Pete's voice cracked on his last word.

Franco and I drove on. Heat blasted through the glass of the windows, turning the car into an oven.

Sweat trickled down my face, dripping into my eyes and down my neck.

"Keep going," Pete told us.

"Can't see a thing, mate," Franco said. "*I can't see.*"

"Hugh can see you," Pete said. "The helicopter's got heat mapping. I've got a relay on a computer screen, and I'm watching on."

Franco wiped his hands on his trousers, then replaced them on the wheel. "It's nothing but hot down here. Flames everywhere. You sure the mapping can work in this?"

"Hugh can see you," Pete assured us.

Franco continued to drive. Behind us, I could barely make out the headlights of Bigley's SUV.

We were running a gauntlet.

Pete did as he said he would. He kept talking to us. "Keep going… keep going. Around the bend. To the left. Left, left, left. Go right now. Straighten up."

Pete was leading us along the road… but there was nowhere to go. He must know that.

And at any second, we could swerve off the road. And then either crash into a tree or tumble down into the gully.

But I was grateful Pete was there. I held tight to the sound of his voice.

Franco swore constantly under his breath as he tried to keep the car on the road.

"Kate, Franco, Andrew—prepare to go right," came Pete over the radio again.

My stomach clenched as I turned to look right. "Pete? It's nothing but a field of fire over there."

Pete rushed his words. "There's a break coming. Take it when I say. It's a lagoon in a clearing. I don't know how deep the lagoon is. I don't know the exact perimeters. You have to be careful you don't drive straight into it." He paused. "Listen. There's a steep drop just past the lagoon. Once you leave the road, drive for a count of ten seconds, going at twenty kilometres per hour. Then stop. Everyone understand?"

"Got it," said Franco from between his teeth.

"Understood," came Bigley's voice.

"What you need to do when you stop at the clearing is shelter in place," Pete said.

"All right. We'll shelter," Bigley said to Pete in a dull voice. "But I'm not sure we'll survive what's coming. It's a monster."

"Just get down as low as you can in your vehicles," Pete instructed. "Use any blankets you have in your cars and cover yourselves until it passes."

"Copy that," Bigley replied.

"Good luck, Andrew. Clare. Davinia," I spoke into the radio.

"Good luck," Clare and Davinia echoed.

"Look for emergency blankets in your first aid kit, Kate," Bigley answered. "We have two. And yes, good luck to you both."

"Right," Pete said, "I'm gonna start a countdown to where you pull off the road. Approach at twenty kilometres per hour, okay? Ready? About to start countdown. Sixty seconds… fifty-nine seconds… fifty-eight seconds… fifty-seven seconds…."

Pete counted the moments until our exit point.

"Zero," Pete cried urgently.

Point zero was just a wall of thick smoke with embers rocketing through the air.

Franco swung the car to the right. "Hold on."

The wheels bumped and skidded over rocks. I began counting out loud. I heard Clare over the radio doing the same.

Fire reflected bright red in a large body of water.

"There's the lagoon to the left," I cried. "Six… seven… eight… nine… ten!"

Franco brought the car to a sudden stop.

Bigley's SUV moved out of the smoke towards us. He drove alongside and parked his car.

"Pete, we're here!" I called into the radio.

He didn't reply.

"Pete?" I repeated. "We're here."

I locked eyes with Franco as we waited for an answer.

None came.

I put the radio down.

Franco and I rushed to drag the first aid kit from the back of the car. There was one thermal blankets in there, plus some masks.

Lowering the backrests as low as they could go, we hunkered down. And waited.

Outside, the sounds of the fire were growing louder.

"Wakeland," Franco said. "If we get cooked right here and now, I wanna say… we didn't get everything right… but we did lots of good things."

"We *did* do good things."

My lungs battled for air in the small tight space beneath the blanket.

The fire swept over the top of us with the deafening roar of a freight train.

CHAPTER EIGHTY-NINE

The fire front had passed right over the top of us.

With hesitation, Franco and I drew the thermal blanket back.

The air was so, so hot. But it was breathable.

I called Bigley on the radio. "Andrew, Clare, Davinia—are you okay?"

"We made it," came Clare's voice. "Just."

Davinia coughed. "Hard to breathe though."

"Awful air quality for you, Davinia," I said sympathetically. "I hope we can get out of here now."

Bigley didn't speak.

A call came in on the radio. It was Pete.

"Katc, how are you?"

"We made it," I answered.

"Thank God." I heard a quiet jubilation in Pete's voice.

"What happened to you?" I asked quickly. "We lost you for a while."

"We hit a snag."

"What kind of snag?" I gasped.

"A fallen tree."

"Please tell me it didn't fall on your truck?" I kept my breath in check as I waited for his answer.

"Nothing like that," Pete assured me. "It fell right across the road. It's a big old tree with lightning damage—didn't take much to topple it. I'm guessing it fell not long after it caught on fire."

"Can you get past it, Pete?" Clare asked.

"It's a huge tree. No way around it. We need to get some equipment here fast." Pete paused. "I'm sorry."

I wiped a slick of sweat from my forehead. "Okay, Pete. Thanks for letting us know."

"Stay safe. Stay in the cars all of you," he said. "I'll be out of contact for a while. We'll be ripping into the branches with chainsaws."

Pete left the conversation.

"That's some bad luck," Clare said to us over the radio.

"Sure is," I replied.

"Do you need water over there?" Clare asked. "If you need more, we have lots."

"Our bottles of water are warm," I told her, "but we have enough."

"So are ours," she said.

"Well, this trip turned out to be eventful," Davinia quipped.

"You're not wrong," I replied. "Sure is one I'll never—"

My words were drowned out by the roar of a vehicle.

Through the clearing, I watched a small white truck skid down the road. Fire sparked from its undercarriage all the way.

A shriek of wheels and metal followed, then an ear-splitting crash.

Davinia cried out over the radio. "What happened?"

"Sounds like they hit a tree." Franco replied.

"Andrew, you don't have any neighbours close by, do you?" I asked.

"No," Bigley answered. "None." His tone was heavy but gave nothing away.

Franco glanced at me with a dark, tense expression, then spoke into the radio. "We'll go see if we can do anything."

I gave him a rigid nod.

We both knew there shouldn't have been a vehicle out there on the road. Unless the driver was the one who'd started the fire.

Sliding our guns into our vests, Franco and I headed out of the car. We kept the masks on our faces.

Bigley, Clare and Davinia watched us from their vehicle, their faces turned our way. I gave them a quick wave.

Directly ahead, I could see the edge of the drop. The tips of large trees barely speared above that edge, telling me that it was terrifyingly high. It was a cliff. Pete had spared us the details of that.

Franco and I headed for the road.

The ground smoked, hot beneath my feet. The dry air was burning my throat raw.

We were out of the clearing now and onto the smoke-filled road.

I could just make out the sight of a truck wedged against a tree trunk, about thirty metres to the left. A head-on crash.

Fire raced along the side of the ridge, headed for Bigley's house.

"If the driver started this fire," I said, "they weren't prepared. You can't control which way a fire's going to go—not in a place like this."

"And I bet they couldn't get out because of the fallen tree."

"Yeah. If Pete can't get in, they can't get out."

Franco took out his gun. "Let's hope the crash was a good one."

Franco and I walked steadily towards the wreck.

We approached the truck with our guns drawn.

Who would we find in there?

I couldn't be certain. *The Quarry* people could have sent anyone—possibly someone I didn't know.

No sound came from the vehicle, apart from the rattle of the engine. The sparks that'd burned from the undercarriage before had gone out.

Franco opened the driver's side door, while I held a gun on the driver.

The driver's head lolled to one side, blood streaking down his face where it'd hit the window.

Franco held two fingers on the man's throat, feeling for a pulse. "He's alive."

I gasped as Franco moved the man's head around so we could see his face. "It's Doug Overmire."

Franco looked back at me with a taut glance, his skin bright with heat and sweat. "Not strange at all that *he's* here."

I stepped closer. "Mr Overmire?"

I shook his shoulder. He didn't respond.

Reaching over him, I switched off the engine, then pocketed the key.

The front passenger side seat was empty. The back was empty, too. At least, the back seemed empty until Franco opened the door.

A man was wedged into the floor of the truck, his wrists and ankles tied with silver duct tape.

Carlson Green stared up at us, eyes glazed as if waking after being knocked out, a large bruise on his forehead.

So, this was where Carlson had been. Tied up in the back seat of Overmire's truck. I had no clear idea what was going on here.

Franco assisted Carlson, helping him to a sitting position on the bench seat. "What happened, mate?"

"Where am I?" he gasped as Franco took a bandanna away from his face. "Whose damned car am I in?"

"Carlson," I said, "you've been in an accident. You're in a truck with Doug Overmire."

His mouth dropped open. "Doug Overmire?"

"What association do you have with Mr Overmire?" I asked. "Why would he do this to you?"

"I've got nothing to do with him," he answered. "Last I remember, I heard a noise in the garage at my house. I told the kids to wait until I got back. But I got hit over the head from behind." His eyes shot wide open. "*My kids*—Toby and Ollie—they were at home with me…."

"They're safe, Carlson," I assured him. "Toby, Oliver and Jordan are all at an evacuation centre."

Closing his eyes, he breathed deeply.

"So, you were at home when you were attacked?" I asked.

"Yeah." Getting ready to leave. "Wait, what about Angie? Is she okay?"

I nodded. "She's fine."

"Thank God." He leaned his head back against the seat.

Franco took out a small pocketknife from his vest. "Okay, mate, let's get you free of this."

He cut away at the duct tape with the blade.

The sound of a click came from somewhere close behind.

I spun around on my heel.

A tall figure walked up, training a rifle on us.

CHAPTER NINETY

My heart sank.

Melainey stood in the middle of the road, with a sawn-off shotgun raised in our direction.

I cursed as I realised he must have been in the passenger seat of the truck, and he'd gotten out just after it'd crashed.

His shirt was smeared with ash. Sweat was dark under his arms and glistening in the deep lines of his face. He was placing most of his weight on his right-hand side, as if he'd injured himself—possibly in the crash.

"Back away," Melainey told us.

Franco made a small gesture of surrender, turning his fingers up. "Don't try this. You've got nowhere to go with it."

"Back *away*," he repeated. "Hands on heads."

I retreated a step, my head swimming with the heat and smoke in the air. "This is crazy."

Melainey spluttered as he coughed, then spat on the ground. "Crazy? You're crazier. Look at who you just set free. *Carlson Green*. The guy who paid Perdita to adopt Angie."

In disbelief, I looked across to the truck, where we'd left Carlson on the seat.

Carlson emerged from the truck with a gun in his hand. He held it on Franco and me with an almost apologetic expression.

With horror, I watched as Doug Overmire stirred and swung open the door of the truck. He dug in his pocket and produced a pistol. He aimed it at me.

At first, I thought this must have all been some kind of strange, elaborate ambush.

But, no, it wasn't that. Overmire hadn't meant to crash the truck. He still looked groggy from the accident, even as he held his gun on us. And he and Melainey hadn't tied Carlson Green up for any kind of trick. Whatever had gone on between them and Carlson, it was real.

Melainey's mouth twisted into a smirk. "You handled this badly, Wakeland, wouldn't you say? You always *were* just a country cop."

I sucked in a quick breath, recalibrating. "Looks like you're not doing so well, yourself. You three can't get out of here. There's a tree down."

Melainey shrugged, wiping ash from his eye. "We've been in trickier situations than this."

"You know that there are eyes on us, right?" I said sharply. "PolAir has been flying back and forth."

"No, they're not," Melainey said. "It's just an RFS 'copter. Anyway, there's about to be a terrible accident. You and Franco came out here to help the superintendent evacuate from a fire, but you all got caught in it."

"You can't win this," I said. "Too many people know exactly why we came here."

Doug Overmire dabbed at the blood on his face with his fingers, glancing away. "Tracks can be erased."

"Not these tracks. Not this time," I said.

"I'm afraid that's your opinion, Detective Wakeland," Overmire replied.

Doug Overmire's words belied the tense expression on his face. Melainey was the only one who gave the appearance of being in control.

I kept my expression blank as my thoughts spun wildly. There were three of them with guns on us. At least one of them—Melainey—had already murdered people. There was nothing to stop him from murdering again. They'd brought Carlson along by force, but I didn't know the full story. As for Doug Overmire—he obviously thought he could get away with anything.

"Key's not in the ignition. Where is it?" Melainey asked Overmire.

"*She* grabbed it." Walking across, Overmire strong-armed me for the key.

"I should have thrown it before," I hissed.

"Should have," Overmire said, "but you didn't." He reached into and around my armour vest and took everything—my gun, taser, bodycam, handcuffs and radio. He did the same to Franco.

He shoved the items into the back of the truck, then turned to Melainey. "What's the plan?"

Melainey jerked his head towards the road. "We're all gonna head over to the lagoon—the one we found earlier when we were waiting for Bigley to arrive home. If Bigley's suddenly got clever, he'll have a gun at the ready. Won't matter. I'll have him over the drop before he knows what hit him. So, get the truck running."

God. He was going to push Bigley's car over the edge with the truck?

"Have some decency," Franco said. "He's got his family with him."

Melainey looked his way with the coldest of expressions. "None of them will suffer. It'll be quick."

Fear and rage surged within me. "You're a psychopath."

"Not the worst thing I've been called." Melainey said.

Overmire went to start the engine, standing on the road and leaning into the truck. The engine struggled. He glanced back at Melainey. "It won't kick over."

"You used to get the trucks running in the old days on the farm," Melainey said. "And it was going until Wakeland turned it off."

Overmire climbed into the truck and repeatedly tried to get it started.

I prayed the engine was damaged enough to never start up again.

CHAPTER NINETY-ONE

Melainey and Green continued to hold guns on us. They were certain to kill Franco and me straight after they'd killed Bigley.

The truck engine spluttered and groaned with Overmire's efforts to get it started.

Melainey shuffled across to the side of the truck and leaned his weight against it. He made a low groan of pain as he tried to straighten his back.

Terror scattered like broken glass in my mind. But I couldn't show it. I *wouldn't* show it.

I fixed my gaze on Melainey. "All these years, you've been nothing but a criminal."

"We all have to make choices," he said. "Who knows? Maybe if I'd shown you a big stack of money one time, you'd have gone for it, too."

"You were at the carnival raid, weren't you? Back in '89. *You* were the one who took the money."

Melainey nodded slowly. "Jeez, you care about the oddest things, Wakeland. Yeah, I was there. I took half of it. Guess who got the other half?" He glanced towards the truck and Doug Overmire. "Douggie was smarter than me. He invested his half. Mine went up in smoke—in casinos."

"Figures." I coughed in the smoky air. My tongue tasted like ash. "And you went to Witness Mountain to kill Angie and her parents. Why? *Why them*?"

Rolling his shoulders, he adjusted his position, wincing and struggling to find a comfortable pose. I wondered if he'd broken a rib and maybe other bones, too. He'd come out the worst in the crash.

"Not smart enough to figure it out, huh?" he said.

"Humour me," I replied.

"Angie figured out who Perdita was," Melainey told me. "That's what started it all. So, little Angie Green came back home to confront her. Perdita called Overmire in a panic. But she'd just signed her own death warrant."

"Wait," I said, "you were the one following Angie on the island, weren't you? You went to find out what she knew."

Melainey gave a gritty smile. "Yup. I listened in on her conversations. She'd found someone who used to know Perdita—from the old days, when sweet Perdita used to run a brothel. It was a game of dominoes after that. What Angie knew was gonna bring us all down, one by one."

Franco spat on the ground. "And you went to Witness Mountain for a massacre."

Carlson Green was staring at Melainey with an expression of unfiltered hate.

Melainey hooked his eyebrows. "It wasn't a massacre. It was just something that had to be done. Perdita did bad things when she was younger—so, she was no loss. Gus was old and sick. My only regret was for Angie. But she was already living on borrowed time."

"On borrowed time?" I queried.

"She was the kid of the two people we killed on Mulden Farm—better known as the *bunker victims*. She probably should have joined her parents. But, we let her live."

My stomach knotted as I locked eyes with him. "And then you went to kill her thirty years later. How did that day play out, Melainey?"

"Why's it so important for you to know?"

"Just give me this one thing."

"It's burning you up inside, isn't it, Wakeland—wanting to know if you were right or wrong? Okay, so, you were right. I did go after Perdita first. And I shot her. Felt good, too. Hated that bitch. She ran into the house to save her own skin. Gus Iverson tried to stop me from getting to Angie, if you can imagine a weak old guy as a hero. Told him I'd give Angie a head start if he'd agree to shoot himself first. He tried to delay me as long as possible. After he shot himself, I went to take care of Angie. That was no fun at all. Then I returned the rifle to Gus."

"You mean, you staged his suicide," Franco said from between his teeth.

I stared at Melainey. "I'll take a stab and guess that you called in a favour with Detective Farrina. His report of the sequence of events was just a sham. Or maybe he's one of *you*."

Melainey held my gaze. "That's for me to know and you to find out. Except… you won't be finding out anything."

"Keep the smart talk to yourself," I shot back. "Because it's not smart. What you're doing here—it's damned stupid."

"You're welcome to your opinion," he drawled.

"Was that you at the hospital earlier, Melainey?" I asked. "Angie said someone posed as a doctor."

"Ah." He shook his head. "No, not me. Someone else had that job. My face is too well known around town now."

Melainey angled his head around to Overmire. "What's happening, Douggie?"

"Have to hotwire it," Overmire called back.

"Hurry the hell up," Melainey told him.

Something else that Angie had said occurred to me then.

"You might not have been the doctor, but you were the Irish nurse," I said to Melainey. "Angie mentioned that an Irish nurse had been helpful to her. Of course that was you. You were going to see Angie while she was in the coma, weren't you? Pretending to be hospital staff. Making her believe her father was the culprit."

Melainey gave half a shrug, trying to hide the smug look that'd entered his eyes. "Yeah. guilty. I told her that when her father yelled *run*, he was just taunting her. I was a bit shocked that it all worked, to tell the truth."

I stared at him. "But you couldn't have known she could hear you?"

"Seemed like she could," he said. "Her heart rate would go up whenever I mentioned Perdita or Jordan's name to her. But you ended up not happy with us naming Gus as the killer, hey, Wakeland? Which gave us a big problem."

Carlson looked as if he were about to crumble. "I had nothing to do with any of this. I love Angie. You can believe it."

"If you love her," I said to him, "what are you doing helping the guy who tried to kill her?"

"I can't help who I got mixed up with," he replied tightly. "It's all too far gone."

"Tell me, Carlson," I said, "what did Melainey mean when he said you *paid* Perdita to adopt Angie?"

Green just shook his head and looked away.

Melainey burst into a harsh laugh. "I'll tell you. My girlfriend at the time—*Adele*—she brought little, thirteen-year-old Angie to a party. Douggie was having a housewarming to celebrate buying a pad in the city. We were all there. Douggie, Gordon, Nancy Upchurch… Bigley. Perdita was about to get some fresh meat—Angie. But Green took one look at Angie and decided she was *his*."

Carlson Green gazed at me with haunted eyes. "I looked after Angie—I didn't hurt her."

Melainey eyed Carlson. "Is that what you call putting Perdita on a payment plan to look after Angie until *you* could get your hands on her?"

I sucked in a breath at that revelation.

Carlson sounded bitter when he answered Melainey. "Angie looked about eighteen with all the makeup Adele had plastered on her. When I found out she was just thirteen, I didn't touch her. She didn't even notice me. She was drunk… your girlfriend kept giving her wine."

Melainey chuckled. "Adele wasn't a good girl, that's for sure."

"Perdita was terrified of you and was planning on skipping town," Carlson said. "I overheard her telling Doug that. I offered Perdita a way out. I asked her to move to Tallman's Valley with Angie and look after her. She snapped up that offer."

"Ah, the things you do for love," Melainey drawled. "What a sweet story. Man traps kid with the owner of a kiddie porn business until he can have her for himself."

"I didn't know what Perdita did for a living." Carlson's eyes grew wet. "How the hell would I know? No one told me. I only found that out this year. I only just found out… *everything*."

"Should have looked a bit further into the background of the woman you were dumping Angie with," Melainey told him. "I didn't know what she was all about, either. I don't hold with any of that stuff. I used to argue with Adele all the time about her selling pictures of herself. It's damned nasty."

Disgust turned my stomach. These people—they thought they had morals, but they didn't. They all thought they could have whatever they wanted. It didn't matter that Carlson didn't know about Perdita. He'd still groomed a young girl to become his wife when she came of age.

"Carlson," I said, "you lied to us about where you were the morning of the shootings, didn't you? And you got that MP—Gerald Finch—to cover for you. Is he a member of *The Quarry*, too?"

Carlson shook his head. "I didn't lie. Neither did Gerald. He's not with *The Quarry*, and neither am I."

"Then what exactly went on that morning?" I asked.

"I did as I said I did," he told me in a crushed voice. "I'm not with the Quarry, but I know people who are. That morning, I got word that Melainey had been sent to kill Angie and Perdita. It was too late by then. I thought Angie was dead. I thought my sons were dead, too. I wandered around in shock for hours. I came home to kill myself. I looked at photos of Angie and my boys, punched the wall a few times… then went and got myself a rope. I tied the noose, ready to jump. Just before I did that, I checked my phone. That's when I saw Inspector Shintani's message. Angie and the boys were still alive. That gave me a reason to live."

Franco glanced from Melainey to Carlson. "Okay, Carlson, I think I've got the picture. You were angry as hell about what Melainey did. And you went to tell Bigley. But Bigley got scared and blew you off, refusing to listen. Bigley then went into a frenzy, deleting any files that might incriminate him. Then Melainey and Overmire tied you up and threw you into the truck to stop you from going ballistic while they went after Bigley. How am I doing so far?"

Carlson didn't answer.

I gazed at Franco. He'd just clicked a large piece of the puzzle into place.

Behind us, the truck rattled and then roared to life.

Melainey smiled tightly. "Sorry, Wakeland and Franco—but you know what's coming. Can't be helped."

Doug Overmire jumped down from the truck. "What's happening with those two anyway?" He indicated towards Franco and me.

Melainey raised his face to the sky. "I send Bigley over the drop with the truck. Then we put Wakeland and Franco in their cop car and push them over the drop, too."

I met eyes with Franco. There was no way out of this. Even if the cars didn't explode into flames, the crash would kill us.

"It won't work," I told Melainey. "Investigators would be able to figure out what happened."

"Handcuff them," Melainey told Overmire.

Overmire lifted his chin in a nod. "Yeah, okay. I'll get their handcuffs from the truck."

"Never mind." Melainey took a set of handcuffs from his police vest and tossed them to Overmire. "Just duct-tape Wakeland. Shut them up, too."

Overmire pulled Franco's arms behind his back and clicked the handcuffs on. Then he produced a roll of duct tape from his pocket and taped Franco's mouth. Stepping over to me, he wound the tape around my wrists and around my mouth.

For a moment, I thought Melainey wanted to silence us so we couldn't speak to him anymore. But then I realised exactly why he'd done it. To prevent Franco and me from calling out to warn Bigley once we'd arrived back at the lagoon.

Melainey was going ahead with his insane plan.

I held a desperate hope that Carlson would turn against Melainey and Overmire—but he didn't. Instead, he helped Overmire to force Franco and me to walk up the road, towards the lagoon.

CHAPTER NINETY-TWO

Melainey drove just ahead of us in the truck.

We entered the clearing.

Melainey's SUV and the unmarked police SUV were parked side by side next to the lagoon, pointed towards the drop, just as they had been when Franco and I left.

I gasped for air at the thought of what was about to happen—to Bigley, Clare and Davinia, to Franco and myself. Pete and our family dominated my mind. Anger barrelled up from the pit of my stomach.

Melainey moved ahead in the truck.

Dear God. Bigley probably thought help was coming.

Heat and sweat made the hastily applied duct tape peel and then fall from my face.

"Andrew!" I screamed.

It was already too late.

Melainey screeched the tyres of the truck as he drove off.

He careened through the clearing, headed directly for Bigley's car.

The air knocked from my lungs.

I spun around to Franco. "*The oxygen tanks,*" I hissed. "*Davinia has oxygen in the car.*"

I'd forgotten about the tanks I'd seen Bigley pack in there. They'd explode on impact.

Franco and I couldn't save Bigley and his family—but we might be able to save ourselves.

I nodded towards Overmire, crushing my voice to a whisper. "*We bring Overmire down, get his gun and shoot Green.*"

Franco understood instantly, nodding, his eyes large above the tape that still bound his face.

It was a plan with a thread-bare chance of success.

But there was no time for anything else.

Melainey slammed his truck into the back of the SUV.

The two vehicles exploded in a ball of fire.

Franco lunged for Overmire.

With a yell, Overmire fell hard, his gun skidding away from him.

Ducking low, I brought my taped wrists over my head and then scrambled for the dropped gun.

Overmire was quicker, shifting himself far enough out from Franco's hold to get the gun.

He fired at me—the sound exploding in my ear. I didn't know if the bullet had hit me or not.

Overmire's head jerked around as missiles shot from Bigley's SUV, blasting past us. Two of the oxygen tanks.

I made a desperate grab for the pistol now.

I knocked it from Overmire's fist, but my fingers fumbled as I tried to get a proper hold—my wrists too constricted by the tape.

Carlson raced over with his pistol raised.

"Get them off me," Overmire raged at Carlson.

Carlson stood there rigidly, glancing from the column of fire coming from the two vehicles back to us. His hand trembled on the gun.

"Green," Franco said urgently, "What do you think Overmire's gonna do to you? Let you *live*?"

"Don't listen to that," Overmire commanded.

Twisting himself, Franco brought his handcuffed arms around and hit Overmire square in the throat with his elbow. Twice.

Overmire wheezed and spluttered.

"They were planning on putting this all on *you*," Franco told Carlson. "The truck was going over the drop last—did you figure that out? With *you* in it. They were gonna make it look like you were the one sent to kill Bigley. Except, you got it wrong, and you sent yourself over the drop, too—in the truck. Overmire and Melainey would have got away on foot, with no one ever knowing they were here."

"That's not true… not true," Overmire breathed raggedly, struggling under Franco's weight.

My stomach clenched as I waited for Carlson's reply. Franco had Melainey's plan straight—I was sure of it.

Carlson pointed the gun at Overmire. "I'm not your pawn."

"Green?" Overmire yelled, his voice cracking. "What the hell do you think you're doing?"

Wrenching my wrists apart to make the tape go slack, I steadied my hand on the gun. Kneeling, I held the gun on Overmire.

Overmire's expression went blank as he retreated into a frozen shock.

"Put your weapon on the ground," Franco told Carlson.

Wordlessly, Carlson did as Franco had asked.

It was done. Over.

I filled my lungs with the searing, smoke-filled air.

CHAPTER NINETY-THREE

Franco and I remained low to the ground, instructing Carlson Green to do the same.

Two more oxygen tanks exploded through the windows of Bigley's SUV.

That was four. That was the number of tanks I'd seen Bigley pack.

I was numb inside as I watched the two cars burn.

Melainey deserved the way his life ended. As for Bigley—I didn't know the extent of what he'd been involved in. But his family didn't deserve this horror.

I had to turn my head away.

"Wakeland!" Franco called above the din of the fire.

I spun on my heel.

Ahead, our police SUV backed up and began turning.

My mind went straight to Melainey. He must have jumped out in time—without us seeing him.

But as the vehicle turned completely around, there was Bigley at the wheel. Clare was beside him. And Davinia in the back seat.

He drove alongside us and rolled the window down. His hair was ruffled, sweat streaking down his face. His eyes held an expression of shock as he surveyed the scene of Franco and I holding guns on Overmire and Green.

Clare looked in the same state as Bigley, her shoulders quivering and her hair damp.

"We moved ourselves into your car," Bigley told me. "Clare was worried about the oxygen tanks getting too hot… and exploding…."

A dozen thoughts rolled through my mind, but my throat was suddenly too constricted to speak any of them. My eyes grew unfocused as I gazed at Bigley, my mind feeling as if it were filling with smoke.

Bigley opened his car door, fumbling as he pulled a pistol from his vest. He held it on Overmire, white-knuckling the grip. "I'll take over from here."

Franco gazed at Bigley with barely controlled contempt. "A day late and a dollar short, superintendent. Put it away before you end up shooting someone."

Pain radiated through my chest and along my arm. Breathing became much, much harder. I collapsed to my knees.

All around me came the sounds of the distant, crackling fire and a sharp whirr of helicopters crisscrossing each other in the sky.

PART VIII

CHAPTER NINETY-FOUR

DECEMBER 28, 2019

At the same time Doug Overmire and Carlson Green were taken into custody by the federal police, I was escorted away via ambulance.

I'd thought it was a delayed reaction to the shock of watching Melainey ram his truck into Bigley's SUV. But it was more serious than that. I'd had a minor heart attack.

Overmire's bullet had entered my shoulder, too.

I was still here though, while Melainey was gone—gone forever.

At the end of that day, the fires only reached the outskirts of Tallman's Valley. And it failed to jump the river and head into Sydney. But that day—December 21—would go down as the most dangerous day of the 2019 fires for Sydney.

Doug Overmire was now being held in custody. I guessed he was still hoping that his high-paid lawyer would be able to perform miracles and get him out of the worst of the charges.

He had another thing coming.

Superintendent Bigley was also in custody. He'd refused to speak to anyone. It was what I'd expected, but still, there was so much I wanted to say to him.

So much. *So many things*.

All these years, he'd been aiding criminals. While we—the detectives of Tallman's Valley—had been battling against those unseen forces.

It didn't matter—entirely—that Bigley wouldn't open his mouth. Because it ended up that Doug Overmire had kept enough detailed records that it was like having a crystal ball—except that this crystal ball gave us windows into the past rather than the future.

Bigley hadn't taken part in any crimes himself. What he was guilty of was overlooking dubious events that his friends—such as Overmire—had been involved in.

And that was all you needed to do great harm. To look the other way, to cover your ears when alarm bells were ringing, to maintain the old boy—and girls—network at all costs.

Nancy Upchurch was one of those old friends of Bigley's. She never actually engaged with *The Quarry* website, but, oh, did she like the money that came from it. She provided a large part of the finance to buy the supercomputers at CQ—the kind of computers that could run billions of processes, twenty-four hours a day. She was in it, up to her neck, all the way.

Bigley wasn't aware that Melainey was a paid killer—among other things—but he didn't question the things that were very obviously wrong, either. Overmire had wanted Melainey to take the job of lead homicide detective. And, in turn, Bigley allowed himself to become convinced by Overmire that Melainey was the best choice for the role.

The detective that Melainey had brought in to give expert opinion on the multiple shootings at Witness Mountain—John Farrina—was a member of *The Quarry*, too.

Along with everything else, I discovered something that cut me to the core.

Four years ago, when my granddaughter and four other children vanished from a park, Bigley had refused to allow me to join the task force. For three and a half years, he'd held firm on that. But now, I found that Doug Overmire and Nancy Upchurch had been behind that. They'd gotten into Bigley's ear. And he'd listened. *It'll look bad for a detective in the Blue Mountains Area Command to investigate a crime committed against one of her own family*, they'd told Bigley. And so, Bigley had stopped me—even though I was the most experienced detective he had. Overmire had been hoping that being forced to watch the case from afar would destroy me and send me packing from the police force. He'd calculated very, very wrong on that one.

Eventually, in the fourth year after the children had gone missing, Overmire had run a simulation on one of his newly purchased supercomputers, and he'd discovered that the children had been kidnapped by his own sisters. He'd visited Penny and told her it was best that the children were killed and buried.

But Penny had refused, and she'd decided to return the children to their families.

It had been such a thin, thin line between getting those five children back and never finding out what had happened to them. The truth was terrifying in every aspect.

We discovered more details about what we'd learned from Melainey about Perdita and Carlson Green, too.

It was Gordon Quinley—Overmire's brother—who first introduced Adele to Perdita. He'd been one of Perdita's customers.

And at a glitzy party in January 1990, held at Overmire's new house, the sixteen-year-old Adele brought with her the nervous, thirteen-year-old Angelina Kowalski. Adele had told Angelina—who'd just recently run away from the carnival—that she knew people who'd help finance private investigators to find her parents. But the real reason Adele had brought the youngster was to introduce her to Perdita Laurier—and set Angelina on the path to sex work.

The then twenty-one-year-old Carlson Green was at that party. He was from a wealthy family who owned a chain of real estate agencies. Carlson took one look at the tall, lithe dancer named Angelina, and he developed an instant obsession. He was crushed to learn her real age. After finding out that Perdita was desperate to get out of Sydney—after swindling Melainey on a business deal—Carlson offered her a way out. Perdita would legally adopt Angelina and keep her safe until she was old enough to marry Carlson. In the meantime, Carlson would teach Angelina to depend upon him. And Carlson would pay Perdita generously—every year until Angie was eighteen.

Perdita agreed to Carlson's request.

Perdita then fed Angie a false story. Perdita told her she'd always wanted a daughter but was unable to have one. She said she wanted to help her, telling her she'd pay for investigators to find her parents. In the meantime, Angie was welcome to stay with her.

Angie, desperate and out of options, agreed.

Perdita then found a hapless innocent to marry—Gus Iverson.

Doug Overmire, trying to smooth the waters, gave Perdita a portion of his family land in Tallman's Valley. And Perdita moved there with Gus.

After a year, Perdita dangled a carrot in front of Angie's face—she would put Angie through the dance school she had her heart set on, if she'd agree to an adoption.

When Angie turned fifteen, Perdita told her about an afternoon job going at a local real estate agency. Of course, that agency belonged to Carlson Green. And that was the start of Angie being unwittingly pulled into Carlson's world.

Carlson didn't know about *The Quarry* website or the paid killers, but he should have known enough to be wary of the people involved with Overmire.

On December 21, 2019, Carlson discovered something that shocked him. He discovered that Detective Trevor Melainey was the one who'd tried to kill Angie. It was the day his world collapsed and when he realised just how dark the world of Doug Overmire and his network really was.

That same day, a computer programmer named Ben Tremayne discovered something, too. For days, he'd been suspicious of another programmer who managed the computers on the sub-ground level—Elliot Calladine. Ben suspected that Calladine might be behind the mysterious eagle avatar who'd infiltrated the Witness Mountain virtual world. And so Ben kept watch on Calladine.

The day of the fire evacuations, Ben found that Calladine had left open a strange website open on one of the computers. The website had been a dark web meetinghouse called *The Quarry*. Ben immediately realised how dangerous the site was and he'd snapped a photo of the screen. He'd then encrypted that photo on a USB, and he'd given that USB to me.

Unknown to Ben, Leo Dubois had also grown suspicious of Calladine. But Leo had taken the bold step of accusing Calladine of using the CQ computer network for criminal purposes.

Elliot Calladine entered Leo's house in the early hours the next morning. He strangled Leo and then dumped his body in Coldwater Lake.

It did end up that Calladine had programmed himself in as the eagle in the Witness Mountain virtual world. He'd been the one watching me in there.

As for the fire at Witness Mountain on the day of the bicycle test, it remained a mystery. We'd been unable to uncover the instigator. Had it been the careless act of a valley resident or had it been one of *The Quarry* people? No one was owning up to it. Was there something else lurking on Witness Mountain—something someone had wanted to cover up? Perhaps we'd never know....

CHAPTER NINETY-FIVE

As well as finding out about Overmire and his dark network, we were finally able to piece together what happened on the day of the 1989 raid of the carnival—and the years afterwards.

In late 1989, the terrified Tiên and Anthony Kowalski entered Tallman's Valley police station and spoke to the then Sergeant Andrew Bigley. They told him they were concerned that children were being mistreated and neglected on Mulden Farm, and that illegal activities were being carried out.

Mickey Mulden, the owner of the carnival, suspected that Tiên and Anthony had gone to the police, and he wanted retribution. He also wanted to prevent them from becoming witnesses in any court trial. He, Melainey, and his sons Doug and Gordon, carried out the murders of Tiên and Anthony—hanging by noose.

Meanwhile, Sergeant Bigley was arranging a raid. Detective Trevor Melainey of the state homicide squad caught wind of the coming raid, and he decided to join it in secret. But Melainey merely aimed to double-cross Mickey Mulden and scoop up any money and illegal goods that he could find on the farm.

On the day of the raid, when Melainey was looking for the money, Doug Overmire was doing the same thing. Overmire's mother and father had just been arrested. Overmire had quickly decided that he could put all the blame on them and come out clean.

Melainey found Doug Overmire in the bunker, collecting the money. Melainey held a gun on Overmire and demanded he hand it to him. But then the two of them made a deal. They would split the money evenly—an amount close to two million dollars.

As far as I could tell, Bigley didn't receive any of the money. But neither did he ask any questions or properly supervise the raid. All he wanted out of it was a promotion—and he wanted no suggestion of his police force acting badly. He'd been more than prepared to overlook everything.

Doug Overmire rushed away to the city with his half of his father's ill-gotten money. Distancing himself from the rest of his family, he invested the money and began building his business empire.

Eventually, Overmire would become the main financier of the Close Quarters development. CQ had solely been his idea—not the idea of the NineOak corporation. Nancy Upchurch had merely joined him.

Overmire's idea had been to use the CQ development to grow his empire—this time using artificial intelligence. At CQ, he would have supercomputers at his disposal, with the computers capable of carrying out astonishing numbers of processes.

That was it, the whole sordid history.

It was how the silent town had tunnelled beneath Tallman's Valley. It was how the shadowy streets had formed.

But finally, light had reached the silent town.

CHAPTER NINETY-SIX

JANUARY, 2020

I walked onto Sean Macklin's property, past his house and around to the land that spread wide behind it. The grassy fields were peppered with cows and horses.

Jordan and Dakota galloped across a field on two of the horses.

Closer to the house, Toby and Oliver jumped together on a trampoline.

Under a pergola, Angie Green sat cross-legged in a round wicker chair—the size of which made her look tiny. The afternoon sun picked out the gold highlights in her red hair. She wore a purple tee-shirt under green overalls—colours that seemed to suit her.

She waved, and I waved back.

Just then, a woman with steel grey hair stepped from the back sliding doors of the house, carrying a tray of drinks.

"Oh." She looked over at me, blinking.

"Hi, I'm Detective Kate Wakeland. You must be… Sean's mother?"

"Yes. I've come to stay with Dakota while her father is… well…." She shot me a direct glance. "You'd already know all that. You're the detective who arrested Sean, aren't you?"

It was an uncomfortable encounter. "Yes, I'm afraid I am."

She expelled a sharp breath. "He didn't do anything too wrong. He was only trying to protect Angie."

"I know. Look, I like Sean. He seems like a great person. He just… made a mistake that day."

"He always was impulsive. Too caught up in his love for Angie to think straight." She shook her head. "I'm Roberta. Pleased to meet you."

She didn't look too pleased.

"Good to meet you, Roberta," I said.

"Like a lemonade, Detective?" she asked me. "It's a thirsty kind of day."

"I'd love one."

Roberta looked over to Angie. "Lemonade?"

Angie grinned. "Yes, please. You make the best lemonade, Roberta."

Roberta handed Angie a glass. "Well, I'll leave you two to talk. I know she's been busting to see you."

Roberta stepped away towards Toby and Ollie, taking the tray of drinks with her.

I took a seat next to Angie. "How are you?"

"Better. Clearer."

"Great to hear."

"I'm glad you could come." Angie smiled brightly at me. "I wanted a chance to thank you for everything. I don't even know where to start. But please just know that I'm very grateful."

I glanced over at Angie's children and Dakota. "Look at them all—having fun. I'm so happy to see you all together. Makes my heart lighter."

"Thank you. It's because of you we got this chance."

Jordan and Dakota pulled up alongside each other and trotted together on their horses.

"I'm guessing it's going to be a very difficult adjustment for those two," I said.

Angie nodded. "Very. They're both seeing a psychologist to help them through. Dr Li Zhang. She said it would be harmful to suddenly cut them off from seeing each other. So, we're doing supervised visits. Luckily, things didn't go any further with them than a kiss."

"They're both smart kids. They'll find a way through this."

"Yes, they are. But there's no roadmap for this kind of situation. It's messy. Sean and I… well… we totally messed up. And now our kids are paying the price."

"I know you must have been under some pretty heavy-duty coercion from Carlson."

Angie nodded. “Yes, I hope I come to understand that better. Right now, I feel like it’s my fault I wasn’t smarter. All he told me was lies. Terrible, terrible lies.”

“I’m usually good at picking up on character, but I admit I didn’t see through Carlson.”

Her expression went dark. “I was easy prey when I was a kid. As I grew into a woman, he invented different stories to keep me on the hook. He told me his investigator discovered that my parents knew a secret about some terrible underworld of criminals—and that my parents were protecting me by staying away. And I’d hang onto each morsel he threw to me.”

“That’s so awful.”

She bowed her head, picking at a loose strand of wicker on the arm of her chair. “I can’t believe what he did. Paying Perdita to adopt me? What kind of maniac does that? My life was just… built on deceit. The only good things from my past were my adoptive father, Gus, and my birth parents. No one else. As for Polly… she *knew*. All this time. She saw what happened to my parents. And she said nothing.”

Part of me wanted to speak up for Polly, to explain all the things to Angie that Polly had told me. But it wasn’t my place to do that. I hoped that the two of them might get together and talk in the future. Perhaps Angie would never forgive Polly. I couldn’t tell Angie how to feel. It would be her decision entirely.

“I’m so sorry about your birth parents—Tiên and Anthony,” I said gently. “So very traumatic for you to come out of your coma and have to deal with the aftermath of the shootings, and then be hit by that news.”

She kept picking at the wicker, softly sighing. “For the longest time, I believed they were coming back. It was only when Jordan was about ten years old that I understood they couldn’t be alive. Because I knew that the love I had for Jordan would have been the same as the love they had for me. It really hurts to know that all those years, their bodies were lying in a bunker—on Witness Mountain. Practically beneath my feet.”

“My heart broke for you when I realised who they were.”

“Perhaps, in time, I’ll come to feel comforted by the fact that at least they were near me. Maybe they were there, watching over me as I was growing up.” She looked up at me, her eyelashes wet. “Do you think that’s possible?”

“Of course.” I didn’t know what my true feelings were about that. But without knowing, I had to consider that it actually *was* possible.

"Have you come to any decisions about your future?" I asked.

"Sort of. I've decided to go back to Fraser Island for a while. The kids adore Fraser. Sean will be serving a jail sentence for a few months, and during that time, I'm going to do some soul searching. Because of the situation that developed between Jordan and Dakota, I tried to make myself believe that I didn't really love Sean."

"But you still have feelings for him?"

"Yes, very much so. My hope is that my boys and I can return to Tallman's Valley one day soon. I'm sure Sean and Jordan would like to get to know each other as father and son. It all depends on how Jordan and Dakota progress though—they're the priority."

"How did Jordan take the news about his birth father?"

"He was confused. Angry. As you'd expect. But then he said something that surprised me. He said that he was glad to know he was Sean's son and not Carlson's."

"I can understand that."

Angie nodded, sipping her lemonade. "Carlson was never a loving father to Jordan. He knew Jordan wasn't his, right from the start. But he never told me that. He wasn't much of a father to Toby and Oliver, either. He didn't spend much time with them. And his love was always… incomplete."

She looked over to her younger boys jumping on the trampoline, then across to Jordan and Dakota on the horses. "I have to find a way to move forward from here. For *them*. They deserve that much."

CHAPTER NINETY-SEVEN

FEBRUARY, 2020

Normally, January and February would be our risky months for fire in Australia—but so much of our lands had already burned that it seemed there wasn't much left for a fire to catch onto.

February brought my 65th birthday. I'd expected to have announced my retirement from the police force by this date. But there was a massive task ahead with the newly formed investigation called *The Quarry Taskforce*. Retirement wasn't a possibility just yet.

I was no longer going to be on active duty though—no more chasing after murderers. Most of my work would be done remotely now, at home or wherever I chose. Those were the conditions worked out between Shintani and myself.

It was Saturday today. I rose early, took a walk around the property with the dogs, and then headed down to the station to put in a few hours' work. I intended spending the rest of the day with family.

Close to eleven in the morning, I left the station. The air was clear and the sky a stunning blue. With so many days of clear summer skies now, my memories of the former smoky haze were already fading.

As I drove in through the gates of my house, an unexpected sight met my eyes.

A crowd of people were cheering, holding streamers and balloons. Long tables with yellow tablecloths were festooned with food. And a big sign said, *Happy Birthday, Kate*!

Instantly, my eyes were wet.

My birthday celebrations were usually small family affairs. I'd thought we'd have a family dinner tonight, with maybe a bottle of my favourite wine on offer.

Ivy ran to take my hand as I stepped from the car. Bubbling with excitement, she pointed at the paper garlands that the two Maremma dogs were wearing.

"I made them myself, Nan," she said proudly.

"They're beautiful, Ivy." I squeezed her hand.

Pete walked up with a huge grin plastered on his face. "Happy birthday, honey." He wrapped his arms around me.

"How did you manage to plan all *this*?" I breathed.

"I've got lots of helper elves." Pete winked as he glanced down at Ivy.

Abby and Logan approached and hugged me. Their baby—Jasper—reached for me and I took him in my arms. Logan handed me a cold drink.

My family walked me across to where everyone was standing. They broke into a rendition of the Happy Birthday song, ending in cheers and the release of streamers.

I felt a tear slide down my cheek.

I spent the next hour catching up with everyone.

There were friends that Pete and I had known for a long time. And Pete's brother and his family. Angie and her three boys were here, and Dakota and her grandmother, Roberta. Nola and Max were here, too.

Franco made his way over to me, a small bottle of beer in hand. He was wearing the same floral shirt he'd worn to the island.

"Happy sixty-five years, Wakeland," he said, giving me and Jasper a bear hug.

"Thanks." I smiled. "I'm shocked Pete and Abby were able to get all of this together."

"Well, lap it up and enjoy," Franco said. "Because we've got one hell of a week ahead of us."

"Ha! Don't remind me. Oh, and big congrats are in order. Shintani told me there's a new lead homicide detective in town."

Franco grinned. "Guilty as charged."

"You'll be a force to be reckoned with."

I glanced at a dark-haired woman in the distance, who was watching on.

"Is that *Martina*?" I asked Franco.

A smile slid across his face as he shrugged. "We've decided to give things a second spin."

"I'm happy for you."

Shintani strolled over with his glass of red wine. "Perfect weather. Happy birthday, Kate."

"Well, thank you, *Superintendent* Shintani."

"Still getting used to hearing that title," Shintani said.

Franco gave a silent sigh. "Not going to be the same down at the old station. You won't be there anymore, Shintani, now that you're a bigwig superintendent. And Kate won't be there much, either."

"A new start," Shintani said. "Life's full of them."

"I'll drink to that." I raised my glass.

Our small circle of three clinked our glasses together.

"I believe there is a little surprise in store for you, Kate," Shintani told me.

"I'm not sure my heart can take any more surprises," I replied in a light tone.

"I think you'll like this one." Shintani moved aside and a small blonde woman appeared.

"Liz!" I cried.

Liz stood there, hair half-done and shirt half tucked in—the usual Liz. The Liz I loved.

"Just got off the plane and drove straight here," she said in apology, tucking in her shirt.

"Come here, you!" I pulled her into a hug.

"How long are you here?" I asked her, not really wanting to know the answer—because I already knew she wouldn't be here long.

"Just for the weekend," she told me.

"Please tell me you can stay here overnight?" I pleaded.

She laughed. "Yep, I'm here for the night, like it or not. And I have a bottle of champers at the ready."

Liz tickled Jasper under the chin. "This is your grandson? Hasn't he grown?"

"Yes, he's getting so big." I glanced up at Liz again. "I can't tell you how happy I am to see you. Thank you for coming."

"Wouldn't miss it. There's still a lot of work to do, but we've come a long way. A lot of people… they are going to go down. Anyone we haven't gotten already, we're going to get them."

I nodded firmly. "Yes, we are."

Jordan Green approached me. "Hi, Detective Wakeland."

"Excuse me a moment?" I said to Liz. Smiling widely, I turned my attention to Jordan, stepping away with him. "Hi there, young man."

Jordan looked different these days—happier, as if he'd had a weight lifted. He had a computer tablet under one arm and a yellow balloon in the other. He gave the balloon to Jasper.

"I didn't get a chance yet to talk to you," he said to me. "I wanted to say thanks… y'know, for what you've done for Mum… and my brothers."

"I'm just happy the truth has come out." I drew a lengthy breath, glancing across the grounds to Dakota. "Although, I know some truths hit harder than others."

"My psych is making me understand some things," Jordan told me. "She said that sometimes, when you can't have something, it makes you want it a whole lot more." A frown indented his forehead. "So, when Mum took us away to live on the island, it felt like I was being punished for liking a girl. And it made me kind of fixate on the girl. Not to take anything away from Dakota—she's great—but I was mostly just rebelling against being punished."

"I can understand that. I'm the same. You tell me I can't do something, and I want to do it a hundred times more."

"Yeah, you get me." Jordan grinned as Jasper tapped at the balloon. "Mum actually wasn't punishing me, but it sure felt that way."

"So, you guys are heading back to the island soon?" I asked.

"Yeah. I'm looking forward to it—mostly."

"Great." I hesitated. "Jordan, do you mind if I ask just one last question? It's something I can't quite get out of my head."

"Yeah?"

"The accident with your bike and the car that day—did it happen the way you said it did? Sun in your eyes?"

Jordan blew out a breath. Then shook his head. "I was angry. With the world. Angry with Mum for telling me I couldn't leave our house and go see Dakota. Angry with Dakota for telling me to go home. Angry with my dad—Carlson—for not being there to help me. And that morning, I was just… riding along with my eyes shut. Trying to block out the world. And I slammed into the car."

"Oh… now I've got the picture. You poor kid."

"Stupid, huh?"

"Dangerous… but understandable. Well, be sure to keep in contact, won't you?"

"We will. Hey, I've been keeping in contact with someone you know—he and his mum lived in CQ Village. My dad's house—*Carlson's* house—was just on the next street."

"Oh?"

"Yes, he's interested in computers, like me. His name's Ben. Ben Tremayne."

"*Ben*?"

I hadn't spoken with Ben since December—the day he'd slipped me *The Quarry* document. I'd been advised not to. So far, the people involved with *The Quarry* thought that Detective Liz Booth had gained access to their website via the information she'd collected from Adele Hobson's computers. They didn't know that the initial information had come from Ben.

Ben and his mother were still in danger if what he'd done was ever discovered.

"How *is* Ben?" I asked Jordan, excited to hear any snippet.

"He can tell you himself," Jordan said. "He asked me to hook him up today."

Jordan took his computer tablet out from under his arm and switched it on. He connected to a video messaging service and then turned the screen around to me.

The faces of Ben and Ada popped up on the screen.

"Look at you two!" I cried. "I can't tell you how happy I am to see you both."

Ada smiled widely. "Guess where we are, Detective?"

"I can't guess. It looks like you're outside somewhere, but it's very dark."

"We're at the cabin," Ben told me. "Down by the river."

"Oh… you went back to the cabin? I'm so glad you did that."

Ben nodded. "It's freezing cold. And the cabin and grounds need a lot of cleaning up. But it's all good. It's good to be back here."

"Happy birthday," Ada said in a sing-song voice.

"Thank you. How did you know it was my birthday?"

Ada winked. "Oh, a little birdie told me."

I laughed.

I spoke with them for the next few minutes, glad to see that things were looking a little more hopeful for them both.

The call ended, and I returned to Liz and the party.

It ended up being the best birthday I'd had in many years. The previous years that I'd spent when Ivy was missing had passed in a kind of dark vacuum. And before then, so much of my time had been wrapped up in policing. I'd spent many, many birthdays chasing criminals.

Late that night, it was just Pete and Liz and me on the front deck of our house, drinking champagne and catching up together—in the peace of a summer night in the valley.

Abby and her little family had moved out in the afternoon—moving into the house in town that Pete and I used to own. They only had themselves and a few clothes to move, having already moved all the furniture over the past week.

I was sad to see them go, but at the same time I knew they needed to move onto a new phase in their lives.

Close to midnight, Liz begged off—exhausted from her flight. She went to sleep on the sofa-bed downstairs.

After all the chatter and the people who'd been at our house today, it was all so quiet. Just Pete and me. That was how it was going to be from now on.

It was going to take a lot of adjusting to get used to this.

Pete put his arms around me.

"Did you have a good day?"

"The best."

"Time to start planning the next part. You'll have lots of time off with the kind of work you're doing now. We can travel."

"Yep, time to start ticking off our list. Can't wait."

"What'll we start with? The northern lights in Canada… or Iceland? The redwood forests in California? Ummm, a food tour of India? Or a tour of England's fourteenth century castles?"

"All of them."

"Correct answer." He kissed my temple. "We'll have to throw some ideas into a hat."

I half-turned to Pete. "I heard about some new virus in the news. Did you see anything about that?"

"I did. But how bad can it be?"

"I guess so."

"Why don't we just take off somewhere? Give ourselves a day to pack. So, two days and we're out of here."

"Two *days*?"

"Yeah. Why not? We'll just do it. Pick a place, find a flight. And *go*."

Inhaling a long breath, I nodded. "Okay. You've got me convinced. Get your hat, Pete. I'll start writing out our destinations."

DEAR READER

I hope you enjoyed Kate Wakeland and the Tallman's Valley Detective series.

My wish for Kate is that she got to go away on a much-needed trip with Pete!

My wish for Australia—and everywhere in this world of ours that experiences devastating fires—is that we learn how to manage them effectively into the future, when increasingly dire weather events are expected.

Website:
annitaylor.me

BOOKS

Domestic psychological thrillers

THE GAME YOU PLAYED

STRANGER IN THE WOODS

Dark psychological thriller/horror fiction

THE SIX

POISON ORCHIDS

'Tallman's Valley Detectives' series

ONE LAST CHILD

THE LULLABY MAN

THE SILENT TOWN

ACKNOWLEDGEMENTS

THE SILENT TOWN is the product of endless hours of research and very valued advice from various sources.

My thanks and gratitude to:

The Blue Mountains Community Group.
The Fire/Rescue Group. (Facebook)
Cops and Writers - both US & Australia. (Facebook)
The former NSW detective who advised me on rifles.
My great first readers—Tim, Kirsten, Maree and Jeff.

Printed in Great Britain
by Amazon

74310926R00267